Trapped

Bullied, Volume 4

Vera Hollins

Published by Vera Hollins, 2021.

Author's Note

This book is a spin-off. It can be read as a standalone, but it is recommended to read *Bullied* (*Bullied* #1), *Pained* (*Bullied* #2), and *Damaged* (*Bullied* #3) before reading this book to get a better understanding of the story and characters.

There is no time skip between *Trapped* and *Damaged*. Furthermore, chronologically, the first chapter of *Trapped* comes before the scene with Jessica in chapter twenty-two of *Damaged*. Also, the second half of chapter two of *Trapped* comes after the scene with Jessica and Sarah in chapter twenty-three of *Damaged*.

To anyone feeling not good enough. Remember that you matter. You're worthy and special. You are you.

Prologue

SIX MONTHS EARLIER

It was the first day of my senior year of high school. It wasn't quite what I'd hoped for.

I wasn't at my old school in Bridgeport but at a new school that held only the unknown, and I was always scared of the unknown.

The bell rang, marking the end of third period and the start of more unknown things to come. I ignored the stares of my classmates on my way out of the classroom. I just wanted them to stop staring, but I knew that wasn't going to happen.

I was a new girl, which apparently meant I had to be christened with relentless staring, whispering, and finger-pointing, as if they had never seen a new student at this school—as if I were some alien specimen. It was rather intimidating, and I almost chickened out. I'd most definitely have given up on going to the cafeteria if it wasn't for my growling stomach. I was starving.

Students flocked to the hall, which helped me get lost in the crowd. I sucked in my belly and straightened my spine, hoping I wasn't looking as fat as I felt. I was fidgety as I moved, running my hands over the edges of my draped shirt to fix the non-existent creases, hoping it hid the flab above the waistband of my jeans.

It's going to be okay. Look at the bright side. You're starting anew here.

I stopped in front of the cafeteria doors as a dull ache spread through my chest. I didn't want to eat alone and face more staring. It would be better to just pick up some food and go somewhere quiet.

Taking a deep breath, I stepped inside. A quick inspection of the room told me I'd managed to attract some attention, which brought a blush to my face. *Okay. More creepy staring, here we go.*

My insecure steps led me deeper into the lunchroom, until someone stopped a bit too close to me. I raised my head to meet the stunning yet cold gray eyes of a guy who was so tall I felt like a dwarf next to him. I choked on my saliva, confused as to why such a hot-looking guy would approach me deliberately.

1

I studied the chiseled features of his face, noting his high cheekbones, straight-edged nose, and heart-shaped lips that could best be described as "made for kissing." He definitely gave other guys a run for their money, but there was something about him—an air of trouble—that I didn't like, even more so considering I didn't know what his deal was.

He assessed me too, and I didn't miss the cruel calculation on his face or the sudden silence falling on the room.

"Well, you're something new." He spoke loudly for others to hear. A non-friendly grin formed on his face. "What's your name?"

I lowered my head as another blush coated my cheeks. I was growing overly self-conscious, feeling like the thousands of eyes prodded at me.

Too easily, I was taken back to that incident five years earlier. I hadn't been able to deal with that then, and I certainly couldn't deal with this now. I just wanted to get this over with and be out of here.

"J-Jessica," I answered in that squeaky, childish voice I hated. My stammer was followed by vicious laughter from a few students standing nearby.

"Jessica what?"

"Jessica Metts."

"What's that? I didn't hear you. Jessica what?"

"J-Jessica Metts."

"You mean Jessica Fats?"

My stomach dropped at the insult that hurt the most. The insult I heard more than any other. The one that reduced me to this insecure being that could never be truly satisfied with her looks. He was so mean.

His grin grew even bigger. "Because you're so fat, Jessie."

All those faceless people in the room were laughing. The laughter was everywhere, just like that day.

It had been a mistake to come here. A stupid, stupid mistake.

My tears were ready to spill out. I had no idea why this asshole was targeting me, but I didn't plan to wait to find out. I swiveled around, but he reached for me and grabbed my forearm, preventing my escape.

"Where are you going, Jessie? Do you want to miss your welcome party?"

I didn't like the sound of that. "My welcome party?"

"Yes." He glanced at the students around us. "What do you say, guys? Do you want to throw a welcome party for Jessica?"

My heart raced wildly against my ribs; I knew a disaster was about to happen. The guy stepped aside, and reality distorted into something utterly ugly as students started pelting me with food.

Before I could even react, various foods hit me right in the face. I raised my arms to shield my head, but the rest of my body was completely exposed, and I flinched with pain each time I was hit. I was degraded into nothing.

I fell to my knees, my legs too weak to hold me up. I couldn't believe this was happening to me. I couldn't.

Each second brought more pain and humiliation, and my heart started to break into pieces. I burst into tears, hoping for this torture to end. This was unreal. It hurt. It hurt so much.

Why isn't anyone stopping this?
Help...
They're horrible.
Someone... Help me...
Please help me...

Pain exploded in my forehead when a carton of milk hit me and burst open, the milk drenching my whole face, but what hurt more was my heart. I was unable to make sense of this cruelty. It hurt so much.

I opened my mouth to plead for them to stop, but a tall, skinny girl stepped between me and the others to protect me. For a moment, I thought I was hallucinating. My chest tightened with both relief and fear for her.

"Stop this," she yelled at the guy who'd started the whole thing.

His face showed a mixture of fury and surprise. "What the hell are you doing?"

"This is not okay! You're hurting her! Don't you see she is bleeding?!" She looked at me over her shoulder and met my gaze. I wondered if she could see just how frightened I felt—so frightened I hadn't even realized I was bleeding.

"Step aside, bitch."

"No."

He got in her face. "You're going to regret this."

He yanked her by her hair and pushed her to the ground, ripping a few hairs out.

I can't believe him! This jerk was more than vile.

He signaled to the others to throw food at us, but then the cafeteria doors flew open and the principal came in. *Finally.*

"What is going on here?" He reached us in a few quick strides. "Jesus Christ!"

The shock wore me down, and my shaking intensified. I wasn't able to stop crying, aware of how freaky I must have been looking covered in all sorts of food and liquids.

He crouched next to me and placed his hand on my shoulder. "Are you okay?" he asked, but I couldn't find the strength to form the words.

"She needs to see the nurse. She's hurt," the tall girl told him.

He frowned when he spotted something on my forehead, which I assumed was the wound from the sharp edge of the milk carton. He stood up. "Who is responsible for this?"

The silence that ensued was worse than anything. No one would stand up against these bullies? Unbelievable.

"Jones, to my office," the principal said to the guy who had started the debacle.

Yes! There was some justice, after all.

He gave him a murderous glare. "Why me?"

"Don't play innocent, Jones. This is not the first time something like this happened, and most of the time you are involved."

"That's not right, Mr. Anders. I just happened to be here trying to help these girls. Isn't that right?" he asked the two guys next to him, and they nodded in response.

What the heck? They were horrible! They were bullies *and* despicable liars.

"Either way, to my office, Jones. Now. You too, Decker. I want you in my office now."

"Okay," the girl replied. "May I take Jessica to the nurse first?"

"You may, but be quick about it." He faced the whole cafeteria. "Why are you still standing there? I want this mess cleaned up right away!"

I leaned against the girl as I rose up to my feet, feeling like my legs might give out on me at any moment. Everyone stared at me, and shame swallowed me whole. I didn't want to return here ever again.

"Can you walk?" she asked as she put her arm around my shoulder for support. She was a true gem.

"Yes."

"Okay then. Let's see the nurse."

I nodded, immensely grateful, before I looked one last time at the monster who had put me through this. His eyes were two pools of contempt and zero remorse as he stared at me. My stomach churned with revulsion. I'd never felt such a strong aversion toward someone, and I wished I'd never have to see him again.

Somehow, however, I sensed this was only the beginning and I was in for a long and terrible ride.

Chapter 1

PRESENT

End of February

Benjamin Franklin said nothing can be certain in this world but death and taxes.

He was wrong because now, as I sat right in front of my bully in U.S. history, I could easily add another thing to that list.

Nothing can be certain in this world but death, taxes, and Blake Jones' torture.

Blake just had to sit right behind me in this class. He just had to.

I was hyperaware of his nearness every second of this dreadfully long class. Goose bumps broke out on my skin each time I sensed him move, and I could hardly bear it. I had to fight to keep my breathing even, hoping I didn't look like a complete weirdo to my classmate, Marcus, who sat next to me.

That hope waned by the minute because Blake made sure to smear my image in front of him as much as possible. He jeered at me whenever Marcus leaned in to whisper something to me while our teacher scribbled on the blackboard, and I was losing my patience. My heart raced at the prospect of a fight with a guy who was the most complex and callous person I'd ever met.

Blake Jones. Even his name itself gave me the shivers.

He represented a long, distressing story, one that had started on my first day as a senior at this school. He'd bullied me from the moment he laid eyes on me and made my life at East Willow High nightmarish. I'd experienced bullying in middle school and at my previous high school, but that couldn't compare with what I went through with Blake, not by a long shot.

Blake had been crushing me day by day. He tainted my self-image to the point where I disliked everything about myself—from my looks to my personality—and even with therapy, I struggled to remember that I shouldn't care about his insults and should love myself the way I was.

My therapist, Susan, reminded me time and again that I was a beautiful and special girl and Blake was likely only projecting his insecurities onto me, but logical thinking didn't mean much each time he hurt me and brought me to tears.

I was a coward. I was the type of person who would run away at the sight of danger or wait for others to save her, which Blake liked to point out often. He would call me a wimp and double his abuse, just so he could see me crack and beg for his mercy. I constantly lived in fear of his abuse or retaliation if I stood up against him in any way.

I never told anyone about the time he broke into my locker and stole my pads and my period leaked through my jeans by the time my classes finished. The walk out of school was horrifyingly humiliating. Blake was there to document it with his phone, of course.

I also never told anyone he dumped a cigarette butt into my meticulously curled hair as he passed me by, telling me I would catch on fire. Washed over with horror, I tried to remove the lit butt before it burned my hair, only to find out he'd already put out the cigarette before he threw it in. I spent hours crying in my room, unable to understand how someone could traumatize people like that.

Then there was the time he broke into my locker again and left a pile of trash. I reported him to the principal, but he told me I didn't have proof it was Blake who did it and refused to do anything against him. This didn't come as a surprise, as he hadn't helped me after my "welcome party" six months earlier either. The school didn't have cameras, and since no one had stepped up as a witness, it was my word against Blake's. Blake's father was Enfield's mayor, so it was clear whose word had more value in this corrupted school.

Blake had been outraged because I tattled on him to the principal, so he'd gotten back at me by photoshopping my face onto a picture of a woman in a corset and stockings with a whip in her hand and her foot planted on a mini fridge. He sent this to one of his football buddies, who posted it on his Instagram and captioned it "Food Slut." The nickname stuck with me in the following months, reminding me that each time I fought back, Blake was there to make things even worse.

I never knew why he hated me. I never did anything to him, yet he constantly inflicted more and more fear in me until I was close to giving up on my new life in Enfield and returning to my hometown to live with my aunt and uncle. However, I'd made best friends here, and I didn't want to disappoint my parents by giving up.

Blake had stopped bullying me at one point. By some miraculous twist of fate, he stopped harassing me after New Year's, and I thought I could finally have my days free from his cruelty, but then I was proved wrong because he was back at it again lately. I should've known peace wouldn't last.

Now, Marcus had a front seat to my humiliation, and I wished the ground would swallow me up. Or swallow Blake, whichever would be better. The class couldn't finish soon enough.

"Fats," Blake whispered into my ear. I turned rigid because his lips were almost touching my earlobe.

It had been a bad decision to wear a braid today.

"Turn around." His breath caressed my neck, and my stomach flipped.

I pursed my lips as I stared at one spot in my textbook. His fragrance messed me up. It was unfair that he smelled this good.

"You'll turn around, unless you want me to tell your wannabe boyfriend you're a bad kisser."

My cheeks reddened at the reminder of one of the biggest mistakes of my life, accompanied by a stab of pain in my chest because he'd called me a bad kisser.

I glared at him over my shoulder. "Will you stop it already? And he isn't my wannabe boyfriend."

He formed a malicious smile, raising his phone, and snapped a photo of my sneer. "Look at you." He snarled at the photo, as if he was looking at an abomination. "You're a walrus. Now, I only have to use the dog filter and send it to your wannabe boyfriend. I'm sure he'll pee his pants from laughing."

My eyes widened. I reached for his phone in an attempt to delete it along with the other photos he'd taken earlier in class, but Blake wasn't our football team captain for nothing. His reflexes were extraordinary.

"Ah ah ah, not so fast." He held his phone out of my reach.

"Miss Metts, this isn't Starbucks," Ms. Gentry chided, breaking into my bubble of rising anger. I whipped my head around to look at her with burning cheeks. I was mortified that she was taking me to task in front of the whole class. "If you don't pay attention in my class, you can leave."

"I-I'm sorry, Ms. Gentry. I'll pay attention."

Her eyes narrowed as she scowled at me. "You better do that."

I clasped my hands together in my lap, wishing my hair could hide me from everyone. I would not cry. I closed my eyes and sucked in a breath. *Jess, don't you dare cry now.*

I knew Blake was gloating. He enjoyed putting me in the spotlight, and being in the spotlight was something I absolutely despised.

Marcus gave me a sidelong glance and handed me a folded paper when Ms. Gentry carried on talking about Benjamin Franklin. Hiding it under my desk, I unfolded the paper.

Don't pay attention to Jones. He'll stop sooner or later.

I could only wish. Marcus didn't know that ignoring never got me anywhere with Blake. In fact, it only incited him to harass me more. Still, I appreciated Marcus for not thinking any less of me because of Blake's put-downs.

Marcus Robinson was in the school choir like me, and he seemed like a nice guy. He'd asked me out the previous week, which had come totally out of the blue because of the long-circulating rumors that he was gay. I told him I didn't like him and turned him down, but he remained friendly with me.

You don't know him. He can be very persistent, I wrote under his words and returned the paper to him. I glanced at Ms. Gentry, and thankfully she wasn't looking in our direction. Marcus unfolded the paper.

I leaned in to tell him not to accept anything from Blake in case he actually sent my photo to his Snapchat, but too suddenly, Blake yanked me away from Marcus by my braid, and I barely managed to stifle a yelp.

I spun around to face him. "What the hell is your problem?" I hissed, trying to be as quiet as possible.

"Burks isn't enough for you, so you also want Robinson?" he said under his breath, wearing a grimace. "So, you're fat *and* a slut."

I winced, repulsed by his ugly, jealous-sounding words. For once, the urge to put him in his place was stronger than fear, and I blurted out, "Says a guy who's slept with countless girls. It's a wonder your penis hasn't fallen off yet."

His face fell. His gray eyes narrowed to two menacing slits that cut deep into me, and the rest of the classroom ceased to exist. I could feel it—his next attack.

He gripped the wrist I rested on the back of my chair and got up in my face. "Who the fuck do you think you are?" I tugged my arm back to try to free myself, but it was useless. "You know I can ruin you in a second. It's that easy."

"Miss Metts? Mr. Jones?" Ms. Gentry called out, but her voice sounded like it came from far away. Blake and I were too lost in our exchange to care about anyone else, only inches separating our faces now.

"I'll send your embarrassing photos and videos to every college in the state," he said quietly so only I could hear him, and a twinge of trepidation mixed with my anger. "No one will accept you. You won't have any future by the time I'm done with you, so you better think twice before you put my back up again."

I. Hate. Him.

I hate him so much.

"Mr. Jones! What do you think you're doing?"

Our teacher stopped above us, but my anger had reached the boiling point and nothing mattered anymore but hurting him. Six months—that was how long it took me not to care about his sick retributions and pain for once.

Six long months, but better late than never.

He had no limits. He had no shame. And he had absolutely no empathy. It was too much, and I couldn't put up with it anymore. I couldn't just keep quiet and hide under the covers like a scared kid, hoping the danger would pass. No more.

I glanced at his iPhone on his desk—the phone that was there almost every time I was humiliated. That phone documented my tears, my moments of despair, and my moments of mortification. It was abhorrent.

Pent-up anxiety was like a ticking bomb. It could explode at any moment.

Mine finally did.

I stood up before I was even aware of it and grabbed the device I despised so much. I flung it to the floor, relishing the sound of shattering. It was cathartic. His screen cracked in different places, and something akin to satisfaction spread through my chest.

As everyone blended in the background, I raised my head to meet Blake's gaze, and every positive feeling in me vanished. I actually staggered when I saw the hatred like never before in his eyes. The veins on his jaw bulged out as he fought not to lunge at me.

"Miss Metts, this is preposterous!" Ms. Gentry glared at me with her hand placed across her heart. "I won't tolerate such awful behavior in my class. And *you*." She pointed at Blake. "I'm disgusted by the fact that you're bullying your classmate and it's happening right in the middle of *my* class! I can't let that go unpunished. I'm giving both of you detention."

What?! "But he was the one who started it—"

"But you continued it." She pushed her glasses up the bridge of her nose. "I want to see you both here after school on Monday. Now, out of my classroom!"

"You'll be sorry for this," Blake said through his teeth in a voice that chilled me, and I believed him. I truly believed I was screwed. He picked up his phone from the floor and snatched his textbook and notebook from his desk on his way out.

I couldn't look at anyone, unable to shake off the regret and shame. Only now, the consequences of my outburst dawned on me. I'd never gotten a detention before, and my parents weren't going to like this at all.

I scooped up my notebook and textbook with shaky hands and shrugged at Marcus, whose gaze held so much pity. I wanted to rewind the last minute and stop myself from throwing Blake's phone all the more. I couldn't believe I'd thrown it on the ground!

Still dumbfounded by my reaction, I dragged myself out of the classroom and away from the ceaseless whispers of my classmates. I'd just gone around the corner when someone yanked me with a force that left me breathless. My back slammed into a wall, and my gaze met Blake's. His hands on my shoulders prevented me from moving.

"What are you do—"

"You think you can mess with me? You think I'll let you get away with it?!" I flinched as his shout reverberated through the vacant hallway. His six-foot-two body was too close to mine, and my pulse went crazy at his proximity.

I clasped my hands over his to pry them off my shoulders, but he only increased his pressure. "If you hadn't harassed me, I wouldn't—"

"Shut up! I don't want to hear another word coming out of your big, fat mouth." He curled his lip. "And here I thought I could actually give you leeway after New Year's. I thought everything would be better if I just treated you like you don't exist. But you messed up."

He pushed away from me, but instead of feeling relieved by the much-needed distance between us, I felt like I was suffocating, fearing what could happen next.

Facing away from me, he gave me one last glance over his shoulder. "Today, you messed up big time, Fats, and now? Now it's payback time."

Chapter 2

"DO YOU TH-TH-THINK she'll like the bracelet?" Kevin asked me, snapping me out of my gloomy thoughts.

We were on our way to my best friend Sarah Decker's eighteenth birthday party, but I kept dwelling on the incident with Blake.

"Definitely, and even if she doesn't, you know what they say: the best gifts come from the heart. I'm sure she'll love it."

She would definitely love it because she was someone who valued sentiments over material things, and she was the kindest girl I'd ever met. I owed her a lot because she'd always stayed by my side and stuck up for me no matter what, starting with that "welcome party" six months earlier.

I'd always considered myself weak—always resorting to tears and ditching others if it meant saving myself. I felt inferior next to Sarah, but I could never tell her that. I could never tell her I felt even more ashamed of myself when I was around her, so sure no one could ever need me, for how could anyone need a dead weight like me?

Sar never criticized me for being a coward. She never confronted me for bailing on her instead of fighting back against our bullies. She was the girl I admired most because even with all the bullying and difficulties she experienced in her life, she was strong and she kept going. I aspired to be like her, but it wasn't that easy.

I stopped at the red traffic light and looked at Kev. Ironically, I'd met Kev during another "welcome party"—the one Blake, Masen Brown, and their football teammates threw for him. It was as humiliating as mine with the students circling him and throwing food at him, until Sarah and I intervened and helped him get out of the cafeteria.

Kev and I had grown close in record time, especially because I saw my own weaknesses in him. He reminded me of myself—shy, insecure, plagued by the feeling of inferiority—which was all the more reason why I wanted to get stronger and be there for him. I learned through Sarah what it meant to fight for friends, and I wanted to fight for Kev. He also had a passion for music and sang in the choir, and it was cool to finally have someone who could fully understand how much music meant to me.

I flashed him a smile. "That new shirt suits you." The elegant black shirt he wore was a far cry from his usual tartan plaid shirts that swallowed his rawboned 6'3" build.

He blushed. "Th-Th-Thanks. My mom bought it for me. I didn't want to wear it, b-b-but she insisted."

"Your mom has a good taste."

"But I don't like it."

"I get you. My mom also likes to surprise me with new clothes I don't always like." I accelerated when the light turned green. "Still, you look good. I'm sure chicks will dig you tonight." I winked at him. "And guys."

He crossed his arms over his chest and remained silent, letting me know once again how touchy this topic was for him.

Kevin was bisexual, and he'd been struggling to accept his sexuality for years. He'd realized he also liked boys when one boy told him he had pretty blue eyes in third grade, and he had a crush on that boy for a long time. His classmates picked on him for it, making him ashamed of something no one should ever be ashamed of. Nine years later, he was still confused about his emotions.

There was another reason why Kev didn't want to talk about guys or crushes, and that was because he crushed on both Sarah's boyfriend, Hayden, and me. It was beyond awkward, and sometimes, I didn't know how to act or what to say, hoping he would crush on someone else who would be able to reciprocate his feelings. And to think that Blake thought there was something between Kevin and me. If only he knew.

"Wow. The party is already in full swing," Kev said when we reached Hayden's house.

I shifted my car into park at the end of a long row of vehicles that clogged the driveway. The addictive beat of the music blared through the walls, filling me with energy and euphoria. It was a given that I loved everything that had to do with music, which was one of the reasons why I enjoyed parties. There was nothing better than loud heavy-bass songs that sent my blood rushing through my veins and set my body on fire. That was freedom.

"Let's not forget Sar's gift." I grabbed the silver bracelet with flower charms wrapped in silver decorative paper from the glovebox and stepped outside.

"It's cold," he said as he wrapped his arms around himself, despite his thick winter jacket. I, on the other hand, wasn't fazed by the cold, even though I wore a tight-fitting dress that hardly reached mid-thigh and a short coat. I was willing to bet it was because of my excess fat, which hugged me and kept me warm most of the time.

My high heels clicked on the pavement as we approached the house, my anxiety returning in full force because I would see Blake. He was inside and most likely hooking up with some model-worthy girl, and I didn't doubt he would do something to make me regret coming to my best friend's party.

I rang the bell and adjusted the strap of my purse higher on my shoulder. "How do I look?"

"You look p-p-perfect." Aww. He was such a precious cinnamon roll.

"Don't you think I look fat in this dress?"

He shook his head vigorously and pushed his glasses up his nose. "No! You aren't fat at, at, at all, Jess."

A certain person would beg to differ, but it was sweet of Kev to make me feel better about my looks. "Thanks. You look good too. Your hair looks good slicked back like that."

The door opened before he could answer me, and Sarah appeared before us.

"Happy birthday!" I squealed and wound my arms around her skinny frame to pull her into my embrace.

She hugged me back. "Thank you, Jess. You smell nice. Is that a new perfume?"

"It's my mom's. Chanel No. 5." I drew away to look at her with a grin.

She looked gorgeous in a dress that was similar to mine, only hers was blue while mine was burgundy. It emphasized her slim waist and perfectly proportioned hips, which I would never be able to have. All I had was the flab on my waist that I was clearly flashing to the world in this daring dress, although my mom had assured me I was beautiful. I also didn't fail to notice how her long legs looked even longer in high heels. My short, tree-trunk-like legs would never—not in a million years—look as good as hers.

I always envied Sar for the way she looked and wished I could be so effortlessly thin. My therapist had said all of us were unique and I should appreciate what I had, but it was hard not to compare myself to others.

"You look amazing, Sar," I told her. "That's a killer dress."

"I could say the same. Everyone will be drooling over you."

Everyone but the person I want to, my treacherous mind chimed in, but I refused to listen to it.

"Happy b-birthday, Sar," Kev said with a goofy smile as he hugged her.

"Thank you, Kevin. That shirt suits you."

His eyebrows furrowed. "I don't like it. I'm only wearing it b-b-because my mom b-bought it and wouldn't take no for an answer."

"Seriously, you look good in it."

"This is from Kev, Mel, and me." I handed her the gift.

Her brown eyes turned soft, and her pink glossy lips curved in a huge smile. "Thank you so much, guys. Now let's get inside before we freeze to death."

Kev and I linked our arms and entered. The hallway was packed with teenagers, and the sounds of "Ink" by Coldplay played by a live band boomed all around. We left our jackets in the entryway closet and followed Sar through the throngs of people to the living room. I couldn't stop grinning, elated by the music encompassing me. Nothing could beat the way I felt when I listened to the music I liked. It was an unlimited source of inspiration.

The large living room was even more packed and filled with cigarette smoke that stung my eyes. The band played in the corner, while most of the people danced in the middle of the room.

"Jess! Kevin! My dear babies!" Mel emerged out of the dancing crowd with a red Solo cup in her hand. "I was beginning to think aliens had finally come to our precious planet and abducted you. You took forever to get here!"

I giggled and let her pull me into an almost suffocating hug. Melissa Brooks, my other best friend, was as witty and childish as ever.

"I'm sure you'd cross the whole galaxy to save us. Also, if you keep hugging me like this, you'll squash me. Although, I wouldn't mind it if it would cut my weight in half."

"Girl, you don't need that. You're perfect just the way you are." Mel singsonged a melody of her own, shaking her curvy hips as she pulled away from me. She looked amazing in a gray Green Day shirt, black faux-leather leggings, and Doc Martens with a rose pattern on the sides.

Sar rolled her eyes. "Mel is already drunk, so don't mind her."

"Maybe I'm drunk, but that only means double awesomeness." Kevin and I fell into a fit of chuckles at that.

"That's true," Kev said. "It's like awesomeness is your s-s-superpower."

"You bet it is! Superman got nothing on me!"

My skin tingled with strange awareness, and I looked around us, my pulse picking up. I always reacted this way whenever Blake was nearby, but before, it was out of pure fear. Now? Now it was because of something I refused to acknowledge and fiercely hoped would disappear. I could almost feel his eyes on me, expecting to see him any moment, but I found Hayden Black's gaze instead. He was headed our way.

He looked handsome in a dark gray T-shirt and jeans that fit his muscular form very well, demonstrating why he was considered one of the most attractive and popular guys at school. A few scars dotted his face—most of them a memento of the night he left the gang—but they did nothing to diminish his good looks. My eyes went to the tattooed words and various small shapes decorating his upper arms. They intrigued me, but I'd never asked Sar about their meanings because I guessed they were too personal.

I was curious whether Blake had any tattoos, though there were hundreds of reasons why I shouldn't have been interested in that. I looked around Hayden, but Blake was nowhere in sight.

He stopped next to Sarah and slipped his arm around her waist, pulling her against him. "Hey, Jessica."

"Hey," I said as I smiled at Sar, who was positively glowing next to him. She wore a radiant smile that spoke volumes about how happy Hayden made her feel. It was touching, even more so after everything they had gone through together. She'd rarely smiled when I first met her, but these days she couldn't keep a smile off her face.

Hayden nodded at Kev. "Burks."

Kevin blushed, his eyes downcast. "Hello, Hayden." Melissa and Sarah glanced at each other.

Even after two months, Kev was still shy around Hayden. It was painfully obvious to everyone how much he was attracted to him.

Hoping to erase the awkwardness hanging in the air, I said, "This band sounds amazing."

"Yeah," Hayden said. "They're Hawks and Roses. They have a YouTube channel where they post their original songs and covers. Their debut album comes out at the end of this year."

My heart gave a flutter. I also had a YouTube channel with covers and my own songs, and I hoped to release my own album one day. I had yet to show myself in my videos because I wasn't confident enough to do that, using watercolor pictures as backgrounds.

"Okay, let's get you something to drink," Sarah said, leading us to a table with Jell-O shots and other alcohol.

Kev and I grinned at each other as we took shots. "Cheers," I said, throwing mine down.

Just as I reached for another one, I spotted Blake on the other side of the room, and my breath hitched in my throat. He sat on the couch with a girl on his lap. She leaned toward his ear to tell him something, but he wasn't paying attention to her. Instead, he was looking directly at me.

I gripped the shot in my hand, growing insecure under his stare. Even with the distance separating us, I could clearly see those cold, cold eyes tracing each part of my body, and I felt naked. I felt like he was stripping me, leaving me with nothing but heat and insecurity. He did this on purpose. He did this to intimidate me since there was no way he would look at me like this because he was attracted to me.

He most definitely found me fat, and I could just imagine the kind of thoughts going through his head. I could bet he was laughing internally at me.

"Today, you messed up big time, Fats, and now? Now it's payback time."

His words played in my mind on repeat; I was sure he already had his next humiliation planned. All I wanted was to have fun tonight, but I remembered very well what had happened the last time Blake and I were at the same party, which was on New Year's Eve. It had ended badly.

I downed the second shot and told myself to ignore him and make the most of the moment. *These shots better start working fast.*

Kev and I had another one before we went to dance with Mel. I felt Blake's eyes following me, but I refused to look his way, growing hotter and extremely self-conscious.

My determination didn't last long. As Kev spun me around, something drew my gaze to Blake, and our eyes met. They met again and again, until the alcohol kicked in and everyone and everything else blurred, the world becoming a mixture of excitement and joy.

• • • •

IT WAS WAY AFTER MIDNIGHT, and I was way drunk. Mel was telling me something as she twirled me around, but I couldn't make it out. I couldn't make out anything, and my vision was too blurry. I wondered if Kev's glasses could make me see any better.

I reached for them and tried to put them on, but they slipped out of my hands, and Mel almost stomped on them. All three of us burst out laughing. *Oops.*

Sar and Hayden were long gone, probably somewhere getting it on, and I envied her once more. I wished I could find someone I could get it on with... I wished—

"*Watch it*," Mel shouted at Masen, Blake and Hayden's friend, as he danced next to us with some brunette.

He turned around, but his arm never left the brunette's waist. His seductive smile vanished when he saw Mel. He was three sheets to the wind, if his glassy eyes were anything to go by.

"What's your problem now?" he snarled at her.

"You bumped into me, you jackass. I almost fell because of you!"

He raised his eyebrow. "Seeing how canned you are, you're going to fall on your own any moment now."

Mel's nostrils widened. She reminded me of a furious dragon, and I wouldn't have been surprised if she'd started spitting fire at Masen.

Melissa and Masen didn't get along. No, that was an understatement. Mel hated Masen's guts, and he didn't hide just how much she disgusted him. He never missed the opportunity to call her ugly or whatnot. If Mel, who was super pretty, was ugly to him, I could only guess what a girl had to look like for him to consider her beautiful. She had to be Miss Universe.

Masen himself didn't look bad, which explained the hordes of girls who were always after him and his reputation of being a womanizer. His light bronze skin accentuated his crystal blue eyes, making them more notice-able. His blond hair was short and unruly, and his body was honed into hard muscle. He could easily pass for a model. It was too bad his personali-ty lacked virtues.

"You're more irritating than diarrhea," Mel slurred, swaying as she took a menacing step toward him with her fist raised in the air.

Masen didn't move an inch, unimpressed. "Right back at you, Satan. This isn't WWE. Knock it off."

He turned around and planted his hands on the brunette's hips. I couldn't hear him clearly, but it sounded like he told her not to pay atten-tion to Mel. They continued dancing, completely dismissing her, while she looked like she was about to go nuts on them.

"It's Sar's birthday party." I placed my hand on her shoulder to calm her down. "Don't do this now."

Kev twisted his hands together. "Yes, Mel. Leave th-them be."

She watched them dance with a sneer. "Okay. I won't do it. I'll just have to break Barbie's nose the next time I see him."

Kev and I glanced at each other, and he shrugged his shoulder. Yep, she was that drunk.

"He didn't do anything wrong, Mel," I said. "He's just dancing with that girl."

Mel's brows quirked up. "He did nothing wrong? He exists! He should be wiped off the face of the earth!"

I snorted. "You're being a drama queen. And remember that anti-bully-ing campaign of yours, Miss Vice President? What would the student coun-cil say if they heard about this? They would call you out on your double standards."

Her only response was to roll her eyes. The band started playing a bal-lad, which was my cue to finally go to the kitchen to fetch some water. I was parched, and my feet hurt too much in my high heels. The blisters were go-ing to be a nightmare to deal with.

"I'm going to get some water."

"Have a nice trip," Mel said before sticking her tongue out at me.

I wore a goofy smile as I pushed through people, struggling to see anything beyond the hazy lines of my surroundings. The sweat was coating my skin, and I hoped my makeup was in place. If not, I was most probably looking like a clown. I giggled at the thought and sashayed my way into the kitchen, which brimmed with activity.

Some guys played beer pong on the kitchen island, while a blonde girl and a guy who looked old enough to be in college played flip cup on the dining table. There were a few couples kissing, and I exhaled a wistful sigh. I wanted to have someone to kiss, too.

The unwanted memory of my last kiss rushed through my mind, and blush spread all over my cheeks. The lips that drowned me in desire. The hands that reveled in me. And then the words that came out of his mouth that destroyed everything.

I tucked my curls behind my ear and opened the fridge with a pout. Everything about Blake was complicated. The walls around him and his complex past were too high, impenetrable, and dangerous. The depth of contempt in his eyes each time he looked at me was too much, and I asked myself for the hundredth time why I'd had to let him take a piece of my heart.

We weren't meant to be, and even though Sarah had just told me earlier that he might realize how wrong he was and change, it was hard to get over all the things he'd done to me.

I took the water bottle and placed a cup on the counter, humming to the ballad playing. I unscrewed the cap and tilted the bottle to pour the water, but someone flicked my cup aside, and I jerked back when the water splashed all over the counter and my dress, bumping into someone standing too close to me.

"What—" I started to turn around, but he grabbed the counter and pressed himself against me, two arms corded with muscle caging me in.

I was ready to panic, disgusted by this perverted stranger, when the voice in my ear said, "That dress doesn't suit you. You're too fat for it." *Blake.* "Your flabby stomach and sagging ass are on full display."

I closed my eyes shut and squeezed the bottle in my hand tightly. It hurt. It hurt so much, and shame and anger invited more self-hatred and self-doubts. I was more than aware of his hard body behind me, my pulse hammering madly. I imagined dumping the rest of the water from the bottle on his head.

I wasn't Mel though. Dumping liquids on annoying guys was her specialty.

"Looks like someone couldn't take their eyes off of my body," I replied with faked confidence courtesy of alcohol.

He snorted. His lips were so close to my earlobe I got goose bumps. "I didn't have to stare at you to figure out how fat and unattractive you are."

I bit into my lip and put the bottle down on the counter with a thud. "You can't seem to stop talking about the way I look. Are you that obsessed with my body?"

"Obsessed? You think I'm obsessed with your body when I get to sleep with girls who are way better looking than you?" Another snort traveled over his lips. "You're pathetic."

I refused to let his words get to me. He was a prick. "Leave me alone."

He spun me around too quickly and got into my face, creating a whirl-wind of emotions within me. I pressed myself against the counter to get as far away from him as possible and tipped my head back so I could meet his gaze. His icy gray eyes promised me pain.

"I won't leave you alone, because you broke my damn phone screen today. You can't mess with me."

"I'll pay you for the screen. And you're the one messing with me—all the time."

He grimaced. "I'm messing with you because I can't stand you. And don't think you can just pay for my screen and that's it. You won't get away with it that easily."

He is unbelievable! "You're sick, Blake, and—"

He grabbed my shoulder. "Now listen to me and listen to me carefully. I'm not that fool Burks who kisses the ground you walk on."

"He's not—"

He shook me. "Don't interrupt me. As I said, I'm not him, so don't think even for a second you can have me wrapped around your finger."

A few seconds went by as we glared at each other, our faces only a breath apart, and heat spread through my chest. He looked at my lips. Something feral passed through his eyes that said everything opposite of what had just come out of his mouth, and for a crazy moment, I thought he was going to kiss me.

However, whatever held us together was gone as quickly as it'd come, and again, we were nothing more than enemies.

He let go of me abruptly and stepped away. "You broke my screen today, and I won't leave you alone after that stunt. So you better think twice before you open your mouth again." With that, he spun around and walked away.

Chapter 3

IT WAS ELEVEN IN THE morning when I dragged myself out of bed. I felt like I'd been sleeping for ages. I didn't need to look at myself in the mirror to know my hair resembled a nest and my mascara and eyeliner were smeared all around my eyes. My foul breath was the real winner though.

I brushed my teeth, washed my unusually puffy face, and tied my long hair up in a messy ponytail, ready to haul my way to the kitchen in my PJs. My stomach was howling with hunger.

I hummed the tune I'd just come up with as I descended the stairs. It was a ballad that played in my head on the piano, but I wanted to memorize it and try it out on my guitar later.

"Good morning, sweetheart. You look like you came straight out of the washing machine," my mom, Julie, told me when I entered the kitchen. She was making lunch.

She wore a sports shirt and sweatpants that showcased her slim hourglass figure, which was a complete contrast to the clothes she wore at work. She worked as a PR manager, and I saw her in formal suits more often than not.

I yawned and picked up my plate of ham and eggs before I slumped down on the kitchen stool. I was dying to wolf down my late breakfast. "Good morning to you too, Mom."

Her amber brown eyes twinkled with amusement. "Did you sleep well?"

Yes, if you didn't count two hours of tossing around in my bed and trying to get some sleep after that encounter with Blake at the party. But she didn't have to know that.

"Like a baby."

"When did you come home last night?"

I groaned. "Mom, don't do that."

"I just want to know. Is that so bad?"

It wasn't bad, but it was irritating. My mom was the sweetest mom in the world—minus her tendency to be curious about my every move.

"You know I didn't break curfew."

"I don't know that. I was sleeping."

I sighed. "I didn't. Cross my heart and hope to die."

She tossed me a smile over her shoulder. "That's good. Was there someone who caught your attention?" She wiggled her eyebrows.

I dropped my gaze to my eggs. "Nope."

"And Kevin?"

"You know I'm not into him," I mumbled as I chewed with my eyes set on my plate.

"But that boy is so sweet!"

I took a big bite as I thought about the last time Kev was at my house. It was totally embarrassing. We watched *American Idol* in the living room—or more like tried to. My mom kept coming in and giving him the third degree, and I almost expected her to request he show her his family tree before he professed his undying love for me.

Poor Kev couldn't even imagine why she was so interested in him. He was the only boy I'd brought to my house since my ex- and only boyfriend, Rory, so it was no wonder she thought there was more to Kevin's and my friendship than there actually was.

"But I don't like him."

"Oh well. When are you going to invite him to our house again?"

"Mom, stop it. I won't fall for him, if that's what you're thinking." I chuckled. "We're just friends!"

My dad, Owen, walked in the kitchen. "Who's friends with whom?" he asked.

I glanced at him with my mouth full of eggs and bacon and got another reminder that I'd gotten the short end of the genetic stick. Just like Mom, he looked too handsome for someone in their forties with his defined chest, broad shoulders, and solid muscles, proving that weekend jogs really pay off. I had his deep blue wide-set eyes, freckles on the nose, and lighter complexion, but I'd gotten my mom's sand-colored hair, perky nose, and luscious lips.

I had a pretty face if I excluded my double chin and chubby cheeks, but the rest of my body... My mom, my therapist, Mel, and Sar always told me I looked gorgeous and had great curves, but it was hard to believe them. The mirror didn't lie, and the mirror showed a fat stomach, cellulite, and huge flabby thighs. It was hard to love those parts of myself.

"I'm friends with Kevin."

He took a water bottle from the fridge. "He's a good kid. You should invite him here more often."

I groaned. "Dad, not you too."

He raised his hands in the air. "What? I'm just saying. He can have a positive influence on you. You know school is important."

Count on my parents to underscore hanging out with good kids and getting good grades. My family and relatives had tried to drill into my head their high expectations of me my whole life, and they never even asked me what *I* wanted to do with my life.

My dad was a lawyer, and he represented important public figures. He owned a law firm that had merged with another hotshot firm from Enfield, which was why we had moved from my hometown, Bridgeport, to Enfield. It was only natural for my dad to think I was going to follow in his footsteps.

This was why I hadn't yet told them I'd applied to a few music colleges. I was still gathering the courage to tell them about it, and my stomach knotted each time I thought about that moment. It was going to be disastrous.

"Speaking of school," I started quietly, "there's something I need to tell you."

Dad stopped halfway through the kitchen door. "Tell us what?"

"You look like you're about to drop a bomb on us. Are you pregnant?" my mom joked.

I snorted. At this moment, even that felt better than the truth. I wished I could delay telling them about the detention, but my dad would be so angry if I didn't tell them now.

"I got detention."

They frowned and glanced at each other. "*Detention?* But how is that possible, Jessica? What did you do?" Mom asked.

It was almost like they expected me to say *Gotcha! There's a hidden camera.* I wished there were a hidden camera and this weren't real. I wished I hadn't thrown Blake's phone on the ground to start with.

"Jessica?" Dad prodded, his tone revealing an impending argument.

I should've finished my breakfast first. I pushed my plate with the half-eaten eggs aside. "I threw my classmate's phone on the ground."

Mom brought her hand to her chest. "Jesus."

Dad's face turned so grim I felt like I'd committed a felony. "Why did you do that?"

I kept my eyes firmly on my plate, bristling at his rising voice. My parents weren't aware of how much I was bullied in school, because I was too ashamed to tell them all the details. They thought it was something temporary and insignificant, something that would pass if I ignored it. They told me to ignore bullies and focus on my studies and they would leave me alone. *Little do they know.*

I'd mentioned Blake to my mom once, and all she told me was to stay away from him and report him to my teachers. As if it was that easy. As if Blake cared about school authorities—*he* was the authority, all thanks to the cash his parents threw around in the name of school donations.

"The boy I told you about," I began, glancing at Mom. "He bullied me in class again today. He didn't stop no matter how much I pleaded for him to. He was horrible...so I just snapped."

The silence in the kitchen was too loud. "So you just snapped," Dad repeated.

"Yes," I replied with red cheeks. "I grabbed his phone and threw it on the ground...and his screen broke."

Dad ran his hand through his hair. "I can't believe you would do something like that. That boy should be punished for his actions, but you didn't have to stoop to his level. I thought we raised you better than that."

"I know, and I'm so sorry, but he just wouldn't stop—"

"Then you should've reported him to the teacher," Dad interrupted.

"That doesn't help, Dad! The teachers in our school are not like you. Our principal is not like you. They don't care."

"Well, it's high time they start caring now that the school board is changing." He stopped next to me and put the water bottle down on the counter. "I'm going to talk to your principal again and demand he do his job."

"In the meantime, you're going to apologize to the boy and pay for his phone screen," my mom said.

NO. That was an absolute no. I didn't even want to imagine how badly that would go. Blake didn't need my apology, and he'd already said paying for his screen wouldn't do me any good.

"I'm afraid of him, Mom, so I don't want to go anywhere near him. And he's the one who should apologize to me! For everything he's done to me."

Dad scowled deeply. "Has he ever hit you or physically abused you?"

I chipped away at my nail polish. "It's complicated."

"Jessica." His stern voice demanded obedience. "Did that boy hit you?"

"No, he never hit me. He just manhandles me most of the time."

He let out a long sigh. "We'll talk to the boy's parents and—"

"No!" I exclaimed. I was horrified just thinking about that. I didn't want to drag Blake's and my parents into this, which most likely wouldn't do anything to help me. It would only anger Blake, and then all hell would break loose. "I-I'll talk to him and apologize."

My dad looked at me as if he didn't buy it. "Will you?"

The blush on my cheeks intensified. "I will."

There was no way I would actually talk to him and apologize for the broken screen. *I'd rather eat glass.*

"Good," Mom said. "And I really hope you won't resort to damaging people's property in order to deal with them again. What you did is never the solution. Owen will talk to your principal and make sure something like this doesn't happen again."

"That isn't necessary—"

"Of course it's necessary," Dad said. "I don't want students to harass you. Also, that can affect your grades, and we've already told you how important your grades are. You can't hope to get accepted by top universities if you start getting bad grades and detentions. So if I hear you got one more detention or made any more trouble, I won't buy you a new guitar."

My jaw dropped. "What? But I've been asking for that guitar for years!"

"Then you better make sure not to make another mistake."

I wanted to cry. They weren't being fair. All my life I'd been studying hard, always obsessing over my grades, and now that I'd gotten a detention for the first time in my life, they were treating me like I was going to become a delinquent.

I dashed back to my room and closed the door with a bang, angry tears spilling from my eyes. I felt the need to shout my resentment to the whole world. I hated being so impotent.

When I was seven, my grandmother taught me how to play a guitar and gave me her Martin—an acoustic guitar she'd owned since she was in her twenties—as a birthday present. It was special for me because it had guided me into the world of music and helped me discover who I was, and I'd grown to love it more than anything else I had. It was my anchor when I felt lost and my source of joy when I felt blue. It'd led me to singing.

However, its tonal quality wasn't as good as it could have been. So, I'd been asking my dad to buy me a new guitar ever since I realized I wanted to be a singer and started imagining myself on a stage, just me and my guitar, performing my songs for my audience.

Now I was one detention closer to not getting it, as if years of being an exemplary student could be easily annulled with one freaking detention. It was downright ridiculous.

I dropped face down on my bed and grabbed my iPhone.

I told my parents about the detention, I texted Kev.

And what did they say?

That I should apologize to Blake.

You're kidding, right?

And that I should pay for his phone screen.

Are your parents on drugs?

It gets better. My dad says he won't buy me a new guitar if I get one more detention.

It's confirmed. They're on drugs.

Tell me about it. I hate it. I've been stressing myself out over the pop quizzes last week, but it's all for nothing because good grades aren't enough for them.

But this wasn't your fault.

Technically, it was my fault, and it doesn't matter that Blake is a jerk. Plus, now I have to 'apologize' to him.

But this is Blake we're talking about. Apologizing to him is useless.

I rolled to my back and looked at the posters of my favorite indie pop singers on the walls. I thought about the lyrics of "Running with the

Wolves" by Aurora, wishing I could break free from the chains of fears
that held me back and be free, starting with Blake. He was everywhere. He
owned my mind and hurt me on different levels, and it sickened me that I'd
given him so much power over me.

The chains of fears... Now that could be my new song.

I know. So you can just kill me and put me out of my misery, I messaged
Kev back.

I have a better plan. Let's go out and eat something.

I smiled widely. Food was always the solution.

You're a genius, Kev :) I'm totally down!

After we decided when and where to meet, I went to my makeshift
recording studio. It was actually a walk-in closet, which was so big it served
perfectly as a studio. When we'd moved into this house, I had picked this
room only because of it. I'd turned it into a studio, soundproofed it with
foam, and equipped it with an audio interface, studio microphone, and studio headphones. I'd spent all the money I'd received from my family and
relatives over the years on it, and I didn't regret a single cent.

I took my guitar and sat on the chair. I was dying for my daily dose of
playing and singing. I strummed a chord and allowed the music to envelop
me in its empowering arms. Closing my eyes, I started singing, letting all
my worries and stress out and forgetting about everything but the melody
that carried me over to a place far more magical and peaceful than any other.

• • • •

"MMM, THIS IS HEAVEN," I said with my mouth full as I looked at my
delicious cheeseburger. It was a real treat.

Kevin grinned at me from across the booth, and I spotted a piece of lettuce stuck between his teeth. "It's d-d-delicious."

I chuckled. "Eww, Kev! You have lettuce stuck between your teeth!"

He went beet red and covered his mouth with his hand. "Really? Give
me your compact."

I chortled. He was adorable like this.

"Here you go." I fished the pink mirror out of my bag.

He grabbed it and faced the window so I wouldn't see him while he removed the piece. I took a sip of my Coke and looked through the window at the people passing by. A large layer of snow lay thickly on the ground, promising children snowy adventures. The dark, cloudy sky indicated there was more to come as the howling wind propelled snow particles around.

"Your p-p-parents are really s-strict." He handed me back my compact. "One detention isn't the end of the world."

I took another bite of my cheeseburger and swallowed it quickly. I always scarfed my food down and ate it rather sloppily, but I had to slow down if I didn't want to disgust other diners. The place was full of people from our school and college kids. I looked at my food sadly. It almost begged me to stuff it into my mouth with its deliciousness.

"It sure is for them. All my life I've been told how great my dad is. I'm always reminded of his achievements. The best in his class, graduated summa cum laude, owns his own law firm. And if that isn't enough, they keep reminding me not to be like my cousins, who are either too lazy to study or mingling with the wrong crowd."

"They're p-putting too much pressure on you."

I reached for my cup and took another sip of my Coke. "Yep. They always wanted me to be their perfect child. I have to be responsible and think about my future, blah blah blah. Sometimes, I feel it's never enough. I feel tired of proving myself to them."

"You still haven't told them you want to be a singer?"

I took a bite. "Nope. Seeing the way they are when it comes to something as minor as detention, I'm scared to imagine their reaction when I tell them about this. They think singing is just my hobby." I grinned at him. "If you don't hear from me, it means they've killed me."

He chuckled. "I'll make sure you're remembered." He pushed his glasses up his nose. "I think you should tell them you want to be a s-s-singer. Singing makes you happy, so they should understand it."

"I hope so. Let's keep our fingers crossed."

Then again, even if they accepted it, that would solve only one part of my problem. The other part was much bigger, and I didn't know how to deal with it.

I had stage fright. I'd had it ever since I was twelve and that incident happened. I couldn't sing in front of others. Sar and Mel had tried to convince me to join the school choir for months before I finally caved. The first few weeks were disastrous because I couldn't find my real voice. All that came out was a high-pitched squealing, and it was humiliating.

Our teacher tried to help me overcome it. She told me there were twenty more people in the choir, so the attention wasn't solely on me. The choir wasn't about me. It was about all of us—the unity. Gradually, I was able to relax enough and perform at a satisfactory level, but we had a school festival in about a month, right before spring break, and I was absolutely terrified of singing at it.

I watched him slurp his Coke. "How did your therapy go?"

Kevin had a speech disorder, and he'd started speech therapy a month earlier. He'd lived with his stutter his entire life, which put a huge dent in his self-esteem and desire to pursue his dreams. It made him afraid of communicating with others or meeting new people.

Once, he'd told me he felt his stutter defined him. He said nothing brought him more shame and frustration than when he did his best to speak fluently only to fail and be met with misunderstanding or ignorance, especially from those who deemed him stupid just because he couldn't put his thoughts into words or took a long time to form a sentence. He faced mocking, pity, and annoyance day after day, which squashed his hope for change, so he chose to speak as little as possible. I wished I could help him somehow.

"It was so-so. We worked on easy onset. *Again*."

"What's that?"

"You s-start to use your voice gently and ease into the rest of, of, of the word." He took a deep breath and demonstrated the technique. "We read s-s-some passages from a book."

"How was it?"

"Exhausting. I don't see any progress."

"It takes time, Kev. You've only been going there for a month."

"But I t-told you I went to therapy as a kid. Nothing helps. It's not curable."

"Maybe you just haven't found the right therapist or therapy for you."

He didn't look convinced. It was true that many stuttering cases couldn't be treated successfully, but I hoped that wouldn't deter him from chasing his dream of becoming a singer. As unusual as it was, Kevin didn't stutter when he sang, which was remarkable.

"Oh no," he said with a suddenly pale face, looking at something behind me with wide eyes. "Look who's here."

My pulse quickening, I glanced over my shoulder. My cheeks warmed when I saw Blake, Mel's brother Steven, Masen, and two girls enter the diner together. I whipped my head back and moved my hair to hide my face behind it. *Just my luck.*

"Please don't let him see me," I whispered to myself. "Don't let him come anywhere near us. Make him sit at the far end of the room. Make him disappear into thin air."

"I-I don't think that's gonna help, Jess. They're heading our way."

I sucked in a sharp breath. "You're joking, right?" I pinched the bridge of my nose. "Please tell me this is just a bad dream. They're not really here," I muttered, staring at my cheeseburger which, all of a sudden, became much more interesting to look at than anything else.

"Would you look at that? It's Burks!" Masen exclaimed, stopping right next to our table. I didn't move, refusing to look away from my cheeseburger. "And Metts. I'm not surprised to see you here, Metts. You *have* to replenish your supplies of fat somewhere."

The girls who were with them giggled, but I didn't dare raise my head and look at any of them. Or at Blake. Almost instantly, I regretted eating this giant cheeseburger that probably had enough calories to last me a week.

"Why is she pretending to be a statue? Knock-knock," Steven said, knocking on the top of my head twice.

"What do you want?" I said in a whiny voice as I snapped my gaze up to meet his, which was difficult since he was 6'5". "Leave me alone."

They went into a fit of laughter, and color rose to my cheeks. I still couldn't look in Blake's direction, though I saw him in my periphery behind Masen and the girls.

"Just checking if your brain is still there," Steven said. His friendly smile didn't feel right.

There was something about Steven that was totally off-putting, and I didn't know if that was because he was a heavy user and typical bully or because he looked like a hyena with bloodshot eyes. I had to hand it to Melissa for putting up with her brother.

"You won't find it," Blake said, and I met Kevin's gaze. He looked embarrassed. "She's a stupid freak."

I. Hate. Him.

"Come on," Steven cooed. "She's not all that bad. Maybe she's got no brains, but she's cute."

I grimaced with another dose of mortification, feeling more and more eyes on us. I didn't want to be in the spotlight. I wanted to bolt from here right away.

"Now, are we going to spend the whole day standing here or what?" Steven asked.

They finally moved to go sit down, but my relief was short-lived because of all the booths, they sat in the one right next to ours.

I almost groaned when Blake sat facing me. He raised his eyes to meet mine, and a jolt raced through my stomach. He held me in his unblinking gaze, rendering me immobile. My chest ached with unspoken feelings, which came from a twisted place that dismissed the fact that he was abusive toward me all the time.

I lowered my head and tried to hide behind my hair once more, but I knew it was useless. I could never hide from him.

I racked my mind for anything to talk about with Kev, but I couldn't come up with anything, and I bit into my cheeseburger forcefully. It was like all ears and eyes were on us.

"Hey, girly four-eyes," Masen started after the waitress took their orders. He turned around, patting Kevin on his shoulder. *Oh come on! Leave us alone!* "Look at you. Mama's boy is finally on a date."

I dug my fingers into my thighs. If there was anything I hated more than being bullied, it was seeing others bully Kevin. Someone always picked on him in one way or another, and I couldn't stand it.

Jumping out of my shell, I snapped at him, "We aren't on a date. And don't call him that."

"You could've fooled me," Steven interjected. "You defend him like a real girlfriend."

"We need to give her a medal," Masen said to Steven.

"Exactly," he agreed, sporting a creepy grin.

"Give her a medal—for the fattest girlfriend in the world," Blake joined in, and the girls chuckled. I squeezed my hands into fists, feeling like I could start crying any moment now.

"Since when do they let trash in this place?" Blake asked, sounding and looking bored. "We have to talk to the manager. His staff has some cleaning to do."

I bit the inside of my cheek and glanced at Kev's and my unfinished food. I itched to run away, but I didn't want to give them the satisfaction of seeing me running. They had seen me running too many times already.

"Ignore them," I mouthed to Kevin and picked up my phone to go on Instagram, relying on it to help me endure this.

"They are no fun," Steven said in a fake whining voice. "They don't want to talk with us. So rude! *Boohoo.*"

He exploded into a loud hysterical laugh, probably gathering the attention of the whole diner. Who knew what drugs he'd used today?

Kev sent me a message. *Do you want to go?*

Yes, but I don't want it to look like we're running away.

Then we'll finish this and go. Okay?

Deal.

The waitress brought them their drinks, and Kev signaled for the check. I took a bite and chewed quickly, each passing second seeming like an eternity. I could feel *his* stare on me, but I refused to look at him. My cheeks burned as I bit into my cheeseburger again. I didn't taste anything as I chewed, scrolling through my Instagram feed so I wouldn't have to look at him.

"Tonight's races are going to be fun," I heard Steven say. "I'll make good money."

"They're not that fun because they're a piece of cake. It will be an easy victory for Blake or me," Masen said.

"Like always," Blake replied in his deep voice, and before I could stop myself, I pulled my gaze from my screen to look at him. My stomach back-flipped because he was already looking at me, his fiery gaze making me feel like there was no one else here for him but me. It didn't make sense. If he hated me so much, he shouldn't have been paying attention to me. He shouldn't have been looking at me like that.

"Don't sound too smug, bro," Steven told him, and I broke our eye contact. "I heard rumors about some guy who's supposedly unbeatable. T said he's going to race at the track soon."

"Let him come. We'll show him how it's done," Blake said, talking a big talk.

I took the last bite of my cheeseburger. Sar had told me about their revolting gang activities. They participated in illegal races and fights, and some other members were also involved in theft and drug dealing. T was their gang leader. I just couldn't understand why someone would ever join something as horrible as a gang.

Blake, Masen, Steven, and Hayden had been in that gang for a long time, but more than a month earlier, Hayden had finally gotten out of it, leaving his troublesome past behind for Sarah and himself. He had to go through hell in order to leave, and even had a brush with death when other gang members jumped him out. It had taken him weeks to fully recover.

Just imagining Blake in that same situation filled me with inexplicable fear. I shouldn't have cared about that. That was his life, not mine. Yet, I was afraid for him. I wanted to laugh at myself for being afraid for my bully. I was so susceptible.

Kevin finished his burger and took the last gulp of his Coke just as the waitress brought us the check. *Finally.*

"Let's go," I said when we paid for the meal and stood up. My cheeks turned red as tomatoes because they all turned and silently watched us leave.

I hurried past their table, too aware that I had to pass Blake to get my freedom, but he moved quickly. He threw his Coke at me, and the liquid landed all over my jacket and jeans. I halted with a gasp.

My embarrassment hit an all-time high when the countless stares of the customers around the place were pinned on me in prolonged silence. One young teenager raised his phone as if he planned to film me, and I turned my head away from him. I felt like a zoo attraction.

Anger, shame, and hurt boiled to the surface, getting stronger when I met Blake's gaze, which was full of contempt. He smiled sardonically.

"Oops," he said, loudly enough for the people around us to hear him. "My hand slipped."

I had difficulty swallowing. "When? When will you stop doing this?" I could barely say it, my voice breaking. He showed zero remorse as usual.

His smile disappeared in an instant. "I'll never stop," he said in a low voice only I could hear. "You can run, Fats, but it won't make any difference."

My eyes filled with tears, which meant I had to escape before I got humiliated even more. I wasn't going to let him see me cry. The stains on my clothes represented the shame, regrets, and pain I'd carried for a long time, and I was so sick of it. I wished all my problems could be magically eliminated. I wished a day would come when I wouldn't have to fear Blake or others and could live my life in peace.

I couldn't look at anyone as I rushed with Kevin to the door and out into the cold. Only then did I succumb to the tears, regretting leaving my room in the first place.

Chapter 4

I WENT BACK HOME AND locked myself in my room, where I spent the most of my Saturday evening and Sunday. Following my earlier spurt of inspiration, I created the lyrics and melody for "The Chains of Fears" and recorded myself performing it, which I later uploaded on my YouTube channel, Valerie.

It was my pseudonym since I didn't want to use my real name on my channel. Hiding my identity worked in my favor since people were intrigued to meet the face behind the voice, and it was thrilling but also intimidating. The incident from five years earlier had scarred me, and the best I could do at the moment was make music anonymously.

Sunday passed too quickly, and another Monday morning rolled around. I almost stayed home, tucked safely under the covers in my room, but I didn't forget the argument I'd had with my parents the last time I had decided to cut school and stay home. They had been furious with me, and I feared their reaction if I ever skipped again.

Having managed to convince myself I would survive today's detention with Blake, I quickly ate leftover Chinese and got ready for school.

Luckily, I didn't see Blake before lunchtime, but I was met with a few "Fats" and "Fatty" from some students in the hallways, which already made me regret showing up. One girl called me a "Food Slut" in French class and almost brought me to tears because it felt like that nickname was going to haunt me for the rest of my senior year. Students never forgot. They enjoyed picking on those who displayed weakness, and boy did I display it in more ways than one.

One part of me wished I could transfer to another school, but Sarah was right—if I ran away, they won, and I was supposed to overcome my weakness.

I met Kevin at his locker, and then we went to join Mel and Sar in the cafeteria.

"Hayden is also th-there." Kevin pointed at our table, and I followed his gaze.

Hayden sat next to Sarah, his arm around her waist as he said something to her, and I felt a familiar pang of envy at seeing them so in love. Hayden never missed the opportunity to show how smitten he was with Sarah, looking at her like she was his reason for existing. He smiled most brightly when he was with her. I wanted an all-consuming love like theirs, but at this point it felt like a pipe dream.

"Is something wrong with that?" I asked Kevin.

He blushed. "Nope." He didn't look at me even once as we made our way to the lunch line.

I tucked my hair behind my ears and pulled in my belly. I regretted wearing these jeans. They were too tight, and the high waistline cut deep into my skin. I sneaked a glance at Blake's table and saw him talking to a girl sitting next to him. The girl laughed at something he said, looking even more beautiful with a smile, and my chest clenched. I tore my gaze away from them.

She was another skinny girl, of course. Where did he find them? They all looked like they came straight from a runway.

Suddenly, chicken nuggets didn't look as appealing as they had seconds earlier. My stomach growled when I glanced at the roasted veggies, as if begging me to take the former. My scale had said I'd gained extra weight recently and should go on a diet ASAP, so it would be best to take only veggies...

Oh, darn it! Absolutely no one could resist those delicious-looking chicken nuggets.

Pushing my regret and guilt aside, I took my food and followed Kev to our table.

"Hey," I said as I sat down next to Mel.

Kev stood contemplating where to sit. There was an available place next to Hayden, but he opted for the seat on Mel's other side, his cheeks two red blotches.

"You look like you're going to shit yourself, Burks," Hayden told him in an amused tone. "Relax. Breathe."

"Hayden!" Sarah said sharply.

He raised his brow at her. "What? I'm just trying to help the guy. He always looks constipated around me."

Mel smacked her forehead. "We're all going to look constipated around you if you don't stop," she told him.

If Hayden's looks could have killed, Melissa would have already been a ghost. "You look constipated all the time," he said.

"And you—" Mel started, but Sarah interrupted.

"Okay, enough. Can we please eat without you two bickering?" She looked at Hayden with a plea in her eyes and kissed him on the cheek. "Please."

Hayden clenched his jaw, clearly battling with his emotions as he looked at Sar. Hayden had borderline personality disorder, which manifested in moments like this, when each little thing could provoke him and lead to an immense and uncontrollable anger. It was connected with his extremely low self-esteem and severe trust issues he'd had basically his whole life. Mel and Hayden hadn't gotten along until recently, but even now they had a spat every once in a while. I could only imagine how hard it was for him to simmer down, and I admired that he tried his best to control himself.

His face was taut as he reached for his Coke. "She should learn when to shut it," he muttered.

"Mel," I mouthed at her when she parted her lips to respond, telling her with my gaze to drop it.

Melissa was temperamental, fiery, and occasionally aggressive, and she never failed to give others a taste of their own medicine. It was no wonder she aspired to be a social activist, already working her butt off as vice president of the student council to root out bullying from this school. She was passionate and brave, but she had a thing or two to learn about controlling her aggressive impulses.

She rolled her eyes. "Yeah, yeah." She shoved a few French fries into her mouth. Her sullen face was rather funny. "Anyway, have you heard about the theme of the school festival?" A slow grin formed on her face. "All my efforts have paid off because The Uneducated Swine And Pain In The Ass agreed to it being anti-bullying. Hooray."

Hayden snorted. "What did you do to make it happen? Threaten to chop his dick off?"

She raised her eyebrow at him and harumphed. "I'm promoting anti-violence here, although I wish I could do just that. He had to agree seeing that school board policies are changing. We're finally getting people who are willing to investigate just what the hell is going on in this pit of hell and make changes for the better."

It was true. The days of Principal Anders' corruption and poor work ethic were slowly coming to an end. Two weeks earlier, two seniors had pushed a freshman's head into a toilet, and a third had recorded it then posted it on Instagram. East Willow High students often posted bullying content on their private or public social media accounts, but so far they had managed to stay under the media's radar.

However, a niece of a Connecticut senator had stumbled upon this video and showed it to him. In one day, the news of brutal bullying in Enfield's high school spread across the state, and the authorities demanded a thorough investigation of our school's administration. We had the media on our doorstep more often than not these days.

Of course, the principal refused to take responsibility for this issue. He claimed he wasn't aware there were severe cases of bullying at his school, but I didn't think the investigators bought that.

So now that our school was in the public eye, Mel was using the opportunity to start her anti-bullying campaign. She even claimed she would film bullies if she had to and would send the videos to the media until Anders finally quit.

"We'll organize events to raise bullying awareness and spread the message of peace. I thought we could invite victims of bullying to speak about their experience, so people can understand more easily," Mel continued.

"Now that's a great idea," Sarah said enthusiastically, and I agreed with her. I had to hand it to Mel for her ideas and willingness to make things right. We needed more people like her who were passionate about making the world a better place.

"We can also play bullying documentaries," Mel added.

"While you're at it," Hayden interjected evenly, "why don't you also show the side of bullies?"

Mel frowned at him. "Their side? What do you mean?"

"I mean, if you're preaching, don't speak just about victims. Speak about bullies too. Show our side. We aren't all demons from hell. If people could understand us better, maybe we could have better chances at being less shitty."

We all gaped at him. I was surprised he was admitting out loud that he was one of the bullies, but what surprised me more was how I'd never thought about it that way. I'd never thought understanding bullies could make a difference, but it made sense. If they were ostracized and treated in the worst way possible, chances were slim to none that they would become better people or make something out of themselves.

Hayden was a real example of this. He was able to change more easily because he had Sarah with him. Her understanding and support fueled his strength and will to change.

Blake, on the other hand... I glanced at him. He talked with Masen and Steven at their table, with an ever-so-serious face, and I wondered once again what his story was. I was conflicted. Sarah had said some people could be so lost in their pain they were blind to how awful their actions were, but as much as I could understand it, that didn't change the fact that I'd suffered so much.

Even if what she said was true—that Blake could realize his mistakes and start to change—it would be difficult for me to get over everything he'd done to me. Maybe I'd be able to forgive him because holding a grudge would only make me more miserable, but anything beyond that would be pushing it.

The small part of me that harbored these feelings I refused to accept lived with an illusion that there could be more to Blake and me and we could find happiness just like Sarah and Hayden, but I couldn't keep having my head in the clouds. Reality was too painful for me to just get over it that easily and embrace Blake with all his flaws.

Sarah wrapped her arms around Hayden and left a kiss on his lips. "I love that idea, Hayden." She looked at Melissa. "It would be great if we could see bullies' side of the story. I think it would also be good for the victims because that way they can deal with their issues in a healthier way. They would be able to better understand their past and see it wasn't their fault for being bullied."

Mel rubbed her chin, deep in thought. "Hmm. I'll consider it. Although I think bullies deserve the worst, you do have a point there. Then again, I have a bully in my own house, and I know very well what happens inside his head, so I can understand to some extent why he behaves the way he does." She raised her index finger in the air. "*But*, this doesn't mean I'm defending him or anything. He deserves to be put in his place after everything he's done to all those poor students." She popped another French fry into her mouth. "Speaking of bullies"—she nodded in the direction of Blake's table—"I think your friends miss you."

Blake and Masen were looking right at us, and my cheeks warmed. This wasn't the first time Hayden had eaten with us, but it was still unusual. I glanced away from Blake, unable to hold his derisive gaze.

"Barbie can't stop looking this way. I guess you're more interesting than that chick next to him."

Hayden arched his eyebrows at her. "Are you jealous?"

She nodded. "Madly. I'm so sick with jealousy I'm so going to puke these fries on you right this minute." She rolled her eyes. "Actually, the whole cafeteria is staring at us. One can't eat without all these nosy busybodies." She pointed at him. "It's like you're a celebrity!"

"It's always been like that," Sarah said. "He attracts attention wherever he goes."

"It's b-b-because he's beautiful," Kev blurted out.

We fell into heavy silence, and he went crimson red. Sarah shifted in her seat, looking at him with pity.

Hayden cleared his throat. "Burks—"

"I'm s-s-sorry," Kev said with his eyes fixed on the ground as he jumped to his feet. "Forget about it."

"Kev," I called after him, but he dashed away from our table and made a quick exit. Without thinking, I went after him, ignoring everyone's stares.

"Kev, wait!"

His long legs carried him all the way to the other side of the school before I could catch up to him.

"Kev!"

"Leave me alone," he cried out over his shoulder, giving me a glimpse of his teary face. My stomach sank.

I grabbed his shoulder and turned him to face me with all the force I could muster. Each of his tears nailed new pain to my chest, and it bothered me that I couldn't do much to help him deal with this.

"I won't leave you alone," I replied with conviction that was rare for me. I glanced down the almost empty hallway and pulled Kev into the nearest empty classroom. I closed the door behind me. "Talk to me."

He walked over to the windows and remained with his back to me. His shoulders were shaking, his hunched form telling me just how distressed he was. My heart ached for him.

"It's not important."

"It's obviously important since you're like this." I approached him with a sudden surge of strength coursing through me. I felt protective of him.

He was so much taller than me, but he looked so small and fragile I wanted to wrap my arms around him and shield him from the whole world.

"Sharing is caring, right?" I said.

He sniffed. "I s-swear I'm not a crybaby."

I placed my hand on his shoulder. "It's okay if you are. I'm a crybaby too." I giggled. "We can be crybabies together."

A raspy chuckle slipped through his lips as he faced me. He quickly wiped the tears off his red cheeks. "I'm ashamed of talking about this with you."

"Don't be. You're my bestie. You can talk to me about anything you want."

His brows knitted together as he closed his eyes. "I feel awful."

"Because of what you said in the cafeteria?"

"That too." He sniffed a few times. "I feel awful for b-being...for being attracted to him." His cheeks reddened again, and he turned away from me. "I'm a guy. I...I'm not supposed to feel this way."

I grasped his upper arm. "Don't say that. You have the right to feel however you want to feel. That doesn't have anything to do with your gender. It's who you are."

He snapped his angry eyes over his shoulder to meet mine. "I don't like it! I've been living with shame ever s-s-since I realized I...I like boys too. Even my mom thinks it's weird!"

I shifted closer to him, the urge to protect him becoming stronger. "She's wrong. Just because she doesn't understand your sexuality, it doesn't mean it's bad. Straight, bi, or otherwise, that's who you are, and there's nothing wrong with that."

"So you don't think I'm messed up?"

I pulled him around to look at me. "Absolutely not. You're normal, and you should never be ashamed of that. I think you should embrace it and live your life however you want."

"But what if others find out? They'll bully me even more!"

I let out a heavy sigh. "It's true that there are close-minded people who act like this isn't the 21st century, but truth be told, bullies can find any reason to bully others, whether it's their sexuality, appearance, or something else entirely."

At least this was what my therapist told me all the time. She encouraged me to embrace the way I looked and be proud of it because that was who I was. It was easier said than done.

"I don't know, Jess. I...I'm scared."

My lips curled into a half-smile. "I understand." I understood it well because I was scared too. I was scared of living my life the way I wanted to live it.

He pushed his glasses up his nose. "I'm a horrible friend. I guess S-Sarah hates me."

"She doesn't hate you. She understands because we can't choose who we fall for."

"You don't think she's angry?"

"Not at all. So don't worry about her."

He rolled his lips in. "But I'm so embarrassed to even look at Hayden. How can I face him after this?"

"Act like it didn't happen? I don't know. I think it's not that big of a deal. I mean, it's not like you can do anything about it." I patted his shoulder. "So don't worry about it."

He shrugged. "I'll try." He wiped his nose with the back of his hand and adjusted his glasses. "Thanks. You're amazing."

He was so sweet. "You too."

"By the way, it sucks that you can't go to our choir practice. Marcus is going to miss you."

Tension coiled in my stomach at the reminder that I had detention with Blake after school. I wanted nothing more than to miss it, but there was no escaping it.

"Marcus?"

"Yeah. You know he keeps asking me about you when you're not there."

"Really?"

"Yeah. I mean he always wants to talk to me for some reason."

"Hmm, that sounds interesting. Maybe I'm just an excuse for him to talk to you."

"Nah. No way." I gave him a pointed look. "No way. He asked *you* out."

"That's true, but honestly? I don't feel like he likes me. He's friendly to me in U.S. history, but I think that's all there is to it."

"I see." He looked away. "He's cute," he said quietly, blushing.

"He's cute? Now that sounds interesting." I wiggled my brows at him and laughed when his whole face went red.

The bell rang, and my anxiety intensified. Just one more period and I would have to go to detention. I wrung my hands together, wishing a time-skip existed so I could just step into tomorrow.

We left the classroom. "Good luck with detention, Jess."

"Thanks. I'll need it. See you," I mumbled in response and headed to my next class, hoping one more time that this detention was just a bad dream and I was about to wake up soon.

• • • •

THE LAST PERIOD ENDED too quickly. I dragged myself to Ms. Gentry's classroom with anxiety bubbling in my stomach.

"It's okay, Jess. It will pass quickly. He won't do anything to you. Don't be afraid," I whispered to myself, my pulse accelerating rapidly.

It was no use. I couldn't calm down.

I reached the classroom just in time and exhaled in relief because it was empty. I sat down at the desk on the far side of the room, hoping Blake wouldn't show up. It was too quiet, which didn't sit well with me.

All my hope was squashed when the door opened and Blake entered. He looked ever so intimidating in a dark gray shirt and black jeans, but as always, there was more to him, and I couldn't look away. His piercing gaze held me captivated, wiping away all my coherent thoughts as we looked at each other. The silence in the room suddenly became deafening.

He crossed over and halted right in front of my desk. He looked down at me with his arms folded across his chest, and I felt at a big disadvantage sitting with him standing above me. I caught a whiff of his distinctive scent and frowned, reproaching myself for liking it.

"Did you have fun with Burks?"

My heart rate doubled as I stared at one spot on the blackboard, ignoring his unexpected question.

"You two are perfect for each other. Both of you are losers no one wants."

I tugged at my shirt, my fingers clenching around the material. He supported himself with both hands on the desk and leaned toward me. I dropped my gaze with a start. *Go. Away.*

"Only a loser would want to fuck a whale."

I winced and dug my fingers into my thighs as my face warmed up. My hair couldn't hide me enough.

"Shut up," I said, hardly more than a whisper.

"You like them weird, Fats? Does he stutter when he fucks you?"

My chest burned with anger. "Please shut up."

"I bet he couldn't keep his dick up for even a minute."

I was pressing my fingers into my thighs so hard it was going to leave bruises. "*Shut up.*"

He chuckled. "Maybe two minutes tops—*if* he imagined Hayden's dick."

"I said, shut up!" I stood up, forgetting all about fear as my anger took over. "You're absolutely disgusting! I won't let you speak about him like this!"

He raised one eyebrow at me and straightened himself up. "Or what? What are you going to do to protect your *boyfriend*? Whine? You're just making a fool of yourself."

"For *friends*, I'm ready to do anything."

Not even a muscle moved on his face as he studied me, his eyes ablaze. "Those are brave words for a total coward. Why don't you go to some corner and hide like usual? Before you shit your pants."

Just a few months earlier, that was exactly what I would've done. I wouldn't even have been able to speak my mind, but I couldn't keep quiet anymore—just like that day in the cafeteria more than two months earlier, when I'd confronted him for the first time ever.

"I'm aware that I'm not the bravest person out there, but I can change. I *want* to change."

"Aww, so touching. Do you want applause? Here." He clapped his hands hard. Each clap brought me more shame and pain, but I didn't back down.

"You can mock me all you want, but that doesn't change the fact that I'll be out of high school soon and won't have to see your face ever again." He clenched his jaw. "One day, I'll be a better person, but you'll never change. You'll always remain this horrible jerk without a heart." Something flashed in his eyes, and the veins at his temples bulged out. "You'll stay alone."

He fisted his hands. "Shut your damn mouth."

"Why?" I let out a taunting chuckle, which was so not me, but it was oddly fitting in this moment. "It's the truth. Does the truth hurt you?"

He grabbed the collar of my shirt and yanked me toward him. "If you don't shut your mouth right now, you'll regret it."

The adrenaline and anger silenced all the warnings that told me not to provoke him. "What's the matter, Blake? It hurts? But I'm just telling the truth! No one is ever going to love you—"

He shoved me into the nearest wall and pressed me against it, shaking with rage. "Shut the fuck up! You don't know anything about me!"

"And I don't want to!" I grabbed his hands with mine and tried to remove them from my collar, but to no effect. "I want to stay as far away from you as possible!"

He got into my face. "You'll never stay away from me!"

"Why?!"

"Because you're my fucking trigger!" His shouted revelation echoed sharply in the classroom. "You brought everything back! And for that, I'll make you pay!"

I was dumbstruck, my gaze darting between his eyes. "What are you—"

"Miss Metts? Mr. Jones? What in heaven's name are you doing?!"

Releasing me, Blake stepped back and faced Ms. Gentry, who stared at us with eyes wide open. My legs turned wobbly now that I was coming off my adrenaline high, so I supported myself against the wall.

"I-I'm sorry—" I started.

"What the fuck does it look like?" Blake growled. He looked like he was about to explode, which was nothing new because he'd always been volatile and easily angered when confronted.

"Watch your mouth, Mr. Jones. You can't talk to me like that."

He sneered at her. "Or what?"

She narrowed her eyes. "Or I'll talk to the principal about your suspension."

"Do that, and I'll talk to my father about having you fired." I gaped at him. The audacity!

"I'm not afraid of your father, Mr. Jones," she said in a slightly raised voice with her hands placed on her hips, and I looked at her with newfound respect. "And you would be wise not to talk to him because I'm not afraid to go to the press and expose your father if that happens. I'm not that easily intimidated."

He clenched and relaxed his hands as he glared at her, staying silent. I hoped he wouldn't make this harder than it already was. I just wanted this detention to be over with.

"I see you two have some serious issues with each other, and I'm not sure you really understand the ramifications of your deeds. I'm going to let you go home now." *Huh?*

"You're letting us go home," Blake stated in a monotone voice, his eyes zeroed in on her.

"Yes, but hang on. I'm not finished yet. Our janitor has work for you, so you're going to help him out until Thursday. You'll start tomorrow after classes."

I stared at her open-mouthed. This couldn't be happening.

"You've gotta be kidding me," he said, crossing his arms over his chest.

"Afraid not, Mr. Jones. This is your punishment, but also a valuable lesson. Just writing reports or essays won't cut it. You two have to learn to communicate better, and working together can help you with that."

"*No*," I blurted out. This was madness! I was sickened that I had to spend the rest of the week doing who knew what with Blake. No amount of time spent together would make our communication any better.

"You can forget it," Blake said. "I'm not doing it." He went for the door, but Ms. Gentry didn't plan to let him have the last word.

"Then you will face a suspension and possible expulsion."

He looked at her over his shoulder with his hand on the door handle and snorted. "Expulsion? There's no way I'd get expelled. You seem to keep forgetting who my father is."

"And you seem to keep forgetting that your father's connections don't matter much now that the whole world knows what is going on at this school. I've seen your record, Mr. Jones, and I can say with certainty that your bullying days are coming to an end. I'll personally make sure you're expelled if you refuse to attend detention."

He marched over to her with a murderous expression. "If you think you can make the rules, you're dead wrong."

She wasn't fazed in the least. "I won't repeat myself, so you better choose your next words wisely."

Wow. Just wow. I looked back and forth between them with admiration for Ms. Gentry. No teacher had stood up to Blake because they were afraid of his father, so this was the ray of hope Mel had often talked about. Mel believed individuals could change the world, and Ms. Gentry in action definitely confirmed that.

"The same goes for you, Miss Metts. Don't even think about trying to evade it."

I gulped, terrified just thinking about getting expelled. I could *not* let that happen. My parents would disown me!

"I'll help the janitor."

"Good." She nodded at me then looked at Blake. "Mr. Jones?"

His glare was startling. He just stood there and looked at Ms. Gentry and me like we were his worst enemies. Seconds and seconds ticked by, tension rolling off him in waves until he finally gave in.

"Fine," he spat out. "I'll do it."

"Excellent. Look for Mr. Maynard tomorrow. He'll tell you everything you need to know."

Giving me a glance full of hatred, Blake spun on his heel and stormed out of the classroom, but I couldn't breathe any easier. All I could think about was that I was stuck with him for the next three days, replaying in my mind that one sentence that reached the deepest corners of me.

You're my fucking trigger.

Chapter 5

I YAWNED AND RESTED my head in my hand. I struggled to stay awake in English. If only I was in my bed and sleeping. Ms. Dawson droned on about Virginia Woolf, but I didn't hear the half of it. I thought about Blake and the way he'd acted the previous day, unease clawing at my insides. He was so fixated on me, and I didn't know what to make of it.

To make things worse, my mom had given me the money to pay him for the broken screen. This meant I had to approach him and humiliate myself in order to fix this. The money in my pocket felt like lead, weighing me down.

I glanced at Sarah. She doodled something in her notebook, obviously not paying any attention to Ms. Dawson. Hayden, who sat on her other side, was on his phone. He looked even less interested in the lesson.

Sarah and I now sat the back of the classroom instead of the front, having taken the seats of Hayden's buddies. It was only natural for Sarah to sit next to him after they got together, so switching places was a no-brainer.

I took my phone out of my pocket. I was going to see if Sar knew something about Blake that I didn't.

Has Hayden told you anything about Blake?

She stopped doodling and reached for her phone in her pocket. She cast me a curious glance before she opened the message. Her reply arrived a few moments later.

Like what?

Like what's his goddamn problem?

Did something happen between you two in detention?

We had a huge argument before Ms. Gentry arrived. And we have to help the janitor until Thursday as our punishment.

Are you serious?

Is Mel vegetarian?

She texted me back, and I glanced at Ms. Dawson to confirm she wasn't looking in our direction—not that it mattered much because she couldn't have cared less that the half of the classroom was chatting or texting. I opened the message.

That's not good.

Yeah. He mentioned something weird.

What?

He said I was his trigger. Do you know what it could mean?

Not really. Hayden hasn't told me much, except that he never dates.

That much was obvious, considering he went from one model-like girl to another like they were candies. She sent another text before I could reply to her.

I have a theory.

Boy, I had more of those than I could count, and each one was more absurd than the last.

Shoot.

I think something happened to him that prevents him from falling for anyone.

I just stared at the message, taken back to the time in the school gym a couple of months earlier, when I'd found him alone crying. That was the moment that had changed my perspective on him, and it was then that I'd heard him mention a girl's name that piqued my curiosity. *Emma.* Did this have anything to do with her?

Sar's new text popped up on my screen.

I noticed something.

Yes?

I think he was or is abused because he doesn't like being touched from behind.

I frowned. I recollected my every encounter with Blake, but I failed to find anything that would confirm her words.

How do you know this?

Remember when you drove me home last year? He went berserk when you touched his shoulder.

My pulse quickened as the memory of that day rushed back to me. I'd thought he was just mad because I, someone he hated, had touched him. I hadn't found anything about it unusual.

You think that's a sign of some trauma?

It's possible.

How about a phobia?

She frowned, deep in thought, before she typed a new message.

Like a phobia of touching?

Yeah.

Who knows?

I thought about this as the day went on, but I was unable to connect the dots. Even if he had been or was being abused, it didn't justify the way he treated me. This meant he'd shifted the blame onto me for something that had nothing to do with me, and it was inexcusable. I didn't deserve his anger.

U.S. history was about to bring me more time with Blake, and it didn't help that we had detention right after it. I had to pass next to his locker on my way to the classroom, and my heartbeat accelerated before I even spotted him going through his stuff there. I quickened my pace to move past, but then I drew up. This could be my chance to give him the money for his phone screen.

My stomach spasmed. I wanted to bolt away, but I remembered my mom's face when she gave me the money. It was either give him the money or die trying.

I forced my unsteady legs to move before I lost what little courage I'd gathered. It was like I was walking straight into the lion's den, and I was clueless about what was waiting for me in the end. I stopped at a safe distance and took the money out of my pocket.

My traitorous eyes slid down his body, taking advantage of the opportunity before he turned around. My chest ached with sweet pressure that morphed into displeasure when I realized I was gawking at him.

Stupid, stupid me.

I tugged at the end of my shirt, remembering to suck my belly in when a few girls passing by glanced at my stomach. It was a good thing I wasn't wearing a tight shirt today.

"Blake," I called out, and his back muscles turned rigid. I swallowed hard, clutching the bills in my hand. *I must not wimp out. I absolutely must not wimp out.*

He turned to face me with a hostile expression. "The fuck you want?"

As much as he drove me up the wall, I had to put up with his horrible attitude and be a better person this time. "I owe you for your broken screen." Each word hurt; everything in me was set against this. "So I want to pay for it."

My racing pulse went crazy when I moved two steps closer to him and extended my hand with the money toward him, silently begging him not to make this harder for me and take it.

He looked at the bills as if he didn't understand what the hell I was doing. Frankly, I didn't understand myself either, but I'd broken his screen, and it was time for me to own up to it.

"You're paying me for my broken screen," he stated flatly.

"Y-Yes." My hand was shaking, and I was sure he could see it. He was most certainly feeding on it, enjoying seeing me at his mercy. "I-I'm sorry for breaking your screen." There, I'd said it. I'd managed to say my apology. "Please. Take the money."

He tilted his head to the side. "You're sorry for breaking my screen."

"Yes."

After several long seconds, he reached for the money, and I met his gaze, relieved but also surprised he wasn't going to give me trouble. It seemed things would work out in my favor. I held my breath when our hands met and his touch lingered on my skin for a second longer than necessary before he pulled his hand away.

I expected him to put the bills into his pocket, but he didn't do that.

Instead, he ripped them into pieces, his expression blank as he stared at me. My eyes widened as he dropped them to the floor. A couple of students stopped to see what was going on, and my face flared hot.

"You can go fuck yourself with your shitty apology."

Those torn bills were the ripped pieces of my dignity, thrown to the floor to be stomped on and tarnished. My dignity would always be trampled. Tears collected in my eyes.

"Why do you have to be this way?" My voice was whiny—too whiny.

"Did you already forget what I said? You won't get away with it that easily."

A tear escaped my eye, and I brushed it off furiously, angry at myself for allowing him to see me shaken. He shut his locker with a bang and walked away.

I trembled hard as I stared at the bills on the floor. *I. Hate. Him.*

Hiding behind my hair, I ignored everyone's stares and hauled myself to the classroom. A knot of nervousness in my stomach grew stronger when I stepped inside and reached my seat with my eyes fixed on the floor. I felt like I could erupt into tears at any moment, but it was out of the question, and I tried my best to smile back at Marcus when I sat down, pretending I was perfectly fine.

Blake's proximity to me was torturous, but Marcus provided a good distraction as we messaged each other on Snapchat. This helped me forget about Blake at least for a little while.

When the class was over, Blake was the first to leave. He didn't look at me even once, which was completely fine by me. I fiercely hoped he would skip detention and go somewhere far away. Like to the moon.

Ms. Gentry cast me a long glance that said loud and clear: *Don't even think about missing detention.* I nodded at her, my stomach twisted in knots.

"Can I talk to you?" Marcus asked me in the hallway. "I need to tell you something."

"I'd like to, but I have detention now."

"It won't take long."

"Okay then."

We stopped at the corner that coincidentally looked right at Blake's locker across the hall. He was there, leaning against it as he talked to some girl, and my stomach churned with misplaced bitterness. I pulled my gaze away from them so he wouldn't notice me looking and focused on Marcus. He seemed uncomfortable.

"What's up?"

He scratched the back of his neck and ran his hand over his twist out. "I guess you've probably heard the rumors that I'm gay?"

I shifted on my feet. *Okay, this was unexpected.*

"Yes."

"I thought you didn't want to go out with me because of the rumors."

"No, that's not it. I just..."

My gaze darted to Blake, and my stomach somersaulted because his eyes were already on me. Aversion was written all over his face as he looked between Marcus and me, and once more, the world narrowed to the two of us. Anger flickered in me, reminding me of how degraded I was when he ripped my money into pieces.

He would never change. That simply wasn't possible.

Blake's stare became too intent, and I blushed profusely. He didn't even pay attention to the girl talking to him, until he suddenly pulled her against him and made a great show of kissing her. His hands slid down from her shoulders and cupped her butt right in the middle of the half-empty school hallway. I dug my nails into my palms, pursing my lips as I tried to suppress the increasing anger.

"Jessica?" Marcus called out to me, and I forced my gaze back to him.

"I'm sorry, Marcus. I really don't want to hurt you, but I don't feel that way about you. I see you as a friend—"

He grinned. "That's okay. It's good that you see me only as a friend, because I lied to you."

I eyed him carefully. "You lied to me?"

"Yes. I don't actually like you."

My heart contracted painfully because for a moment, I thought he was going to say he'd asked me out because of some stupid bet he'd made with his friends or something.

"Then why did you ask me out?"

He slumped his shoulders, avoiding my eyes. "Er, the rumors are true. I'm gay." I was only able to stare at him, confounded. "And I asked you out because I thought if I got closer to you, I'd also get closer to Kevin."

I tipped my head to the side. "You asked me out because of Kevin?"

"Yes. I...I like Kevin."

I couldn't find the words right away as I processed this latest piece of information. Seeing how vulnerable he looked, I didn't think it was the right moment to tell him his "strategy" was absolutely not the way to get anyone. It was beyond me how he could've thought that by asking me out he could be with Kevin one day, but I didn't have it in me to get angry.

Now that I thought about it, Marcus and Kevin would look so cute together. I could already imagine them walking together holding hands. So cute.

"Then you should talk to him and tell him that."

"Er, I don't know." He rubbed his neck. "It's not easy to say that. And what if he's not into guys?" Aww. The blush that covered his light brown face was adorable.

"You won't know that unless you talk to him."

"How about you talk to him?"

"Me?"

"Yes. Please. I'll owe you forever. Just tell him I like him and want to ask him out."

I wasn't sure that was a good idea. "Marcus..."

He looked away. "Look...I'm sorry." His quiet words were dripping with shame. Out of the corner of my eye, I saw Blake coming in our direction, and I grew very still.

"Why are you sorry?" I asked Marcus. *Please don't stop. Just go somewhere far, far away.*

"Because it sounds like I wanted to use you. Okay, I did want to use you, but I didn't have any bad intentions. I swear." He looked at the floor. "Now I see how stupid it was. It was so, so stupid."

Blake was only a few feet away from us, and I tried my hardest to ignore him...

"Don't worry. I'm not angry. I—"

"Whore," Blake spat out without stopping. The word was so harsh and demeaning it felt like a slap on my cheek, and I recoiled in shock. I flexed my hand into a fist.

Ugly. Fat. Stupid. Disgusting. Whore. All those powerful insults...they only produced more pain and insecurity until I was reduced to an unworthy being. Until I believed them.

The words were burning in my throat, echoing in my mind louder and louder as my anger rose. First my money, now this. I was tired.

I was tired of him, and I was tired of fear and shame.

Of his continuous insults.

Of waiting for him to change.

Of my heart going against my logic.

Screw this.

"You're a whore!" I exploded loud enough for the whole hallway to hear it. "You're the only whore here, Blake Jones!"

He stopped mid-step, and I was sure I was done for if he got his hands on me. I grabbed Marcus's hand and ran, leading us away from that hallway. I didn't stop until we reached the foyer and I was sure he hadn't followed us.

I supported myself against my knees to catch my breath. I was astounded by the courage I'd had to talk back to him like that.

Marcus burst out laughing. "You're amazing. His face when you said that was priceless! He totally deserved it."

I let out a short chuckle, but I wasn't actually amused. It was just to hide how awful I felt.

With Blake, I couldn't expect anything but an infinite loop of embarrassments and insults. I'd gotten back at him now, but the bullying wasn't going to end. There would always be another day filled with his hatred. Always and always.

I cast Marcus a fake smile to mask my pain. "I guess you think I'm a freak because of the way he treats me."

"Why would I think that? You're not weird at all."

"But Blake keeps saying nasty things to me. It's too much."

"It's not your fault he's too stupid to realize what a great person you are."

Everything in me warmed, and a real smile broke out on my face. "You really think that?"

"Yeah, and it's not just because you're Kevin's friend and you might help me with..." He smiled sheepishly. "You know."

"Right, Kevin—you want me to talk to Kevin about you. Sneaky." He shrugged his shoulders, chuckling. "I can't promise anything, but I'll try to talk to him."

Marcus didn't need to know how bad his chances were, seeing that Kevin crushed on Hayden and me.

"Thank you! I said this, but I'll say it again—you're amazing!"

"It's good to know at least someone thinks I'm amazing," I muttered to my chin. "I need to go now."

"Sure. See you tomorrow."

"See you."

I waved at him and headed to Mr. Maynard's office. Each step that took me closer felt heavier. I expected Blake to retaliate, so I figured this would be a good time for him to skip detention. Or have sudden amnesia and forget about my outburst.

Tugging at my shirt so it wouldn't show my stomach flab, I knocked on the door and entered Mr. Maynard's extremely small office. Blake was already here, sitting on the only chair in the room beside Mr. Maynard's. His jaw was set hard as he glared at me, and I hoped for a miracle that would allow me to get out of this detention unscathed.

There was barely a place for me to stand in the room illuminated by a weak light bulb hanging from a cord. I had to be squeezed between the janitor's desk and his small drawer cabinet. The desk was loaded with an old computer and stacks of folders and papers, which threatened to tip over to the ground.

"Miss Metts, you're here. Good," Mr. Maynard said with a smile. He was a kind man in his fifties, and I found it easy to return his smile. I glanced at his receding hairline and wondered if he was dying his hair black because I couldn't spot even a single gray hair.

Blake shifted on his chair, and I sucked in my breath. He was too close, his appealing scent drifting up to my nose. If I moved only a little, the hand he had resting on his thigh would touch my leg.

"So will you finally spill what this is all about?" Blake asked gruffly, but Mr. Maynard—always so nice—didn't take offense.

He smiled and nodded. "Of course. Now that Miss Metts is here, I can tell you what's expected of you this week. There are a few rooms in the basement that need to be refurbished."

I sensed Blake tense, and I glanced at him. He had an expression that was completely unexpected. It was terror.

"You're not going to refurbish those rooms, if that's what worries you," he joked with a chuckle, but Blake wasn't amused. He wasn't amused at all, staring at him completely frozen.

"In order to refurbish the rooms, we need to remove the things that are in there. It's some old school equipment that hasn't been used for more than a decade now. All you need to do is pack them into boxes and throw them into dumpsters."

"Did you say a basement?" Blake asked slowly through clenched teeth. It was as if he'd ignored everything Mr. Maynard said except for that one word.

"Yes, Mr. Jones. They are in the basement." Blake fisted his hand on his thigh, his artery pumping furiously in his neck, but he didn't say anything. "Those old rooms were used as storage, but we have a serious mold problem, so we need to renovate them as soon as possible. You will work for one hour after school each day, and you'll start with one room. If you finish cleaning it before Thursday, you will go to the next one, and so on. The boxes are already down there. Now, do you have any questions?"

He looked between Blake and me, but neither of us said a word. I glanced at Blake and saw him staring at the ground with a vacant gaze, like he was out of it. His breathing grew ragged.

"Mr. Jones?" he asked him, but Blake didn't move an inch, let alone acknowledge the question. His gaze never moved from the floor.

"No," I answered, staring at Blake in confusion. "No questions."

Mr. Maynard clasped his hands together and cast us another one of his warm smiles. "Good! Then I'll take you there and leave you to it. Come with me."

I was the first to step out, wanting to put as much space between Blake and me as possible. The school was mostly empty now, and our steps echoed in the long hallways. I glanced at Blake over my shoulder. I didn't miss his heavy steps or stiff posture as he stared at the ground with scrunched-up eyebrows. He was rubbing his left hand incessantly.

"Here we are," Mr. Maynard said, opening the double doors that led downstairs. He turned the light switches on and continued down the slippery-looking steps. I followed closely behind him.

I'd never been down there, and after hearing Mr. Maynard talk about dilapidated rooms with mold, I expected a long, dark corridor out of a horror movie with eerie sounds and shadows looming higher with every step.

The real thing was less dreary than my imagination, but it could make a person feel claustrophobic or uneasy with its low ceiling covered with mold, poor ventilation, stale smell, and rusty pipes that ran along the ceiling and white brick walls.

Mr. Maynard stopped in front of the first discolored door and turned to face us, but then his gaze fell on Blake. "Mr. Jones? What's wrong?"

I looked at him over my shoulder. He was unusually still on the last step of the staircase, his hand gripping the banister. Even with the distance separating us, I could see how pale he looked. His eyes were wide and terrified as they darted all over the long passageway.

"Mr. Jones? Are you all right?"

"I can't do this," Blake said breathlessly, and before Mr. Maynard could even say anything, he rushed up the stairs and got out.

Chapter 6

"YOU'LL CHOKE IF YOU eat that fast," my mom said with a chuckle as she poured coffee in her cup. She wore her business suit, ready to go to work.

I swallowed a big bite of my toast with peanut butter, savoring its rich taste, which was to die for. I loved peanut butter so much I wanted to own a gigantic warehouse with an unlimited supply so I could eat it every day for the rest of my life.

"I can't help myself. You know I can't resist this sweet, sweet peanut butter." I took another bite. *Mmm, so good.*

As I chewed, I scrolled on my phone through the comments on "The Chains of Fears." I already had loads of positive reactions. Many people complimented my distinctive voice and the way I was able to pour my soul out and make them feel my pain and helplessness. This gave me a huge boost.

"My new song is getting positive reactions," I told Mom.

She leaned against the kitchen island as she took a sip of her coffee. "I told you people would like it. It's such an emotional song. Although, it's very sad and a bit on the dark side."

"Yeah. It is."

She placed her finger on her chin. "'You shackled me to yourself and led me to tears. You're nothing but the chains of fears,'" she said softly, reciting lines from the chorus. "Is this coming from your personal experience?"

I cast my eyes down and bit into the toast to buy some time. The blush on my cheeks didn't help.

"No," I said between swallows. "It's just random."

"I see."

I returned my attention to my phone, but I didn't see anything, my mind drifting to the previous day. Since Blake had skipped our detention, I was forced to work alone, which was ten times better than sharing that rundown space with him, but it meant I was all alone with my thoughts. Whenever I thought I was done with him, I witnessed something that

63

touched the hidden corners of my heart, and a new cycle of want, doubt, and pain would start.

I wasn't supposed to feel sorry for him. I wasn't supposed to care about his problems, let alone feel the need to help him in any way, but I couldn't help the way I felt.

As I filled the box with the dusty equipment, I mulled over his unusual behavior in Mr. Maynard's office and on those stairs, and I came to the conclusion that he must be afraid of basements. His fear was evident when Mr. Maynard mentioned the basement, as well as when we got there and he was rooted to the last stair, as if the basement was lava and he was terrified of taking even one more step.

His inexplicable fear only added to the mystery of him and gave me more proof that he wasn't as invulnerable as he'd seemed when I met him. As much as I despised him, I wanted to push through his layers of poison and anger and see what made him tick. I wanted to see the real him.

"Owen spoke to your principal yesterday."

"He did?"

"Yes. He guaranteed the school was working on a new program that imposes stricter punishments for problematic kids."

I rolled my eyes. It was typical of Principal Anders to try to save face after the tabloids had labeled our school as "The Lair of Bullies."

"He even confirmed that all personnel will go through extensive training to learn to deal with bullies more effectively."

"Wow. It's a real utopia in there. I'll give up cheeseburgers forever if that actually happens."

"Only time will tell, but in the meantime, make sure you stay out of trouble, okay? If anyone harasses you, report them."

I rolled my eyes again. "Sure."

She sipped her coffee and glanced at her watch. "I need to hurry because we have an important meeting today."

I giggled. "You always have some important meeting." I took a huge swallow of the toast.

"That's how it is when you have a drunk local singer who doesn't know when to shut it on a podcast. So now I have to do damage control."

I was overcome by a fit of chuckles. I knew very well what my mom was dealing with in her PR firm. The dirty things she knew about some of her clients were enough to fill tabloids for the whole year.

"Right. Before I go, I want to ask you—have you received any admission decisions?"

A piece of bread stuck in my throat, and I started coughing. This was *not* the topic I wanted to discuss early in the morning.

I'd received a few responses, but how could I tell her I didn't care about any of those colleges she and Dad had made me apply to? There were only two responses that truly mattered to me, and those would come from music colleges in Hartford and New York. I still didn't know how to break the news to my parents.

"Yes..."

"You did? Why didn't you tell us anything? What did they say?"

I shrugged, my eyes downcast. "I wanted to surprise you?" I gave another shrug. "I'm still waiting for some responses, but so far, I've been admitted to three of them."

"You have?" She clasped her hands together, her face a picture of joy. "Oh, dear!" In a second, her arms enclosed me in a tight embrace. "I knew it! I'm so proud of you, Jess. I knew my sweetie would get in." She kissed the top of my head and looked at me with pride in her eyes. This only made my chest ache.

I forced a smile on my face. I couldn't tell her now. I didn't want to see her face fall with disappointment. "Yeah."

"We have to celebrate! I'm going to call Owen and tell him the great news. He's going to be thrilled! And wait until I tell your grandparents!"

I smiled more widely, feeling like I was getting deeper into a mud trap with no way out. My stomach churned when I got into my car. There was no way they would ever accept me going to a music college.

They'd never thought much of my passion for singing. They were full of praise for my voice and liked to boast about it to our relatives, but they never regarded it as something serious. Dad had once told me singing couldn't pay bills and I should be realistic, claiming becoming a lawyer would be the smartest and most responsible thing to do. I never mentioned wanting a singing career again.

I parked in the school's parking lot as I sang along with "What the Water Gave Me" by Florence and the Machine playing on the radio. I was instantly calmed by the notes coming out of my mouth and could breathe more easily. I closed my eyes and leaned my head against the headrest, buzzing with energy as I hit the highest notes. At this moment, I was invincible, and the best years of my life were about to come.

I got out of my car with a smile and headed into school, trudging through the snow that had accumulated overnight. It was the first day of March, but the weather was unforgiving and promising more cold days to come. I rubbed my gloved hands together and picked up my pace until I reached the foyer.

My phone vibrated in my pocket, and I drew it out. It was Dad.

Mom just told me the news. Congratulations, Jess! We're going to have a big celebration.

I grimaced at the message. They would most likely have a barbecue in our back yard and call all our relatives. I was under more and more pressure.

Thanks, Dad. Maybe just us three can celebrate for starters. I'm still undecided on which college I'll attend.

That's just a minor detail. We'll help you decide which option is the best for you.

I stopped at my locker with heaviness in my chest. My thumb hovered over the keyboard before I gave up on answering and shoved my phone back into my pocket. I had to tell them before this became a bigger mess.

I opened my locker, but someone slammed it shut and caged me in with his body, flattening his palms against the lockers on both sides of my shoulders.

"Don't move," Blake growled into my ear before I could make a sound, creating flutters deep down in my stomach. My body stirred at his nearness.

"What do you want?"

"I want to make sure you won't open your fat, ugly mouth and say anything about yesterday."

I squeezed my eyes shut and inhaled a long, raspy breath. I may have been pushing my luck, but I wasn't going to keep quiet anymore. I suffered whether I stayed silent or not.

"Which part? You being a jerk all the time or you running away like the coward you accuse me of being?"

He slammed his fist against the locker and got in my face. "Shut the fuck up."

"What? The truth hurts again?"

He grabbed my chin and made me look at him. "I think you forgot you shouldn't talk back to me because if you do, I'll get back at you and it will be real ugly."

"More than it already is?" His fingers pressed into my skin, and I winced. "It...hurts," I said through my gritted teeth, frustrated that he was using aggression to subdue me.

He lessened the pressure, but he didn't remove his fingers from my chin. "That's what you get when—"

"That's what I get?!" I chuckled, but it didn't contain even an ounce of joy. It was an expression of utter pain that resided in my heart because he was so cruel and merciless. "Do you even hear yourself? So when you can't win using words, you use aggression? What's next? Are you going to raise your hand against me? Beat me?"

He released me and stepped away, and I spun around to face him. I pressed my back against the lockers as I took in his frown and lips pressed together in an unforgiving, thin line.

"Is that what you think of me? You think I would *beat* you?"

My heart fluttered at the brief display of hurt that shadowed his face, but I didn't allow that to stop me from saying what I'd kept inside for so long.

"Are you seriously asking me that? You're a bully! I expect the worst from you! And how could I not? How many times have you pushed me around? How many times have you grabbed my arms or shoulders so hard it left me with bruises?"

He staggered back with widening eyes, but instead of feeling satisfaction at seeing him like this, I only felt more pain.

"You keep threatening me whenever I piss you off, which is *always*, so I'd be a fool not to expect you to hit me or worse." I clenched my fingers around the hem of my shirt, holding back the tears that came so suddenly. "I don't even know why I'm telling you this. It doesn't matter."

Ignoring how weak my limbs felt, I turned my back to him and opened my locker. The hair on my neck bristled as I waited for his reaction. I expected him to do or say something that would hammer more pain into me, but he didn't do anything. I pulled out my French textbook and *Le Père Goriot* by Honoré de Balzac, which we were going to read in class.

I closed my locker and turned to him, expecting to see his eyes drilling into me, but he was already gone.

What gives?

I smiled.

I didn't know if this was a small victory or not, but it was definitely progress.

. . . .

I STOOD IN THE MIDDLE of the dank room, singing quietly as I filled boxes with wall maps, old lab tubes and bottles, VHS tapes, and other stuff. Dust was everywhere, and I sneezed at least ten times. I was glad I'd brought an old shirt I only wore at home because I was totally covered in it.

Blake wasn't here, which came as no surprise, although I wondered if he would be suspended for skipping, or if he would manage to turn this around in his favor. I was betting on the latter.

My muscles hurt from all the work, and I hoped I could shed a few pounds. The jeans I wore were already too tight, and I'd bought them only three months prior. I stopped and looked at my thighs, which rubbed together when I walked, and pulled a face. They did seem thicker than three months earlier...

I knew I had to cut down on my sweets and snacks, but it was an impossible mission. It wasn't fair. These days it seemed I could gain weight just by drinking water, and I wished I were like Sarah. She was so skinny with her thin arms and remarkably slim, long legs, and she wasn't even trying. I wanted her thigh gap. I wanted her weight. And most of all—I wanted to eat pizza without worrying about those horrific calories.

Think positive, Jess. You're beautiful the way you are. You're beautiful the way you are...

I heard quick footsteps in the distance, and I tensed. I hoped it was Mr. Maynard and not Blake. I reached for the flasks on the shelf next to me, my pulse quickening with each footstep. I put the flasks in the box and raised my gaze. Blake entered the room with a big box in his hands and a scowl on his pale face, and my heart dropped to my stomach.

Uh-oh.

"I'm not a coward," he told me, referring to what I'd said to him this morning, and went to the other side of the room. I didn't say anything in response as I watched him put one of the VCRs into the box roughly, surprised he felt the need to defend himself to me.

We worked in silence for several minutes. I threw occasional furtive glances at him, noticing that he'd never looked more on edge than he did now, with his face taut and eyes guarded.

Standing on my tiptoes, I took the desk globe from the top shelf, but the sphere separated from its mounting and dropped all the way down to the floor with a loud clunk.

"Fuck!" Blake jumped back and placed his arms in front of him as a shield. He met my eyes, his fear ebbing into rage. "What the fuck are you doing?!"

"I'm sorry," I mumbled and picked up the sphere from the floor. "The globe wasn't connected to the mounting well. I didn't mean to scare you."

He tightened his jaw. "What are you talking about?" He picked up a couple of tubes, avoiding my gaze. "You didn't scare me. I just hate clumsy people."

I wanted to tell him it wasn't my fault the sphere had fallen off, but I swallowed the remark. I thought about what he'd said to me on Monday.

"What did you mean when you said I was your trigger?" I asked, ignoring my inner voice that told me to keep quiet.

He grew still and snapped his eyes up to look at me. "Forget about that."

His tone left no room for argument, but I didn't heed the warning that suggested I would regret this. "Why?"

"Because."

Vexed, I put the sphere in the box none too gently and placed my hands on my hips. "Why do you bully me?" He flexed his hands at his sides. "Why do you hate me?"

He returned to packing, refusing to give me an answer. My heartbeat took off at a gallop. Something deep in me pushed me to get closer to the truth amid the rising anger and warnings in my head.

"Blake, stop ignoring me and, for once, tell me the truth!"

He dropped the projector into the box and pinned me with a glare. "You want the truth?"

"Yes!"

"Okay. Here's your truth." He approached me with a sneer, his steps slow. "I hate everything about you."

I recoiled and grabbed the edge of the table behind me for support.

"You're a whiny bitch. You always hide behind your friends and live like a coward." Something splintered inside of me, and it was painful. "I hate girls like you the most."

My nails dug into the unyielding surface of the table, but even that hurt less than the growing wound in my chest.

"You're always crying and crying and *crying*, and I'm really curious how you have any more tears left to cry."

I was cold. So cold. "Okay. Enough."

"No, *sweetheart*. You wanted the truth—now handle it."

He stopped with less than two feet separating us, and I pressed myself against the table as much as I could.

"You're fat—like do you even have limits?" He pinched my belly, and I yelped, astounded by it. "Look at this. Tell me, do you really think there would be a guy who could like this? Or this." He gave my cheek a squeeze and tugged at it. "Or this." He pinched my inner thigh, and I scrambled away from him with a cry.

"Don't touch me!"

I backed away until I hit the cabinet next to the table. All my insecurities rushed back to me, my self-loathing topping everything, and tears sprang to my eyes. Never had I felt uglier or fatter than under his hateful eyes in this moment.

"You're hideous from the inside out."

I whimpered and lowered my gaze to the floor. My hair wasn't enough to hide me from him—nothing was ever enough to hide me from him—and shame pushed away all the self-esteem I'd managed to gain these last few months with the help of my therapist.

He snorted. "Just like I said—you're all tears and nothing else."

I couldn't take this anymore. I darted for the exit, blind with tears. To hell with detention and everything. I was about to reach the door, but I remembered too late I'd left a packed box near the doorway to dump it later. I tripped over it and crashed down on the floor, my knees taking the biggest hit.

For a moment—just for a moment—I allowed myself to close my eyes and wallow in utter humiliation. My knees hurt badly, but I didn't stop to inspect them. I picked myself right up without even turning to look at him. I was just giving him more reasons to hate me. I was giving myself more reasons to hate myself.

I took two steps toward the door, limping.

"Jessie, wait...," he said in an unbelievably soft voice that was laced with regret, and I halted, unsure if I'd just imagined it. Warmth spread through my chest, spurring me to stay.

Of course I didn't acknowledge it or him.

I just got out and never looked back.

Chapter 7

I SPENT HOURS IN MY car parked in front of my empty house, the dark sky gradually enveloping me in shadows. I wished my tears had dried a long time ago, but they kept coming, and my chest ached under the on-slaught of self-denigrating thoughts.

I shouldn't have been complaining about his cruelty. I'd asked for the truth, and I'd gotten it. I couldn't expect anything else from him, because who could love me like this?

My mind raced back to the two-year relationship with my ex-boyfriend, which had ended a year ago. Rory was the son of my mom's best friend, so we'd known each other since we were in diapers, but we'd never been particularly close. Not until I went to his birthday party in ninth grade.

That night we danced, talked, and then talked some more, and something changed between us. We ended up kissing on his porch, and he asked me out on a date. Rory was pretty, but he wasn't quite my type. He was short and had a few too many pimples on his face, but he was sweet and good-natured. As someone who had been invisible to boys, I was hungry to be seen, and I basked in his attention, so I wanted to give us a shot.

If I could explain our relationship in one word, it would be plain. He was a nice guy, but there was no spark. Despite that, I gave him my virginity because I felt comfortable enough around him and believed he wasn't going to mention anything about my weight or criticize me.

He never said a bad word about my body, but he rarely complimented it, and he generally avoided any conversation that touched on the topic of my weight. He would say I was cute, but I had eyes and I noticed the way he looked at slim girls. It wasn't the same expression he had when he looked at me.

I'd acted like I was okay with it—like that was something I had to ac-cept—but month after month, it just created a bigger dent in my self-confi-dence until the harsh truth was drilled into my mind. No one could like me like this.

I gripped my steering wheel and leaned my forehead against it, closing my eyes.

How I envied them. How I envied the girls who didn't have to worry about the next calorie or those who could easily slip into their bikinis without worrying about their fat or cellulite. How I wanted to be thinner. To actually be noticed, and not for the bad reasons. I wanted a day when I would be completely satisfied with myself and didn't have to suppress this inner dissatisfaction that hounded me each day.

Now, all those words about self-love and self-acceptance my therapist had fed me felt fake. They seemed like a wrapper that was supposed to hide the real thing inside, which was my ugliness. This wasn't only about my looks. This was about my cowardice and weakness. There wasn't actually anything good about me, was there?

I closed my eyes and wished that when I opened them, I would magically be skinnier. I wouldn't have this overlapping stomach fat. I wouldn't have cellulite. I wouldn't be this unhappy.

All those years, I went on diets, tried eating only healthy food and limiting my food intake, and a few times, I even exercised, but I was miserable because I wasn't cut out for it. It just wasn't my thing. I wasn't Sarah. I didn't think much about healthy living or being in good shape, and I found it unfair that I had to submit myself to something I hated in order to change myself. Why did I have to change myself? Why couldn't the world accept me the way I was?

The whole world was built upon the standards of beauty that movies and TV shows forced on us constantly. All those pretty, slim actors parading across our screens. Then, all those fat jokes and harassment. I couldn't even count the number of times people had stared at me in disapproval, their faces telling me I wasn't fitting into the labels our society put on us.

So I was stuck between loving myself the way I was and wanting to be someone I was not. I was stuck between losing myself in that rich, amazing taste of food and being ashamed of eating it.

And I was stuck between reason and liking the monster who only hated me.

"*Why am I here?*" I sang the lyrics I'd come up with just now as the sad piano melody played out in my head, my voice shaking with tears. "*Why am I here when I'm like this?"* I sniffed. *"Why am I here when you hurt me? You hurt me."* My voice was shaky, going deeper and deeper. *"Why do I like you? You'll never like me—"*

I started sobbing. Why did I have to fall for him?

I was stupid. So stupid.

"Jess? Honey?" My dad knocked on my window, making me flinch.

Just great. I wiped my tears quickly before I raised my head to look at him.

"What are you doing in your car? Why don't you come into the house?"

I took my backpack from the seat and got out, avoiding his gaze. "I was about to go inside."

"Honey, are you okay?" He made me look at him and frowned when he noticed my face, which was probably all puffy. *"Jess.* Why are you crying? Did something happen to you?" He looked at me as if he was checking me for any injuries.

I sniffed. "Dad, am I fat?"

"What? Of course not, sweetie."

Resentment surged through my veins. "You're lying! You're only saying that because I'm your daughter!"

"That's not true. You're beautiful and normal-looking—"

I rushed into the house, refusing to hear another word. He was biased, so he couldn't be telling the truth. I wasn't normal-looking. I was fat, and there was no denying it.

I locked myself in the bathroom and sat on the floor, lowering my head between my knees. I rocked my body back and forth as the fresh tears burst out. I hated myself for looking this way. I hated the hideous balloon that was my stomach and the trunks that were my legs. I hated the number on the scale. *Hate it, hate it, hate it.*

The old urge to throw up reared its ugly head for the first time in several months. It came from the recesses of my mind that reminded me how disgusting I was for being this way.

I stood up on my shaky legs and looked at myself in the mirror, repulsed by what I saw. Each bite of the food I'd taken today created guilt and shame that pressed in on me from all sides. I felt like my heart pumped acid, and the pressure to relieve myself and get rid of the toxins in me prompted me to get down on my knees and empty the contents of my stomach into the toilet.

And I did that. I grabbed my hair to keep it from getting into my face as I hunched over the toilet and pushed my fingers deep into my mouth, making myself throw up until I was dry-heaving and my chest burned. I flushed the toilet and slumped against the wall, my whole body shaking and breaking out in sweat. I felt tired, but for a few moments, it didn't matter, because I was overcome with peace. I felt good.

But, as always, the high was gone as quickly as it had come, and I was left with more shame, disgust, and disappointment. I'd promised my parents I wouldn't do this again. I'd promised myself.

The knocks on my door ripped through my thoughts. *No, no, no, no, no. Not now.*

"Jess? Honey? Please open the door," Mom said, rattling the handle.

I couldn't let her see me like this. "No. Go away!"

She knocked harder. "I won't go away, Jessica. Open the door."

"Leave me alone!"

"Jessica Metts! I swear to you, if you don't open this door right now, you'll be grounded for a whole month!"

I pressed my forearm against my eyes, terribly ashamed. She'd caught me throwing up the first time I did it, and it had been one of the most humiliating experiences of my life.

I picked myself up and forced my unstable feet to carry me to the door. Shame hit me even harder as I unlocked the door and stepped aside. She barged in and took me in with a gasp, realizing immediately what I'd done.

"Sweet Jesus!" She wrapped her arms around me and pulled me into a firm embrace. "Oh Jess...oh dear..."

A fresh wave of pain washed over me, and I burst into tears. I wound my arms around her waist like I was drowning and she was my lifebelt. I might as well have been drowning because I couldn't find the way out, and I didn't know what to do with myself.

"I'm sorry, Mom," I said into her shoulder as I clutched her shirt in my hands. "I said I wouldn't do it again...I'm so sorry."

"Oh Jess. Don't be, honey. Don't be sorry for anything." She leaned away and cupped my cheeks. Her eyes filled with tears. "Talk to me. You know you can always talk to me, especially when it gets this hard."

"I know, but I...I don't want to worry or disappoint you. Or Dad."

Her eyes widened. "No, honey. Don't ever say that. You can never disappoint us." *That's not true*, my inner voice said. *You're disappointed whenever I act the way I shouldn't.* "Please don't hide things from us. Your dad and I are here to help you." She put the toilet lid down and made me sit on it. She kneeled in front of me, taking my cold hands. "I know it's hard, but you know you only hurt yourself by doing that."

I nodded and sniffed. My eyes were swollen from crying.

"I understand how you feel because I've been there. I went through all kinds of things as a teenager with bulimia, and you know what happened in the end."

I nodded again. A fear of dying, which I knew too well, seeped back into me. Mom had struggled with bulimia since her early teens. She'd binge-eaten and purged by vomiting, using diuretics, and exercising excessively for many years. These recurring cycles lasted until her first year in college, when she had a cardiac arrest and escaped death only by miracle.

After that, she made a fresh start and changed her life completely. She devoted herself to healthy living and balance, and when I began struggling with my body image after the incident at the end of sixth grade, she recognized it immediately and sent me to a therapist before my issues developed into an eating disorder.

However, even with therapy, I had moments like today when everything became too much and I just wanted relief from the pressure, allowing my brain to lead me into this.

"I know, Mom. I really know I put myself in danger by throwing up. I know I shouldn't have done it."

She caressed my hands, never taking her worried gaze off me. "You'll get through this, sweetheart. I'm here. Don't forget about that. You're never alone." She smiled at me and caressed my hair with slow moves. "You're amazing and strong. So amazing."

My gaze dropped to my lap. I wanted to believe her words, but it was so hard. "I don't know. I feel so fat, and I don't like it."

"You aren't fat, honey."

"But look at me, Mom." I opened my arms widely. "The mirror doesn't lie."

A few tears spilled out of her eyes. She palmed my cheek. "Oh, it does. The mirror lies, and do you know why? Because it all comes from here." She tapped her head with her forefinger. "The way you see yourself defines that image in the mirror." She stood up and kissed my forehead. "So instead of telling yourself you're fat, tell yourself you're the most gorgeous girl. You'll see. In time, the image in the mirror will change. It will be better."

This was hard because I couldn't feel it inside. Words weren't enough, but I repeated them anyway, hoping one day I would accept myself.

"Everything about you is beautiful." She smiled a watery smile. "Every single thing, including your flaws. Your flaws make you *you*. No matter how much you weigh, you'll always be this special girl with a heart bigger than her body will ever get." She tucked a strand of my hair behind my ear with her trembling hand. "And at the end of the day, that is the only thing that matters."

I sniffed. "Thanks, Mom."

"It's the truth. Just make sure you talk to Susan about this, okay? She'll be able to help you overcome it."

I picked at my nail polish. "I will. I have a session with her this Friday."

"That's good. And honey?" I raised my head to look at her. "I love you."

A bit of warmth returned to my body. I managed to smile at her. "I love you too."

• • • •

TOMORROW WAS A NEW day. So the next morning, I got up, closed all my negative feelings and thoughts in a box, and went to school with a renewed determination to not let Blake mess with my mind. Sarah's inner strength must have rubbed off on me at some point because I was able to bounce back from my low more quickly than usual and keep going.

My second period was psychology, which I shared with Mel. We sat closer to the back of the classroom, talking with each other in hushed whispers whenever our teacher turned to write something on the blackboard.

Masen was also in this class, and Mel didn't hide how much she disliked
that fact even though he hardly paid any attention to us.

Today, he flirted with a pink-haired girl sitting next to him in the second row, who giggled almost every time he said something, and Mel's eyes
were plastered to them.

My lips curled up at the corner. "You look like you're about to go ballistic," I told her.

"I *am* going to go ballistic. Shreya Wilkins—you know, one of the student council members and the president of the math club—had a nervous
breakdown right in the middle of our meeting yesterday, and we didn't
manage to discuss anything because she was crying like the apocalypse is
coming! She cried so much she could've flooded a desert!"

Since the desks in this classroom were very close to each other, it was
easy for Masen to place his hand on the girl's thigh as he leaned over to
whisper something in her ear. Mel clenched her fists under her desk, grimacing.

"Shreya is soooo madly in love with Barbie, but apparently, he doesn't
give a flying fuck about her feelings. He just used her for sex last weekend
and hasn't looked twice at her since."

I shrugged my shoulders. There was nothing new about that. It was
known that Masen never, *ever* dated. For him, girls were pieces of meat, and
he never slept with a girl more than once, or so the rumors said.

"To be fair, I think she knew what she was getting into," I said. "I mean,
it's not a secret that he isn't looking for a girlfriend."

"But that doesn't give him the right to treat her like she's worth no
more than the shit in his toilet." I gave her a sidelong glance, surprised by
the amount of venom in her words. "That's why I despise guys," she gritted
out. "They're disgusting pigs who only use girls for sex."

I gaped at her. I was confused as to where all this aversion came from.
I wanted to ask her if that was the reason why she didn't want to date anyone, as she'd mentioned on numerous occasions, but I couldn't, because the
teacher turned to face us, so we had to stay quiet. I focused on my textbook
as she held forth on Pavlov's experiments.

The moment she turned to the blackboard, Mel leaned toward me.
"Looking on the bright side—I managed to propose our dearest council set

up booths manned by psychologists who can counsel victims of bullying during the festival."

Mel was fired up about the festival, and she was working like a beaver to make it successful. "Now that's brilliant," I told her. "Maybe some victims will feel less reluctant to seek help if they have this option."

She played with the edges of her textbook. "True. I was also thinking about what Haydee Bumblebee said on Monday."

I rolled my eyes at her nickname for Hayden. "What's up with you and those nicknames? You have one for everyone except for Steven."

"Hey! I have many nicknames for Steven! I call him idiot, moron, pea-brain, imbecile, annoying poop—"

"Okay, okay. I get it."

"Anyway, Haydee Bumblebee actually said something I could agree with. Hallelujah!" I chuckled, shaking my head at her. "The psychologists can also help bullies—that is, if those bullies are willing to open up to them and cleanse their minds of their evil ways."

"You're being overdramatic," I told her, and she stuck her tongue out at me. "Maybe they would open up more often if all of society didn't look at them as if they had a contagious disease."

"Whaddaya mean?"

I glanced at our teacher, who went overboard with scribbling on the board. No one was going to write all of that down anyway.

"I guess it's hard to come out and admit you're a bully because that means immediate public shunning or worse."

She looked at me like I was out of my mind. "And what do you think they deserve? A big round of applause for their heroic efforts in destroying other people's lives?"

"I think they deserve a second chance. If they want to change, of course."

She snorted loudly, attracting the attention of two girls in front of us. They glared over their shoulders at her. "What?" she mouthed at them with a raised eyebrow. "Our teacher is that way." She pointed. "Eyes to the front."

The girl in front of me whipped her head back around, red with shame, but the other girl gave Melissa a dirty look. "So rude," she sneered.

"Says the girl who keeps staring at me. Didn't your mommy teach you that staring is rude?" Mel said.

Realizing she couldn't go up against Mel, the girl grimaced and looked back to the front.

"That's a huuuge *if*," Mel said as she turned to me, returning to our topic. "Look at my idiotic brother—a freakin' bully! Do you know how many times I've told that nuthead to get his act together?"

A small frown formed on my face. One thing was certain: Steven was spiraling. Rapidly. He and Mel were arguing more often these days, and I could see it was wearing her down. She never showed it, her happy, energetic mode turned on at all times, but I saw the real her in the moments when she thought no one was watching. She worried about Steven, and for very good reason.

These days, he didn't look well. Previously extremely muscular, his 6'5" body was rapidly becoming gaunt. His dark blue eyes were often unfocused, his jet-black hair was straggly, and his clothes were rumpled. He acted like he was angry at the whole world, skipping a lot of classes and hanging out with other junkies in the school's back yard. I was worried about him too because if he continued walking down this dangerous path, it wasn't going to end well.

"Is he still not sleeping at home?"

"Still not sleeping at home? He doesn't even know where his home is these days! Ever since our mom bought us a house and we moved from our grandparents' place to what I call a Cruella de Vil mansion, he's MIA."

I was unable to contain a chuckle at her description of her new house. She often repeated that her mom had gone overboard with the new property, seeing that the house had nine rooms, a huge indoor pool, and a botanical garden, which was more suitable for a president than a single mom with two teenagers.

"*Some women cut or dye their hair after a breakup,*" Mel had said a few days earlier. "*My mom buys a ridiculously extravagant mansion that costs an arm and a leg.*"

Both Mel and Steven were unhappy with their mom's drastic decisions. In addition to that, Mel wasn't coping well with the divorce of her parents.

"How about your dad?" I asked her subtly as I glanced at our teacher. She'd returned to her desk and could look our way at any moment.

"Too busy with his work to care. I got sick of only speaking to his assistant, so I left him two voicemails yesterday. He didn't call me back."

Mel's dad was a lawyer like mine, but I couldn't imagine my dad working to the point of not seeing our family. Even when he worked his fingers to the bone, we were his top priority. He was always there for me.

When class ended, Masen placed his hand on the small of the girl's back and led her out of the classroom, keeping her close to him. Mel couldn't resist throwing a jibe at him as we passed them in the hall.

"Barbie, wrap your willy. You don't want that poor girl to get an STD."

The girl gasped, her eyes darting between Masen and Mel, while Masen looked at Melissa with animosity that was almost palpable.

"Don't worry, sweetheart," he said to the girl in his naturally raspy voice. He sounded laidback, but I could discern the anger hidden beneath the surface. "Satan is just jealous because she wanted to suck me off last night, but I told her I'm not desperate enough to get it on with Shrek's doppelgänger."

Mel placed her hands on her hips with a chuckle and looked sweetly at the girl. "Honey, he's lying. He wanted it so badly, but he totally couldn't keep it up." She extended her pinky and bent it, mimicking a deflating dick, and pointed at it. "He's that small, yes."

I grasped her arm and pulled her away from them. "Okay, Mel. Leave them alone. You'll be late for your next class at this rate."

Laughing under her breath, she let me drag her until we got around the corner and out of their sight.

"Did you see his face?" She erupted into another fit of laughter and smacked her thigh. "If someone ever makes him a wax sculpture at Madame Tussauds, they better capture *that* expression!"

I shook my head at her with a smile and went on my way, heading to the restroom to pee before I picked up what I needed for my next class from my locker. I passed next to the staircase in an almost empty hallway and froze when I heard Blake's voice nearby. My good mood evaporated into thin air, my pulse accelerating at once.

"Is Isaac sure he's the new racer?" he asked, and I looked all around me, trying to determine where his voice was coming from so I could escape in the other direction. "That means I may be closer to them than I've thought," he said, and I realized he stood behind the staircase and wasn't able to see me from that spot. There was no answer, which could only mean he was on the phone. "No. Don't do anything. Let's see if they'll show their faces at the track."

I moved slowly, planning to tiptoe until I was a safe distance away from him.

"Don't worry." His hushed voice drifted to me. "I've had this planned for a long time, so I won't mess it up."

The hairs on my neck stood up. *Mess what up?*

My Vans skidded soundlessly across the polished floor as I picked up my pace and rushed around the corner. With a sigh of relief, I allowed myself to run, stopping only when I reached the restroom.

Heaving, I leaned against the wall and placed my hands on my knees. I was disappointed with myself. I shouldn't have cared about his affairs or cryptic conversations, yet my heart beat faster because the conversation was about something that was obviously extremely important to him.

I should've been better than this. I always followed my heart, but this time, I had to stop being that hopeless romantic who believed in happy endings. There were no happy endings here. Blake would only ruin me, and if I kept obsessing over the hidden side of him, I would only get burned. Badly.

So, I had to be smarter than this.

I had a hunch, however, that my heart wouldn't get the memo.

Chapter 8

BLAKE WASN'T IN THE cafeteria during lunch, and by the end of last period, the rumors spread like the wind. One of them said Blake was necking some girl in an empty classroom. Another said he was banging her. And then there was the one saying he'd been caught in the act with a teacher.

As I packed things into boxes, surrounded by silence because Blake was late again, my mood went downhill. It wasn't the first time such rumors had circulated around the school, but they bothered me nevertheless, which led to more self-reproach.

I was attacked by mental images of Blake holding some magazine-cover-worthy girl in his arms and making her feel everything I'd felt in that pitch-dark closet at the New Year's party, and jealousy ate away at my stomach. I gripped the U tube and threw it into the box, dying to take my guitar and strum the strings until all my anxiety was gone.

Everything would be easier—way, way easier—if I could like someone like Kevin. Kev would never break my heart or devalue me. He would be sweet and nice, and I wouldn't have to feel this hopeless because of my stubborn, stupid heart.

Blake stormed in, and I almost dropped the microscope I held in my hands, startled. He didn't even look at me as he picked up an empty box and carried it to the far side of the room, which was probably for the best after our last run-in. I'd expected him to mock me for my fall or do a number on me, but he never even glanced my way as we worked quietly, which helped me relax. He wasn't going to make this detention harder for me. That was a first.

A new tune dashed into my mind—an up-tempo song with guitars and a bit of violin in the chorus segment—and excitement swirled through my chest. There was nothing better than having my creative juices flowing. If I was inspired, I could come up with a couple of new songs in a day, but I couldn't record all of them, so I had to opt for those that spoke to me on a deeper level.

Immersed in my song, I almost forgot Blake was there, when suddenly darkness covered the whole room. I stopped mid-step and clutched the small cardboard box filled with VHS tapes in my hands.

"What the...?" Blake shouted. "I can't see anything!"

The fear in his voice sent a tremor through me. "The electricity must have gone out," I said, taking two steps toward the table where I planned to set the box down, but they felt like a hundred because I couldn't see a thing in this tangible darkness.

"No shit."

I turned in the direction of his voice, which sounded closer to me now, but it was a mistake because this only messed with my orientation. "You don't have to be so rud—"

"Where's the goddamn light?!" His words were heavy with panic, spoken through bursts of heavy exhalations. "I need to get out of here."

He fumbled close to me, hitting the chairs scattered around us twice before he dropped something. His fear hit me hard, and a piece of me deep inside yearned to help him. I had to get my phone before he had a panic attack or something equally scary happened.

"*Fuck.* My phone." He tapped the floor, apparently searching for his phone, his breaths fast and shallow. "Where is my fucking phone?!"

I all but dropped the box on the floor and reached for my phone in my pocket. "Wait. I'll turn on the flashlight—"

"Finally," he said, not even paying attention to my words, presumably having found it. It seemed only inches separated us, and my body tingled with his nearness. "I need to find the door."

I was about to turn on the flashlight on my phone, but he tripped over the box I'd lowered next to me and collided with me. We lost our balance and fell on the floor.

The air was sucked out of my lungs when nearly all of his hard-muscled body ended up on top of me, both our phones lost somewhere in the darkness. I brought my hands to his waist to get him off me, fazed by his warmth and his scent that stirred my insides.

"Blake, you're crushing me," I said, but he barely shifted his weight off me. He was breathing so fast it was becoming alarming.

"I can't stay here," he cried out. His shaking got stronger. "I can't stay here. I can't stay. I have to get out of here."

He scrambled up to his feet, but he ran into something next to me and dropped right back down with a curse. He was wheezing. Feeling the floor around me, I reached him on my knees. I could sense him better now that I wasn't relying on my sight anymore. My concern for him won out over any distance I wanted to put between us, and I decided to help him get through this.

"Hey, calm down. You'll hyperventilate if you keep going like this," I said softly. He whimpered. I outstretched my arm toward him on impulse. "It's all right." My hand found his shoulder, and he flinched. "You're going to get out of here, but first, take deep breaths."

He was still panting, and I stroked his back in a reassuring way, reveling in the feel of him. In this darkness, we weren't enemies. In this darkness, our painful past didn't exist. In this darkness, there was just his hurt and my need to make it disappear.

"Everything's okay," I whispered.

A few minutes passed, but I didn't stop caressing his back until his breathing returned to normal and he stopped trembling. We slid into complete silence. His addictive warmth seeped into my palm through his shirt, and only then did I realize I shouldn't have been touching him. I whipped my hand back, trying to even out my erratic breathing as I waited for his reaction.

His attack never came, and the atmosphere between us shifted. The air filled with anticipation. I could have sworn he'd turned around and was now facing me on his knees.

"Why did you help me?" he whispered, rousing butterflies in my stomach. He was so, so close, and I was sure he was able to hear the wild pounding of my heart.

"You needed help. I couldn't just stand aside while you had a breakdown."

"Anyone else would have done exactly that in your place."

I shrugged my shoulders, even though he couldn't see that. "Well, I'm not like that."

His breath fanned my face, and I curled my fingers into fists on my lap, glued to the spot.

"You're right," he said quietly. "You're not like that at all."

He placed his hand on my waist, and I sucked in air. My pulse went crazy at the sudden contact. I was astonished that he was touching me, reminded of the exact moment we'd shared in that dark closet two months ago. It was just like this...

"Only you," he said.

My chest ached. "Only me?"

"Only you managed to make it go away."

Whoa. I could feel his face only inches away from mine as his breath caressed the side of my neck, and I couldn't recall a single reason why I shouldn't let him do this. He nuzzled my neck, creating an explosion of emotions in me, and it was like a dream come true. My heart embraced this greedily even though my mind tried to fight it.

"Blake..."

"You smell like jasmine...," he whispered into my skin, removing my hair from my shoulder. And then...then he grazed my earlobe with his lips, a touch so light it could've been my imagination.

I breathed hard, struggling to remember everything he'd done to me. I shouldn't have been allowing him to do this...I should have pushed him away right this second, and I raised my hands to do just that—

"Kids? Are you there?"

I jerked and looked at the janitor standing in the doorway with a flashlight. Blake had already pulled away from me before the beam of light reached us, confirming that the moment we'd shared was just an illusion and a big mistake.

"There you are," Mr. Maynard said in relief. "The electricity's out, but it should be back in an hour or so. Are you two okay?"

I cleared my throat. "Yes. We're okay," I replied and looked at Blake.

"Then let's go. I'll get you out of here."

I could hardly process Mr. Maynard's words as I took in Blake's expression.

He just stared at me like he couldn't believe what had just happened between us. Something resembling regret passed over his face just briefly, but it was enough to cause another gash in my heart. He shut himself off, the all-too-familiar ice back in his eyes.

Without a word, he picked up his phone before he sprang up and darted out of the room.

• • • •

ANGRY WITH MYSELF, I got back home and spent the whole evening playing my guitar, singing until my throat was sore. It was my refuge but also punishment for allowing my compassion to rub away all those bad memories. I shouldn't have touched him. When I heard him panic and lose control, I should've done something—*anything*—else instead of breaking the barrier between us and initiating contact.

As if that wasn't enough, as if I'd lost my brain somewhere along the way, I hadn't moved away when he came so close to me and said those rousing words. I'd practically served myself to him on a silver platter.

At least our detention was over, and I didn't have to stress myself out about spending time alone with him. Blake didn't come to school, so I had the whole Friday away from him, which was the only bright spot after the week's recurring disasters.

Friday evening meant a new session with my therapist and opening up to her about my latest setback. The last time I had self-induced vomiting was in November last year, after the "Food Slut" photoshopped photo. Blake had had a field day that time.

It'd taken me several sessions to regain a piece of the tenuous confidence I'd gained, and the recent argument with Blake threatened to annul that, throwing me back into those dark, old times when I felt like my body was too big for me and suffocating me. This was all the more reason for me not to let my heart rule because of those few minutes in the basement, but when it came to Blake, I had to deal with many conflicting and unwanted emotions.

"You're my dilemma. A continuous chase. You break me. You mess with my mind. And in the end, there's nothing else." I sang the lyrics I'd come up with just a few minutes earlier as I drove to the clinic, the last rays of sunset

lighting the road ahead. The melody was ingrained in my mind, and each line I sang alleviated my tension.

Halfway to the clinic, I pulled into Stop & Shop to get a pack of gum and a bottle of juice. I'd just left the store when I spotted Masen in front of a grocery store nearby. He walked next to a quadriplegic boy in a power wheelchair, and the surprise made me stop.

Masen smiled as he talked with the boy, who couldn't have been older than thirteen or fourteen. My chest filled with sympathy for him. He was a younger version of Masen with his blue eyes, blond hair, and striking face, which could have meant he was his brother or a cousin.

Masen seemed like a completely different person. There was no usual smirk or conceited look on his face, and his constant swagger and air of arrogance were gone. In fact, for the first time, he looked approachable, leaving the womanizer-douchebag attitude he had in school behind. I didn't fail to notice that the clothes he wore now looked much cheaper than those he wore at school, which were always brand name and fashionable.

He carried grocery bags around an old silver minivan and to its cargo space at the back while the boy waited for him on the side. There was a grocery bag on his lap, but as he moved the controller with his spastic hand to reposition his wheelchair, the apples slid out and dropped to the ground.

My heart clenching for him, I rushed to pick up the apples. I knelt in front of him, collected the fruit, and took the bag out of his lap to put them back inside.

"Here you go," I told him with a smile, touched by the innocence and shyness on his face. I was about to put the bag on his lap when Masen snatched it away from me and grabbed my upper arm, jerking me up to my feet.

"What are you doing?" he hissed. His previously nice demeanor was completely gone, replaced with something frightening. I'd never seen him look this scary, with his blue eyes boring into me as if I'd attacked this boy.

"I-I was just—"

"Stay away from him."

My lips parted. I was astounded by how protective he was being. "I... Sure. I didn't mean anything—"

He tightened his grasp around my upper arm. "And don't say a word about this to anyone. You got it? Especially not to that bitch Melissa. I don't need her to harass him just because she's neurotic and gets a kick out of putting others down."

"Mel isn't like that. She—"

He bared his teeth. "Tell me you won't say a word. *Tell me.*"

"Mace?" the boy said tentatively. "What's going on?"

"Nothing, Eli," he answered in a soft voice, though his unforgiving eyes remained on me. "I'll take the fruit and put the ramp down in a sec." He got into my face. "If you say even one word about Eli to anyone, I'll make you regret it, Metts." He said it so only I could hear him.

I fully believed him. I could clearly see he was ready to do anything to protect this boy, and despite not understanding why he wanted me to stay quiet about him—why it mattered so much that no one knew about him—I didn't want him as my enemy. I had too much on my plate with Blake as it was. Besides, I'd heard stories of how brutal Masen could be. He'd bullied three girls into leaving school, and he'd sent a couple of guys to the hospital. Better safe than sorry.

"I won't mention this to anyone. You can trust me."

"I don't trust anyone," he spat out. "And especially not girls." He pulled away from me. "This is your only warning. Cross me, and you and I are going to have a problem."

I nodded and hurried to put some distance between us, taking one last glance at the boy, who looked at me silently with sad, wise eyes resembling those of a much older person. I got into my car and drove away.

• • • •

"TELL ME HOW IT ALL started again," Susan told me, her notepad in her lap.

I sat in a recliner across from her, my gaze darting between her PhD certificate and a painting of fruits gathered in a metal bowl. I studied the shades of the colors for the hundredth time as I formulated the answer about the moment I'd relived in my mind so many times.

"I was in a school play in sixth grade. I played a supporting role." I closed my eyes; the old pain coated my chest. "I was extremely nervous about singing in front of an audience for the first time. It was a dream come true, but I couldn't get rid of the stage fright."

"What happened then?"

She knew well what came next, but her question helped me refocus and recollect the incident in more detail.

"The moment I appeared on the stage, my peers in the first row broke into hushed whispers. I thought it had something to do with my oversized dress, but I was wrong. It all had to do with my weight."

"What did they say?"

I sharply sucked in a breath, my eyes still closed. This memory never failed to bring back the humiliation and fear I felt that time.

"They called me a pig. Hippo. Fat. Fatty." My long nails were pressed hard into my palms, but the pain was good. Pain kept me rooted to the present.

Susan's face was sympathetic as she waited patiently for me to continue.

"They said I would surely sound like a squealing pig when I opened my mouth." *It's in the past. Remember, it's just a memory.* "So when I started to sing...nothing came out. I tried and I tried, and the only thing that came out was a high-pitched sound that couldn't even be called singing."

"And then?"

I glanced at the golden pencil she held in her hand. I'd found out the first time I saw her that that golden pencil also helped me stay in the present. So I stared at it, transfixed.

"And then they started booing and laughing. Even some of the classmates I considered friends laughed or pointed fingers at me. It was terrible. They said I didn't know how to sing. They said I should never sing. They said I was too fat for the stage." I buried my face in my hands. "It was cruel and vicious."

"How did you feel in that moment?"

"Shocked. Then ashamed. I was so ashamed I couldn't stay on that stage anymore. I couldn't sing. So I rushed away and swore to never go on a stage again. I never tried singing in public after that."

"And that is how your weight and singing insecurities started." I nodded. "Did you consider yourself overweight before that incident?"

I wiggled my lips back and forth. "Hmm, maybe. I don't know. It wasn't that big of a deal. I mean, I didn't pay that much attention to my weight. I kinda knew I was fat, but it didn't bother me. I was a kid, and I couldn't have cared less about the way I looked. But it all changed after that day, and I started thinking about dieting and calories." I snorted. "Up until then I didn't even know what calories were, but all of a sudden, I was all about calories, the number on the scale, and the size of my clothes."

"What did you do to lose weight?"

I shrugged. "Nothing special. I used to diet from time to time, like trying out some popular diets I could find on the internet, but I would usually get bored of them after a few days and start eating normally. I also tried exercising a couple of times. I never actually lost any weight, and for a while I just tried to learn to live with it. Like: oh okay, I'm fat—well, it's not like it's going to change any time soon, right? I just have to live with it." I let out a chuckle.

"What led you to make yourself vomit?"

A faint blush covered my cheeks as I inspected my hangnails. "My back-then crush, who never even noticed me, made fun of me with his friend in eighth grade. His friend loved to taunt me about my weight, but one day he joined in too and...and it was horrible.

"He said no boy would ever be interested in someone as fat as me, which hit a nerve, because I was always invisible to boys. All my friends had boys crushing on them or were dating someone. I had nothing. That night I thought if I couldn't be slimmer by dieting, maybe I could make myself throw up. That...that was the first time."

"So you threw up because of what your old crush said?"

"Yes."

"How did you feel afterward?"

"Relieved. I felt I had control. It was nice for a change, but then I felt guilt and fear because I remembered my mom, who had had an eating disorder. I was afraid I would end up like her if I kept throwing up. She also caught me that time, which was totally humiliating. So, yeah."

"And did you keep vomiting?"

"From time to time. Maybe like once or twice a year. I don't know. I went to therapy then, but I wasn't fully convinced I had a problem."

"I see. And what brought about those moments?"

"At that point I was in a relationship, and while it gave me a confidence boost in the beginning, I kind of always felt that Rory could find someone better. One time, we went bowling with friends, and everyone ate just a sandwich or a couple of snacks, but I overdid it and ate my weight in food."

I watched her golden pencil move as she scribbled, remembering the embarrassment too well.

"I came home, locked myself in the bathroom, and made myself puke."

"And now? Do you feel compelled to do it?"

"Compelled? Not really. It's like it's an isolated incident. Sometimes, just sometimes, I think about it, but I don't feel the need to do it. I do it when things become too hard and I feel cornered, and it's like a way for me to let all those negative feelings flow away."

"What made you do it this week?"

I grimaced and told her what Blake had done in the basement, and then about the pressure I'd felt when I got home.

"Did it provide any relief?"

"Only for a bit."

"Do you think that relief was worth it?"

I tucked my hair behind my ears and dropped my gaze. I was fully comfortable around Susan, who had been my therapist since I'd arrived in Enfield six months earlier, but it wasn't easy to open up about my tendency at all times.

"In that moment, yes. But then I felt disappointed in myself because I'd promised myself and my parents I wouldn't do it anymore. So, no. The relief was not worth it."

"Considering how you feel about it, on a scale of one to ten, how likely would it be for you to do it again?"

I ran my hands down my face, contemplating yet another difficult question. Susan was good. She bombarded me with questions until we reached the root of the problem, but I wasn't always ready to face the truth. It took great courage to be able to look deep into myself and see who I actually was.

"I don't know. I think three. Four?"

She wrote something down in her notepad. "We talked about how bad self-induced vomiting is."

I nodded. "Yes, I'm aware of the consequences. My mom is a living example of how unhealthy it is."

"That's right. Your mother is a clear example of this. It may feel like just one episode isn't a big deal, but after that may come another, and then another, and soon it can become worse, and before you know it...things can get really bad."

I stared down at my shoes, swallowing hard. I was aware of my repetitive mistakes. I just didn't want to return to that scary place where wrong seemed right and pushing fingers into my mouth was the way out of my problems. I had to overcome this.

"I know. I know it's not a way to deal with my problems and it won't lead me anywhere." I pursed my lips. "I've been thinking...yes, an event or person is what causes me to do it, but if I wasn't already having doubts and insecurities, I wouldn't do it. Right?"

"In your case, yes, there is an underlying process, and it ends when you solve what troubles you. You aren't satisfied with the way you look. You feel you're not good enough."

"Yes."

"But the number on the scale doesn't define your worth or the worth of your body. It doesn't define who you are. Weight doesn't define you. Who are you, Jessica? Think about it."

I looked at her pencil. I didn't need to think about that one. The answer had been burning in the back of my mind all this time.

"I'm just someone who clings to others to solve her problems. I always take the easy way out. I'm a coward who can't even follow her own dreams. I would rather live in the infinite cycle of my mistakes and complain about them day after day than break that cycle and fight for what I actually want to be." I chuckled. "I can't even look at myself in the mirror without that silent voice telling me I'm not good enough. I'm not good-looking, I'm not brave, I'm not myself."

I finally met her gaze, realization dawning on me. I couldn't even begin to love my body if I felt so much self-hate. I kept focusing on my bad points, without ever thinking about the things I'd never want to change about myself. If I was to look myself in the mirror, everything beautiful I saw would be devoured by negatives. I loved my big breasts and thick butt. I loved how sexy I could look in dresses that emphasized my curves. It wasn't all bad.

I always compared myself to others and envied all those slim girls, always wanting to be like someone else and never like me. I knew I had to embrace my imperfections and remember that all of us are imperfect in one way or another if I wanted to be happier, but I'd never actually tried to do it.

Sure, I would have been ecstatic if I weighed a few pounds less, but more than that, I had to stop letting everyone, especially my parents, determine my life without ever trying to fight back. I wanted to be respected for what I could do. I wanted to follow my dreams and stop living in fear.

"There you have it," Susan said. "The first step is to identify the problem. Now you should think of a way that will help you resolve it—a bridge between what you are now and what you want to be." She leaned toward me. "It's your choice, Jessica. You can choose to live your life blaming yourself or others, or you can actually do something about it."

· · · ·

I LEFT SUSAN'S OFFICE feeling unburdened for the first time in a long time. It was like a piece of what had been troubling me had been removed and replaced with something much better, much healthier. I had a long way to go, and I still wasn't sure if I could do it, but I felt more determined to improve and stop living with regrets and complaints.

I rounded the corner, buttoning up my coat, when the door across the hallway opened and a tall guy dressed in all black came out of an office.

It took me a heartbeat to process whom I was actually seeing, and my pulse accelerated, all my thoughts rushing to a halt.

Blake.

Chapter 9

BLAKE'S PREVIOUSLY vacant eyes widened when he saw me, rooting me to my spot. He was here. He was actually here. The memories of that darkness in the basement hit me hard as we stared at each other, and blush spread all over my cheeks.

He took a step toward me, anger replacing surprise on his face. "What are you doing here?"

I had no intention of staying a second longer. I bolted, passing by the people who gave me weird looks for running through a clinic. I didn't care. I just had to get away from Blake.

I stopped next to my car and reached for my key in my pocket, but I didn't manage to take it out, because Blake pressed me against my car. *Damn, he's fast.*

"You think you can run away from me?" His hot breath caressed my ear, in contrast with his harsh voice. "You didn't answer my question."

"And what do you think? I was visiting a therapist. It's not like I went on a picnic, Blake," I bit back, surprising us both with my guts.

He spun me around to face him, his eyes nearly dark with fury. "You don't get to talk to me like that."

Flaring up, I fisted my hands. With the way he was acting, it was like we'd never had a moment in the basement. I just wanted one day of peace—free of confusion and these feelings brewing in me each time he was nearby.

"And you do? You've been abusing me since the first day of our senior year, and I've always stayed quiet, but you've never stopped. I'm tired of the same cycle. Why are you so obsessed with me?"

The muscle in his jaw ticked. "Careful now."

"No!" I hated how good he smelled and how much I wanted to lean into him. It was absurd, yet my body basked in it. It basked in his nearness and his attention. *So sick.* "You keep bullying me, and I'm losing my mind here!"

"*You* are losing your mind?"

"Yes!"

95

"Then what can I say about everything you're making me go through?! It's killing me. It's destroying my life!" He stepped away from me, on the verge of exploding, his veins protruding from his neck.

"What are you talking about?"

"I want my life back, but I can't have it when you're around! I've been trying to get you to leave East Willow High, but no. Despite everything I've done, you've *stayed.*"

I'd suspected he wanted me out of school, but I'd never known why. "If that's the case, then get away from me. I'll stay out of your sight—"

"I CAN'T!" His roar rattled all of me, attracting attention from a few people in the parking lot, but he didn't care, never taking his eyes off of me. "That's the thing! *I. Can't.*"

My chest throbbed. "Why?" A question I'd asked myself a hundred times already.

He didn't say anything, observing me silently for a long time. The part of me that wanted his attention reveled in this; it clung to the fact that he obviously wasn't immune to me. Something shifted in his expression, and he crossed the distance between us. I backed up against my car, struggling to breathe. He supported himself against the roof and leaned close to my face. A slow smirk formed upon his lips.

"My patience with you can only go so far, so you better watch your mouth." He tilted his head to the side. "Because who knows? Maybe I see a therapist because I'm a psychopath. So I wouldn't mess with me if I were you."

My eyes darted between his. I didn't believe him, but the words ventured out of my lips anyway. "Are you? A psychopath?"

His smirk widened. He cast one lingering look at my mouth then walked away.

• • • •

"THIS IS RICH," MELISSA said, lounging on the couch in Hayden's living room. She and Sarah had a day off from their part-time job at the retirement home, so we were spending Saturday morning in Hayden's house—and Sarah's. This was also her home now since she'd moved here after her birthday more than a week earlier.

"Hayden goes to therapy," Mel continued. "Sar goes to therapy, you go to therapy, Kev goes to therapy—although for his speech—and Blake goes to therapy! Let me guess...Barbie goes to therapy too?"

Sarah shrugged her shoulders. She sat cross-legged in the armchair across from Mel and me. "You are who you hang out with?"

"Do you go to therapy?" I asked Melissa.

"No, but I did a few years ago. Does that count?"

"Yes. That makes you a certified member of our 'freaks' club," I said with a soft smile.

Mel rolled her eyes and sighed. "Oh goodie. We're all fucked up."

I giggled. "That we are."

"So how was your session?" Sar asked me.

I looped my hair behind my ears as my smile turned into a thin line. They knew about my struggles with weight and self-image, but I'd never told them about throwing up, because I was vulnerable and ashamed to admit it. I was terrified of them judging me. One day, I might be ready to talk about that, but not now.

"It went better than I expected. I was on a downward spiral after Blake's insults during our detention—"

"What did that gorilla say?" Mel's sharp tone sliced through the air.

I stared at my hands as I recounted his put-downs, choosing to keep what'd happened the next day in the basement to myself.

"Just the usual: I'm fat and no one would want me like this. But this time, it hit the mark, so I felt down and really, really fat—"

"Geez, Jess," Mel interrupted me and grabbed my hand. "Are you serious? So what if you have a few extra pounds? There's nothing wrong with that. And you look sexy. I would kill for your curves."

"You already have curves." I pointed at her hips.

"Yeah, but not like yours. And I'd pick thick thighs over skinny thighs any day—no offense, Sar." She patted Sarah's shoulder.

Sarah chuckled. "None taken."

Mel shook her head. "Damn that asshole Blake. Don't listen to him, okay? You're a knockout."

I melted a little inside because of her sweet words. I smiled at her. "This isn't just because of him. I've been unhappy with the way I look way before I met him."

"But why?" Sar asked me. "You're beautiful."

"Exactly," Melissa agreed. "You look good the way you are. Like, I get how you feel because all of us complain and manage to find something wrong about ourselves, but we should accept it. Nobody is perfect. Not even those top models."

"That's easy for you to say," I told her. "You're hot and your face is super attractive."

She rolled her eyes. "And I have pimples all over my shoulders and upper back. My nose is slightly crooked. See?" She showed us her profile, pointing at her nose. "My left boob is smaller than my right one, and my right foot is bigger than my left foot. Oh, and my feet easily get sweaty and stinky...do you want me to continue?"

I laughed, shaking my head at her.

"So, as you can see, there are plenty of things I hate about myself," she said. "We all have flaws, girl. So don't listen to that stupid gorilla, because his opinion isn't worth a dime. If he really thinks you're fat, there's something horribly wrong with his brain—*if* he even has one."

"Mel is absolutely right. And since we're talking about flaws," Sarah started, "I hate my protruding hip bones. It just feels so uncomfortable when I lie down on my stomach. My breasts are non-existent, and I have a huge thigh gap that makes me feel like everyone is staring right at it. You see? I'm not perfect either."

"I disagree," Hayden said, walking into the room. He wore black sweatpants and a black Nike t-shirt, looking as handsome as ever.

But not as handsome as Blake, my inner voice said, and I almost rolled my eyes at myself.

"You're perfect from head to toe." He stopped behind her armchair and left a kiss on the top of her head. "That is, if we exclude unshaved legs, nasty pimples, and cellulite."

"Hayden!" Sarah shrieked.

"What?" He shrugged and looked between Melissa and me. "I'm just speaking the truth."

Sar blushed. "Have you been listening to us?"

He raised his brow. "Like I don't have better things to do than listen to girl talk."

"We all know about your stalkerish tendencies," Mel said, sticking her tongue out at him.

"It takes a stalker to know one," he replied to her, deadpan. "Here." He extended the sheet of paper he was holding toward me. "I improved a few lines."

I took it, curious to see them. Sar had suggested Hayden and I could collaborate since he wrote poems and lyrics, and I'd been excited to try it out. My lyric-writing skills were solid, but Hayden knew how to add depth and shake people to the core. These lyrics were very personal, and I wasn't fully comfortable sharing them with anyone, but Hayden had been cool about it and hadn't made a face when I jotted down the chorus.

I smiled as I went over the words. "They're amazing. Thank you."

I read them a few more times, memorizing the changed lines. This song went perfectly with the melody I'd worked on the night before.

"So? Let's hear it." He pointed at my Martin resting next to me on the floor. I'd brought my guitar after Mel badgered me to bring it, but I hadn't planned on playing it.

Blush settled on my cheeks. "I can't."

"Come on," Hayden said. "Why not?"

I lowered my head so that my hair hid most of my cheeks, thinking maybe I should get bangs because they would help me hide my forehead too. "I have a fear of performing in front of others," I admitted reluctantly, wanting their attention on anything else but me.

"But why?" Mel asked. "It's just us. We won't judge you."

I picked at the thread sticking out of my jeans. "Yeah, well, I'm afraid anyway, okay?"

"That's all the more reason for you to do it," she said. "Face your fears. That's the only way you'll be able to conquer them."

"We won't look at you if that will make it easier for you," Sar added with a faint smile.

"Or you can close your eyes and pretend we're not here," Mel said.

If only it were that easy. I wanted to sing and play my guitar in front of them—I wanted it so badly—but I was afraid I wasn't going to be good enough or would screw something up.

"I can't."

"Then Blake is right," Hayden said as he sat in the armchair next to Sarah's. "You really are a pathetic coward." I flinched, crimson red.

Sarah glared at him. "Hayden, don't speak to her like that."

He looked at her impassively. "Why not? It's only the truth." He met my gaze. "And you say you want to be a singer? How? Do you think your fear will disappear on its own? Or do you plan to run away from singing your whole life and do some 9-5 job you hate, until you're old, wrinkled, and having stupid regrets? Are you going to realize then how stupidly you're acting right now?"

His blunt words cranked up the ache in my chest. He was absolutely right. I was ready to ignore my dream my whole life if it meant not facing the very fear that kept me away from it. How many times had I told myself I was going to regret not being braver? It stung. I wanted to sing so badly and see the admiration in their eyes as I carried my notes, but I stayed in the dark and didn't allow myself to shine.

So what if I made a mistake? So what if my voice or playing wasn't good enough? I had to start somewhere.

Maybe it was time for me to take a leap of faith. Maybe I should embrace the spotlight for once and show the world who I was.

"Don't pressure her," Sar told him. "Do you think she doesn't know that already? It's not that easy—"

"No, he's right," I said in a shaky voice, my guitar already in my hands. I ignored the shaking of my hands and the furious pounding of my heart as I plucked the strings. *I'm actually going to do this.* "He's absolutely right." I started strumming the guitar, hoping I wouldn't mess this up. "Don't laugh."

"We won't," Hayden replied and entwined his fingers with Sarah's over their armrests.

Okay. I can do this.

One, two, three, four.

"*I'm tired of being a coward.*" I sang the words tentatively, which resulted in a weak voice and bright red cheeks.

I closed my eyes and cleared my throat as I played the soul-wrenching notes. I had to forget about my shame. There was no place for it now.

I'm tired of being a coward
Wasting my life on nothing at all
All those lost chances
All because of my fear
I feel so small

A paradox that ensnares
I'm between happiness and pain
But I'm repeating my mistakes
And everything is in vain
I'm so foolish
So foolish, yeah

I'm a coward, but then I'm not
I'm a girl who wants a way out
Of the problems and the pain
So she won't have to run off in shame

My fear, all that fear
Cutting me, creating doubts

And everything is in vain
I'm so foolish
So foolish, yeah

I strummed faster, emotions resonating within me, pouring out of me.

I'm a coward, but then I'm not
I'm a girl who wants a way out
Of the problems and the pain
So she won't have to run off in shame

I'm so foolish, so foolish, yeah
I want to fight
And cure my lows with light
But I'm so foolish
Losing it all

I want to wake up and be strong

I used vibrato on the G string and plucked the strings, playing the last notes. Just like always, I was immersed in my music, unaware of everything and everyone as the song carried me somewhere far away, and it was the closest I could get to complete bliss and peace.

My eyes still closed, I played the last note and smiled as silence wrapped around me. I felt like I was on top of the world, invincible. Music pumped through my veins and filled me with happiness that was larger than life. This was all I'd ever wanted.

Loud claps broke out, and I snapped my eyes open, remembering I had an audience. Mel and Sar watched me with stars in their eyes and smiles as big as mine, but Hayden was nowhere to be found. I looked around for him and let out a startled gasp.

He stood in the arched doorway...right next to Blake.

Blake's eyes were liquid fire as he watched me, stripping me of everything. His face had an expression I'd never seen before—all traces of his constant disdain gone—and it was like I was seeing a completely different person. My heart throbbed, bound to him in a world where no one existed but us.

"That was amazing, girl! Bravo!" Mel was the first to break the spell, and I tore my gaze away from him. Mortification filled every inch of me.

Blake was here. He'd heard me sing. He'd seen me play guitar. He was here, and he'd heard every goddamn word that had spilled out of me.

Oh hell no.

Unable to look anyone in the eyes or stay here a moment longer, I did the only thing that came to mind—I grabbed my guitar and jacket and fled from the house.

Chapter 10

MY PARENTS HAD INVITED all our relatives from Bridgeport—more than twenty of them—to a Sunday BBQ to celebrate my college acceptance. The weather was on our side, allowing us to jam-pack our small back yard and spend time outside until the evening.

My dad, never one to miss a chance to give a speech, repeated a bunch of times how lucky he was to have such a good and responsible daughter who was going to follow in his footsteps. I couldn't look at anyone when he said he'd never been more proud of me. My stomach churned with guilt and a fierce need to tell him I didn't want to go to his or any other law college.

Each smile and laugh I shared with my parents and relatives felt fake and shallow, and a voice inside screamed at me to take the bull by the horns and stop this gigantic charade.

I didn't say a word, but I promised myself I would tell them by the end of this month. I'd tell them I would finish music school and become a singer. I had weeks to find the guts.

Now all I had to do was conquer my fear of performing in public, which was even tougher when Blake was included. My moment of triumph had been cut short when our eyes met across Hayden's living room, and I'd felt more vulnerable in front of him than ever. I had probably looked like a serial killer was after me when I rushed to my car and passed Masen, who had arrived at that time.

Mel had left me a dozen messages, checking up on me. She'd even said she should kick Blake where the sun doesn't shine.

Did Blake say anything after I left? I texted her.

Nope. He was serious as the Statue of Liberty.

He didn't mock me?

Nope x2.

Sarah had also texted and told me I was awesome and there was nothing I should be ashamed of.

I wasn't ashamed. Okay, I was a little ashamed, but most of that shame came from the fact that Blake had witnessed a very personal moment I'd never have chosen to share with him.

I didn't even want to imagine the taunts that would come out of it. He would eat me alive. Sure, he hadn't said anything in front of my friends, but it would have been silly of me not to expect him to give me a hard time at school.

What was Blake even doing there? I messaged Sarah.

He and Masen came to pick Hayden up to go out.

Of all times? I'm so unlucky.

They usually hang out on weekends. But I wouldn't call it unlucky, because he looked floored by your performance. You should've seen him when he saw you.

My heart drummed wildly as I reread her message time and time again. I wanted to ask her for all the details, but that felt desperate even to me, so I refrained myself from asking anything. But oh boy, did I want to know.

On Sunday night, I gave in to my curiosity and went to Blake's Instagram before I hit the sack. I must have been a glutton for punishment because there was no other way to explain why I was compelled to scroll through his photos in search of...what?

His account was all about parties and moments with different girls or friends, and all of the photos painted a picture of a bad boy life. Cigarettes, booze, fast cars, and bikes—it was a world so foreign to me, yet I was enthralled by it. I was drawn to the adrenaline and danger he seemed to experience every day, unable to forget his pain on that basketball court in the gym when he cried for Emma, whoever she was. That pain was unlike anything I'd witnessed, so deep it had completely changed the way I saw him.

He was a mystery I would never get to unfold. He was an abuser who didn't deserve a single thought, but he had it and much more every waking moment. What did that make me? A fool? A hopeless romantic? A stupid girl with a way-too-big heart? Maybe all three together.

I scrolled back to the top of his profile and looked at his bio, which had just a single sentence.

You live only to encounter pain.

I slipped under my covers and closed my eyes. I willed myself to forget about him, but my mind was the weakest right before I drifted off to sleep, always wafting to him.

This time it was all about the moment we'd shared in that closet at the New Year's Eve party. A drunk me thought it would be a great idea to play seven minutes in heaven. Blake wasn't even playing the game, but he was sitting right behind an empty spot in the circle. So when someone spun the bottle, it ended up pointing at him.

I expected him to refuse. He wasn't playing and it was me he would have to take to the closet, but he didn't refuse. He stood up and pulled me after him, shocking me. Before my shock could wear off, he pushed me inside the closet and closed the door behind him.

He backed me into the wall, and even in the complete darkness, I could feel his lips painfully close to mine. I could smell alcohol on his breath, mixed with mint and a taste that was purely his. He placed his hands on my waist, and through a fog, I sensed the panic that he was going to feel my stomach fat and see for himself just how fat I was. It was short-lived because my desire took over and pushed my insecurity aside. It was hard for me to pretend I didn't like him this close to me.

"What are you doing?" I asked, my thoughts and senses in a state of disarray. Everything was happening so fast, and what I thought I knew about Blake turned into nothing as his short breaths fanned my face.

"What both of us want," he said.

He buried his head in my neck and kissed it slowly, in a way that awoke my every single nerve and made me pliable under his mouth and hands. It was tantalizing. It was mind-numbing. It was absolutely wonderful, and I found myself gripping his hair.

He groaned in response and ran his hands through my hair, pressing himself against me. I could feel how much he desired me, the clear evidence flush against my stomach. I threw my inhibitions and doubts out the window and clung to him, starving for his kiss.

He left a line of kisses that stopped right next to my lips as a way of taunting me. I moaned in response, a second away from kissing him.

"What? You thought I was going to kiss you?" His breath caressed my lips softly. "Think again."

If I'd been sober, I would have drawn away from him as if he'd slapped me. I would have refused to touch him for a moment longer.

But I didn't.

Spurred on by alcohol and an overwhelming desire, I crushed my lips to his, surprising us both.

He didn't need even a second to respond; he gave in to me in a way that seemed like he'd been suppressing something for so long until he couldn't anymore. He grabbed my face and pushed me further against the wall, his moans creating strong sensations in my stomach. We couldn't contain ourselves as our hands roamed across our bodies restlessly, and it was leaving me breathless and needy for more. Much, much more.

Minutes passed—or maybe an eternity—before he pulled away from my lips, panting just like me. He threaded his fingers through my hair and leaned his forehead against mine. He was breathing heavily as the silence stretched on and on...

Until his body grew stiff.

"No," he said in a voice dripping with regret as he removed his hands from me. "Fuck no."

"Blake?"

He didn't answer for a second, two, three...ten. And then he released a chuckle that cut me deep.

"So not only are you fat, you're also easy." This time I recoiled, appalled by the complete change in his actions. "First, Burks. Now, me. Who's next?"

I couldn't speak. The first tears had already found their way down my cheeks.

He let out another chuckle. "I didn't even need to do anything to have you eating out of my hand. So easy."

"I...I hate you." It was all I could say, but I managed to pour all my resentment into it.

He snorted. "What else is new?"

I pushed him to the side and lurched toward the door. I was about to open it when he said, "Happy New Year, Fats. And learn how to kiss better."

I hit my fists against the mattress. I was reliving those minutes as if they were happening right now. I was a masochist, tormenting myself with memories that would only bring me pain.

What hurt the most was that it had been one of the best moments of my life. For a few blissful seconds, I'd felt closer to him than anyone, and it had mended all my scars. There was no better way to start a new year.

Only, he'd managed to destroy it, cruelly reminding me that we would always remain enemies. Our kiss meant everything to me. It meant nothing to him.

And now, three months later, I was still stuck between my feelings for him and my reason. If only things could have been different.

If only I could be free.

• • • •

MONDAY MORNING ROLLED slowly by. Too slowly. I was mentally exhausted and bored by lectures, and I counted the minutes until lunchtime. Kev had texted me to tell me not to wait for him because he had to run some errand for his Spanish teacher, so Mel and I were the first to get to the cafeteria. Mel kept staring at me for some reason, and it was getting hard to ignore it. I went for roasted veggies, thinking about my calorie intake.

I thought about what Susan had told me before. I understood it better now, and it wiped away some of the shame I felt for craving unhealthy food.

"You're stressing yourself over whether you're eating the right or wrong foods, which can have bad consequences for your health. Food isn't your enemy. So instead of depriving yourself of the foods you like, think about balance and moderation."

Okay, maybe pizza contained extra calories, but I'd feel even more miserable if I had to deprive myself of every single food I liked. Maybe I should finally give that balance thing a try, instead of giving up on all the foods I liked.

I repeated one of Susan's mantras to myself, feeling more comfortable about it: all choices had consequences, but instead of regretting them, I should take responsibility for them, enjoy them while they lasted, and then see how to continue from there.

"What?" I asked Mel when we brought our trays to our table and sat down.

"You like Blake," she stated, no hesitating whatsoever.

A stupid blush covered my whole face. "No, I don't," I denied quickly.

I'd told Sar about my feelings for Blake because she'd been through the same thing and could understand me better. Mel, on the other hand, was not so understanding or tolerant, having been anti-Hayden until only recently. She would never approve of Blake.

"And now you're lying to me."

"I'm not." Another lie.

"Look, it's pointless to deny it. The sooner you accept it, the better for you."

My jaw almost dropped. "You won't criticize me? Not that I'm interested in him or anything." I wasn't a good liar at all.

She sighed and rested her face against her hand, picking at her French fries. "I did that a lot with Sar, and what good did it bring? I just want you to be careful. Blake is not a good person. He can seriously hurt you."

Her words were the truth, but my chest ached nevertheless. "And how do you know that?"

"Because I've seen how brutal he can be. I can show you, if you want, so you'll see it firsthand too."

"Show me what?"

She bit into her fry. "His life in the gang."

Gang. Yet another proof of how wrong I was to like him of all people. I didn't know much about that aspect of his life, but it was enough for me to draw a conclusion that he lived extremely dangerously and was associated with all kinds of lowlifes.

"You want me to see him fighting?" I was surprised she would suggest something like this.

"Actually, I'm talking about racing. There's this race on Thursday Steven won't stop talking about. It will bring the first three places a tidy sum. So, we can go there, and you'll see for yourself what kind of life Blake leads. Maybe it will change the way you see him."

I doubted it would make a difference since I already saw him in bad light.

I bit at the cuticle on my thumb. "Are you sure it's safe for two high school girls to go out there all by themselves?"

She snorted. "*Please.* I used to go there all alone and drag Steven out of their lairs, so this is nothing. Sarah also came with me once before Hayden got jumped out. Besides, no one will even notice us at the track. People there only care about the racers and their cash."

I shuddered at the thought of getting jumped out. I could only imagine what Sarah had gone through the night she witnessed Hayden take a beating from several gang members, which happened only a month after he got out of coma and recovered from a serious car accident. She wasn't the same after that, spending days in the hospital next to Hayden, who had been in a critical condition.

If Blake wanted to leave the gang, he would have to get jumped out too. I inhaled a deep breath as a pang of concern hit my chest.

"Fine. You've convinced me."

"Good. I'll use this opportunity to keep an eye on Steven."

"Why?"

"Because that idiot could be risking his life with the way he's acting right now. He's dead set on racing this Thursday. I argued with him and tried to knock some sense into his empty head, but he's like a train in motion. I can't stop him."

She frowned and crammed a few fries into her mouth. Only now did I notice she looked like she hadn't slept a wink the previous night.

"What's with the sour mood?" I asked her. "You don't look good."

"Tell me about it. I stuffed myself with energy drinks until I was ready to die from diarrhea."

I giggled. "Oh no. Not diarrhea."

"Everyone's worst enemy." She ran her hand through her hair and exhaled a sigh of exhaustion. "Steven and I had a huge fight last night."

"Why?"

"I found coke under his bed and flushed it down the toilet."

"Oh gosh."

She ran her hand across her face. "He went crazy and acted like he was ready to be admitted to a mental hospital."

"I can't believe he's using coke."

"Coke, heroin, LSD...you name it. He's getting worse, and it's scary. Up until now, my mom always gave him big allowances, but now that she bought us a new house, we have to cut down our expenses a lot. So she finally refused to give him more money."

I swallowed a piece of broccoli. "Finally."

"Yeah, but—surprise, surprise, Steven doesn't like that. He can't spend a day without drugs, so he's in a pinch. He needs to find cash, which brings us to that race on Thursday."

I took another bite of the vegetables. "Does your mom know about it?"

"Steven threatened me and made me promise not to tell her anything."

"He threatened you? How?"

"He said he'd run away from home if I ratted on him."

"I'm so sorry, Mel. I wish I could help you."

"I know. You should've seen him last night. It was worse than a horror movie. He was terribly aggressive."

"How aggressive?"

"He hit our mom."

My hand rushed to cover my mouth. "What?"

"We were arguing, and he was screaming so loud I was sure I would go deaf. Our mom barged into my room and tried to reason with him, and when he asked her for more money and she refused, he hit her."

"I can't believe this. He hit his own mother?"

She poked at her fry, grimacing. "Yep. And then I punched him in the face and almost broke his nose." She put her head in her hands. "It was awful. He left after that and only returned at six this morning."

"Have you tried suggesting rehab?"

"He doesn't even want to hear about it."

"So what are you going to do?"

She raised her head to look at me. "Take a pan and hit his face so hard it turns into a shovel face."

I burst into giggles just as Hayden appeared with Sarah by his side.

"Why so serious?" he asked Mel. "You look like someone kicked the bucket."

"Yep. My rat Pepito died, and now I don't know what to do with my life," she said dramatically with her hand raised in front of her, all previous worry gone from her face.

Once more, I was surprised by how quickly Mel could recover, or rather, hide her pain when needed. She never cried. She rarely harped on her problems, always pushed forward, and never said *I can't do it.*

"You don't have a rat," Sar told her as she took a seat between Hayden and me and placed her tray on the table.

"I did when I was eight and thought it was cute to keep rats in the house. My mom flipped out when I came to our doorstep carrying a rat by its tail. Sadly, he died a tragic death."

"What happened?" I asked.

She put two fries into her mouth. "Our cat Butcher ate him."

Hayden raised his eyebrow while Sarah and I broke into laughter. "Butcher? Let me guess—he ate rats for breakfast," he said.

"Exactly. He lived up to his name. He butchered all those rats in the neighborhood with no mercy."

Sar and Hayden glanced at each other as if looking for the other's reaction to this. Hayden squeezed her hand underneath the table and leaned in to leave a kiss on her forehead.

My heart swelled at the sight. Seriously, they were goals. They did these small signs of affection all the time, and I wasn't sure they were even aware of it.

If I had to compare their relationship from six months earlier to their relationship now, it would be like comparing the sky to the earth. From enemies to a sweet couple everyone envied, starting with me. The way Hayden looked at Sarah was so intense that even I, an outsider, felt it, and the romantic in me craved experiencing that. I craved having someone look at me like I was his reason for his next heartbeat.

No. Not someone, but *him.*

As if I'd conjured him with my thoughts, Blake entered the cafeteria, but he wasn't alone. He walked next to some girl, their bodies too close, and my stomach churned up a storm. It was hard not to notice how attractive she was, with her waist half the size of mine. His eyes found mine immediately, as if drawn to me, and it was like a kick in the gut. My pulse began drumming.

I tore my eyes away from them and met Hayden's incisive gaze. I blushed and glanced at my food. I could feel him seeing right through me.

How long would this new girl last? One hour? Two?

"He changes them more often than I wash dishes," I grumbled. I didn't mean for it to be heard, but Hayden picked up on it, all right.

"Do you have a problem with that?" he asked.

His question hit too close to home. "I'm just curious as to why he doesn't pick one," I replied, trying to downplay it.

"Because he doesn't want a relationship. He's with those girls just for sex and nothing else."

I frowned. "That doesn't sound right."

His face remained blank. "If Blake and his girls are enjoying it, who are you to judge?"

Were those girls actually enjoying it? What if they developed feelings for him?

"But why doesn't he want a relationship?" The million-dollar question.

He stayed silent, and I could see from the corner of my eye that he was observing me over Sarah's head. I couldn't look back at him, feeling like I'd asked too much.

"Look, you're Sarah's friend, and if you get hurt, Sarah will get hurt too. So, I have to warn you—don't waste your time on Blake. You'll only get burned."

Blush pervaded my face. I glanced sideways at him and opened my mouth to say I wasn't interested in him, but Hayden beat me to it.

"Don't deny it, because you're too obvious."

Talk about embarrassment. Okay then. Since it was already like this, I figured I might as well satisfy my curiosity.

"Let's say hypothetically that I'm interested in him. Although, I'm absolutely not." Mel snorted, and I glared at her. She snorted again. "I'm not interested," I repeated. "But hypothetically, if I wanted to be with him, why would I get hurt?"

He narrowed his eyes at me. "Because he can't love you. Satisfied now? There are reasons why he doesn't date girls."

Reasons. Not a reason, but reasons. My curiosity reached its highest peak, and I threw all my shame and caution away. "Reasons? What reasons?"

He looked away from me and reached for his pizza. "I'm not telling you that."

He was unbelievable. Both Blake and him with their half-assed answers.

"The bottom line is that you better forget about him," he concluded.

As if it was that easy. My gaze moved of its own volition and locked with Blake's, who already observed me from his table, and my heart jolted in my chest.

Forget about Blake? I could only hope.

Chapter 11

THE REST OF THE WEEK was uneventful, slowly bringing in Thursday night, which had my nerves humming with doubt. I was in luck when I told my parents Mel and I had to finish a school project and asked them to let me sleep over at her place because they didn't question it one bit.

I wrestled with my contradicting thoughts during the entire ride to the track. I didn't want to be near Blake, but at the same time, I wanted to know more about him. I wanted to put an end to the mystery that he was.

Why couldn't he love? Why had he been so gentle in the basement? He'd clearly dropped his guard, just like on New Year's Eve, but such drastic changes in his attitude gave me whiplash. Either he hated me or...

No. That was a dangerous way of thinking. It didn't matter. However he felt didn't matter, because I couldn't get over everything he'd done to me.

Or could I? I didn't know if I was capable of wiping the slate clean. He didn't deserve me. He was obviously so full of anger, and I took the brunt of it, and for that sole reason, I knew I had to get away from him. He wasn't good for my sanity...yet I wanted to help him.

"You're awfully quiet," Mel told me, her gaze unmoving from the dark road ahead. This area outside of Enfield was unfamiliar, dotted by woods that provoked fear and unease, and once more, I asked myself why I was going to a place where nothing good dwelled.

"I'm still not sure this is a good idea."

"What exactly?"

"Prying into Blake's business. I should stay away from him, not chase him."

"You're not chasing him."

"I know, but I feel like I am. So what if he's in a gang? That doesn't concern me."

Oh, what a lie that was. I even had nightmares that revolved around Blake's life in the gang, and it made me want to wrap my arms around him and protect him somehow.

"Tell that to your heart," Mel said as she headed down a bumpy pathway in the woods that only led us deeper and deeper into encompassing darkness.

After ten minutes of rocky ride, the forest gave way to a clearing filled with parked cars. In the distance, a crowd of people stood by what I assumed was a track, which ran around a farm.

Mel parked her Volvo next to a red Sedan, and we stepped out onto a thin layer of snow, greeted by the icy cold air. I shivered, but it wasn't only because of the low temperature. Adrenaline pumped through me as I took in the people surrounding us.

They looked like the kind of people I would never willingly associate myself with. Most of them were dressed fully in black and wearing leather jackets, looking like they could crush me with their little finger if they wanted to. A lot of them were much older than us, with menace carved into their faces along with the scars that testified to cruelty.

Following Mel's suggestion, I'd worn all black too, which allowed me to blend in easily. I double-checked that my phone was in my pocket in case something went wrong and followed Mel to a nearby group of guys.

Steven was the tallest of them and easily the loudest; his high-pitched laugh grated on my ears. Masen stood next to him with a cigarette in his hand as he talked to a short guy on his other side. Blake was nowhere in sight, and the ball of tension in my stomach shrunk a bit.

"Oh look. Here's my nosy bodyguard," Steven said out loud and pointed at Mel, the bruise on his nose impossible to miss.

The whole group turned to look at us, and I blushed to the roots of my hair. I got the urge to hide behind Melissa as they checked us out. Masen raised his eyebrows, clearly surprised to see me. I would have felt the same if I were him. I felt like a fish out of water here.

"Oh look, it's the brain fart! Oops. I mean, my brother."

The group burst out laughing, everyone except Steven, whose eyes turned into slits. "I told you not to come here."

"Yeah? And I told you I don't follow anyone's orders. I just want to make sure you don't break a bone or two."

"Cue the eye roll," Steven said to Masen, matching his smirk. He turned his gaze back to Mel. "Yes, Mommy. Anything else, Mommy?"

She slapped the back of his head. "Get serious, you jerk."

"Ouch! Your signs of affection never fail to amaze me, sis. I wouldn't be surprised if I woke up with bruises tomorrow." He pointed at his nose. "You already gave me one."

Mel grimaced but covered it quickly. "You'll end up with broken bones or worse if you race while you're this stoned."

"Shiiit, Brooks. Why didn't you tell us your sister was a savage?" The guy standing next to Masen winked at her. "So hot. I'd totally do you."

Mel gave him a murderous glare that made even me shrink with apprehension.

"You don't know what you'd be getting yourself into," Masen said to him, his smirk long gone. "She'd chew you out before you even took your dick out."

Mel fisted her hands. "Steven, give me your knife."

Steven tipped his chin down. "And why would I do that?"

"Because I want to cut this asshole up," she said with her glare fixed on Masen.

"Sheesh! They're at each other's throats, but the sexual tension between them is off the charts! Kinky," a redhaired guy on Steven's other side said to another guy. He smirked at Masen. "Why don't you two blow off some steam in the back seat?"

If Mel was furious before, now I was sure she was on the path of becoming a murderer.

"Mel—" I started, wanting to reason with her, but she didn't pay attention to me.

"And why don't you shut up and stop sticking your nose where it doesn't belong, you stupid asshole?" she bit out, ready to swing at him.

The redhead's smile dropped, and he drew himself up to his full height. "What the...? I'm gonna knock this bitch out."

He lunged at her, but before she could react, Masen slid in between them, surprising us all.

"Don't do it, man," he told him. Mel's eyes widened and went down Masen's arm, which was now placed against her waist and holding her behind him. She inched away from the contact, but she kept looking between his arm and the back of his head, her lips parted.

Steven moved to stand next to Masen as he finally decided to side with Mel. "Yeah. Don't mess with my lil' sis."

"You're defending this chick?" the ginger asked Masen through his teeth.

Masen snorted. "I'm defending *you* from her. Ending up in the ER because of this nutcase isn't worth it."

The confusion on Mel's face was replaced by fury, and she spat at Masen's feet. "Go to hell and drown in the hottest pits of fire." She grabbed my hand and dragged me away from the hollering group.

"Oh yeah? I'll make sure to drown you in those pits first," he shouted, his murderous glare following us all the way to Mel's car.

She let go of my hand and hit the hood of her car with her fist. "Jackasses! They are all jackasses."

Worry sprouted in my chest as I observed her quietly. She was so full of anger. It was almost tangible.

"Don't take it to heart." I placed my hand on her shaking shoulder. Her white-hot rage wasn't healthy at all. "They're not worth it."

She pressed her fists against the hood, clenching them so hard her knuckles turned white. "It's just that...it's not fair. I hate that kind of people. I hate all of them. The world would be a better place if people like them didn't exist."

I flinched at her venomous tone. "It's just that they don't know any better."

She snorted. "They don't want to know better. They just enjoy living their miserable lives and bullying others."

"Don't be so judgmental, Mel."

"I'm not judgmental. I'm a realist."

She was more like a pessimist, but I didn't tell her that. The truth was that sometimes she had to back off and refuse to engage, but she never considered that possibility. She could be too explosive, and her anger issues got the best of her far too often.

"Anyway." She took a deep breath and exhaled it before she faced me with a gigantic smile. "I'd have totally broken that guy's nose if I'd gotten the chance. I'd have made pudding out of him!" She swung her fist around in the air, going for a comical effect.

She was back to old Mel pretty quickly, too used to putting a mask on, and it only made my heart ache for her more. I wanted to help her get rid of her demons, but how could I help someone who refused help? Whenever I tried to talk about it with her, she dismissed me and said she was completely fine. She always told Sar and me to open up, but she never opened up herself.

A few cars parked nearby, and I raised my head in time to see Blake stop his red Dodge Challenger Hellcat about fifty yards away from us. He hadn't even gotten out of his car and a group of girls already flocked around his car, half of them wearing black leather skirts and leather jackets that fit their perfectly proportioned bodies like a glove. I pushed my envy aside and willed myself to remember I should embrace the differences between our bodies and stop being so bitter.

Blake got out of his car. He looked immensely attractive with his spiky dark hair, the sides shaved close, and black clothes that added to his appeal. Two girls attached themselves to him as if pulled by a magnet.

Before I could look away, he glanced over and caught my gaze, and even with the distance between us, I could see he was surprised to see me here. I dragged my gaze back to Mel, definitely feeling like I was here chasing him.

"I'm surprised a good girl like you is here. You look nice tonight," a voice said into my ear, and I jumped back. I came face to face with Steven, who had left his friends to join us.

"She always looks nice, moron," Mel told him.

I stepped away from him, but he closed the gap between us immediately, and my stomach coiled. He reeked of what I assumed was weed.

"But tonight, she looks even better. Wanna have some fun with me after the race?" He put his hand on my shoulder as he leaned close to my face. "I feel all lonely, and I need someone to warm my car seat. So what do you say, doll?" He winked at me.

I shifted away from him once more, breaking our contact. "I'm not interested."

Mel scowled at him. "Last time I checked, junkies don't score high on the attractive-boys scale. Maybe you'd stand a chance with her after you clean up your act, but for *dating*, not fucking, you jerk." She smacked the back of his head for the second time this evening. "Although, I wouldn't suggest she date you even then, considering your horrible personality."

"Will you shut up already? You're yapping all the time. And what's with the hitting? I'm not a punching bag, so chillax." He flashed me a smile that gave me the creeps. "So, doll, what's it gonna be?"

"I'm really not..." My voice trailed off as I met Blake's glare from where he stood only a few feet away.

"So?" Blake cocked his head to the side, not taking his eyes off of me even once. "Are you with Brooks too?"

Anger choked off my reply, but *still*, my heart missed a beat or two because of his obvious jealousy.

"What's that supposed to mean?" Mel asked him, placing her hands on her hips.

"It means I'm not talking to you, clown face," Blake told her, but his eyes remained on mine.

"What the hell did you just call me now?"

Steven burst into chuckles. "Clown face! I like that. I'll be using that often from now on."

"Go back to those girls and stay away from Jess," Mel said, stepping in front of me to protect me from Blake, but for the first time ever, I didn't appreciate the gesture or her words. I could see it in Blake's eyes—the same feeling that now churned in my chest: disappointment.

Once more, I was unable to fight back. Once more, someone else was fighting my battles. Once more, I was a coward.

I stepped to the side so Mel wasn't shielding me anymore. "You're asking me if I'm with Steven? Then what about you? Are you with some unknown girl, number five hundred?" I fired off the first thing that came to my mind and motioned with my head toward the girl who had been wrapped around him just a minute before. "What a hypocrite."

His eyes flashed with liquid anger, but he didn't say anything. Instead, he pulled me after him.

"Hey!" I yanked my arm to set it free, but my strength was nowhere near his. "Let go of me!"

"Where are you taking her, asshole?!" Mel rushed to catch us, drawing the attention of all the people around us.

Blake halted and cut his eyes at her. "Stop following us unless you want this to turn ugly."

"I won't step aside! She's not property! You can't drag her wherever you want."

He snarled. "You keep barking, Brooks, and it's really getting on my nerves."

Steven approached her. "Sis, stop making a mess out of everything. Step aside and let them go."

She looked at him incredulously. "Drugs have really destroyed all your brain cells. Of course I'm not going to do that—"

"I've had enough of you today, Melissa." Steven changed his tone completely, a sharp edge to his voice that added to his vicious appearance. "You're not her mother, so stop fricking treating her like a child. She can handle herself." He gave me a pointed look. As much as I was afraid of Blake, this altercation just prolonged the inevitable. He always got his own way.

"I'll go with him," I said weakly.

"Are you crazy?!" Mel exploded, but Blake didn't wait a second longer, dragging me after him as Mel watched us in disbelief. I swallowed back my resentment, fear showing its ugly head because I didn't know what he was going to do.

He stopped next to his car and glared at two girls sitting on his hood, who were apparently waiting for him. "Get the fuck away," he snarled.

They shared a puzzled frown before they scurried off.

Blake released me and pointed at his car. "Get inside."

I glared at him. "I'm not going anywhere with you."

He caught my shoulder and leaned in. "We're not going anywhere. I need to talk to you, so get inside."

His lips were too close to mine, and I tore my gaze away from them, cursing him for attracting me even at a time like this. "I'm not crazy enough to get in the car with you."

"Right now, you're safer with me than with any of these people hanging around. Now. Get. Inside."

His breath on my lips tickled, and my pulse quickened. *He's too close to me.* I wiped my clammy hand against my jeans and opened the door, getting into the space that was all Blake with its black and red leather and impressive interior that exuded power and control.

It was overwhelming, and I realized just how truly dangerous it was to be here with him. I had to fear him *and* my stupid heart for finding something in this moment that didn't exist.

Blake got in and slammed his door shut. His nearness affected me in more ways than one, and I had to make an effort to breathe slowly as I stared straight ahead into the darkness. His tinted back and side windows hid us from any onlookers, and knowing he could do *anything* and get away with it... *Not good.*

"What are you doing here?" he asked.

I blushed. I could never tell him I was here because of him. "Why does it matter to you?"

He snorted his derision. "It doesn't." He chuckled. "Who would've thought? You really are an easy girl. First Burks, then Robinson, and now Brooks. And let's not forget New Year's Eve in that closet."

I crossed my arms over my chest. I was fed up with his insinuations. "You're such a hypocrite," I bit back. "You're a hypocrite *and* jealous."

His eyes grew wide before they slid all over me. "You give yourself too much credit. You think I'm jealous? Because of you?" His condescending look called forth a crushing sensation in my chest.

"Then why am I here? Why did you want to talk to me?"

"It's because I want you to stop messing with my mind."

I sucked in air. "Messing with your mind?"

"Ever since I met you, I feel like shit and it's getting harder and harder. I want you to stop."

"I'm not doing anything! I just want to live my life in peace and away from you."

"It's too late for that."

"What do you mean?"

"How many times do I have to repeat myself? I can't stay away from you." Flutters spread through my belly at the words that sounded intimate despite their real meaning.

I let out a chuckle that contained no humor. "You make no sense! You blame me for making your life difficult, but you can't stay away from me?"

We were now facing each other, our eyes never straying away from the other's face. His scent—a mix of cigarettes and his cologne—created the heat in me that opposed the pain that spread at his cold words. This toxic circle of insults and hate would go on forever. Maybe there was good in him, but I would never get to see it.

"I don't get you, Blake. I don't get you at all." My voice cracked. I was a hopeless fool.

He seemed to want to say something, to give me some explanation, but his expression darkened, and his lips formed a wry smile.

"Come on—start crying. It's what you do best."

I curled my hand into a fist. I hated the venom that rushed through me, that pushed me to say hurtful things.

"Yes. I always cry, and I'm weak, but no one is weaker than you." He flinched. "Look at you, all worked up because of me. You don't even have a clue how to deal with your mess, so you're going in circles and acting like a big bully."

He grabbed my upper arm and jerked me toward him, rage and hurt flashing in his eyes. "Don't fuck with me, Metts."

My eyes darted between his, too many emotions clogging my chest. "I'm just speaking the truth. You don't have an answer, so you're just using aggression, threats, and insults to make yourself feel better."

"Shut your mouth."

"No. I was silent for far too long, and it didn't do me any good. This is not some punishment for I don't know what. This is a pathetic attempt to deal with your anger. You can't direct that anger to the right target, so you're using me to get rid of it and get rid of your frustration."

His face twisted in pain, and his eyes turned the color of tempestuous clouds. I hadn't expected such a reaction from him, but instead of satisfaction, I felt pity.

He looked away and pursed his lips, but he didn't let go of me.

I smiled sadly. "Don't you see? It never gets better, because making my life shitty doesn't make yours any less shitty, and you know it. And it will only get worse for you."

He lowered his head, his grip on my arm turning shaky and breaths heavy. He didn't say anything, and I didn't know what to do. I should get out of his car, but I didn't have it in me to move, bound to him for a reason I still tried to deny. My chest constricted at seeing him this vulnerable.

"Fuck you," he said suddenly.

I recoiled. He grasped my other arm and raised his head to look at me. His red eyes darted all over my face, tracing each inch of it.

"Fuck you for making me this confused. Fuck you for all the pain. Fuck you for bringing back the nightmares. And *fuck you* for making me break the promise I made her."

I didn't dare speak. I didn't dare even move. His words were so harsh, but his eyes...they were fire.

"I'm betraying her because of you." He shook me, his face distorted by despair. "I'm not supposed to feel like this!" My chest hurt so much. It was too much. "I'm supposed to hate you."

His eyes fell on my lips and lingered there. I still couldn't move, holding my breath...

"Fuck you for making me do this," he whispered and leaned in too quickly—

The knocks on the window froze us in our tracks before his lips could touch mine.

"Blake?" Masen said. "The race is about to start, man."

"Shit," Blake muttered as he released me and looked away.

I closed my eyes with shame. This took the cake.

What was I thinking? I would've let him kiss me. No, not only that—I'd been *anticipating* it.

Bad. That was so bad.

I needed to get away from him. This was more proof that I couldn't trust myself when I was around him. I rushed to get out as I opened the door, but he grabbed my wrist and made me look at him, back to his old self.

"Don't say a word about this to anyone."

I didn't reply. I just scrambled out of his car, completely flustered and confused.

Chapter 12

I COULDN'T EVEN LOOK at Masen as I closed the door. I rushed between the cars and headed back to Melissa, but not before I managed to hear Masen say something to Blake that sounded like "You don't look good." I was curious as to why he'd say that, but I didn't turn around or slow down to hear more.

If Masen hadn't appeared, I would have been kissing Blake. He'd wanted to kiss me. I groaned, forcing myself not to think about that. It was a disaster and not something I should be excited about. Not at all.

I joined Mel close to the starting line. She was surrounded by a group of girls in leather jackets who looked like they would pummel us if we even looked at them the wrong way. I shivered. The cold in my limbs contrasted with the rising anticipation in the air.

Mel's eyes slid down my body as if looking to see if I was in one piece.

"I'm alive," I told her. I hoped she wouldn't ask for details.

"And strangely flushed." She narrowed her eyes. "What happened in his car?"

"Nothing," I fired back quickly.

"Mhm. And I'm Spider-Man's bride."

"He didn't hurt me, so you can relax." She raised her eyebrow, but she chose to stay silent. "How many laps do they have to make?"

"Five. There are eight miles in total. Look, they're starting."

Six cars lined up on a wide circuit track that was lit by generator-powered flood lights. Blake's Dodge Challenger Hellcat and Masen's yellow Chevrolet Corvette were parked in the middle. Steven's silver Audi TT was between Masen's Corvette and a green Mustang with a black skull painted on the hood. The furious rumbling of engines roared through the air, and the spectators cheered louder.

He was close to kissing me...

Shut up, stupid brain. Close the door on it.

I couldn't. He'd mentioned something about a promise to a girl and betraying her, and my mind took me back to Emma and his connection to her.

A race girl wearing knee-high boots and a mini skirt that barely covered her butt sashayed her way to the starting line, breaking through my thoughts, and marked the start of the race.

The cars left the starting line in a cloud of smoke, and my pulse quickened with excitement. I'd never cared much about racing and didn't understand what was so special about it, but watching it in person with the sounds of engines and the ecstatic crowd all around filled me with energy.

I was sucked into their world, my eyes plastered to the cars. Steven was in the lead, closely followed by Masen's nimble Corvette and the green Mustang. By the end of the first lap, Masen passed Steven and sped up, putting more distance between them before the first turn.

I was amazed by Masen, who seemed to rule the track. He killed the turns, accelerating way before any of the other drivers could. I faintly remembered Hayden mentioning that Masen's specialty was racing, which was clear as day now.

I'd also overheard him saying Masen needed cash badly, which wasn't a surprise, because unlike Blake or Hayden, Masen didn't come from a rich family. I doubted his father's salary as a local TV news editor brought in a great deal of money. Then there was that boy, Eli, who needed care as a quadriplegic, and I could only imagine how much that cost.

My eyes went to Blake's car. He was falling behind the Mustang. His Challenger oversteered at turns, which left him struggling to keep the fourth position. I was bewildered that he didn't drive that well.

Masen had said Blake didn't look good, and I wondered if that was because of me. Maybe my words had a bigger impact on him than I could've possibly guessed.

Masen ended the second, third, and fourth lap in first, but the Mustang got pretty close to him at the beginning of the final lap, almost sending Steven off the track at one of the sharper turns. Blake was struggling to stay in fourth place, until the last car managed to take his position in the middle of the lap.

Steven's engine roared when he stepped on the gas and almost pulled ahead of the Mustang, but the Mustang's driver swerved to block Steven and passed Masen at the last possible moment, finishing first. The crowd

burst into cheers. Blake crossed the finish line last and veered to a screech-
ing stop next to Masen's car.

The viewers darted to the track to greet the winner, some of them
taking pictures of his Mustang. The excited murmurs carried one name
through the air, which I assumed was his: Bobby Q.

"It's over," Mel, who had been unusually quiet during the race, exclaimed in relief and grabbed my hand. "Let's get to Steven."

We rushed to his car, which was parked right behind Masen's. Steven
got out and hit his fist against the rooftop, baring his teeth. Mel collided
with him and pulled him into a crushing embrace.

"I'm going to steal your car and sell it so you can't race again. You scared
the crap out of me!"

Steven didn't return her hug or reply. He glared at the winner, who was
now surrounded by two busty brunettes. A shiver ran down my spine when
my eyes stopped on the guy's face. He had shoulder-length raven hair, and
he looked at least ten years older, with an even scarier expression than the
rest.

"I could've won," Steven gritted out as he separated himself from Mel.
"That money should've been mine!"

I inhaled a sharp breath, taken aback by his hysterical tone. His scraggy
face was twisted as if he was in pain, and my heart ached for Melissa. I
didn't know much about drug addicts, but I could guess the addiction
messed him up real bad when he was this furious and desperate.

Mel scowled at him. "You should be happy you're alive, you punk."

"Knock it off, Melissa. You're acting just like Mom, and it's driving me
nuts."

They didn't stop bickering, but I tuned them out as my gaze fell on
Blake's profile close by. My stomach twisted into knots at the look on his
face as he stared at Bobby Q. It was hatred unlike anything I'd seen before,
but there was also terror, which was further accentuated when he closed his
eyes and pinched the bridge of his nose.

Masen joined him. "What's wrong?" I heard him ask in spite of the
constant chatter and shouts around us.

"Isaac was right. It's him." It was hard to make out his words from this distance, but moving closer to them be dropping the ball. He nodded toward Bobby Q. "He came to the surface."

Masen followed his gaze. "Shit. Are you sure it's him?"

"I'm positive." He added something else, but I couldn't hear it.

"Do you think he knows who you are?"

I glanced at Mel and Steven, who were in the middle of their tiff and paying zero attention to me.

"Not likely..." I wasn't able to hear the rest of his sentence. I flexed my hands, which had turned sweaty in the meantime. Blake really didn't look good.

"Will you be able to handle him with your...? You know."

With his *what*?

Blake glared. "It doesn't matter. I'll do whatever is necessary."

"So what now?" Masen asked, and I held my breath, my heart thumping harder in expectation of his answer.

"Now I finally..." The rest was lost in the roar of a nearby engine.

• • • •

I COULDN'T STOP THINKING about the cryptic conversation between Blake and Masen and the way Blake had looked after the race. He knew that driver, and everything in me told me he was in for big trouble.

It wasn't my business. I shouldn't even have been thinking about Blake's fears or his mysterious words, but here I was, chewing it over *again*.

I shoved the thoughts of Blake aside and looked at Ms. Donovan, my choir teacher, who played piano while Shelly, a sophomore, practiced the solo she was going to perform at the school festival.

Ms. Donovan was still trying to convince me to perform a solo, assuring me I had the voice of an angel that would reach many hearts. I was totally terrified of it, but I couldn't deny I liked the idea. Only two weeks were left until the start of the festival, and she'd said I had to make my decision by today.

Kevin nudged me with his elbow and whispered, "Marcus is, is, is watching you."

I glanced at Marcus. He was looking in our direction from where he stood with the rest of our group across the room, but his chocolate eyes weren't on me—no, they were on Kev, and it was a look of so much longing I wished I were Cupid so I could get those two together.

This reminded me—I hadn't talked to Kev about Marcus.

I inched closer to Kevin so I could talk to him without others pricking up their ears. "I talked to Marcus last week."

He gave me a side glance. "Yes?"

"He told me he's gay."

Kev did a double take at me before he looked at Marcus. Almost immediately, Marcus looked away and scratched his neck. *That was so cute!*

"Marcus is gay? But why did he ask you out th-th-then?"

"Brace yourself. He asked me out because he likes you."

His eyes bugged out, blush paving its way across his face. He gaped at Marcus, who was now staring at his phone.

"B-B-But I don't understand. It doesn't make sense."

I shrugged. "He wanted to get closer to you. I know it's not the right way to go about it, not by a long shot, but I think it's sweet."

His blush intensified. "So he doesn't like you at all?"

"Nope, and he asked me to talk to you and tell you he wants to ask you out."

"Ask me out?" he said in a high-pitched voice, wide-eyed. "I...I don't know."

"Do you like him? You said he was cute."

He fidgeted as he stared at his shoes. "He's really cute, but I, I, I've never thought about him that way."

"Well, think about it. You two would make a nice couple."

He gave me a tight-lipped smile. "If you think so."

"I do. He also likes music and sings, as you can see, and he told me once he's a hardcore Star Wars fan. Just like you!"

"Really? That's awesome." The lack of excitement in his voice produced a sinking sensation in my stomach.

I knew well where this mild reaction came from, but I tried not to think about it. I couldn't expect him to be ecstatic about Marcus, but I hoped he would find someone who could reciprocate his feelings.

I suppressed a fresh wave of guilt and focused on Ms. Donovan. Shelly had just finished her song, and it was time for all of us to practice for the festival performance.

Marcus often looked at Kevin, but Kev constantly stared at his shoes, singing with zero enthusiasm, and I felt like a terrible friend. We ended the song, and Ms. Donovan called it a day. Wanting to cheer Kevin up, I headed out of the classroom behind him, but the teacher called out for me.

"Jessica, may I have a moment of your time?"

I twisted my hands together. I'd forgotten I was supposed to tell her my decision about my solo.

"Sure." I glanced at Kevin and offered him a huge smile. "See you tonight." One of Hayden's friends was throwing a party, and we'd all been invited.

He nodded, half-smiling, and rushed out of the classroom. I caught Marcus's gaze and read the question in his eyes. I shrugged my shoulder. Kevin hadn't refused to go out with him, but he also hadn't agreed.

Ms. Donovan turned to face me when the classroom emptied. "So, have you made your decision?"

I bit the inside of my cheek as my pulse sped up. I felt I was standing at a crossroads, and my decision would determine who I was going to be: a coward or a fighter.

My stomach hurt just imagining myself out there, all alone in front of the whole school, doing what I'd dreaded all these years. It would be the most horrifying experience of my life that could lead to the ultimate embarrassment I wouldn't be able to recover from.

Then again, running away from it would enforce my being a coward. It would prevent me from moving forward and actually doing something important in my life. I couldn't become a singer if I couldn't face my fears. I would have to kiss my dream goodbye and regret it for the rest of my life.

I didn't want to confront my fears.

I was dying to get rid of them.

This could prove to be the worst decision of my life.

This could prove to be the best decision I'd ever made.

Follow your dreams, Jess.

I swallowed the bile that rose up my throat and raised my head to look at her. "Yes," I answered in a shaky voice. "I'm going to do the solo."

Her eyes filled with pride. "Excellent! That's the best decision you could've made, Jessica. Let yourself shine."

I returned her smile, but inside, I was absolutely terrified. How I was going to get my voice to work in front of an audience was beyond me.

I just hoped I'd made the right call.

Chapter 13

THE UBER DRIVER PULLED up behind one of many cars parked in the driveway of a large three-story house. I got out thinking about the session I'd had with Susan earlier. I'd told her about my decision to do my solo, and she'd praised me for taking charge of my life. She was sure I would be able to perform when the time came. As much as I wanted to share her enthusiasm, most of the scenarios my brain concocted weren't good.

She was positive that the solo would boost my self-confidence and improve the way I saw myself, and somewhere deep down, I knew this could be a way to deal with my self-loathing. If I could prove to myself I had actual worth, I would, for once, enjoy being myself.

She also gave me homework. She told me to take a look in the mirror and find one positive thing for every negative thing I saw on myself and write it down. I did that, and it turned out I had more features I liked than I'd thought. I taped the list to my mirror, determined to focus more on the positives than the negatives.

I checked my reflection in my compact mirror when the Uber driver drove away and smiled. My blue eyes stood out with eyeliner and a mix of light and dark shadows that made them appear bigger. A fine layer of blush brought color to my fair face, while baby pink lipstick coated my lips. I wore black jeans, black five-inch high heels, and a floral low-cut waist-belted shirt that hid my love handles and emphasized my big boobs.

I looked beautiful. I took my phone out of my purse and snapped a few selfies, smiling at the camera. I chose the last photo and posted it on Instagram, feeling unusually confident.

Wait until Blake sees me.

Hold on. What?

I clenched my phone. After the previous night's "almost kiss," my mind was playing tricks on me, forcing me to think about him and his kiss. It didn't help that he was a good kisser and extremely good-looking, which shouldn't have mattered at all. He was my bully. I had to remember that. My bully. Nothing else.

I ran fingers through my straight hair to fix it. The music was blasting out of the house, and my blood pumped faster with excitement. Humming to the electro-pop song currently playing, I glanced at the cloudy sky before I texted Mel.

I'm here. Where are you?

Kev and I will meet you at the front door.

I maneuvered around tightly parked vehicles, my pulse accelerating. Mel and Kevin waited for me at the entrance, and they both looked like they were already tipsy. Kev wasn't wearing his glasses, dressed in khaki jeans and one of his favorite tartan plaid shirts, which was a sharp contrast to Mel's leather mini skirt and a black shirt with a white "My Eyes Are Up Here ↑" slogan across the chest.

"Wow," Mel told me as she looked me up and down with round eyes. "You're a bombshell."

"It's nothing special." I tucked a strand of my hair behind my ear.

Kevin was also staring at me, but it was the kind of stare that said I was the most beautiful girl in the world. My stomach knotted.

"Ha ha. Nothing special, she said," Mel replied. "If that's nothing special then I look like I've emerged out of a swamp."

"You look beautiful. Both of you," I said.

Kevin blushed. "Th-Thank you. You too."

"Let's go inside and get you something to drink." Mel wound her arm through mine and headed inside.

The loud music and smoke surrounded me, and the strong beat caused my heart to pound harder. Mel guided us around the crowds of teenagers that transformed this big house into a matchbox, considering how many people were here. She led us to a room with three pools and a mini bar in the corner, and the hairs on my neck stood up. I could feel him. He was here somewhere.

My eyes darted over various faces until I found him sitting between Hayden and Masen at the bar, and I pulled my belly button in. His eyes were already on me, taking all of me in, making breathing difficult. He didn't look away from me even once as we approached them, stripping me of everything, and that part of me I despised enjoyed it too much.

He was getting to me more and more, and I couldn't control it.

"Where's Steven?" I asked Mel.

She frowned, a hint of shadow passing over her face. "He's probably doping up with his junkie pals at some shitty place. Let's not talk about him tonight, okay?"

"Okay," I agreed, seeing how much it bothered her.

"Hey," I greeted Sarah, Hayden, and Masen when we joined them, ignoring Blake's stare. Masen nodded at me and took a gulp of beer straight out of his bottle before he turned back to the gorgeous blonde he was talking with.

"Hey, Jess," Sarah said and leaned in toward my ear. "You look so beautiful!"

My eyes met Blake's over her shoulder, and a pang hit my chest. His stare was too intense, robbing me of breath and reason, and I needed to force myself to look away from him.

"Thanks. You also look beautiful," I told her. "That dress is amazing on you."

She wore a navy bodycon dress that showed off her thin waist and small hips, paired with ballet pumps with ankle straps. Hayden's heated eyes were plastered on her, and I smiled inside with joy for them. He wrapped his arm around her waist when she moved back to him and pressed a kiss on her lips with such intensity that I grew a bit hot just watching them.

My eyes flitted over to Blake again, who idly swung his beer bottle by its mouth between his fingers. I caught him staring at my breasts and blushed excessively. I pushed my hair to the front to hide my face.

"Okay, if these two ever kiss in front of kids, they're going to traumatize them forever," Mel said as she watched Sarah and Hayden kiss and passed Kev and me the drinks.

I rolled my eyes at her and took a cup of something that looked like water, but I knew better. I needed alcohol if I was going to get through Blake's confusing mood changes. I downed the whole cup in a few gulps, butterflies wreaking havoc in my stomach. I was supposed to hate having his eyes on me. I had to hate it. I couldn't let him reduce me to a pathetic fool that easily.

Mel handed me another cup, which I accepted eagerly, but then I noticed how down Kevin looked as his eyes shifted to Sarah and Hayden, and I realized he'd barely spoken two words since I arrived.

I placed my hand on his upper arm. "Kev? Are you okay?"

His arm tensed under my hand. "Yes."

"You don't look okay."

He grinned and raised his thumb at me. "I'm great."

"You know you can tell me anything that bothers you, right?"

"Yep." His grin grew even larger, if that was possible.

"Guys, let's go dance," Mel told us before I could answer him. "We didn't come here to be utility poles."

"I guess you don't want to dance with us," Sarah said to Hayden, her lips swollen and eyes glazed.

He gave her a flat look. "Fuck no."

"Right." She kissed him one more time and yelped when he smacked her butt playfully. She smiled at him and linked her arm with mine, shaking her head.

I grinned and followed Mel out of the room, feeling Blake's gaze on my back but never returning it.

• • • •

THREE HOURS AND A COUPLE more drinks later, I was a carefree bundle of joy. I'd danced my feet off to the music that made me high—or maybe that was the alcohol. Either way, it felt good, and I couldn't stop smiling.

Sarah had gone somewhere with Hayden while Mel, Kevin, and I ended up playing truth or dare gathered around the kitchen island. Mel hadn't wanted to play the game; she'd claimed it was stupid and would quit if she was asked to kiss someone, but Kev and I managed to convince her.

Masen and Blake were playing too, and I pretended I didn't notice Blake's continuous stares, looking at everything and everyone but him. The whole time my heartbeat refused to slow down.

The bottle had stopped on me only once so far, and I'd chosen truth, not brave enough to do a dare because most of the dares were about kissing someone or doing something horrifyingly embarrassing. A guy across from me had asked if I was a virgin, and I'd felt embarrassed by the question even with all the drinks in my system.

"No, I'm not," I answered then, which was met with whistles. Blake's eyes widened, followed by a glimpse of disappointment on his face before he put his neutral mask on. My mind fought to get to the bottom of that, but I was too drunk and distracted.

"Cucumber, right?" Masen added loudly, referring to one of the comments on that "Food Slut" Instagram photo that said I'd lost my virginity with a cucumber.

I blushed hard, but I met his amused eyes, speaking my mind before Mel could. "The only cucumber I know about is the one stuck in your butt."

A few guys howled at this, and Mel grinned at me.

"That's my girl," she said, high-fiving me.

After that, Mel got dared twice and Blake once. He had to kiss the girl on his right, and my stomach twisted with something ugly as I watched him lean closer to her. I expected him to give her a long and deep kiss, however, he pulled away from the girl the moment their lips touched, his face expressionless.

A girl with purple hair on my right spun the bottle, and it stopped on the guy on Mel's left. "Truth or dare?"

"Dare," he said with no hesitation.

"I dare you to get on all fours and meow for the next two minutes." We all burst into laughter.

The guy glared at her. "Really? Do you want me to purr too?"

The laughter around me grew louder. "If you want to." The girl winked at him. Kev and I looked at each other, and our grins went wider.

"Bro, don't make this harder on yourself," his friend told him.

The guy groaned and went down on all fours. Masen pulled his phone out and directed it at him, ready to film.

"I feel s-sorry for him," Kev told me.

I giggled. "Me too."

The guy scowled at Masen over his shoulder. "Hey! Don't record me!"

"Start meowing!" the purple-haired girl said, and the guy obeyed reluctantly.

"Meow. Meow. Meow," he said, voice monotone as he crawled around the kitchen island.

"You sound like you're on the verge of dying," Masen told him, following him with his phone. "Louder! Embrace your inner cat!"

I doubled over with laughter, holding my stomach, which started to hurt. Masen and his antics.

I glanced over to Blake without thinking, and the laugh froze on my lips. He wasn't laughing. He wasn't even smiling as he observed no one else but me, his eyes strangely heated.

I couldn't look away from him, not until the dare was over and the guy spun the bottle. It stopped on the blonde next to him, who chose dare and had to do a lap dance with him, but I couldn't have cared less about it as Blake's darkened eyes haunted me.

The bottle pointed at Mel next, and she chose dare. "I want you to kiss his neck," the blonde said to Mel, motioning toward Masen. *Oops.* That wasn't a good idea.

Mel's jaw tightened. "Say what?"

"No way," Masen said with a deep frown. "I refuse."

The blonde looked at him like he'd said the earth was flat. "Why?" She cast a determined gaze at Melissa. "Come on. Don't spoil the fun. Do it or you're out."

Mel crossed her arms over her chest; her eyes carried only contempt for Masen. "Then I'm out. There's no way I'll touch him."

Masen sneered. "There's no way I'll let you touch me."

"I'm glad the feeling is mutual, Barbie." She stomped out of the kitchen before I could even say anything or stop her. I blinked a few times to clear my blurry vision.

"Do you think she's going to be all right?" I asked Kevin.

He shrugged. "That's Mel. You know she, she, she can handle herself."

"What's up with you and that girl?" the blonde asked Masen.

"Nothing. I just can't stand that nutcase."

"Don't call her a nutcase," I snapped. As much as I hated drawing attention to myself, I felt proud for finally standing up for my friends. Even if it did take a couple of drinks.

"All right, all right, all right," the blonde said before Masen could answer. "Let's not turn this into drama. I'll spin the bottle again."

This time, the bottle ended up on Kevin, and he surprisingly chose dare.

"Hmm. Let me think." The blonde pressed her finger to her lips.

"You sure you want to do this?" I said into his ear, giggling. "Seeing the way they are, they will ask you to lick the floor."

Kevin nudged my shoulder with a chuckle. "I'll be fine."

I could feel Blake observing my interaction with Kevin too carefully, and heat surged to my cheeks. The whole night he'd been staring at me, and I couldn't figure out his deal. I expected him to bully me, but it didn't happen.

"Okay. I want you to kiss my friend." The blonde pointed at the black girl with braids across from her, and Kev blushed furiously.

"S-Sure," he said, but he visibly swallowed.

"Does this faggot know how to kiss a girl?" a guy next to the black girl said, stunning us into silence.

Kevin paled and dropped his gaze. I balled my hands into fists with the growing need to protect him.

"He's *gay*?" his friend asked him. "Eww. Hell no."

"There's nothing wrong with being gay," I bit out, shaking with anger. Kev was motionless next to me. Too motionless.

"It is if you can get STDs," the purple-haired girl said, and I gaped at her.

"Have you ever heard of condoms?" I asked her in a quivering voice. Kev was almost in tears.

"As if they can actually help."

I was ready to have words with her, but Kevin darted from his spot, pushing through people to get out of the kitchen, and I rushed after him right away, hoping I wasn't drunk enough to fall over.

"Kev!" I called out. *Those ignorant and awful people!*

I reached him on the back porch. There was no one in the back yard, and the music wasn't loud out here, the smell of the imminent rain present in the air. It got colder, but the alcohol was warming me up.

"Don't pay attention to them." I stopped behind him.

He didn't turn around. "It's not easy to, to do that, because th-those kind of people are everywhere! How can I tell p-p-people I'm b-bisexual if they're going to react like that?"

A lump formed in my throat. I placed my hand on his shoulder. "I know. It's not fair, and there's a lot of injustice in this world, but not everyone is like them. There are good people out there, Kev. There are people who won't judge you or look at you any differently because of your sexuality."

"I know th-there are good people out there, but that doesn't mean anything when this happens. It's difficult to accept who I am when I'm b-bullied for it. I wish I could change it."

I moved next to him and peered into his face. His red eyes and the pain in them left a deep gash in me, and I pulled him into my embrace, already sobering up. I understood him perfectly. I understood firsthand what it was like to suppress yourself because you were afraid of what the world would say. They held the power over us, silencing our voices, dreams, and desires, turning them into dust and us into shells of who we really were, and for what?

Everyone should have the freedom to be themself, but it is so hard to achieve it. We live only once, but we spend out time pleasing others and forgetting our own happiness—forgetting we are the ones who have to live with our choices, not them. Why does it matter so much? Why does it matter whether we are bi, gay, fat, ugly, stupid, unsuccessful, or any other label society puts on us?

"It's going to be all right," I said reassuringly. "Just don't hide or suppress who you are, no matter what. I've been doing that for as long as I can remember, and now I'm struggling to find a way to live free of my fears. So don't let them win. You and I will find a way to be ourselves."

He pulled away, but he didn't break the contact between us, holding me by my elbows. "Why are you so nice to me?"

"Why shouldn't I be? You're my friend."

"No one has treated me as, as, as nicely as you have. I'm nobody. I'm not worth your t-t-time."

I shook my head. "Don't put yourself down. You're so sweet, Kev." I pinched his cheek. "You're the best friend anyone could wish for."

He dropped his hands. His lips curled into a sad smile as he stared at the sky. "A friend, huh?"

I opened my mouth to confirm it before I stopped myself. I felt like I was treading a thin line. "You know I really care about you."

"Yes, I know. You care about me...but as a friend."

"I..." I sighed. "I'm sorry. I know how you feel about me, but...I just don't feel that way about you."

He looked more upset with each word I spoke, and I hated hurting him like that. He grasped the railing as his eyes shifted to the sky. "I know. But I hoped you would like me too and I...and I could also forget about Hayden. It's so s-stupid of me to crush on him. Or you."

I observed his profile. "Is there maybe someone else you like? I mean, what about Marcus?"

He frowned at me. "Marcus?"

"Yeah. I know maybe you don't see it that way, but I think you two would look amazing together."

He let out a long sigh and pushed himself away from the railing. "I'm not sure I can be with him, Jess. And how can he like me with my s-stutter?"

"And why shouldn't he like you with your stutter? Your stutter is not who you are, remember? I can see Marcus doesn't care about that, and neither should you. Stutter or not, you're a sweet, nice person, and you deserve the best."

"Then why can't you like me?" He ran his hand through his slicked hair, managing to ruin it. "Is there no way for you to like me?"

My eyes traced the clouds hiding the stars, a thick layer of regret blanketing my chest. A shiver swept through my body. "Kevin, I...I can't. I like someone else."

"I know. It's Blake, isn't it? Even though he's always b-bullied you, you fell for him."

I didn't like the accusation in his tone. I didn't turn to look at him, fisting my hands on the railing.

"Yes. I fell for him even though he's my bully. Sick, right? You probably see me as stupid, but do you think I haven't tried to get rid of these feelings? It's not easy."

He grabbed my hand, and I looked at him. The longing in his eyes was too much for me to bear. "I can help you forget him. We can both forget our s-s-stupid crushes and be together—"

"Do you even understand English, Burks? Or do you need me to translate 'I like someone else' for you?" a deep voice said, and my heart stopped.

Hell no.

Blake stood only a few feet behind us with his arms crossed over his chest and an unreadable expression on his face.

He'd heard everything.

Chapter 14

MY WORLD CRUMBLED. He'd heard it. He'd heard I liked him.

I was going to be sick.

"She likes *me*, not you, so stop trying to force her to like you. Now, beat it," Blake said, motioning with his thumb at the back door for Kevin to leave.

"No. I-I-I won't leave Jess alone with you. And Jess and I are t-talking, so you're the one who should leave."

Blake's nostrils flared, and he lunged at Kev, grabbing his shoulder. "Are you actually talking back to me? Do you want me to force you to leave, Burks?"

"Don't touch him!" I jumped to separate him from Kev and pushed him away, shielding Kev with my body. "He did nothing to you, so don't you dare touch him."

His scowl deepened. "I need to talk to you, and he's just in the way."

"I don't want to talk to you," I said, but it was a lie. I wanted to talk to him, as stupid as it was. I wanted to know why he was here and how much he'd heard. I wanted answers to the questions that grew louder in my mind day after day.

He inclined his head, his eyes narrowing at me. "You're not a good liar. I think you're dying to know what I have to say about your little confession."

A strong blush colored my cheeks, and I glanced away. My skin tingled at his closeness. *I hate him, I hate him, I hate him.* "Fine. We'll talk."

"Jess," Kev said in a disappointed tone, but I didn't look at him—I couldn't—staring at my shoes instead.

"It's okay, Kev. Go. We'll finish our conversation later, okay?"

He didn't answer immediately, and I could feel him watching me. "Okay. I'll find Mel. T-Text me if..." His voice trailed off, and Blake snorted.

"What?" Blake taunted. "If she gets hurt by the big bad wolf? Are you going to be her knight in shining armor?"

Kevin tipped his chin up as he looked at him defiantly, which left me open-mouthed. "I might."

Blake's smirk fell. "You really do have a death wish."

My heart twisted in fear for Kevin. I didn't want him to get hurt because of me.

"Go, Kev. I'll come inside soon."

"Fine," he mumbled and dragged himself back into the house.

I descended the porch stairs and went down the stepping stone path away from Blake, needing that distance between us. The air got cooler. Despite being in the open space, I felt like I was enclosed in a small bubble where nothing existed but Blake.

I could hear him following me closely, and my shivering intensified. I stopped near the back shed and folded my arms across my chest. The smell of the rain spread around me as a poignant tune depicting this moment between us formed in my mind, but I would never get to finish it.

"You wanted to talk, so talk," I said boldly, facing away from him.

He shifted closer, stopping only inches behind me, and the thumping in my chest grew stronger. "Who would've thought you'd fall for me?"

I rubbed my arms to get rid of the cold that penetrated my skin, choking back my shame. "So you're here to rub salt into the wound. Congratulations—I feel even more miserable and ashamed. Will you leave now?"

"Since when?"

I frowned. "Since when—what?"

"You know what I mean."

I closed my eyes, and the image popped up behind my lids. His fragile, hunched form on the floor in the gym that day had shattered my heart. The words that had slipped through his lips were filled with pain that went so deep I wasn't even sure if it had an ending.

The last thing I'd heard before I left was a whispered "I love you, Emma," and even now, I remembered the all-consuming longing in those four words that echoed through the corners of my mind.

"Since I thought I saw something else beneath your cruel exterior, something good. But I was wrong."

"Something good." It wasn't a question. It was a statement said in a tone that revealed he didn't believe he contained anything good to begin with.

I took a few wobbly steps away from him, looking at the sky. "It was when I saw you heartbroken because of some girl named Emma." I started turning around. "It made me realize you aren't that heartless—" My words turned into nothing when I saw his cold expression.

He erased the distance between us in two angry strides and towered over me. "What do you know about Emma?"

The anger rolled off his body, and I had to take a step back, shocked by the sudden change in his mood. "Nothing," I said quickly. "Except that she's someone you obviously care about a lot."

He stepped toward me, eliminating the distance between us again. "Don't mention her name ever again."

I flinched. "*Jesus*. She's really gotten under your skin—"

His eyes flashed with rage, and he launched himself at me. With a yelp, I backed away until I hit the wall of the shed, but he followed me all the way and pressed his palms on each side of my head.

"Don't ever speak about her again!" He slammed his hand against the wood. "You've got no right!"

Pain pierced through me. I could see the love in his eyes that burned so fiercely for that girl, devotion so strong that made me yearn to have something like that. My eyes filled with tears, old wounds opening up.

"I see. I won't mention her again." I moved to the side to walk away, but his arm didn't budge, keeping me in place. "Let me go."

"Why? Isn't this what you want?" He ground against me, fully aroused, and I gasped at the sudden, offensive contact. I squeezed my eyes shut and fisted my hands, hating this. I hated him for breaking me like this. "You like me, so I guess this is exactly what you want."

The first tears dropped, and I turned my head to the side, avoiding his stare. "Not like this," I whispered. "Never like this." I bit into my lip. "Don't degrade me like this. Please."

I felt so cold. Cold and lonely.

He pulled away, and the grip that had been clasping my heart lessened its hold, but I couldn't meet his stare. "Then what do you want?"

The words came out of my mouth before I could regret them.

"What do I want?" I lowered my head, closing my eyes. "Even a fragment of what you feel for that girl. A tiny bit of it. Your smile. But I'll never get that, so what's the use of being around you like this? What's the use of my stupid feelings? This is toxic."

A droplet fell on my cheek, and I opened my eyes to the sky as the first drops of rain cascaded down upon us. A strong shiver rocked my body as I brought my gaze to Blake. My heart contracted at the fiery look in his eyes, which devoured me in the prolonged silence.

"Yes. It's toxic," he finally said. "But it doesn't have to be."

My eyes widened. So many thoughts rushed through my mind at his words, his closeness, his eyes... We were getting soaked, but neither of us moved or acknowledged it. The earthy scent of the rain meeting the ground mixed with his smell appealingly.

"We aren't supposed to be like this," he said, cupping my cheek as his gaze fell to my lips. "I'm not supposed to feel this way." He ran his thumb over my mouth, and a sigh escaped me. I should've moved away. *Any moment now...* "I hate it."

"Then let me go," I said weakly through my chattering teeth. The rain was a real downpour now, gluing our clothes to our bodies.

"I can't. I want that, but..."

"Stop playing me. Over and over again. Enough."

"I'm not playing you."

"So what are you doing exactly?" I asked tiredly, squinting through the deluge. "All this time, you've been giving me mixed signals. So, what do you really want? Please be honest with me for once."

It seemed like he was still trying to resist something, but then resignation settled into his features and he took the last step that separated us. I shivered, but it wasn't because of the weather.

"I want to stop feeling guilty for being this way. I want to stop feeling. Period."

I willed myself to breathe evenly. "And what are you feeling?"

His eyes darted all over my face. There was no hate. No anger. Just need. He cursed under his breath.

"I can't get enough of you. I can't stop thinking about you. And as much as I'm telling myself what we're doing now is wrong...I'm not able to fight it."

He grabbed the back of my head with his hand and crashed his lips against mine before his words could even settle in my mind, swallowing my gasp of surprise. His kiss was fierce, igniting everything in me, and for a few moments, I allowed myself to enjoy this, to forget the pain...to pretend this was okay. I pulled him closer to me. I was starving for the kiss that was ruining me as much as it breathed happiness into me.

His hands roamed up and down my back, seeking the next inch of me like he'd been dying to touch me, and the feel of it was incredible. His body radiated warmth that was stronger than any cold, sheathing me in its addictive cocoon. My heart went wild when he deepened our kiss and his tongue clashed against mine, and it went on and on until I lost my reason. Until I craved more, more, more.

He moved his hands under my thighs and picked me up with stunning ease. I grabbed his shoulders, and my legs wrapped around his waist reflexively as he pressed me against the shed.

"No, wait. Let me down. I'm too heavy."

His heavy-lidded eyes were two dark pools of lust. "No, you're not. You're not heavy at all."

He kissed me again, pressing himself against me, and the contact created a sweet sensation in my core. The scariest thing was that the way our bodies molded to each other felt natural, and I never wanted him to let go of me.

His hand traced my waist and ended on my flabby hip, grasping it. Panic spread through my chest, and I broke our kiss, too aware of the extra fat I had there.

"No...don't touch me there." I tugged at his hand to move it from that spot.

He leaned away to look at me. "What are you doing?"

"I just don't want you to touch me there."

His brows scrunched together. "Why not?"

I blushed, glancing away. "Because I..."

"Because what?" he pressed further.

Damn him. "Because I'm fat, and touching my flab doesn't feel nice."

He lowered me down, all lust in his eyes gone. "Are you for real?"

His tone killed the short-lived warmth in me, bringing back the pain. This was what I got for being so weak and allowing him the kiss he didn't deserve.

I curled my lip. "As real as all those times you called me fat and Fats."

He backed away and ran his hand through his hair. "That's not..." He shook his head. "You're not fat."

Say what?

I gaped at him. "I'm not fat?"

"Yes. You're not fat," he repeated, getting angrier, but his anger couldn't compare to what I felt in this moment. I was beside myself, all those months of insults coming back to me to mock me.

"Then why did you make all those fat jokes at my expense? Why did you insult me all those times, calling me fat and many other horrible things?! Why did you make me remember how much I hate my body?!"

He staggered, his eyes widening. "Jessie, I..." He hissed and kicked away a small rock on the path. "I never wanted to..." He fisted his hands. "*Fuck.* Look, I'm sorr—"

"Don't even say it!" I screamed and pushed against his shoulder. "Don't even say it, because one sorry will never repair the damage you've already done. Don't say it when you don't even mean it! Because tomorrow, you'll send another 'fat' insult my way, and I'll end up making myself throw up in the toilet all over again, feeling awful and like the fattest person in the world!"

Silence fell upon us as shock settled on his face. And then I realized what I'd just said.

I whimpered. I'd actually told him about throwing up.

Kill. Me.

I'd reached the very bottom of humiliation, giving him yet another thing he could use to break me. How much more stupid could I get?

Unable to stay here a second longer, I hid my face in shame and darted away.

Chapter 15

SATURDAY WAS A BLUR of tears, self-hate, and replays of our kiss. Not only was I at a low ebb, my throat was sore too. I couldn't even sing, stuck with homework and dreary thoughts.

He'd kissed me like his life depended on it. He'd told me I wasn't fat. He'd tried to say he was sorry.

He couldn't stop thinking about me. He couldn't get enough of me.

Big deal.

None of that mattered. It didn't matter when everything would remain the same. There was no respect, trust, or love.

But nothing from the night before topped Blake's expression when I'd told him my most embarrassing secret, and it gnawed at me. I wished I could glue myself to my bed and stay in my room until I graduated and was gone from this town.

My parents had other plans, though. My dad valued Saturday dinner gatherings of our family and those of his key clients, which served to strengthen his business relationships with them. Those dinners always bored me to death, but as the obedient daughter that I was, I never refused to go.

So that was why I was waiting all dressed up in the living room for my parents to come downstairs. I wore an elegant white flowery blouse and black pants, with braided hair and makeup that hid all the gigantic pimples that had popped up before my period. Add a sore throat and terrible cramps into the equation, and you got a girl who just wanted stay home, make hot chocolate, and watch Netflix in bed.

My phone chimed with a message from Kev.

Can we talk?

My parents took their time to get ready, so I probably had a few more minutes to spare.

"Hi," I said when he picked up, feeling a flicker of guilt because of our last conversation.

"Hi." His voice was raspy.

"You don't sound good. Are you sick?" He didn't reply immediately, and the heavy silence made me frown.

"No."

I pressed my hand against my cramping stomach. "Then what's wrong?"

"First, I want to apologize for last night. I was too drunk."

"It's okay, Kev. You don't have to apologize. You just said how you felt."

"But I don't want to put p-p-pressure on you."

"You're not. Don't worry about it. I'm just..." I bit at the cuticle of my thumb. "I'm just sorry I don't see you that way. I want to, but you know you can't force your heart to love someone, right?"

He sighed. "I know, and I understand. You like B-Blake, and after last night, I think he may like you too."

I chuckled coarsely. "Yeah, right."

You're a liar, Jess. What about that kiss? And the almost kiss at the track?

"No, seriously. The dude has some serious issues, but I don't think he hates you."

No, he only hates the way he feels, which is equally messed up.

"Even if that's true, it doesn't mean anything. I'm all for forgiveness, but he's still my enemy. And he's hurt me a lot."

"True dat," he said.

"But enough about him. I feel like there's something else that's bothering you."

"Umm...I told my dad I'm bi."

"You did?! What did he say?"

He let out another sigh. "He s-said he doesn't understand me. He didn't get mad, but he looked disappointed."

I could imagine the look on his dad's face. It was the same look I dreaded seeing on my parents' faces when I told them I was going to a music college.

"I'm sorry, Kev." I glanced over my shoulder to confirm my parents were still upstairs. "Our parents can suck sometimes."

"Tell me about it. You know my mom also isn't s-supportive of it."

"I hope they aren't pressuring you to change or act like you're straight."

"No, they aren't. They said they won't p-p-prevent me from dating any-one I want, but they hope it will be a girl."

I shook my head. "Who cares what they think? If you want to be with a guy, it's your right. You're in control of your life, not them." This last sentence came from Susan, and it was one I'd repeated like a mantra the last few weeks, drilling it into my mind.

"I'll try to remember. But..."

"Yes?"

"You really think Marcus and I would look amazing t-t-together?"

I grinned. "Absolutely."

"He's d-d-definitely cute."

My grin grew bigger. "Mhmm."

"I saw him at a restaurant earlier."

I quirked my eyebrows up. "Oh? And?"

He cleared his throat. "And nothing. He was with his, his, his parents, and I was with mine."

"I sense a 'but' in that sentence."

"But our eyes kept meeting, and I..."

"Yesss?"

"I liked it."

I could feel excitement bubbling up in me, imagining the moments their eyes met in the restaurant. *So, so cute!*

"He even s-smiled at me."

"Aww. And how did you feel?"

"Nice...but strange. I haven't noticed him until now, and it feels a little too s-s-sudden."

"I get what you mean. But it's a start, right?"

"Yeah...but I don't know."

"You don't know what?"

"I don't know if I want to be with a guy..."

"But Kev, there's nothing for you to be ashamed of—"

"No, you d-don't get it. I'm not fighting against it. I know it's p-point-less."

"Then why?"

"I'm going to be bullied for it."

I closed my eyes as another wave of pain hit my belly, ready to disagree, but I stopped myself because I knew better. If I was bullied for my weight, what could non-straight students expect? There were people at our school who were homophobic, and they had a whole slew of expletives ready to go for people they disliked for this or that reason. While I hoped the anti-bullying festival would bring bullies to their senses, unless we worked on understanding and accepting all our differences, I wasn't sure if the festival would have a long-term effect on them or not.

"Mel would tell you to screw them all and do whatever you want, and my therapist would say not to fritter away your opportunities—especially not because of those who absolutely don't deserve your attention."

"I guess you're right. I'm just s-scared."

I pressed my lips into a thin line. "I know, Kev," I whispered. "I know."

"Jess?" my mom called from the hallway. "We're ready to go."

I stood up. "Kev, I have to go."

"Sure. See you at school."

Ending the call, I followed my parents outside to my dad's Tesla, taking a deep breath when my cramps got worse.

I got inside and buckled up just as Dad pulled out of our driveway. I needed something to get my mind off the pain, so I went to Instagram and opened my story, which was a selfie I'd taken before the party, a different one from the one I'd posted on my feed. My eyes skimmed over the usernames of the people who had seen my story before I spotted one that sent my heart spiraling.

blake.j1

That was Blake's username.

I tapped on my story again just to check if my eyes were playing tricks on me, but I wasn't mistaken. It was him.

My body heated. After the words I'd blurted out to him, I expected only the worst from him. *He looked at my Insta story.*

It didn't matter. His attention didn't matter. I shouldn't even think about it.

My fingers didn't care about my thought process. They took me to his Instagram, and my eyes went over the line in his bio again.

You live only to encounter pain.

His last photo was of him and Hayden at the party; both of them looked at the camera with no smile on their faces. They looked intimidating but super hot nevertheless, and of course, the photo garnered a lot of "You're gorgeous" and "Sooo hot" comments filled with many heart emojis. I moved my fingers over Blake's face on the screen, imagining I was touching his face for real. Before I knew it, my fingers slipped over the like button beneath the picture.

I flinched. Had I accidentally liked his photo?

I breathed through my open mouth, gaping at the empty heart icon as my heart pounded fast. I hadn't liked it. Good. *Phew.*

I stuffed my phone in my bag before I did something more stupid.

Mom turned around in the passenger seat to look at me. "Why are you so quiet, honey? Is it because of your sore throat?"

"Sorta. I think I might die from my period."

"Maybe you're catching cold." She extended her hand. "Come here." I leaned closer to her, and she felt my forehead with the back of her hand before turning back. "You don't have a high temperature. Did you take Advil for your cramps?"

"Yep, but it doesn't help. My stomach hurts like hell."

"Don't think about it, and it will pass," my dad said, his eyes set on the road.

My dad always looked so serious when he was driving. He didn't like to talk, listen to the radio, or answer phone calls so he could fully focus on the road, which was bad because I needed music in the car. I should've brought my headphones.

"If only it were that easy."

"You can always learn to meditate," my mom said, and I rolled my eyes. Recently, she had this obsession with yoga and meditation; she'd bought lots of scented candles and lit them all around our house. She said they would help us cleanse our spirits or something equally uninteresting.

"Or you can make me chocolate cake. You know that always works for me."

She grinned and turned to look at me over her shoulder. "Since you got into Owen's college, you deserve a little treat, right?" She winked at me, and my stomach churned with unease.

"She deserves more than a treat for that." Dad glanced at me in the rear-view mirror. "I'll finally buy you a new guitar."

I willed my lips into a smile, but it was so fake my chest ached. These days, he kept asking me if I'd responded to his college, assuming I would accept its offer of admission, and the pressure I felt got stronger. I couldn't be happy about that guitar when I knew they wouldn't take well my decision to accept the offer of a music college.

"You don't look happy about it," my mom remarked.

Grin, Jess. Make it convincing. "I'm thrilled! But I'll drop dead any moment now from this pain."

My dad tsked. "Women and periods. I'll never understand."

"What's there to understand?" I asked. "It's obligatory hell."

"I can imagine. Anyway, have you accepted the admission?" There he was again. I needed a distraction right this moment.

"I've been busy with school assignments, but I'll find some time soon. Sooo, what's up with this client? Who is he? Or she?" I crossed my fingers that the diversion tactic would work.

"He's the mayor."

I choked on my spit. "The *mayor*?" My voice reached the limit of its shrillness. *No. Just no.*

He gave me an odd look in the rear-view mirror. "Yes. Mayor Jones."

My mom glanced at me over her shoulder. "Is something wrong, sweetie?"

Something wrong? *Wrong?*

Just a level-seven catastrophe!

"Nope. I just didn't know you were working for the mayor."

"You know Owen's firm works with some politicians too," Mom said. "Enfield's mayor is one of them."

"His son is your age," my dad added. "You must have heard of him. His name is Blake."

Hearing his name created flutters in my belly, which was mixed with queasiness because I didn't want to see him. Not after my shocking revelation.

"Yeah, I've heard of him. It's impossible not to when he's one of the most popular students in our school." *And he's also my bully.*

But I couldn't say that. My mom knew about the boy who bullied me, but I'd never told her his name. I hadn't even told her much about him, keeping most of his relentless bullying under wraps. I couldn't admit to her or Dad how horrible my school life was and destroy their image of me. They would most certainly think it would affect my grades and put more pressure on me to be a good student.

"Is he going to be there too?" I asked them, hoping my voice didn't give anything away.

"Probably," Mom said.

Just great. I should've insisted on staying home.

I had to force myself to breathe evenly as I looked through the window at the houses we passed. The difference between them and mine was clear-cut. These mansions looked like they came out of celebrity home magazines.

However, the Jones' estate was in a class of its own. I did a double take of our surroundings when Dad passed through the ornate main gate and proceeded down a long, tree-lined driveway.

Holy moly.

It was an enormous property that told tales of money. The white brick and stone mansion in the distance was ten times bigger than my home. There was even a gigantic fountain with angels carrying water pots at the end of the driveway.

"They're loaded," I muttered, twisting my hands in my lap. I was getting more nervous with each second that took me closer to Blake's home.

"Their house is beautiful," my mom said, awe coating her words. "And huge."

"You chose the wrong profession, Dad. You should've been a politician."

He let out a chuckle as he parked the car in front of the entrance. "Not all politicians can afford this luxury. The Jones are one of the wealthiest families around here. Old money and such."

"I can see that. This estate clearly cost a pretty penny," I replied and got out of the car. My hands were becoming sweaty.

Only now did it dawn on me that I was going to meet Blake's parents, and I felt curious but also intimidated. I'd been wondering what his parents

were like for a long time. I couldn't imagine them as sweet and warm people, seeing as they had a miscreant son.

I shouldn't have been surprised to see a maid open the front door, but I
was anyway. She was middle-aged and extremely polite, wearing a uniform
that probably cost more than all the clothes I owned combined. She ush-
ered us inside, and a gasp of surprise almost slipped through my lips.

Their foyer was an ostentatious display of their wealth with its marble
floor, two grand staircases, and a crystal chandelier hanging from the ceiling. Everything was made in white and gold, and I wondered how they kept
it so clean. I couldn't keep my white sneakers spotless even for a day, so I
could only imagine the amount of effort their maid had to put into cleaning.

She took us to a grandiose living room I could've easily gotten lost in,
which was also made and furnished in white and gold. It was a lot to take
in as my eyes darted from a white-tiled fireplace and decorations to a large
wall-mounted TV and the white leather sectional couches that put our single three-seat couch to shame.

"Owen, it's good to see you." A man I recognized as Nathaniel Jones
from the newspapers and TV programs approached us with a smile that
was the epitome of charm. It was a nice and convenient mask he used for
the public, but despite the refined appearance, there was something fishy
about him.

Blake didn't look anything like him, since Nathaniel was a lanky
blond—*seriously, does this man dye his hair?*—with a huge nose and close-
set green eyes beneath bushy eyebrows.

"I'm glad I'm able to finally meet your family. Thank you for joining us
for dinner tonight."

They shook hands, and Dad introduced my mom and me. I swiped my
hand down my thigh, hoping it wasn't as clammy as it felt, and shook his
hand. His grip was firm; his smile never faltered as he assessed me, and I
could barely look him in the eyes. Meeting new people and shaking hands
with them had never been my strong suit.

"It's nice to meet you, Jessica."

"It's nice to meet you too, sir," I replied, trying to clear my throat. It was even more sore, and my nose had started running, which meant I would be down with a cold tomorrow.

His wife appeared behind him. She was a tall and classy brunette with a beautiful face that hadn't aged at all. Now I knew whose looks Blake had inherited. He was his mother's replica. She even had the same posture as Blake, with an air of cool indifference oozing out of her. It was like an invisible wall that shielded her. Her icy gray eyes that were so Blakeish locked on mine, and my breath caught.

"This is my lovely wife, Daniela," Nathaniel said with a smile. I wrapped my fingers around her cold, slender hand and shook it shyly.

"It's a pleasure to meet you," she said in a mellifluous voice, donning a smile that didn't reach her eyes.

I smiled back at her and retracted my hand quickly. I looked around the room to see if Blake would pop up from somewhere, but I came up short.

"Please excuse our son, Blake," she said. "He is unable to attend our dinner since he has already made some other plans for tonight. He sincerely apologizes for his absence."

Wow, she was so formal. The translated version: he was out partying and couldn't have cared less about this stupid dinner.

And I doubted he ever apologized for it.

I was relieved that I didn't have to see him, but I also felt a flicker of disappointment when I heard he wasn't going to be here.

Something about being in the house of my enemy, the person who'd given me the best kiss of my life the night before made my heart beat faster. I could almost feel him—the memory of his fragrance, the feel of his warmth, his skin against mine...

I wondered if he'd known my family was supposed to come here.

"It's understandable," my father replied, although I doubted he meant it. Punctuality and precision were virtues he put great stock in, but it wouldn't have been wise of him to put their business relationship on the line, now would it?

The meal was served in a dining room with a round table that could seat ten and floor-to-ceiling windows leading to a stunning stone balcony. Daniela mentioned they had three dining rooms when we sat down, and my eyes almost bulged out. How many bedrooms did they have then? Thirty-three?

My mom complimented her on the interior design, which was a cue for Daniela to start talking about the renovations they had started the previous month.

I hardly paid attention to her, not the slightest bit interested in demolition, refurnishing, and other specifics she spoke about so proudly. The food they served was sumptuous and delicious, especially the salads and the chowder, and I had to remind myself time and again not to gulp it down but eat slowly.

I thought about Susan's words from our last session to ground myself. Food was not my enemy. Balance was my friend. So, with the right portions, I could eat anything I wanted without blaming myself for it. This was as good a time as any for me to practice this.

"...Blake's room in the left wing," Mrs. Jones said, and I perked up, my attention fully on her now. "I have already prepared a new room for him on the third floor close to us, but he wants to stay on the second floor. He says he likes his privacy there." She let out a quiet chuckle, but it was blatantly fake.

"Teenagers. You can't win against them," Nathaniel said, and my parents laughed in response. I coughed and suppressed the urge to sneeze.

"We don't have such problems with Jessica," my mom said, always taking any opportunity to gush about me. "She's such an obedient and responsible child."

"Is that so?" Daniela asked, her sharp Blake-like gaze fixed on me. I glanced away, blushing.

"And what college will Jessica go to?" Nathaniel asked.

"She'll go to my alma mater. She's going to be a lawyer," my dad replied. I turned rigid as I stared at the salad on my plate.

"Really?" Nathaniel asked. "That's good to hear. My son will also go to law school."

I whipped my gaze to him. Blake and the law? It was like he'd said you could eat Nutella with salads.

"He's going to become a lawyer?" I asked, unable to stop the words from coming out.

"Most likely."

"That's good. That's the most promising career choice," my dad said, which led to a talk about colleges, and I couldn't handle being here a second longer. If I heard my dad say how proud he was of me for following his path one more time, I would scream in frustration.

"Excuse me, but may I go to the bathroom?" I asked Daniela, silently cursing my stomach cramps. They wouldn't let up.

"Of course. All bathrooms on the first floor are under renovation, so you will have to use the one on the second floor. Our maid will take you to it."

I nodded and waited for her to come and show me the way. I didn't say a word as I followed her upstairs to the left wing, which sent my heart into overdrive. That was where Blake's room was.

She led me to the first door on the right and left me to it, going back down. There were two more doors in the hallway, and my heart sped up because I was so close to Blake's room. I took deep breaths and entered the bathroom, knowing nothing would stop my cramps for at least another hour.

I finished in the bathroom and headed to the staircase, but my legs stopped midway. My eyes went over my shoulder to the second door on the right, and then to the door at the far end of the corridor, and I got an inkling that was his room.

My chest tightened with a strange sensation as an idea formed in my head. It was beyond outrageous, but I wanted to do it all the more. I was supposed to go back to the dining room and continue being the obedient and responsible kid.

Instead, I headed up to the door at the end of the hallway.

I must be going crazy, I thought to myself. *I'm turning into a stalker.*

I told myself I was doing this so I could get some advantage over him in case he wanted to use my greatest vulnerability against me on Monday. His room could contain some incriminating answers.

But it was a lie, and I knew it. I just wanted to see his room. Nothing more, nothing less. It was like a hidden treasure that was so close I could practically feel it, and it felt like a once-in-a-lifetime opportunity. Me in Blake's room—it didn't get more personal than that.

If I got caught, I could always say I'd gotten lost.

Yeah, right. Like they would buy that.

My hand turned sweaty as I reached for the knob, hoping it wasn't locked.

It wasn't locked, but in the split second it took me to open the door, I realized Blake could be inside. Maybe he'd been home all this time and just didn't want to come down.

Well, crap.

I bit into my lip with my heart in my throat, expecting to see him in the room, but I was met with complete darkness. It was his room, all right, but he wasn't there. I let out a sigh of relief.

I slipped inside and closed the door behind me. I needed a few seconds to get used to the dark, inhaling his scent that was *everywhere*.

I was crazy. I was so crazy for coming here, but that didn't stop me from going deeper into the spacious room, my eyes darting around to take in as much of it as possible.

Thanks to the faint light coming from the back garden through the floor-to-ceiling windows, I could discern his king-size bed that stood across from them and a 75-inch TV mounted above a TV stand that was positioned diagonally from his bed. The stand contained a PlayStation, a cable box, and a couple of other gadgets. A few of his shirts had been thrown over his made bed, and a few pairs of his Air Jordans lay messily on the floor next to it.

There wasn't a lot of furniture or personal things, which denoted an emptiness that added to the mystery that was Blake. If you took away the basketball lying next to his built-in closet, the two framed photos of Infected Mushroom album artwork on the wall—*he listens to psytrance?*—and the video game discs stacked on the floor close to his PS4, you would get a room out of those home & lifestyle magazines that looked like no one actually lived there.

I glanced at the door, fearing someone could come inside at any moment. I stood in place, listening carefully for any sound, ready to hide if needed, but I couldn't hear anything except the furious pounding of my heart. Like a stab, a cramp hit my lower stomach, and I had to press my hand against it and breathe deeply so I could endure it.

Okay. Only a few more seconds, and then I'd be out.

I moved across the black and white striped carpet to his desk next to the bathroom door. My eyes studied the dark screen of the laptop before they caught sight of a manila folder with some photos sticking out of it. They sent a tremor of discomfort through me, and I frowned as I took out my phone and turned on the flashlight.

I cast another glance at the door. My brain told me to stop snooping around and come to my senses, but my hand didn't listen, directing the light at the photos. They were all pictures of some run-down houses and guys taken from a distance and in the dark; their low quality made it difficult for me to make much of the faces or the buildings. A note lying next to them said in big handwritten letters: *Never forget.* My pulse quickened. Never forget what?

"What are you doing with these, Blake?" I whispered.

I noticed one photo peeking out from under the manila folder, and I reached for it, freezing when I saw what it was. It showed young Blake hugging a beautiful girl with short, curly black hair and dark brown eyes somewhere outdoors. She was thin and tall, and her megawatt smile matched Blake's as they looked at the camera. I felt a sudden rush of longing because I'd never seen Blake smile like that before.

He looked so...carefree and happy. He was nothing like the cold and reserved guy I'd known from day one at East Willow High. His eyes shone with joy, and it was clear that they were madly in love. It just beamed out of the picture.

On the bottom, written in black marker:

Emma & Blake forever

A dull ache curled through my chest, a yearning and sadness for young Blake bringing tears to my eyes. What had happened to them? Where was she?

Deciding to leave before I ran out of luck, I returned the photo to where it was, but I bumped the mouse next to it with my hand in the process, and the screen of the laptop lit up. In the dead center was an open folder containing a video with a grainy thumbnail and the title *Blake Jones and Emma Hoover, day 11.* Upon closer inspection, I could make out a boy tied up to a chair in it... No, not any boy. It was *Blake.*

I clamped my hand over my mouth as a shiver ran down my spine. What the heck?

My instinct told me to step away and forget I'd seen this. Whatever was going on here, it wasn't my business. I had no right to look at it. It would be utterly wrong, and I would just ensnare myself more deeply into his web of secrets and darkness.

But something terrible had happened to Blake, and even with guilt and fear churning in me, I couldn't just ignore it. I took one quick look over my shoulder at the door and moved my trembling finger over the mouse, hoping the video would be over soon and I would be out of here before anyone came in.

The first few seconds showed a grayish, filthy surface I recognized as a floor only after the camera moved upward. This person was in an extremely small basement with dirty and damp gray brick walls that gave me chills.

The camera focused on young Blake in the chair, and I could barely recognize him through the many gashes that marred his face. The room was semi-dark, but the hanging light bulb provided enough light for me to distinguish each bruise and cut. My stomach curled.

"Are you recording?" a guy in the background said; the sound was just loud enough for me to hear it.

"Yeah," the one holding the camera replied.

Blake looked exhausted and malnourished, his tortured gaze fixed on the floor as the guy holding the camera circled around him. He was motionless, in his own world.

The guy recording grabbed Blake's chin and forced him to look at him. His dull eyes had lost all their light.

"Smile for the camera," the guy said. Blake didn't move a muscle, remaining silent. "That's not good. You don't want your parents to see you like this when they get this video, do you?" I let out a gasp of disgust just as he grabbed his chin. "You keep ignoring me, and it's starting to get on my nerves. Let's see if you're going to ignore this."

The video was shaky as the guy moved to the other side of the room, where a disheveled girl lay curled on the floor in the corner, her hands and legs tied up with a rope. She was the girl from the photo. Emma.

"Let's play with your girl."

"Don't touch her!" Blake's sudden shout hit me hard, and the first tear slid down my cheek. The other guy, who was dressed in all black and wearing a ski mask that showed only his eyes, grabbed the girl and dragged her closer to Blake. "Don't touch her! Leave her alone! LEAVE HER ALONE!"

The guy ignored him completely. He removed the ropes from her and straddled her as she lay on the ground without putting up a fight or even moving. It was as if she'd accepted her fate, and it shattered my heart.

The guy with the camera moved back so that the frame showed both Blake and Emma. Blake was thrashing against the chair and shouting curses, straining to set himself free, which seemed to only amuse the guys.

"She likes this," the guy said as he ran his hand over her face, pinning her arms above her head with his other hand.

He groped Emma's breasts over her shirt and then moved his hand over her stomach, going even lower. He pushed his hand into her sweatpants, and I felt a rush of nausea. My hand hovered over the mouse to stop the video, but I couldn't stop it, compelled to watch the horror unfold in front of me.

Blake pushed against the ropes, screaming as the guy recording chuckled in the background, and the force of his moves tipped his chair over. He fell down on the floor with a loud crash, his head hitting the floor with a thud.

"Blake," Emma screamed, looking at him with teary eyes.

This seemed to amuse the guy in black, who now touched Emma in the most inappropriate way while she just lay down there and stared at Blake.

"Don't touch her! Get away from her!" Blake raised his head from the floor as he watched them, crying. "I'll kill you! I swear, I'll kill you!"

The guy didn't stop touching Emma, not sparing Blake a single glance. "But she liked it the last few times, isn't that right, kitten?"

No. My breathing turned more and more shallow.

He grabbed her chin to make her look at him. "Answer me!" He pulled his hand out of her sweatpants and slapped her with such force it made her nose bleed.

"Leave her alone!" Blake's shrill voice rang in my head, filling me with the most profound pain.

"This is to teach you to be more obedient next time," the guy said to him, and then the monstrosity I feared happened...

He ripped the sweatpants and underwear off Emma and pulled his jeans and briefs down, starting something that was brutally etched into my mind forever. Blake's and Emma's screams reverberated in my mind, mixed with the cruel laughter of their captors that never stopped.

And then the gruesome act was over. Everything in me was cold as I watched the girl who looked lifeless. She didn't move from the spot on the floor where the guy had left her, staring at the ceiling with eyes that petrified me. The sick bastard zoomed in on her and then showed Blake, who had somehow managed to free his hands in the seconds when the focus wasn't on him.

Blake pushed the ropes wrapped around his waist off him and propped himself up with his ankles still tied together.

"I'll kill you!" He pounced at the guy and wound his hands around his neck, sending them both down as he strangled him.

"*Shit*," the guy with the camera said and lowered it on some piece of furniture before he joined in to help his friend. I couldn't see much, but it was enough, my heart pounding furiously as he separated Blake from the guy, which allowed the guy in black to punch Blake in the stomach.

Blake cried out when the guy landed another punch to his abdomen, which was followed by more and more merciless hits.

"No!" Emma picked herself up and launched herself at the guy punching Blake, wrapping her arm around his neck to yank him away.

"Get off me," the guy shouted and threw her off, sending her flying down to the floor. "I'm sick and tired of this bitch. We don't need her anyway."

"NO!" Blake fought against the guy who held him, but he couldn't set himself free. "What are you going to do to her?!"

"Do it," the other guy said. "It's long overdue."

The guy took his gun out of his jeans and aimed it at Emma. "Time to say goodbye."

"NO," Blake screamed as the gun went off, and the bullet landed in Emma's head.

She was gone. In a heartbeat.

The camera showed everything. Her upper body hitting the floor. Her lifeless eyes as she stared at nothing. The abundant amount of blood that gruesomely pooled beneath her. Blake screaming until the guy knocked him unconscious with the handle of his gun.

And then a heavy silence.

The guy picked up the camera and directed it at his face covered in a gray ski mask. "You want your son to end up like this too? If not, you better have that goddamn money ready by the end of this week."

Chapter 16

I MADE SURE THE DISPLAY went back to sleep and returned downstairs. I barely managed to keep my face neutral as I sat through the rest of dinner, extremely disturbed by the gore I'd witnessed in the video. Only after we returned home and I closed myself in my room did I let it all out, crying for hours in my bed.

I cried for Emma. I cried for young Blake. I cried for their tragic love. I cried for the injustice in this world that had sent those evil people their way and confined them to that basement.

I never could have imagined something so devastating and gruesome—something so *sudden*. One moment, she was there. The next, she was gone, her last seconds—no, *days*—spent in the utmost horror.

That footage played behind my eyelids over and over again as I tossed and turned, trying to sleep, and when I finally managed it, I was tormented by nightmares.

Blood, death, rape...it was all mixed together until I couldn't take it anymore, so I gave up on sleep and went into my recording room to play my guitar at four in the morning. I plucked the strings as I chased the happy melody to soothe me, but it was hard to brighten up.

I regretted entering his room. I was such a fool for prying into his business, getting way more than I'd bargained for. Way, way more.

What was he doing with that stuff, anyway? Now I understood what that "Never forget" note related to and why he had the phobia of basements, but what was going on with those photos? Why did he need a reminder not to forget what had happened?

This new mystery only threw me further into a tizzy, so I pushed all my thoughts aside and focused on my music. Managing to calm myself enough to try to sleep again, I left my guitar and wrapped myself tightly in the sheets, finally falling asleep.

My cold was worse when I got up, and I had a fever, so I slept almost the entire Sunday away. I woke up around noon the next day when my parents were at work and found my favorite tomato sandwich in plastic wrap on the plate on my nightstand, along with Mom's note that said to rest the whole day. She'd also left me some cash in case I wanted to order food.

Starving, I bolted the sandwich down and ordered pizza, then I switched out my pajamas for sweatpants and a t-shirt and went to the bathroom to do my daily routine.

I planned to spend the next few hours watching *House* for probably the hundredth time, so I ended up lying on the couch in the living room. I'd already made a pile of used tissues next to the tissue box on the coffee table, and my nose was dry and sensitive after all the blowing. My cramps weren't as intense as they had been on Saturday, but it was enough to keep me cranky.

Mom called to check up on me, making sure I ate well and wasn't running a fever. I still had a temperature and felt so exhausted I wanted to stay glued to the couch for the rest of the day. My nose was stuffed, and each time I swallowed, it was like I was swallowing a marble.

The pizza delivery was quick, staying true to the twenty-minute delivery time they advertised. I paused the last episode of *House*'s first season, took the money, and hauled myself to the front door, ignoring the protest of my muscles. At least there was something positive about this—I didn't have to go to school.

I opened the door and curled my lips up in a smile, but my smile froze because on my doorstep was none other than Blake. After a brief moment of confusion, that video appeared in front of my eyes. All I could see was young Blake in it. Beaten. Devastated. Hopeless.

He saw his girlfriend get raped and killed right before his eyes...

I blinked, clearing my mind of those nauseating thoughts. I spotted his red Ducati Panigale R many chicks at our school drooled over parked in my driveway, and I frowned. Unless Blake was a pizza delivery boy, I couldn't even begin to understand what he was doing here.

My heart started racing. *Maybe he's found out I was in his room.*

"What are you doing here, Blake?"

His gazed moved down my body slowly, so slowly, and my cheeks flamed. I'd humiliated myself in front of him on Friday night, and now that he was here, my words came back to taunt me. My cheeks grew even redder, if that was possible. As always when I was around him, I sucked in my stomach, hoping my muffin top wasn't as visible as I thought it was.

I coughed and sniffed. The small frown on his face grew deeper when he met my gaze. "You didn't come to school." I raised my brows. "I heard Sarah say you got sick, so I came to see you."

What? I was tempted to pinch my arm, just to check if I was imagining this or not. The school day wasn't even over yet, and he was here *checking up on me*. This must have been a prank. He would smile another of his cruel smiles and show me he was just messing with me.

At least he isn't here because I was in his room and watched the video. This meant he didn't know about that.

"You..." I started in a voice both squeaky and raspy. I coughed. "You're checking up on me?"

His eyes seared into me. "You could say that, yes."

I believed I must've been transported into another dimension; that was the only explanation for why Blake Jones—my enemy and bully from day one—was here, checking if I was okay.

"Why? We aren't friends."

He opened his mouth to reply, but then the pizza guy brought his scooter to a stop next to Blake's bike. Blake crossed his arms over his chest. His face didn't reveal any emotion as he observed the interaction between the pizza guy and me. I couldn't do anything against the shame that he was seeing me buy pizza. I didn't want him to judge me for my eating habits, too aware of the fact that he was only drawn to super thin girls.

Until you, my mind chipped in, but I didn't let that treacherous thought sink any deeper into me.

"That'll be $11.99," the guy said as he handed me the pizza.

I gave him fifteen dollars, coughing. It was the middle of March, but it was cold as if it was February. "Keep the change."

He smiled at me. "Thanks. See ya." He cast a quick glance at Blake, who didn't move an inch from his spot, and left.

I gripped the box with the pizza as I wondered what I should do now. Chills rushed down my neck when the cold breeze swirled around me.

"What's with this sudden attitude change?" I asked. I still expected him to say this was a prank and I was a fool for believing it.

"Can I come inside?"

I gaped at him. He didn't bulldoze his way in but asked for permission? This was getting more surreal by the second.

"Why?" I wasn't going to drop my guard just because he was acting all nice.

"Because you're clearly freezing." He pointed at me, and I looked down my body. I was visibly shivering. "Also, I want to talk to you, and I'd like to do it inside."

I'd always wanted Blake to treat me like a human being, but I couldn't just act like we didn't have a painful history. I couldn't be all happy about it, even though my heart rejoiced at him being here.

"You've never cared about what I want, so why should I care about what you want?"

He scowled, his arms folded over his chest and flexing. "Okay, I get it—you're getting back at me for everything I've done to you, but will you give me just five minutes? That's all I'm asking for."

Another bitter remark was on the tip of my tongue, but I couldn't say it. For reasons I couldn't explain to myself, I stepped aside and motioned for him to enter, my gaze on the floor. He strode inside like he owned the place, and I stood mesmerized by the confidence he exuded, drinking in his body clad in a black leather jacket and dark jeans.

I erupted into a fit of coughing as I joined him in the living room and lowered the pizza on the coffee table. The flicker of appetite I'd had earlier was completely gone. I felt vulnerable because he was seeing me like this. My gaze darted over to the disgusting tower of used tissues on the coffee table, but he didn't even look in that direction.

He pointed at the TV screen. "You like *House* too?"

My stomach fluttered, and I glanced away. "Yes."

"It's the best show." I didn't know what to say, dumbfounded by him.

He went to the fireplace and stopped to inspect the photos of me with my family on the mantel. I grimaced when his gaze landed on the image of ten-year-old me. I was the fattest then but blissfully ignorant of how much I actually weighed.

"So? What do you want to talk about?" I asked, hoping he would stop staring at those embarrassing photos and turn around.

He didn't. To my mortification, he took the photo of me when I was seven and had just received my Martin from Granny. I was missing a front tooth, but my smile was bright nevertheless as I held the guitar in my hands like I'd found a chest filled with gold. My heart skipped a beat when a small smile tugged at his lips.

I darted around the coffee table and snatched the photo out of his hand. "Stop."

His smile disappeared. "Stop what?"

"Stop acting like it's normal for you to just come here out of the blue."

He ran his hand through his hair, his gaze moving around the room. "I'm trying to make things right, Jessica."

My pulse accelerated at hearing him call me by my name. His eyes met mine and stayed on them, captivating me.

"Maybe I want to turn over a new leaf," he said.

A warm sensation shot through my chest, and I allowed myself to bask in it for a little while. Sarah had said love could empower us when we were at our lowest and illuminate even the darkest of places, and at this moment, I could feel that. I could feel some of the pain that had held my heart hostage beginning to dissolve. I wanted that. I wanted to turn over a new leaf with Blake, but I had to be real. His words sounded too good to be true.

"And you think you can just snap your fingers and we'll start anew? Do you have that little respect for me? No, wait—forget about that because you obviously don't respect me at all. You showed me that the first day of our senior year."

He clenched his fists at his sides. "What do you want me to say? I won't lie to you. Yes, I didn't respect you. Ever since the day I met you, I felt only hate for you. Do I wish things were different now? Maybe. But back then, I felt there was no alternative for me."

I lowered the photo on the mantel with a thud, glaring at him. "But there was an alternative! You could've ignored me. Instead, you chose to bully me!" My sore throat closed up on me, protesting against the yelling. I sniffed a few times. It was high time to use a tissue.

He went to the coffee table and plucked a tissue out of the box. "Here you go." He offered it to me.

My cheeks grew scorching red. I grabbed the tissue out of his hand and turned my back to him, refusing to let him see me blow my nose. I could hear him chuckle as I blew it, and I cast a glare at him over my shoulder, still pressing the tissue against my nose.

"This is not funny," I said, but because I was squeezing my nose with my tissue, my voice sounded like Bugs Bunny's, which, I had to admit, sounded too funny.

He broke out in laughter, and I just stood motionless as I watched him, captivated by it. He was laughing. It was full-on laughter that illuminated his whole face and erased all traces of the ever-present cruelty. I couldn't stop looking at him.

Young Blake came to my mind again. His bleeding pain was such a contrast with the smile decorating his face now. What had happened after that eleventh day? How much time had passed until he could laugh freely like this, away from that devastating darkness that was his and Emma's life in that basement?

"Your snot is stuck to your nose." He pointed at it.

"What?!" I screeched and pressed the tissue back against my nose. He doubled over with laughter, smacking the mantel with the palm of his hand.

"You're something else," he said through his laughter, looking at me with a shine in his eyes that made my knees go weak. "I'm just teasing you."

My head began to throb. I sat down on the couch and grabbed a new tissue to blow my nose.

"Since you obviously can't resist picking on me, I'm going to have to ask you to leave. Besides, my parents will come home soon, and I don't want them to see you."

He straightened himself up and grew serious. "I already told you you're not a good liar, and it's only one o'clock. Both of your parents are working, so I find it hard to believe they will return home so early."

I leaned my head against the back of the couch, not even bothering to deny it. My high temperature was getting to me.

He sat down on the other end of the couch, making sure there was enough space between us. I could feel his stare on me, but I refused to look away from the tissue I twisted in my hands on my lap.

"You didn't answer," I said. "What's with this sudden change?"

"Maybe I finally saw how much damage I've done."

I dumped the tissue next to the others on the table and crossed my arms over my chest.

"As I told you, back then I felt I had no alternative," he continued. "You brought me a real shitstorm when you came to our school, and I needed you out so I could stay sane. I hoped you would finally have had enough and leave because each time I saw you at school... Each time, I had to relieve something that was destroying me." He looked away and squeezed his eyes shut.

His words ripped through me, dousing what little warmth I'd felt in the last few minutes. "You needed me out so you could stay sane? But what about *my* sanity? You made my life shitty. You destroyed piece after piece of me, making me so small. Do you know how many times I cried myself to sleep or couldn't sleep at all because of you? It was horrible!"

He stood up and went over to the windows, crossing his arms over his chest. "Then why didn't you leave?"

Tears pooled in my eyes as I raised myself from the couch. "I wanted to. So many times, I was so close to leaving. But I couldn't, and I would've hated myself even more if I'd let you chase me away from here." I closed my eyes briefly to hold back my tears. "And to think you hurt me to make me leave just because you couldn't handle my presence... It's awful. You're awful."

His whole form tensed visibly, but he didn't turn around, standing motionless for a while. He flexed his hands.

"I know. And I'm sorry." The words were barely whispered, but they were there, locking me into disbelief.

I gritted my teeth. "You're *sorry*?"

"Yes."

"Is this a trick? You want me to fall for your apology so you can hurt me more later?"

He turned around to face me, frowning. "What? Of course not. You think I'd tell you how I felt then if it was?"

I just crossed my arms over my chest, studying his expression for a long moment. It looked sincere enough.

"I turned what you told me on Friday night over in my mind, and I realized I've gone too far. I'm sorry for causing you all that pain. I'm sorry for treating you the way I did. You didn't deserve it."

I didn't feel his apology, even if it was real. I couldn't after what he'd just admitted to me.

"Well, I don't accept your apology."

He scowled. "Why?"

"Because I don't feel you're really sorry, and you've gone too far since way back. Since day one, actually. I was even bleeding that day, and it was all because of you. Sticking my finger down my throat because of you is nothing compared to all the messed up things you made me live through. So no, we can't turn over a new leaf. There's too much bad blood between us."

He clenched his jaw. "You really have to make this hard?"

I coughed. "*I* make it hard?"

"Yes, because I didn't come here to fight. I came to apologize."

I looked away as I drew in a shaky breath, refusing to dwell on the pain in my chest. I wanted to forgive him. I wanted to say we were cool. But I wasn't ready. It didn't feel right.

I crossed my arms over my chest. "Maybe it's too late, Blake. Maybe I don't care about your apology anymore."

I didn't hear him move, but in an instant, he was right in front of me. I gasped when he pulled my chin up and made me look into his tormented eyes, the urge to touch him strong. He was so close to me, and it would have been so easy to just lean into him and seek his embrace.

"What do you want me to do? Grovel at your feet?"

I moved my chin out of his grasp. "Yes, Blake. That's exactly what I want you to do," I snarled before I could stop myself. "You think one half-assed apology is enough for me to get over everything you've done to me?"

His eyes hardened. "*Half-assed apology?* What kind of game are you playing?"

"Game?"

"You say you like me, but you're playing hard to get."

I frowned at him, hating that my feelings were fully exposed to him. "I'm not playing hard to get! I don't even want to be with you."

The muscle in his jaw flexed.

"Good," he said. That one word wasn't supposed to hurt me, but it did. "Because I'll never be with you."

I recoiled as another nail got hammered into my heart. Of course Blake would never be with me. We would never get together, and it was high time for me to chop off the roots of that sick fantasy. I'd let it grow for too long.

"I wasn't expecting you to get over everything, but I thought this could be a start. However, now I see it was a mistake to come here."

How much more humiliated could I feel? I went over to the tissue box and grabbed another one as the first tear escaped down my cheek. "Yes, it was." I was barely able to keep my voice even. "Now, please leave."

"Fine. Whatever. I'll leave you alone. *For good.*"

I swallowed hard, more tears pouring out. "Sounds great."

His leaving footsteps were the only thing that could be heard until he stopped. I held my breath as I waited, completely still.

"Just don't make yourself throw up, okay? Take care of yourself."

My heart contracted too painfully. I didn't say a word. Seconds went by in complete silence, as if he was waiting for me to react, but I didn't turn around. I didn't even move. After what seemed like an excruciatingly long time, he left, and only then did I allow myself to move. I dropped down on the couch and burst out in more tears.

This was good. He was leaving me alone. Perfect.

Only, I couldn't feel an ounce of joy.

Chapter 17

BLAKE STAYED TRUE TO his word. I returned to school on Thursday, and he acted like I didn't exist each time we were near each other. I was supposed to be relieved and embrace this new chapter in life where I didn't have to worry about him, but I kept looking for him, partly because of the habit born from a deep-rooted fear and partly because...because I couldn't stop thinking about the kiss or the change in his behavior.

I was the last person who held grudges, always ready to forgive, but when it came to Blake, I wasn't allowing myself that. Still, these days I had nothing to do but cry and reflect on the harsh words I'd said to him. I cared about his apology. I cared about it a lot, but I was scared he would change his mind and go back to his old ways. Six months of bullying couldn't be erased that easily with a few soft-spoken words.

Sarah and I texted each other during English, and I mentioned the kiss and his visit on Monday. She was surprised, to say the least.

That explains why I haven't seen him with any girls this week, she texted me.

My heart palpitated, finding foolish hope in her words.

He likes you. A lot. Maybe one day he'll even grow to love you.

I held back a snort and glanced at Ms. Dawson. Her eyes were on the students in the first row.

Love me? I don't think so. He won't let himself love me, I texted her back.

And if he did, what would you do?

My heart contracted hard with longing. I stared at her message for a minute as contrasting feelings fought for dominance in me. *Kiss him and lose myself in his strong arms...*

No, no, no, absolutely *not*.

Nothing.

Why?

I met her brown eyes, which held sympathy for me, and sighed.

Because he's a mess and I feel he's going to hurt me. Just like always.

She tucked a strand of her hair behind her ear and made a kissing motion with her lips toward Hayden. A slow smirk spread across his face as he reached with his hand under her desk to squeeze her thigh. I glanced away, blushing. Almost instantly, I imagined Blake doing that exact thing to me...

My phone vibrated in my hand.

I get you. You feel it's better to stay safe than be sorry, right? she wrote.

My fingers hovered over the screen as I thought about the answer. She messaged me again before I could come up with anything.

If you ask me, he's just trying to fight it off.

I thought about Blake's words the night we kissed at the party.

Maybe, but how come you're so sure about it?

Because that's exactly what Hayden did before he confessed to me. He was confused by his new feelings when all he knew was hate, and then he tried to get rid of them.

Her next text arrived a few seconds later.

But I don't think Blake can fight them off.

Because you can't win against your heart?

You can win, but not always. I couldn't win against mine.

Do you ever regret it?

Out of the corner of my eye, I saw her smile.

Never. Even these days, when Hayden and I get into a huge fight, I feel we're a step closer to mutual recovery because we're able to learn to communicate better and overcome obstacles one by one.

Overcoming obstacles one by one... I couldn't take my mind off her messages for the rest of class, thinking about how I always let my heart lead me. If Sarah hadn't been able to do anything against her feelings for Hayden back then and she was more rational than me, what could I do? I was in too deep. I'd even watched YouTube videos and read blogs that talked about moving on, but it was like I was trying to build a rocket. I could only hope that once I was gone to college, the distance and time would do the trick.

Third period was free since the teacher had called in sick at the last minute and they couldn't find a sub, so I went to the library, thinking I could write the sheet music for my solo there without being disturbed. The school festival was in a week, but I hadn't gotten to practice my guitar or sing with a sore throat much these last few days. At least I'd been able to plan and compose. I already had a melody in my head, one that just begged to be let out into the world, making me giddy.

I headed to my locker to retrieve my headphones, intending to use a music app I'd downloaded to create music when I wasn't home. I passed the gym, and the continuous thumps of a basketball and squeaking sneakers greeted me through the wall. My heart accelerated, associating those sounds with Blake, and I shook my head at my silly reaction. That could be anyone inside, and even if it was Blake, it didn't matter—

A cry that sounded like it came from the depths of the person's soul stopped me short. It was followed by another that was on the verge of a scream, suffusing me with concern. My legs carried me to the gym doors quickly.

I cracked the door open and peeked inside. Blake was playing basketball alone on the court, and I had to stifle the gasp that yearned to get out. He moved fast across the floor, dribbling aggressively and jump-shooting over and over again. He scored a basket each time.

The tormented look on his face spurred a bitter feeling in me, and I found myself wishing I could do anything to help that expression disappear. It looked like he was running away from his demons, his every move full of anxiety that took over his body. My mind drifted off to that shocking video.

I closed my eyes under the onslaught of the gruesome images. I was finally able to understand him better. Whatever he'd gone through before and after that day didn't justify his ruthlessness, but it explained all that endless anger and hate.

With another blood-chilling cry, he swung the ball at the basket and supported himself against his knees, panting and covered in sweat.

The ball hit the backboard and bounced off the floor in my direction. It kept rolling until it stopped close to me, but Blake didn't turn around to get it. Instead, he stayed in the same position.

I'd found him alone on the basketball court enough times to know it was his way of getting rid of whatever was troubling him, and after seeing that video, I could only imagine the extent of his pain. Basketball was his outlet, allowing him to pour out his pent-up anger and aggression on the court, but it wasn't enough because he was a walking bomb of tension that could explode at any moment, provoked or unprovoked.

His gaze was now fixed on one spot in front of him, and his eyes had that faraway look that made it seem like he wasn't here but at some scary place. My instinct told me to help him. *But help him with what?*

I curled my fingers into a fist as I looked down the hallway that led to my locker. I knew very well I should stay away from him. He'd told me he would leave me alone. I was finally having my freedom. The healthy and logical thing would be to keep my distance from him as much as possible and forget about him. That was the only way I could move on.

So what the hell was I doing now?

I entered the gym and took the ball. He didn't move an inch; his eyes were still on the same spot on the floor.

"Hey, Blake." My heart was pounding too hard. He remained motionless, his hands fisted against his knees. "Blake? Blake, do you hear me?"

It took him a few seconds to react. He straightened himself up and turned around, his face taut with pain and fear as he just stared through me, looking out of it. I observed him to try to find out why he would feel fear at all, but I came up with nothing.

I bounced the ball to the basket, fighting to keep my gaze on him. "Are you okay?"

His face took on a guarded expression as his eyes finally focused on me. "What..." He pinched the bridge of his nose and shut his eyes, breathing heavily. "What are you doing?"

I'm trying to help you with your demons because apparently I can't just walk away when you're in pain.

"Let's play one on one."

He opened his eyes and narrowed them at me, and my face turned red. My proposition sounded ridiculous even to my own ears given our circumstances.

He started taking deep breaths as he rubbed the back of his hand with his other hand, looking way too guarded. "After everything you said on Monday?"

I stopped at the free-throw line before I aimed at the basket, growing more flushed under his hard stare. This was very uncharacteristic of me, but I liked the fact that I hadn't run away yet. I coughed twice and sniffed.

"I just want to play."

I shot at the basket and felt the familiar rush at the motion. I knew I was going to miss the shot because the last time I'd played the basketball was with my cousins in my hometown during the last Christmas holidays, but that didn't douse the excitement. I loved basketball, despite being an average player.

I missed the basket by a few inches, and the ball passed right under it. I needed to put more force into my shot the next time. I went to the ball and picked it up.

"I don't want to play with you, so pass me the ball and leave."

In an unusual spurt of courage, I gave him a small smile and looked at him under my half-closed lids. "And if I don't?"

Distress ebbed away from his face, as if whatever demons holding him prisoner started to disappear. His eyes filled with a completely different emotion as he erased the distance between us in slow steps. He stopped too close to me, and I had to raise my head to maintain our eye contact, unable to breathe.

"Careful, Jessie," he said quietly. "You don't get to toy with me."

I was sure he could hear the maddening pounding of my heart. It was impossible not to notice how hot he looked in his black basketball jersey and shorts. The beads of sweat sliding down his chiseled cheekbones and jaw only added to his appeal.

"I just want to play basketball. Nothing else."

He cocked his head to the side. "Do you even know how to play?"

With a sweet smile, I dribbled the ball to the basket. I bent my knees and shot, having a hunch that I would make it this time. The ball balanced on the rim before it went through, but at least I didn't miss. I grinned, feeling smug that I'd proved my point.

"It's not that hard," I said as I turned around to face him. My heart fluttered when I met his intense stare. It pierced through me and warmed me in many places. "I often play with my cousins in my hometown."

"Aren't you still sick?"

My lips curled into a smile against my will because he sounded like he cared.

"You sound like my dad." I couldn't resist the joke. He didn't find it funny, scowling at me, but this only made my smile bigger.

I jogged to retrieve the ball that had stopped a couple of feet behind us. I shouldn't have been playing because I still hadn't recovered completely and had to sing at the festival the following week. If I got sicker, I wouldn't have enough time to practice for my solo. Yet, I was full of excitement and energy.

I'd suggested Blake play one on one with me. I was going crazy.

But at least he didn't look as troubled as he had before I got there. Mission accomplished.

I picked up the ball. "Since you're curious, my nose is still runny and sometimes I feel like I'll cough my lungs out, thank you for asking. But I'm not crippled, so let's play."

His lips twitched. "You think you're funny?"

I bit into my lower lip, which drew his attention to it. "Maybe."

He flicked his gaze up to my eyes. "Now this is interesting."

"What?"

He motioned at me with his hand. "Your confidence. You aren't a small, scared mouse when you're speaking to me."

I was surprised by myself, too. "You've changed too. You aren't acting like a big, scary wolf anymore. Or at least not as much."

He approached me, and a hint of danger filled the air between us. "You'd be a fool to think like that. I'm as bad as they get."

I was paralyzed by his intense gaze. I couldn't look away from him, my heart thumping loudly in my ears.

He moved so fast I didn't even see it, stealing the ball out of my hands with one hand. He dribbled it to the basket faster than I ever could and dunked, his body twisting in the air agilely.

Just wow. My lips parted as I stared at him in awe. *That body and those moves...*

"Will you stop ogling at me and play?" he asked, pulling me out of my reverie. "First one to twelve baskets wins." He passed me the ball so quickly I almost failed to catch it. "Ladies first," he said in a mocking voice.

"You don't need to do me favors just because I'm a girl."

He smirked. "Don't worry. I won't even need five seconds to get that ball back."

"Is that so?" I bounced the ball out of the three-point line and faced the basket. I wasn't a big fan of challenges and usually backed away from them, but I didn't want to do that this time. I didn't want to act like a coward in front of Blake again.

He went into a stance in front of me, blocking me, and I darted to the side. My adrenaline soared despite the protest of my body against the strenuous movement. I couldn't erase the smile from my face as I dribbled closer to the basket with Blake continuously blocking me. He didn't try to take the ball away from me, which made me suspect he was going easy on me.

"Didn't you say you only needed seconds to get the ball back?" I challenged as I got around ten feet away from the basket.

He didn't need me to say anything else. He smirked and reached for the ball while it was in mid-air, stealing it way too easily. He spun around and did a jump shot, making a perfect basket.

"Hey! That's not fair! You're so much faster than me!"

He smirked and led the ball out of the trey. "So you *do* want me to do you favors because I'm faster than you? How's that fair?"

I harumphed. Of course I wasn't going to use the girl card. I blocked him, but I didn't have anything on his size or technique. He guarded the ball too well, switching hands and spinning too quickly for me to make a good enough move. He scored another point in another flawless move. I was starting to pant and heave.

"What's your hometown?" he asked as he moved away.

"Bridgeport."

He rushed to the side to get nearer to the basket. I tried to grab the ball from him, but he dribbled it between his legs, spun to the side, and raced straight in. He slam-dunked it and hung on the rim. I stared at him. *So hot.*

"Step up your game," he told me before passing me the ball, even though he shouldn't have done that. "It's three points for me and zero for you."

I backed away from him and told myself to focus more on the game and less on his chiseled cheekbones and jaw.

"Do you miss it?" he asked as he stopped in front of me in a defensive stance. My gaze slid along the impressive muscles of his raised arms, and I internally grimaced at myself.

"Miss what? My hometown?" I switched hands, but he didn't even try to steal the ball, never taking his eyes off of me.

"Yes."

I gaped at him, surprised that he wanted to know that. As a matter of fact, this whole conversation was surprising. We were communicating normally. I was supposed to be cautious around him and refuse to reveal anything about myself, but I also wanted to tell him everything. I wanted to open up to him.

I moved to sidestep him, but he didn't let me. "Yes and no."

"Why don't you miss it?"

Since there was no way for me to get anywhere closer to the basket, I hoped for the best and shot. He could've jumped and grabbed the ball, but he didn't move. He was definitely going easy on me.

I missed, the ball hitting the backboard instead. I coughed a few times. I was exerting myself too much, but I didn't want to stop.

He let me have the possession of the ball again, but I returned it to him. "Don't go easy on me," I told him. "If I score, I want to do it on my own."

Something resembling respect passed over his face, and he nodded. He bounced the ball slowly as he went to the other side, and I used that as a chance to steal it. I reached for it once, but he backed away. I reached for it again, thwarting his attempt to sidestep me, but then he caught the ball with both hands and spun on his heel to the side.

I blocked him at the last possible moment, planning to smack the ball so he would drop it, but our bodies collided when he turned around and both of us lost our balance. I crashed down on the floor with him falling on top of me as the ball bounced away from us. For a long moment, his body was fully atop mine, the hard ridges of his frame pressing into each inch of me.

"*Fuck*," he growled as he brought himself up to his elbows, caging me with his arms. His masculine scent enveloped me, and my heart began its wild tempo.

His eyes drifted across my face, reminding me I wasn't wearing any makeup. *Just great.* Without foundation, the imperfections on my face were visible from a mile away, along with my double chin.

But he looked like he couldn't have cared less about my physical flaws. In fact, he kept looking at me, his gaze turning darker and more intense. My chest grew tight. He didn't say anything as he studied my face, and I could have sworn his lips got a few inches closer to mine...

He grazed the bridge of my nose with his fingers, looking at it. "You have freckles."

Blushing, I moved my head to the side. "Yeah. So?"

He didn't smile, but his eyes got a shade softer. "They're cute."

Cute. Blake Jones had just said my freckles were cute. The same freckles I wished I could magically remove.

"I don't like them," I blurted out.

He gave me a half-smile. "You should."

He moved his knee higher between my legs, shifting his weight as he leaned even closer to my lips, and I struggled to breathe, at war with myself. I shouldn't have been allowing him this. *He doesn't deserve me, he doesn't deserve me, he doesn't deserve me—*

"Thank you," he said, voice barely audible.

I snapped my gaze from his lips to his eyes. "For what?"

"You helped me again."

That one sentence affected me a great deal, and I found it harder to fight against the flurry of my feelings. "What did I do?"

"I was able to deal with the pain more easily because you distracted me." His breath fanned my lips, and I moved my head to the side, fighting this, refusing to let him kiss me. I knew I shouldn't let my compassion for him outweigh the bitter truth that I should stay far away from him.

His breath was now on my neck, sliding over it in short, warm puffs...

I closed my eyes and swallowed hard. I could almost feel it. His lips on my neck...

Don't, I thought, or did I whisper it?

The kiss never came.

He got off me and sat next to me. I stared at the ceiling for a few seconds, my heart thudding in my ears.

"So? Are you going to answer me?" he asked, and I looked at him reluctantly. "Why don't you miss your hometown?"

I sat up and sighed, looking at my chipped pink nail polish. I didn't understand why he was interested. He was prodding into my life so he could...what? Satisfy his morbid curiosity? Gather more material he could use against me?

But as I examined his face, I didn't find anything malicious. Unless I was hopelessly naïve, there was no bad intent behind his question.

"I was bullied there too," I finally answered. My face warmed as the influx of bad memories hit me. Back then, I hadn't fit into what some of my peers deemed acceptable or attractive, hence all the body-shaming and laughter on my account.

They thought they were funny. They thought they had the right to make fun of me like I was any less worthy because I had extra weight. Like there wasn't a person with feelings beneath that outer appearance. Like all that mattered was that you were considered beautiful on the outside. So they mocked me and laughed at me, making me feel like I didn't belong anywhere.

"Who would've thought?" I said when he remained silent.

"Why were you bullied?"

I let out a chuckle of disbelief. He, of all people, should have known the answer to that. "You tell me." I stood up. "You're the one who labeled me as fat the day I got here."

He frowned and jumped to his feet. "I didn't actually mean it."

My eyes rounded. "Come again?"

He went to take the ball, avoiding my gaze. "When I first saw you in the school cafeteria, I didn't think you were fat." He began bouncing the ball. "You weren't skinny and you had curves, yes, but that didn't stop me from checking you out."

I scowled at him. "Let me get this straight—you didn't think I was fat that day in the cafeteria."

"Right."

"You thought..." I had to brazen it out and ask the question I was burning to ask. "You thought I was attractive?"

He glanced away, tilting his head down. "Yes."

My stomach did a few flips, betraying my anger. I ignored it.

"But you told me I was so fat."

He bounced the ball harder. "Yes."

"Why?"

"Because I guessed it could be your weak point. So I used it against you."

"You used it against me because, for some reason, you disliked me from the moment you saw me."

He stopped bouncing the ball and finally looked back at me. "Exactly."

I clamped my hand against my mouth. I didn't know what was worse, Blake thinking I was fat and fat-shaming me because of that or the actual truth—that he didn't find me fat but fat-shamed me because he wanted to use my weakness against me.

"And why did you dislike me?"

He remained silent as he began to bounce the ball again, and each bounce brought more tension and anger that spread fast and owned more of me. So that was another question he was going to refuse me an answer to.

"Do you have any idea what you've done? I already have a bad enough image of myself, but you had to make it worse?!"

He dropped the ball and ran his hand down his face. "I already told you I realized how wrong it was. Something has changed in me these last few days. I'm not that same guy who didn't care about how much you're hurt. If I could take those words back now, I would."

I shook my head. My chest hurt with raw pain that had resided in it for so long. "If you only knew...if you only *knew* how deep each of your insults cut. If you only knew how much I hated myself." I sniffed and turned my back to him. "You broke me," I whispered.

He didn't say anything for quite a long time, and I was starting to think he wasn't going to at all.

But then he said, "If you'd told me this back then, I probably wouldn't have even cared. But now...now, it hurts. It hurts me that I caused you so much pain. It hurts me to know I messed you up so bad and I'll never be able to take everything back."

I closed my eyes, telling myself not to get swayed by the regret and guilt I could hear in his tone. A few soft words couldn't replace the horrors of his actions—or so I kept trying to convince my heart.

"But there's something I don't understand," he continued. "Why haven't you ever fought back? Why do you let people walk all over you?"

I snapped my eyes open and swiveled around. "*Excuse me?*"

"Why do you let people abuse you?"

"I *let* them?"

"Yes."

"Are you seriously asking me that? You, who controlled me and inspired fear in me *every single day*?"

"That's all in your head. Fear and inability to defend yourself are all in your head. I'm not reducing my blame here, but you let your mind mess with you, allowing me and others to exploit that."

I gritted my teeth, seething. "You don't know what you're talking about."

Tightening his jaw, he crossed the space between us. "I don't? You have no fucking idea what I've gone through."

I froze, the frames from that video intruding into my mind once more. His eyes grew stormy as he grabbed my shoulders and pulled me until our faces were a breath apart. He was shaking.

"I know fear the best. Hell, fear destroyed my life! But I never stopped fighting it. Every second of my life, I'm fighting it. You? You just run away from it, but running away *doesn't make bad things disappear*. So instead of playing the role of a little, weak girl who waits for Sarah and others to save her ass, tough it out. Fight back. And even if you get hurt in the process, at least you aren't a pathetic coward in the end."

He released me, picked up the ball, and left the gym, leaving me rooted to the spot.

Chapter 18

BLAKE HAD TOLD ME TO tough it out. He was right about that because overcoming my cowardice was long overdue. His words stayed with me the whole day long, playing on repeat, inviting each bullying memory back into my mind.

If I'd fought back, would things have been any different? Mel seemed to have it under control. She never let others walk all over her and always fought her battles on her own.

How many times had I thought about fighting back but not been able to because I felt smaller than a mouse? After all, what could one girl do against so many people? And even if I defended myself, who could guarantee it wouldn't get worse? If you defeat your bully, who can guarantee they won't come back tomorrow with someone to back them up?

I'd seen that scenario too many times before. I'd seen boys punch their tormentors back, only to get beaten to a pulp in the school's back yard the next day by those same tormentors and their friends. Victims couldn't win. They were brutally silenced.

So I suffered in that lonely silence and hoped for all the bullying to stop one day. But it never did, becoming even worse when I came to East Willow High and met Blake.

"And even if you get hurt in the process, at least you aren't a pathetic coward in the end," Blake had said.

I was ready to fight back for Kevin. So why couldn't I fight back for myself?

Fighting back at all costs or remaining a coward.

Both choices could cost me a lot, but I'd been a coward my whole life, and what had that brought me? I was even ready to sacrifice my future—my whole life—and go to a college my parents preferred just so they would be pleased.

So when Melissa asked me to come with her to the track on Friday night because Steven hadn't come home for days and she wanted to make sure he was okay, I agreed without a second thought. If I wanted to become stronger, I had to break out of my shell and experience some excitement in my life. I needed a bit of danger to prove to myself I wouldn't break that easily.

I didn't like lying to my parents again, feeling like the pile of lies I'd told them had grown a lot bigger lately. This time, I said Mel had invited Sar and me to a sleepover at her house, and they only let me go after I promised I would spend the whole weekend studying and working on my assignments.

The old guilt seeped in. I was supposed to be their perfect daughter who remained in her bubble that kept her away from the horrors of the real world. I wasn't supposed to mingle with people who had one foot in a prison cell.

But then again, I was tired of trying to be perfect for them. I was tired of the limited freedom.

I glanced at Mel, who was deep in her thoughts as she drove us to the track. She looked exhausted, with worry lines embedded deep into her forehead, and I guessed it had a lot to do with Steven. Apart from not coming home, he'd also missed a whole week of school, and no one knew what he could be up to.

"Are you okay?" I asked her.

"Never been better," she replied, her gaze fixed on the unlit road.

Her dark eye circles and face told a different story. "How are you sleeping these days?"

"I'm not sleeping at all. I've become a vampire, and now I function at night too."

I went into a fit of giggles, shaking my head at her. "It's that bad?"

She tightened her grip on the wheel. "On a scale of one to ten? It's thirteen plus three."

"So that's why you've been popping those energy drinks lately."

"Yep. Red Bull is my new best friend, my future boyfriend, and also my future husband."

"Wow. I wish Red Bull and you all the best in the future."

"Thanks." She switched gears and ran her hand through her shoulder-length hair. "Between my idiotic brother and the school festival, I barely have time to breathe. Add in my anti-bullying campaign and the vice president duties, and you get a zombie."

"Now, you can't be both a vampire and a zombie. You have to pick one."

"Vambie?" I chuckled. "I've been so busy with the festival. I had to confirm the participants of the workshop and make sure we got all the necessary rights for the bullying documentaries."

"The workshop?"

"Yeah. We're going to create clay figurines and sell them. All proceeds will go to anti-bullying organizations."

"That's so cool! I wanna join."

She glanced at me. "You do?"

"Yeah. I used to make clay figurines in elementary school. It was fun."

"Great! I'll count you in. Sar will make some too, and she'll also create drawings with anti-bullying messages."

"That sounds cool."

Mel's Samsung, which was in the dashboard holder, chimed, alerting her to a new message from her dad.

She snorted. "So he finally decided to text me back."

"Finally?"

"Yeah, finally, because he's sooo busy. He never has the time to even respond to a call."

"That sucks."

"Big time. He keeps working extra hours, and whenever I go to see him, he has only a few minutes for me. Last week, he forgot we were supposed to go out for dinner, and I had to wait for him at the restaurant. When I texted him to see what was going on, he just sent a short apology and rescheduled for 'sometime in the future.' It's a damn mess. Ever since my parents filed for divorce, our family has been falling apart."

"Maybe his work is his way of dealing with the divorce?"

She clenched the steering wheel. "That doesn't mean he has to neglect his children. It's as if it's not enough that Steven and I have to go through hell because of them—we also can't have a normal relationship with them?"

"You still think it would be better if they got back together?"

"Two hundred percent yes."

I didn't say anything in response, unsure of what to say to that. I knew if this were happening to my parents, I wouldn't want them to stay together and be miserable just for my sake. That would be selfish of me. I'd want them happy, even if that meant a divorce.

But I understood Mel's perspective. It was a big change, and it created a huge family rift. She and Steven were going through a lot because of their parents, and it could leave a mark.

Mel slowed down when we got closer to the track. Just like the last time, the clearing was filled to the brim with cars and crowds of people wearing black, promising another night of excitement and adrenaline. I got out of the car, and the cold breeze bit deep into my cheeks and nose. I pushed my hands into the pockets of my jacket to keep them warm.

"Let's find that idiot," Mel said, and I followed her.

The smell of weed was strong in the air. It came from a nearby group of guys in their twenties who wore black hoodies and permanent scowls on their faces. Once more, I felt out of place. If my parents knew I was here, they would both have a heart attack for sure.

I looked around, searching, but not for Steven. My pulse sped up, a prickle of awareness hitting the back of my neck because I knew *he* was nearby.

This was proved right a couple of seconds later, when I found him talking to a red-headed guy I didn't recognize in the distance. Blake wore a neutral expression on his face, but there was something about the two of them together that didn't feel right.

"There he is," Melissa said then rushed to Steven and Masen, who sat next to each other on the hood of Steven's Audi TT and smoked. Masen's smile transformed into a deep scowl when he saw Mel.

Melissa stopped in front of Steven and placed her hands on her hips. "Do you even remember that you have a home, punk?"

I gaped at Steven now that I saw him up close. He looked like he'd aged ten years in the last few days, and a rash lined his mouth. My stomach crawled, and when he met my gaze, his eyes bloodshot and pupils dilated, I actually recoiled, wanting to be at least a mile away from him. His look screamed danger, but most of all, it was alarming since it was obvious he was ensnared by something that led nowhere good.

"Who are you?" Steven asked her as he licked his lips, completely serious. He glanced at Masen while pointing at Melissa with his cigarette. "Do you know her?"

Masen snorted and took a drag of his cigarette, but his eyes remained hard as he looked at Melissa. He let out the smoke through his nose. "She's Fart Stench."

Mel moved to Masen with a sneer and slammed her hand on the hood next to his thigh, getting into his face. "Why are you letting him be like this?"

Masen glared at her, but he didn't back away, only inches separating their faces now. "What the fuck are you talking about?"

She smacked the hood with her open palm. "Aren't you supposed to be his friend? What kind of friend just stands by and does nothing to help someone who's ruining his life right in front of their eyes? Look at him!" Melissa gestured at Steven, who observed their interaction with no emotion on his face. "He's completely high and looks like he's about to dissolve into nothing! Don't tell me you'd let him get in his car and race in this condition?!"

Steven rolled his eyes. "Sis, you're making a big deal—"

Masen moved so quickly Mel couldn't even react, throwing the cigarette on the ground and flipping them around so that she was pressed between the hood and him.

"I'm sick and tired of you jumping to conclusions," he told her, pressing her hands together against the hood behind her back. "You don't know shit about me, so don't act like a know-it-all."

His tone of voice and the expression on his face were unlike his usual easygoing, playboy attitude, and it chilled me even though his anger wasn't directed at me. It reminded me of that day when I met Eli and Masen flew off the handle. He could be terribly scary when he wanted to.

"Get away from me, you germ container!" She thrashed against him to set herself free, but Masen predicted all her self-defense moves and caged her in using his strength and experience. She had no advantage over him, even with her Krav Maga skills, and a sudden fear flickered on her face.

"I never hit girls, but when it comes to you, I want to the slap the shit out of you," he growled into her face.

Steven slid off the hood and placed his hand on Masen's shoulder. "Bro, let her go. You know how she is. I'm used to it, so just drop it."

Masen didn't move immediately, each of them glaring at the other with undiluted hatred. After a few seconds of high tension, he released Melissa and pushed himself away from her.

"Fuck this shit," he muttered, walking away.

Mel frowned at Steven, her face cracking to reveal pain. "Real nice. You really know how to pick friends, Steven. You nailed it with this one," she said in a shaky voice and lifted her chin toward Masen.

"Are you okay?" Steven asked, ignoring her remark, and I raised my eyebrows at the concern in his voice.

She looked away and rubbed her upper arms. "Yep. Why wouldn't I be okay?"

"Because he pinned you down and you couldn't—"

"We won't talk about that now," she said, glancing at me, which only sparked my curiosity. Steven also glanced at me, and understanding dawned on his face. Mel was hiding something from me, and I didn't know how I felt about that.

"Fine, but will you stop jumping on Mace every single time?" he asked her. "I'm getting new grays every time I see you two fighting. And I want my hair to be perfect, thank you very much."

Mel rolled her eyes. "What are you complaining about? Aren't you always the one who can't wait to grab his popcorn and enjoy the drama?"

"That's true. I'm always up for some drama, but your drama got old a long time ago, sis. And FYI, I'm not racing tonight. Mace, who *is* a good buddy—oh, the shocker!—talked me out of it."

I didn't hear Mel's answer, because Blake's voice reached me from behind. "What are you doing here?"

I turned around, my throat turning dry at the sight of him. His smoldering eyes slid down my body in tight black jeans and a black jacket, and I got strong flutters in my belly. His gaze told me everything—he liked what he saw. A lot.

The old insecurities kicked in, and I folded my arms across my chest, feeling the need to hide myself. I wanted to suck in my belly, hoping the two pounds I'd lost over the last week were showing on my body, but then I remembered I should embrace myself the way I was and stop feeling less adequate than others, especially in front of Blake. He could like my looks or not, but that didn't change the fact that I should love myself however I looked and whatever others said.

I looked at the redhead, who now stood next to Blake. Blake patted his shoulder. "Isaac, go on. I need to talk with her."

So, he was the Isaac I'd heard Blake mention on the phone at school and after the previous week's race. He seemed to be at least ten years older. He gave me a quick once-over, suddenly looking curious about me. There was something calculative in his gaze that didn't inspire anything good in me.

"Sure," he said as he smirked at Blake. "Good luck with the race."

"Thanks," Blake replied, watching him leave before he turned to face me. "So? What are you doing here?"

"I'm here to watch the race." The excuse came out of my mouth too quickly.

"You've gotta be kidding me. You can't be here."

I knew that very well, but that didn't stop me from challenging him. "Why not?"

"Because it's dangerous."

I took immense pleasure in this additional proof that he cared for my safety, but I didn't let it overtake me. "Then what are you doing here?"

His face became closed off. "That's not for you to know."

I frowned at his cryptic answer. I had thought he would say something like *I'm racing, duh*, but definitely not that.

"Fine." I glanced at Mel and Steven, who had moved a few feet away from us and were talking to each other in hushed whispers.

He crossed his arms over his chest. "I can't figure you out. You're all over the place these days. What are you doing now? And don't tell me you came here to watch the race, because I'm not falling for it."

"I'm not here because of you, if that's what you're thinking." *That's not entirely true.*

He took a step closer to me and towered over me. "That's exactly what I'm thinking," he said quietly.

"I'm sorry to disappoint you, Blake, but the world doesn't revolve around you."

He gave me an incredulous look. "This isn't some game, Metts. It's real and dangerous. You should go home. Come on." He reached for me, as if he planned to take me home personally, but I stepped away before he made contact, refusing to let him touch me.

"I'm not going to be a coward, Blake. I'm here to stay. So leave me alone."

I spun around and moved closer to Mel and Steven as the announcer guy declared the race was about to start.

Several engines roared to life, and the atmosphere changed, allowing excitement to take over.

Blake cursed behind me. "*Fuck.*"

I was about to look at him over my shoulder, but he grabbed my hand and pulled me after him.

"Wait! What are you—"

"You wanted to play? Here, I'll give you your danger."

I glanced behind me at Mel, who had a *What the heck?* expression on her face as she watched us leave. It looked like she would come after us, but Steven told her something that kept her in place.

"What are you doing?" I asked him. My skin burned where he held me. We passed by the announcer, who looked at Blake with amusement.

"Taking a chick with ya?" he asked him.

"Call it my lucky charm."

The guy winked at him. "Gotcha."

We stopped next to his car, and he released my hand. "Get inside."

I placed my hands on my waist. "I don't want to be next to you when you're racing."

He rolled his eyes. "I'm not going to crash us into a tree. So get in."

He didn't wait for me to accept. He got into his car, assuming I would follow. I looked around and saw the previous week's winner, Bobby Q. He met my gaze over the roof of his car, which was parked close by. He studied me, unusually motionless, and something terribly cold rushed through me. I didn't want to be on his radar.

Rushing to get away from his gaze, I got inside Blake's car. Instantly, I remembered our "almost" kiss before Masen showed up, and my heart rate kicked up. I was too aware of how attractive Blake looked in his sports car. It didn't help that I was digging guys with said cars.

"I'm not sure this is a good idea," I said, watching his arm flex as he fired up the engine and hit the headlights.

"Relax. This can be fun if you let it."

He revved the engine and shifted into first. The car had a manual transmission, and I couldn't help but be impressed. I had no clue how to drive a manual. My eyes fell on his knuckles. They bore fresh scrapes, which indicated he'd been in a fight recently.

"You better buckle up," he said.

I glanced at him with wide eyes. "So you don't actually intend to kill me, worried about my safety and all," I said, half-joking, half-bickering as I put my seat belt on.

The look he gave me took all the air out of my lungs. "I've already killed you mentally. I don't want to make things any worse than that."

I didn't say anything. I couldn't. I held my hands clasped together in my lap as he lined up with the other cars at the starting line.

Tonight, Blake was racing with two more guys, and one of them was Bobby Q, who was on Blake's left. I looked through Blake's window at Bobby Q. There was something about him that I didn't like at all. I couldn't be sure in this darkness, but it looked like he had a scar line on his face, which gave me a shiver. I whipped my gaze back.

The crowd huddled around the starting line. Blake turned on the stereo, and a remix of Infected Mushroom's "Shakawkaw" filled the cabin. The blaring music made my blood pump.

I grimaced. "How can you listen to this? I can't even hear my thoughts."

His eyes remained firmly on the track ahead. "That's the whole point—I can't hear myself."

I stared at him with mouth wide open, at a loss for words. The race girl appeared at the starting line, and Blake tightened his grip on the steering wheel. His expression became edged and focused, the shadows dancing over his cheekbones and jaw adding to his alluring appearance.

I glanced away from him, biting into my lip. *He's not alluring. He's horrible. He's not alluring.*

The race girl announced the start of the race, and Blake hit the gas, sending us flying forward. I grabbed my seat as adrenaline burst through me. Blake took the lead right before he made the first turn, sending dust kicking up around him. Bobby Q was close behind us. He made a sharp turn on the inner side of the track before he straightened out and accelerated, threatening to pass Blake.

My heart jumped into my throat, and I looked in the side mirror, getting restless. The other driver was right behind us, neck and neck with Bobby Q. Blake accelerated, gaining more distance from them, before he slowed down to take the next turn.

Bobby Q needed only a few seconds to reach Blake's rear side, driving dangerously close to us. I squealed and fisted my hands on my thighs. Unlike Blake, Bobby Q didn't slow down but went into the turn in full speed, which sent his car skidding to the side before he straightened it up and accelerated far behind Blake. *Whew! That was close.*

I glanced at Blake and found him smirking. "What?" I asked.

He didn't look away from the road. "You're acting funny."

He hit the gas as he shifted into the sixth gear, and I grabbed my seat again.

"This is my first time to experience this, so cut me some slack."

His smile grew bigger, his gaze snapping to the rear-view mirror. Bobby Q was nearing Blake's car, but the third car was far behind now.

"Good. I like giving girls first-time experiences."

I arched my eyebrows at him. He barely glanced at me before he lowered his speed and made the next, sharper turn.

I looked in the side mirror and saw that Bobby Q was too close behind us again. I clenched my hands as I took in the last turn in the distance. The previous time, Blake had gotten nothing on Bobby Q, who'd managed to pass Masen right before the finish line. What were Blake's odds now?

"How many laps do you have to make?"

"Two." Blake sped up, his eyes darting between the rear-view mirror and the road. "Shit."

Bobby Q showed up on Blake's left side and passed him, creating a cloud of dust that made it impossible to see the road.

"Son of a bitch." Blake pressed the gas pedal and shifted gears.

Bobby Q was good, gaining more and more distance from Blake. Blake didn't slow down at the turn, which sent the rear part of the car sliding to the side, but Blake managed to regain control.

I looked at him furtively and got engrossed in the look on his face. Danger coated his stern features, but there was also fire in his eyes—a determination. He radiated energy that was contagious, and I loved the adrenaline that kept me high.

"I won't let you win," he muttered to himself. He looked like there was no one in this world but Bobby Q and him; the hatred on his face weaved a tale of something immensely dark. He threw caution to the wind and stopped playing safe, entering each turn at a much higher speed, gambling with so much but refusing to step down.

Our surroundings were just a blur as Blake raced at an incredibly high speed during the second lap, and I held the roof handle like my life depended on it. The last turn was nearing fast, and Blake got so close to the green Mustang that he actually had a shot at victory.

Bobby Q was close to the inner side of the track, but that didn't stop Blake from sliding in between the barrier and Bobby Q's car at the turn. He cut the wheel while speeding up, making a power slide, which kicked up dust all over Bobby Q's Mustang. I squealed in excitement as Blake stepped on the gas, driving side by side with Bobby Q almost until the finish line.

I was on the edge of my seat; the heavy beats of the music fed my excitement, and it was so addictive.

Lost in the mood, I said without thinking, "Come on. You're so close. You can win."

I saw him glance at me out of the corner of my eye. His face registered surprise, but he didn't say anything. Instead, he shifted into sixth only twenty feet before the finish line and gained an advantage over Bobby Q at the last possible moment, winning the race.

"Yes," I screamed. "You won!"

I started squealing and jumping up and down on my seat, before I met Blake's gaze with a face-splitting grin. He skidded to a stop, took his seat belt off, and turned to face me with an unreadable expression that created a burning sensation in my chest.

"Thank you," he said in a voice I didn't recognize, and before I could even respond, he grabbed my face with both hands and smashed his lips against mine.

Chapter 19

WARMTH CLAIMED ALL of me when our lips fused together. The kiss was verging on desperate, something deep within him merging with my pain and desire. The voice of my reason faded into the background as he twirled his tongue over mine.

And then it was over all too quickly. He dropped his hands from my cheeks and pulled away to look at me. He watched me with the intensity I'd always dreamed of, but it hurt because I couldn't fully embrace it.

I turned my head away from him and let my hair hide my face. I didn't want to let him see how I really felt.

"Wait for me here, okay? I'll drive you home," he said before getting out without waiting for my answer.

The crowd surrounded him, and the cheers and claps blasted through the air. I looked at my lap dumbly, pressing my fingers to my tingling lips. *Thank you,* he'd said, and he'd kissed me like he was starving for me. Like our past didn't separate us.

I couldn't believe he'd kissed me. And not only that—I'd let him kiss me. I closed my eyes, in conflict with myself. I should have gotten out of the car right this moment before he pulled me deeper into the pool of regrets and pain.

My phone chimed. I took it out of my pocket and unlocked it. It was Mel.

Tell me that asshole didn't do anything to you and you're still in one piece.

I looked at the crowd on the sidelines, but I couldn't spot her. I pressed my fingers against my lips again, my chest aching at the thought of our kiss. I just had to remember that he was my bully and not let him get to me. This kiss—any of our kisses—didn't matter. They couldn't matter.

I'm safe and sound, I texted back.

I glanced at Blake, who was talking to a clearly pissed-off Bobby Q. Masen stood next to them, and he looked as tense as Blake was now. The traces of triumph on Blake's face were long gone. Blake got into Bobby Q's face, looking like he could punch him at any moment.

My hand clenched around my phone. "Don't fight," I whispered right before I got a new text. I dragged my gaze from Blake and opened Mel's message.

Why are you still in his car? Let's go.

Her next message arrived only seconds later.

And guess what? My idiotic brother agreed to finally come back home. Hallelujah.

I looked at the guys in time to see Masen step between Blake and Bobby Q to prevent things from escalating. He said something into Blake's ear and motioned my way with his head, and Blake glanced at me. Giving Bobby Q one last glare, he spun around and marched back to the car, his jaw clenched furiously.

I bit into my lip and quickly typed a message to Mel, acting on an impulse.

That's great! Btw, Blake will drive me to your place. Sorry. Talk to you later.

I turned off the sound and put my phone back into my pocket. Blake got inside the car, slammed his door shut, and gripped the steering wheel. His breathing was rapid, and it looked like he was on the verge of either exploding in white-hot anger or having a breakdown.

The urge to touch him reared its stupid head, and I curled my hands to stop myself. He leaned his head against the headrest and closed his eyes, taking deep breaths. Bobby Q returned to his car and sped away, kicking up some gravel for the show, and the crowd started to thin out.

I looked at his scraped knuckles again, conflicted. "Blake? Are you okay?" He didn't move to look at me, just clenching the steering wheel more tightly. "Can I...can I help?" I pursed my lips, feeling stupid for even asking this. There was no way he would actually accept my help, but I couldn't just sit there and pretend he wasn't falling apart right next to me.

"I guess not," I muttered.

"You already are," he said, so quietly I thought I'd heard him wrong.

My throat tightened. "What?" He didn't reply immediately, not until his breathing evened out and he raised his head, avoiding my gaze.

"Nothing." He put on his seat belt.

Infected Mushroom's "Becoming Insane" played next, and its strong, Latin-infused beats filled the uncomfortable silence between us as he started the car.

I twisted my hands in my lap. I didn't know how to act around him. He flashed his lights at Masen when we passed, and he waved at us with a knowing smirk on his face. I looked around for Mel, but she was nowhere to be found. I felt a twinge of guilt because I was leaving this place with Blake instead with her.

"Are you even able to drive? Because you don't look so good."

"Yeah, I can drive. I'm not made of glass, Metts," he replied brusquely.

I crossed my arms over my chest. "If you're going to talk to me like that, you can drop me right here and go. It was just a simple question."

He looked at me with parted lips. I expected him to insult me or stop the car so I could get out, but he didn't do either, which floored me.

The lights coming from the generators were replaced by darkness as he drove along the forest path surrounded by endless trees. This only made the atmosphere between us more intimate, and it was confusing. I found it hard to breathe evenly, too aware of how close he was. His smell was everywhere, toying with me, rousing me.

I wanted to ask him what had happened back there with Bobby Q and what he'd done to shake Blake so badly, but I knew I would be stepping into forbidden territory and he would refuse to answer.

"Take me to Mel's house. I couldn't tell my parents about the track, so I said I was going to sleep over at her place." I didn't know why I felt the need to explain myself. "That was the only way they would let me go out."

He raised his eyebrow. "And they bought that?"

"Why wouldn't they?"

"Right. I forgot—you're a good girl who just likes playing bad from time to time." He threw me a smile, but I didn't know if it was mocking or not.

I crossed my arms over my chest, staring ahead. "Why did you offer to drive me home?"

"Because I wanted to."

My breath hitched. I was stumped by this sudden change between us. The lines were becoming blurred, and this gray area we'd plunged into was something I hadn't been prepared for.

I looked at him. "You wanted to drive home a person you despised until very recently?"

He returned my gaze for a second, two... *Breathe, Jess. Breathe.* "Would you rather have me despising you again?"

My eyebrows scrunched together. "Of course not. I'm just confused by this change between us."

"You're not the only one who can't figure out what's happening here. I have no clue what we're doing."

My chest squeezed painfully. "We aren't doing anything. We're nothing, Blake."

"Sure. Lie to yourself if that will make you feel better."

"It's not a lie."

He met my eyes. "Then why are you looking at me like you want me to kiss you again?"

I blushed furiously and looked away, making sure my hair hid most of my face from him. "I don't want you to kiss me again."

He took a turn, reaching the road. "Lie to yourself some more and maybe you'll start believing it."

I bit the inside of my cheek. "Why does it even matter to you? You said you won't ever be with me."

"And I meant it," he replied without missing a beat. "No matter how things go between us, the endgame is always the same—we won't be together."

A bolt of pain struck through my chest, even though we were supposed to be this way. *Why?* burned on the tip of my tongue, but I didn't ask.

"Good to know that because I wouldn't want it any other way," I said as I looked at the lines on the road that passed quickly. I hoped my words didn't sound as fake to him as they did to me, which was ridiculous. *He's your bully, Jess. Don't forget that. Just a bully.*

Another song by Infected Mushroom, a remix of "Demons of Pain", started playing, and its heavy bass hammered nails into my head. I sneaked a glance at Blake, who looked pensive. I fiddled with my thumbs, the bass of the song getting even stronger.

"It's obvious why this song is called 'Demons of Pain,'" I said.

"Why?"

"Because its beat gives me pain." I massaged my temples. "I'm getting a headache from it."

He lowered the volume and glanced at me, the corner of his lips quirking up. "Let me guess—you're all for sweet, lovey-dovey songs."

"Hey! What's that supposed to mean?"

His smile grew bigger. "You wear pink most of the time. You also wear flower hair accessories and bracelets." I shouldn't have been surprised that he remembered all these details, but I was. "You're for sweet things to the bone."

My brows rose. He was right. I *was* all for sweet things.

"I can't imagine you listening to this kind of music. Not after I heard you play your song," he added, and I inhaled sharply. I wanted to remove that embarrassing memory from my mind, but it stood its ground.

I hunched in my seat. "I get it...my song was too sugary."

He frowned. "I never said that."

I didn't respond, waiting for him to say more, burning with curiosity to hear his opinion about it...but he didn't say anything.

"Okay." That's all I said, when I actually wanted to ask what he thought about it.

He tapped his fingers on the steering wheel. "I liked it," he said, barely audibly.

I grew motionless. *Did he say he liked it?*

Fishing for a direct answer, I asked, "You liked what?"

"You know what."

"I don't know."

"Yes, you do, but you want me to say it." He glanced at me, and the raw look in his eyes pulled me in. "Your song. I liked your song. And...I liked your voice."

My breath caught in my chest. "You're just saying that to make me feel better about it," I said, refusing to accept the possibility that he really liked it, because this meant a lot to me, and it scared me.

His forehead wrinkled. "You really like to put yourself down. Don't tell me you've never realized how amazing your voice is."

My lips curved into a big smile. I wanted to pinch myself so I could prove this was real. Blake Jones had just complimented my voice. He actually liked it.

My emotions bubbled up inside me. Had Hayden told him about my dream to become a singer? Was he even aware of how much his praise—*anyone's* praise—meant to me? Did he know how afraid I was of performing in front of others, to the point of not following my dreams?

"You really think so?"

He glanced at me and smiled. Like an actual, real smile. "Yeah."

My smile widened. "Thank you." He only smirked at that, and I fidgeted with the hem of my jacket. "I guess you don't listen to my kind of music."

"No."

"I thought so."

"But I would give your songs a chance."

My heart leapt. "And why's that?" I couldn't resist asking.

"Because they're yours, obviously."

Okay. I had to pinch myself.

I pinched my upper arm. "Ouch."

He snorted. "Why did you do that?"

"Just making sure I really heard you say that."

He burst into chuckles, but then, as if he'd caught himself doing something he wasn't supposed to, he grew serious. He shook his head at me. "You're weird."

We were near Enfield, which meant this ride would end soon. I wished it could last a bit longer. I thought about the moments of tenderness he'd displayed this evening and the last few days, and my body warmed. He was finally letting me see his other side, finally treating me like something more than a bug to squash.

I had so many questions on my mind. We weren't friends. We couldn't be lovers. But we weren't the same old enemies. So what were we?

I was so deep in my thoughts that I didn't realize Blake was slowing down. He went off the road and parked his car next to it, right in the middle of nowhere. The music and all sounds died when he shut off the engine. His car lights were our only source of light.

"What are you doing? Why did you stop?"

He unbuckled his seat belt. "Come out for a sec."

"But why—"

"Just come." He got out and closed the door.

I looked around with a frown. It was so dark I couldn't make out anything in the shadows that converged all over. There were no cars passing. I licked my lips. What was he doing?

Reluctantly, I removed my seat belt and stepped outside, hit by a gust of cold air. He leaned against the hood of his car and tilted his head back to look at the starry sky.

My eyes caught on the sign standing a few feet away, which I recognized from the local news that covered tourist attractions near Enfield. It read: *Enfield's Sunflower Field. Welcome.* I couldn't see that far, but I didn't need to in order to know the sunflower field was vacant at this time of year.

"You do know this is just like all those horror movies, right? You driving me to nowhere and acting all mysterious?" I said.

"If this was anything like horror movies, you'd already be dead."

"Ha ha. That's not funny."

He shrugged. "I wasn't trying to be."

"Yes, I noticed humor isn't your strong suit."

"Says the humor expert."

"At least I don't wear a scowl all the time."

A huge smile broke out on his face, and I stilled, realizing we were going back and forth like old friends.

I crossed my arms over my chest and went to the edge of the field. Now that my eyes had gotten used to the dark, I was able to discern the lines of the empty space. There were no lights, or signs of civilization for that matter, only trees and more trees. I had to remind myself this was Blake I was talking with, but each second spent with him made it easier for me to relax.

"Why did we stop here?"

He took his time responding, looking at the sky. "Have you ever counted stars?"

I tipped my chin down, staring at him with raised eyebrows. Such a strange question. "Yeah, when I was seven or eight. You?"

"Every time I come here."

"Why?"

"Because it calms me down. It helps me stay grounded."

I was confounded by yet another unusual choice of words. "Really?"

"Really."

I half-smiled. "Don't get me wrong, but I didn't peg you as someone who would actually do that."

His expression turned guarded as he met my gaze, and I saw my mistake. He'd just opened up to me, and I'd reacted in a way that could hurt his feelings.

I raised my hands up. "I didn't mean it in a bad way. I just thought you were..."

"What?"

I looked around as I searched for the right word. "Invincible."

He rolled his eyes. "I'm human too."

I fidgeted with my hands. "You didn't seem human whenever you bullied me."

His brows dipped into a frown, and he crossed his arms over his chest. His eyes moved over the field. "You and I are both much more than what we thought of each other, Jessica." He looked like he wanted to say more, but he didn't.

"Fair enough."

A cold breeze enveloped us as we fell into silence. He lay down on the hood and put his arms behind his head, gazing at the sky, and I used the opportunity to observe him. His body. His face that I saw in my dreams more often than I wanted to. Even now, with all the barriers between us, I wanted him to take me in his arms and show me our past was just a nightmare and he was going to wake me up.

"And to answer your question, I just wanted to bring you here," he continued, his eyes darting from one part of the sky to the other. "Besides, you helped me at the track, so..."

I approached and stopped only a few feet short of him. "But I didn't do anything."

"You were there. That was more than enough." He sighed. "I've had shitty days recently and couldn't race, but tonight, with you..." His voice trailed off, and I wanted to beg him to finish that sentence. He looked deep in thought.

"Tonight, with me?" I spurred him on, too curious not to.

Our gazes locked. "It was different. In a good way."

My heart picked up in speed. It was getting harder for me to resist his pull. I wanted to ask him why his days had been bad, but I knew he wouldn't answer that.

I didn't even realize I'd taken a few more steps closer to him. I was now standing right next to the hood, staring deep into his eyes.

"Why this place, though? What's so special about it?"

He sat up. "It's one of my most favorite places. That empty field?" He pointed at it. "Sunflowers will be all over it in summer, and believe me, it's something else."

I stared at him, immersed in his words, his voice, the look in his eyes. He'd just brought me to one of his most favorite places. Another hard layer fell from around my heart, leaving me even more vulnerable to him.

"I can imagine," I said. I was all too aware of how near I currently was to him, only inches between me and his knees, and each new breath added to the sweet pressure in my chest. His body was massive compared to mine, all muscles and height. I had a hard time suppressing my desire.

"I also wanted to thank you." My voice was barely louder than a whisper.

He leaned his elbow against his knee, getting even closer to me. His eyes went to my lips. *Breathe, Jess. Just breathe.*

"For what?"

"I had a lot of fun during the race. I finally see what all the fuss is about."

"Yeah, the rush is the best."

He continued watching me, a half-smile tugging at his lips, and the tension in my chest became almost unbearable. My cheeks were burning. I needed to say something, *anything*, to break the silence.

"So." I cleared my throat. "You like counting stars, sunflowers, basketball, and Infected Mushroom. What else?"

The gust of wind sent a strand of my hair right into his face. He wrapped his fingers around it and moved it, but he didn't let go. He formed a cheeky smile.

"And aren't you curious?"

He tucked the strand behind my ear slowly, so slowly. I shivered when his fingers grazed my earlobe.

He looked at the sky. "What else do I like? I like..." He met my eyes. "You."

I sucked in my breath. He'd actually said—

"...Tube videos," he concluded, bursting my bubble.

I let out a strangled sound, and my whole face flared up. He raised his eyebrows at my expression and erupted into hearty laughter, bending at the waist.

"Your face! You should've seen your face." His laughter grew louder, but I didn't find this as amusing as he did.

I bit into my lip. I was so stupid. I'd really thought he...

He was just messing with me.

I turned my back to him and let out a chuckle that was so empty. "Right. YouTube videos. I like them too." I wished my damn heart would slow down. So stupid.

His laughter died. I stared at the field, telling myself not to take it to heart and forget about it. It shouldn't have mattered.

I folded my arms across my chest. "So, can we go now?"

"Jessie," he said incredibly softly, but I didn't react.

He took my upper arm and pulled me around and between his legs. My eyes widened at the position, heat washing all over me. He wound his other arm around my waist, and I had to place my hands on his thighs to steady myself.

He smiled. "You're so cute like this."

My voice didn't listen to me. I stared back into his eyes completely captivated. My palms on his thighs were burning.

"You really want to know what I like?" He threaded his fingers through my hair. "I like this time here with you." He looked at my mouth, his eyes half-closed. "I like talking to you." He cupped my face with his hand. I trembled.

"How come?"

He slid his thumb over my lower lip. "Because you're so much more than I thought. And this night, you and me here...it feels more real than anything." He leaned his forehead against mine, and I closed my eyes.

I pressed my fingers into his thighs reflexively. It was hard for me to believe this was real. "But for me...it feels like a dream." If I moved my lips an inch closer to his, we would be kissing. "It feels like I'll wake up to another day of hate and insults."

"Jessie..." His fingers tightened in my hair. "We're on borrowed time here, but it's very real." His heavy sigh skimmed over my lips. "I'm sorry." I wanted to ask what he meant by borrowed time, but he said, "I know an apology won't fix shit now, but I want you to know I'm sorry for every insult." His lips grazed my lower lip. "I'm sorry for putting you through all that." He left a tiny kiss on my upper lip. "I'm sorry for everything."

He pressed his lips against mine and wrapped his arms around me, and I gave in, molding myself to him. It was bittersweet—all of this: the kiss, the nearness, the quiet of the night that witnessed our painful dance of forbidden feelings when there was no forgiveness. Nothing about this promised a happy ending, but I was happy to indulge in it for a little while, letting myself get carried away by a wave of illusion.

He deepened our kiss, holding me so close like he was afraid I would disappear at any moment, and I could feel his desperation. It poured out of him with each stroke of his tongue, with each caress of his hands, with each quickened breath that mingled with mine.

He flipped us around and placed me on the hood, never breaking our kiss. His hands pushed me down and moved down my waist and hips, sparking my desire.

He buried his head in my neck and left kisses that stole more of my reason, and when he palmed my breasts over my jacket—a move that felt so natural and left me wanting more—I almost threw all my caution to the wind. But this was an illusion, and when it shattered, its pieces would pierce me and leave even deeper scars than those I already had.

I snapped my eyes open. "Wait." I pushed against his chest. "Blake, wait." He leaned away to look at me, placing his hands against the hood on both sides of my waist. His eyes were filled with desire, his breathing ragged. "You can't kiss me like this. It's not right after everything."

He frowned. "Why do you have to be like this?"

"Why do I...?" I huffed exasperatedly. "Because our past is too painful! Because it's always hot and cold with you. Because I'm afraid I might end up completely broken if I let you treat me like all those other girls."

He stepped away. "I'm not treating you like other girls."

I sat up. "Yes, you are. You'd lose interest in me the moment you had me."

He shook his head. "*No.* You don't understand. This..." He motioned between us. "This isn't about mindless fucking."

"Then what is it, Blake? A game? Because I can't explain in any other way what you're doing with me, especially since you said you won't ever be with me."

He ran his hands through his hair. "Do you think I want to be like this? My mind is telling me to get the hell away from you, but I can't. *I can't.* And I'm tired of keeping myself on a tight leash and denying myself what I want."

I gripped the edge of the hood. His words created intense longing that urged me to pull him back to me and kiss our pain away.

"I'm going against my promise, and you have no idea how much it hurts. I promised her I would never care for anyone else...I said she would be the only one for me..."

I placed my hand over my mouth. My chest ached too much.

He closed the distance between us and palmed the back of my head. His eyes carried a deeply rooted pain. "I made that promise, but I can't keep it. I can't fucking keep it."

He held my gaze, and I saw the truth in his eyes. He was conflicted, torn between his love and devotion to Emma and me. Maybe he even felt he was betraying her, and now, more than ever, I wished we had met under different circumstances. I wished there weren't too many things pulling us apart.

"I just want to lose myself in you for a minute," he said. "Just this time."

He cradled my head with both hands and nuzzled my nose. His warm breath traveled across my skin before he planted a kiss on the corner of my lips and left a trail of butterfly kisses along my jaw, incredibly slowly. Once more, my mind was fogged with desire that turned me into a puppet. His lips skimmed over my cheek before they ended their journey on mine, and I kissed him back with everything I had, our pain converging together.

He stepped between my legs and left kisses along my neck, letting me feel what I'd always craved. He put my legs around his waist and pressed himself against me, which brought his erection to where I needed the pressure the most. I moaned, throwing my head back.

"I want you," he said hoarsely. "I want you in more ways than one."

He started grinding against me, and his kisses grew more heated. His hands explored my waist, chest, and hips, making me feel more wanted than ever.

"If you only knew how good you feel," he said. His eyes roamed all over me, so dark, so full of lust, eliminating all doubts that he really liked my body with all its curves. "You're gorgeous."

And I believed him. The way he looked at me, the conviction behind his words...the lust that matched mine... It was so easy to push everything aside and live in this moment.

He moved his hand and cupped me down there, and I sucked in my breath. Our gazes locked on each other.

"Blake," I whispered, confounded but reveling in his touch.

"Let me touch you."

I looked away, biting into my lip. "I..."

"Let me give you what I've wanted for so long." He increased the pressure, and it was deliciously addictive.

I moaned, leaning into his touch inadvertently, but I couldn't let it happen. I couldn't.

"Just this once," he said, kissing my neck, and I was so close to letting him do it. So close...

But it was pointless. I pushed against his shoulders. "No. Stop."

He groaned. "Jessie, please—"

"No. Not like this." I gave his shoulders another shove, and he drew back, breaking the contact between us. I ignored the furious throbbing of my core as I slid off the hood and stopped a safe distance away. I turned to face him. "You didn't answer my question—what is this? What do I mean to you?"

He let out a loud sigh. "What do you want me to say?"

I scowled at him. "What do I want you to say?!" I pointed at my chest. "I'm not someone you can just use and discard later, Blake!"

"I'm not using you! *Fuck!*" He kicked the front tire and glared at me, his artery pumping furiously along his neck. "I'm still trying to accept the fact that I can't hate you anymore. It was so easy back then. I hated you and everything made sense. You were my enemy and I was perfectly fine with that. But then hate turned into something...something else, and now I have no clue what to do with it."

"How about treating me with respect first? Because I'm also struggling to accept that, for some twisted reason, I've fallen for my bully!" I clenched my cold hands, fighting against the tears. "And what makes it even harder is that all I get from you are half-truths, riddles, and even more riddles. It's too much for me."

He looked to the side. "I can't tell you the truth."

A tear slid down my cheek, and I brushed it off quickly, turning to the side so he wouldn't see my face. "Of course not."

"There are so many things you don't know, but I'm not ready to tell them. I don't think I'll ever be ready."

Another tear escaped my eye as guilt about invading his privacy converged inside me. I wasn't being completely up-front with him either, and now, more than ever, I felt horrible for knowing something he hadn't willingly shared with me—something he probably, as he'd just said, wouldn't ever be ready to share. Hiding it from him didn't feel right at all.

"I'm not the one for you," he continued. "I don't know why we started feeling different toward each other, but we're not meant to be."

He drove another, final nail into my heart. I'd always known this, but it was much more painful hearing it directly from him. I turned to face him, masking my pain with a neutral expression.

"We're not meant to be," I echoed in a flat tone. "Why?" I asked, for the sole purpose of finding closure.

He grabbed the back of his head. His face had a look of utmost agony, and somehow I knew his next words would tear me down.

"Because I have a promise to keep, one that will most likely get me killed, but this promise is the one I won't ever break."

The thumping of my heart in my ears was too loud. *A promise that will most likely get him killed.*

"A promise? A promise of what?"

"A promise of revenge."

Chapter 20

BLAKE DIDN'T ELABORATE on what he meant by that. He returned to his car instead, which was my cue that the night was over, and we continued to Melissa's place in complete silence. I had trouble keeping my tears at bay.

He was going to do something that could cost him his life, and I couldn't do anything against the fear that possessed my heart. I couldn't stop ruminating on it, struggling to connect all the pieces of the puzzle.

I was sure about one thing—it must have everything to do with Emma and their kidnapping. I recollected the fragments of Blake's conversations I'd heard and his reaction to Bobby Q. It could be far-fetched, but what if Bobby Q had something to do with the kidnapping? No, he had to be part of the puzzle, just like those photos I'd found in Blake's room. Then again, what was Blake doing? What was his plan for revenge and when would he execute it?

And that promise of revenge...was it a promise to Emma? Or someone else?

One thing was clear: he wasn't going to back away from it.

It hurt knowing that. I wanted him out of harm's way, but how he looked when he said those words...the fire in his eyes... He was determined to do it, and it didn't matter what he felt for me. He was holding back because for him, his revenge came first.

I was supposed to distance myself from him and stop carrying this constant concern for him, but it was impossible. I knew there was nothing I could say or do to help him, but that didn't stop me from conjuring up various scenarios after he dropped me at Mel's place and drove off without a word. I had a feeling he would get in serious trouble.

I spent the whole night tossing and turning on Mel's sofa, thinking about everything that'd happened in the last week and how I had to apologize to him for intruding into his room and watching that video. My parents and I were going to another Saturday dinner at their house, so I decided to do it then if he was there.

The thought of doing it so soon created a gnawing feeling in my chest, but I couldn't keep holding out on him. I had to own up to my mistake and stop being a coward. As Susan had told me many times, honesty was the best policy. Even if it meant I had to face his fury.

That very thought invoked tears I couldn't stop for a long time. He would hate me more than ever when he heard I'd invaded a piece of his past, and it would be irreversible.

I was preparing myself for it the whole day, but that didn't stop my stomach from fluttering when I got in Dad's car, and the sensation only intensified the closer we got to the Jones' mansion. I jacked up the volume of the Florence and the Machine song coming from my AirPods when my phone buzzed with a new text from Kev.

I'm with my parents at that fancy restaurant that opened last week. Guess what.

What?

The owners are Marcus's parents. And guess who works there as a server.

I chuckled, knowing where this was going.

Santa Claus?

You're close. Marcus. And he's waiting on our table!

My lips curved into a cheek-splitting smile. The day before, Marcus had approached me before our choir practice and asked me if I'd talked to Kevin about him. I told him he should try talking to him himself because Kevin would most definitely appreciate it. After that, Kev and Marcus spent the entire practice talking to each other in hushed whispers, and they looked so cute together. I could see that Kevin was slowly warming up to Marcus. I couldn't have been happier for him.

Ooh. And? Give me some details.

And I can't eat because he keeps staring at me, and my heart does this weird jumping thing. Also, I feel hot.

I giggled, bouncing up and down in my seat. So cute!

Dad looked at me in the rear-view mirror and said something, but I couldn't hear him because of the music.

I took my AirPod out. "What?"

"I said, what has gotten into you? Are you all right?"

I nodded at him, grinning. "Yep. I'm perfect."

"You're acting just like your mom when she stumbles on a sale." He winked at her.

Mom let out an exaggerated sigh and shook her head. "You don't complain when I buy you ties. Or golf clubs."

"You buy them once a year. *Once.* And how many times do you go shopping in a year?"

I chuckled. "Probably a thousand times," I said. "She's obsessed with sales."

She tsked. "I'm *not* obsessed with sales. There's nothing wrong with buying new clothes every once in a while."

I rolled my eyes. "Yeah, more like every once in a week." I put my AirPod back in my ear and sent another message to Kev.

I'm over here smiling like crazy, and my dad thinks I'm ready to be put in a straitjacket. That's so cute!

He replied a few minutes later.

He just slipped a note in my lap!

I squealed and typed quickly.

What does it say???

I tapped my fingers on my thigh, almost on the edge of my seat as I waited for his response. I was seriously living for their budding romance.

It says: Wanna go out with me tomorrow?

"Yes," I shouted, and now both Mom and Dad were looking at me like they were going to lock me up in an asylum.

Say yes. SAY YES.

His text arrived almost immediately.

But I'm stuttering, Jess. That's pretty embarrassing.

I huffed.

Don't you dare say no, Kevin Burks. Marcus isn't like that. He doesn't care.
You think?

I KNOW. You're so much more than your stutter, and Marcus knows that. We all know that. He wouldn't ask you out if he cared about that.

My dad said something, but once again, I couldn't hear him. I stopped the music and looked at him. "Yes?"

"We've arrived."

My smile dropped. I looked around and took in the Jones' swanky front door. My hands started to tremble as I stuffed my phone and AirPods into my backpack. My phone buzzed, but I couldn't focus on it now, taking deep breaths. I would most likely see Blake in just a few moments.

At least my parents didn't notice anything unusual about me. We got out of the car into the surprisingly warm night and headed to the entrance. I clung to the strap of my backpack when my dad rang the bell, and the same maid as before opened the door. She met us with a warm smile that didn't do anything to reduce my growing anxiety before she let us in. Just like the last time, I could almost feel Blake there, and my skin prickled with awareness. I tried my best to play it cool.

"Mr. and Mrs. Jones are waiting for you in the living room."

I stayed behind my parents as we followed her. My mom's high heels clicked on the marble floor, mixing with the sounds of my heartbeat thundering in my ears, and I willed my legs to move no matter how hard each step was.

My eyes swept over the living room as we entered it in search of Blake, but he wasn't there. Again.

"Owen and Julie, welcome," Nathaniel said before he directed his million-watt smile at me. "And Jessica. It's a pleasure to see you again."

I smiled at him weakly and met Daniela's gaze; yet again, she wore a smile that contradicted the cold in her eyes. I felt like she could see right through me.

"Hello," I said, shaking hands with them.

"Come sit." Nathaniel motioned to the couch. "Our son is about to come home any moment now."

My pulse accelerated at once. The prospect of seeing Blake after the night before did something strange to my body. Despite my anxiety and his painful revelation, my thoughts raced to those heated moments between us as I took a seat.

I blushed, remembering well how good his hand had felt on my most sensitive part. His words had brimmed with lust, matching his ravaging gaze that was imprinted on my mind forever. No one had ever looked at me the way he had. No one, but it felt bitter. Whatever we felt for each other was pinned beneath the blocks of past hatred and his promises.

I wrung my hands together. I could see that my dad and Nathaniel had become friendlier since our first dinner, and even Daniela, who had seemed cold and distant the last time, sounded more interested in what Mom had to say now.

The maid served us our drinks—whiskey for the gentlemen, wine for the ladies, and a good old orange juice for me—and Dad and Nathaniel dived into a topic that was as old as time: politics.

I was restless as I listened to them talk, dying of boredom. I was close to taking my phone out of my backpack to spend time on Instagram, but I knew it would be impolite, so I just stared into nothing and nodded at what they were saying, pretending I knew what the conversation was all about. Blake took forever to arrive...

The heavy footsteps resonated in the hall, and my throat turned dry. Seconds passed in soaring nervousness, and then he appeared at the doorstep with a black motorcycle helmet in his hand, dressed in a black motorbike jacket and pants that left me short of breath. He was ridiculously sexy, and when he ran his hand through his disheveled hair, I stopped breathing. I couldn't quite grasp that this guy here had been all over me the previous night and looked at me as if he'd never seen a prettier girl in his life.

He raised his head. His eyes went over my parents before they reached me, and he halted, his eyebrows drawing together as if he was surprised to see me. He looked back at my parents, and then at me again, and it seemed he was putting two and two together.

"Son. You finally decided to grace us with your presence," Nathaniel said and stood up, wearing a smile that was easy to see through. He wasn't pleased with Blake.

"I told you I couldn't make it earlier," Blake told him, not intimidated by Nathaniel in the least.

"And we told you this dinner is important," Daniela said sweetly as she got to her feet. "Meet our son, Blake." Her smile could have cut through ice. "Blake, this is Owen Metts. He's one of your father's attorneys." She motioned at my dad, and he stood up to shake hands with Blake.

"It's nice to meet you, Blake. Nathaniel has told me a lot about you." My dad shook his hand firmly, and something coiled in my stomach at seeing my dad shake hands with a guy who was my bully, my crush, and my ceaseless source of contrasting emotions.

Blake, who was taller than my dad by three inches, returned his gaze with all the confidence in the world. "It's good to meet you too, sir." His voice was so deep, and I squirmed in my seat.

"And this is Julie Metts," Daniela said, continuing with the introductions. Blake stopped in front of my mom, who smiled softly at him. My heart gave a kick in my chest, reacting to his nearness.

"It's good to meet you, Mrs. Metts."

"Likewise, Blake." She took his hand and shook it briefly. The barely visible smile he'd had for my mom disappeared when he met my gaze.

"Blake, this is Jessica. She goes to your school," Daniela said.

I stood up on shaky legs. I partly expected him to pretend he didn't know me. His expression was unreadable as we stared at each other in lingering silence.

"I know her very well," he said quietly, his gaze unblinking. He held out his hand, and for a second, I just stared at it, surprised. I licked my lips and extended my hand, captivated by his darkening eyes.

His long fingers wrapped around my hand, and I felt a tug in my stomach. His touch was warm and intoxicating. Our hands remained connected as his thumb brushed the back of my hand in slow, sensual circles. I couldn't breathe. I couldn't move a muscle as we looked at each other, lost in our own world. My chest grew so tight, and when his eyes flitted to my lips, it was like the previous night all over again. It was obvious that both of us wanted another taste.

Nathaniel said something, and Blake released my hand, bringing me back to our dull reality. He took a seat on the sofa on the other side of the room, putting distance between him and his parents. It was hard not to notice they weren't close-knit.

Whenever his parents tried to include him in the conversation, he fired off some rude remark, openly showing what he thought about his parents' get-togethers. I caught my parents exchanging a few furtive glances, which showed they were also bewildered by this strained family relationship.

Suddenly, disappointment flooded my chest. I hadn't known what to expect from his parents, but I'd thought and *hoped* they would be more supportive of their son. After seeing that video, I had to wonder if they had ever been his pillars of support. It was obvious the event had scarred him, so he should have had someone who would help him and guide him through life.

It seemed he was alone—even with his friends.

We moved to the dining room. This time it was a different one, with a picturesque view of the outdoor pool and flowering hedges surrounding it. Somehow, Blake ended up sitting right next to me, which was a feat because the table could accommodate the whole presidential delegation and he had plenty of seats to choose from.

His fragrance dominated the air I inhaled. I was too aware of his every move, and I had to will my hands to work properly as I put food on my plate and cut it, hoping I wouldn't mess something up. Paying extra attention to table manners was one of the things I disliked about these gatherings, and being so close to Blake made it almost impossible to accomplish.

Our hands brushed when we reached for the salt at the same moment. He turned rigid, and his eyes went to my lips. I looked away, thinking about our recent kisses again.

"So, Blake, Nathaniel told me you'll be going to law school?" my dad said.

I didn't miss the displeasure that flashed over Blake's face. "Yes, sir," he replied, cutting his steak a little too hard. The tone of his voice revealed he wasn't happy about law school, and I wanted to know why.

"And have you chosen a college?" Dad asked.

Blake swallowed his steak and took a sip of his Coke. "You should ask my father that." He glared at Nathaniel. "He calls the shots."

Nathaniel cast a quick scowl at Blake, one I could've easily missed if I hadn't been looking at him. He cleared his throat. "Right. He will attend Columbia."

I whipped my gaze to Blake. "New York?" I asked, unable to hide the surprise in my voice.

I'd accepted my music college admission in New York just a few hours earlier. It was a part of my decision to start owning my life and following my dreams instead of letting my parents decide my future—and now Blake was going to New York too?

Blake just tilted his head to the side and studied me quietly.

"Yes," Nathaniel answered instead of him. "Columbia has one of the best law programs."

Blake sneered at him. "But I still haven't accepted their admission."

"You will," Nathaniel answered in a tone that left no room for discussion.

Blake dropped his fork on his plate; an almost deafening clank stunned us all into silence. My parents glanced at each other, struggling to keep their expressions neutral.

"You've got it all figured out, huh?" Blake mocked. "Ship me off to some faraway college so you don't have to deal with me, right?"

Daniela stiffened. "Blake, this is not the time or place to talk about that matter."

I bit the inside of my cheek. It was like I was watching a tennis match as I looked between Blake and his parents on the other side of the table, only they weren't lobbing a tennis ball but venom. Lots of venom.

"It's never the time or place, *Mom*." He spat the last word with hot anger, clenching his fist on his thigh.

"We talked about this, son," Nathaniel told him. "You're meant for a better school than that measly local college."

So, Blake wanted to attend a local college. I wondered why.

"No. That's not it, and you know it," Blake said. "You just want me far away from here."

"And for a reason, Blake." Nathaniel's knuckles went white as he tightened his grip on the fork. "You'll be better off there with...with your issues."

My thoughts raced through my head as I tried to keep up with them, but then Daniela said, "Blake, why don't you take Jessica on a tour around the house? You can get to know each other better, seeing as you're the same age."

I choked on my saliva. I looked at Blake, who glowered at his mother, both his hands now fisted on his thighs.

"Of course. Anything to keep this dinner civilized. Good reputation and all that." He shot up to his feet, making the chair scrape the floor loudly. "Follow me," he told me gruffly. He didn't even wait for me, rushing out of the room in a few quick strides.

"Please excuse our son," Daniela said, but she didn't sound apologetic at all. "He's just hot-tempered sometimes, but it will pass."

"Teenage hormones," Nathaniel added with a smile that was supposed to be charming, but it had the opposite effect on me.

"Of course," my mom concurred, just to remain polite.

"Um..." I said, unsure of what to do. I glanced between Mom and Dad as I stood up.

Mom didn't look like she wanted me to be around someone so full of negative energy, but Daniela offered another of her tight-lipped smiles and said, "It's okay, Jessica. Go on."

I turned my head to conceal my frown. I was astounded that she cared so little about Blake's feelings. I felt more than grateful that I had a mother who would never treat me so condescendingly, with no care or desire to help me. My legs carried me out of the room hurriedly, my heart urging me to go show Blake he wasn't alone in this world.

It was naïve to think he would accept my company or comfort, because just one glance at him standing with his tense back turned to me in the hallway told me he wanted to be alone.

I gnawed at my lower lip and stopped right behind him. "You don't have to show me around the house, you know." His breathing was ragged, and I wished I could drive that tension out of him.

"I didn't plan to. Come on."

Once more, he walked away without waiting for me and led me to the back porch. I followed him into the quiet night that smelled of grass and exquisite flowers; the air was cold enough to leave little chilly bites all over my skin, so I was glad I was wearing a wool sweater.

He didn't stop on the porch like I expected him to. He proceeded down a stone path that was illuminated by a row of small garden lights, and we reached a garden that had me frozen to the spot. It was dimly lit, but the lack of light only added to its magic.

There was a small pond in the middle, and its surface glimmered under the starlit sky. A stone path that curved around it ended at a deck with a small wooden roof and a wooden bench surrounded by pots of flowers. Flowering vines grew along the lattice panels that enclosed the garden, which brought a unique touch to the space, and I was immersed in the sight.

Blake went over to sit on the bench, which pulled me out of my daze. I moved toward him with slow steps.

"Why did we come here?"

He had yet to look at me, his gaze downcast. My eyes went over his slumped form, then his widely spread legs, and a flicker of warmth danced through me. Shadows emphasized the sharp lines of his cheeks and jaw, giving him a dark allure that was irresistible.

"Because this is the only place on this estate that doesn't make me feel like I'm walled in." He looked at the house with a gaze that told me what I needed to know even before he uttered the words. "I hate that place. It's a prison."

I stopped close to him, but not too close. "A prison?"

His eyes locked on mine, showing me his pain. "Yes. A prison that keeps me stuck in my past."

His words resonated within me, and I just stood there watching him as he stared off into the distance, allowing me to see the myriad of emotions that coursed over his face.

But then, realizing he'd left the door to his world open, he put another mask on.

I cleared my throat and went over to the railing. "I'm sorry about your parents," I said to break the silence. "They aren't fair."

"Don't be. They were never parents to begin with."

I looked at him over my shoulder. "I don't understand. It sounds like you've accepted it."

His gaze was directed at the sky. "I did, a long time ago. I don't really want to talk about my parents."

I nodded and looked at the pond. The fallen leaves decorated its moon-kissed surface in an enthralling pattern. It was magical and peaceful, and if the circumstances had been any different, I'd have considered this moment romantic. I closed my eyes and let myself imagine it. I let myself imagine things were different; Blake would embrace me from behind and I would sink into his body.

I could almost feel him behind me, and I opened my eyes, filled with a crushing and almost unbearable longing. Dog footsteps disturbed my reverie, and I turned my head to find a Rottweiler right next to me.

I raised my eyebrows. Where had this fella come from? He darted his tongue out and wagged his tail, before he sat down in a pose that told me he was waiting for me to pet him. I sat on my haunches.

"Hello," I cooed as I stroked the fur between his ears. "You're such a good boy—or girl." I grinned over my shoulder at Blake.

"That's a first," he said, standing up with his arms crossed over his chest, his brows raised. He stopped right behind me, and I whipped my head back, my heart doing a furious dance in my chest. He was too close!

"What?" I asked, hoping I didn't sound as flustered as I felt.

"That Badass likes someone other than me."

I laughed and met his gaze over my shoulder. "You named your dog Badass?"

His face remained impassive. "He does a good job at scaring people away."

"This dog right here? He's a sweet baby! Look at him! All ready for cuddles." I shifted onto my knees and leaned toward him, petting his head and neck with both hands.

"As I said, you're the only person who's gotten to see him like this besides me."

"I guess that's because animals love me for some reason."

"I'm not surprised," he said incredibly gently, causing my stomach to backflip. I could feel his eyes on me, but I dared not look at him and see the expression on his face.

I giggled when Badass licked my hand. "You like this? Oh, yes you do. Yes you do." I rubbed his neck and head, enjoying this as much as him. I just loved cuddling pets.

Blake shifted to my side, and when I glanced at him, the fierce look in his eyes brought color to my face. It was like he was entranced by me, and it was so intense I grew all shy. I bent my head so my hair could hide me from his gaze, every part of me hot.

"Why doesn't he like anyone?" I asked under my breath.

"He was beaten and hanging on for dear life when I found him on the street. I took him to the emergency vet for surgery and decided to keep him if he survived. He recovered physically, but the beating left him traumatized enough not to let anyone close to him."

My chest filled with sympathy for Badass, and I wished I could do anything to remove his pain and help him regain trust in people. At the same time, Blake's words struck a chord in me because it was like this wasn't only about Badass. It felt like Blake could relate to Badass more than it might seem.

"I'm sorry to hear that," I said quietly as I caressed Badass's ears. At least he had Blake, who'd taken him in and took care of him. I could feel myself melting at this fact, falling more for the side of Blake he hid from the world.

Blake crouched next to me, and his fragrance hit me like a heavy gust of wind, robbing me of breath. He reached out to pet Badass's back, and our hands brushed against each other. A zapping sensation coursed through my arm. I retracted my hand like I'd been nipped by fire, unable to hide how much he affected me.

He looked at me. "Why did you come here?"

I glanced away from him. "You know why. My parents and I were invited—"

"You could've refused to come. You should've refused."

I dug my nails into my palm, sliced with cold and hurt. The previous night had shoved my illusions away, making it obvious that he and I would never work. Yet I was still hurt by his words.

"And miss your warm welcome?" I stood up. "Don't worry, Blake. I assure you this is the last time I step into your house."

He rose to his feet and folded his arms over his chest. "You don't get it." He ran his hand through his hair. "It's getting harder for me to be near you when we can't be together."

He took a step closer to me, and the distance between us became just a space that begged to be reduced to nothing. I was trembling, divided between wanting him and the same old hesitation.

"You have no idea what I want to do to you." He threaded his fingers through my hair, and a sweet ache suffused my chest. "But it wouldn't lead us anywhere."

I crossed my arms and glanced at Badass, who didn't move from his spot as he watched our exchange. "Right. Because of your promise of revenge."

"Yes."

"Promise to who?"

He dropped his hand. His eyes regained their previous hard edge. "Jessica," he growled.

"To who?" I repeated, intent on getting to the bottom of this.

He looked away. "I can't tell you."

I grabbed the railing, tears pricking my eyes. He had no reason to confide in me; however, it hurt so much. I closed my eyes.

"I can ask you what your revenge is for and why you're so hellbent on it, but you'll deny me those answers too, right?"

It took him some time to respond. "Yes."

I took a deep breath. The sky was getting cloudy, the lights of the stars diminishing little by little. Icy fear and pain fenced my world.

"That's okay," I said, bracing myself for what was about to happen. "Because I think I already know."

He was quiet behind me. Too quiet. And then he said in a strained voice, "What do you mean?"

I turned around. "It's about Emma, right?"

His bewildered look told me everything I needed to know. "How did you...?"

I was right. His revenge was about Emma and their kidnapping. Pain unlike anything before hit my chest.

I forced myself to maintain eye contact. "Last Saturday, your parents invited my family to your house for dinner."

He frowned. "That was *your* family?"

"Yes."

I clasped my shaky hands together, feeling too small. My throat constricted, rebelling against the words that were about to come out, but I had to push them out and come clean.

"I had to use the bathroom, so the maid took me to the one on your floor. Being so close to your room...I got curious. You weren't home so I...I went inside."

He winced. "You did *what*?"

I recoiled and pressed myself against the railing. Badass stood up to his feet, sensing something was wrong.

"What did you do in my room?"

I stared at my feet, ashamed of myself. "I went to your desk. I saw some photos sticking out of the manila folder along with the 'Never forget' note and the photo of Emma and you."

His face twisted with a mix of emotions: incredulity, confusion, anger, and then a silent fury that was more tangible with each passing second. My heart took off at a gallop.

"I was going to leave then, I swear, but I accidentally bumped into the mouse, and your laptop screen lit up...there was a video in an open folder—"

"You accidentally bumped into the mouse," he stated flatly.

"Y-Yes."

"You sneaked into my room, looked through my stuff, and stumbled upon that video."

I could barely look at him. "Yes."

"Did you play it?"

The familiar expression of hatred had returned to his face with a vengeance, and I gripped the railing behind me. "I..."

"Did you?!" He got up in my face, slamming his hands against the railing on both sides of me. Badass whimpered.

I bit into my lip so hard I thought I'd draw blood. "Yes. I'm so sorry. I—"

He slammed his fist against the railing. "You had no right!" His scream pierced through the night, and I flinched. Badass let out another whimper, moving around us restlessly. "You had no fucking right!"

Tears blurred my vision. "I know. I'm sorry."

"You know? You're *sorry*?!" He hit his fist against the railing again, and I cried out when I saw blood flowing out of the ripped skin on his knuckles. Badass began barking.

"Was that payback?! Did you do that to get back at me for everything I've done to you?"

"No! No, it wasn't like that." I sniffed and brushed a tear from my cheek. "I admit I told myself I wanted to find something to use to my advantage, but that wasn't it. I just wanted to find out more about you."

He glared at me with hatred that destroyed all the warmth his kisses and loving touches had created. "You wanted to... What the fuck is wrong with you? You had no right to go into my room and snoop around. You had no right to watch that video."

Tears started cascading down my cheeks uncontrollably. "I know that now. I really know that, and I regret doing it. Back then, when I saw that thumbnail—you tied up to that chair—I just couldn't ignore it. I got so worried. But I know it was bad and stupid of me to do that. I'm so sorry."

Without thinking, I raised my hand and touched his shoulder to console him, but he flinched and stepped back, shoving my hand off his shoulder.

"Don't touch me!"

He took a few more steps away from me, staring at me with disgust. I placed my hand over my mouth to stifle my cry. I wanted to dissolve into nothing. I was so stupid for digging into his past.

The barking noise became almost unbearable, and Blake shouted at Badass, "Shut the fuck up!"

The dog whimpered, tucking his tail between his legs, and scurried away.

We fell into silence that was even more unbearable than the previous noise, and it took everything in me not to hightail it out of here. His gaze iced over.

"Did you tell anyone about Emma or what you saw?"

"No." He looked like he didn't trust me. "I swear to you I haven't told anyone about Emma or the kidnapping, Blake." I sniffed, my chest heavy. "I'm really sorry. I didn't want to hurt you. I never wanted to hurt you, and when I saw what happened—"

"Don't fucking say it. I don't want to hear you say a word about it, because if you do, I swear you'll regret ever meeting me."

I lowered my head. This time, I was unable to hide from him even behind the thick strands of my hair. My fingers were clutching the metal railing too tightly, and it hurt, but the physical pain couldn't compare to what

I felt inside. I was a sobbing mess. I tried hard to hold back my tears, but I couldn't.

I wished I could turn back time. I had thought I'd be ready to suffer the consequences, but I wasn't, and it was hard seeing him look at me like this. Just like in the beginning.

"I was such an idiot." He let out a short chuckle. "And here I thought you were someone I could actually trust. I let myself believe maybe, *maybe* if our lives had been different, we could've been together." He shook his head. "I should've never let you in."

I cried out. It was too much. His words, his hate, the distance between us...it was too much.

"I want you to get out of here and never talk to me again."

I couldn't look him in the eyes, scrambling away, but I halted when I noticed Daniela standing next to the pond. Her brows were tightly drawn together as she observed us with her arms crossed over her chest.

"Blake? What is this commotion about?" she asked, shifting her gaze between Blake and me.

I couldn't stay there a second longer. I hurried away, blind with tears.

Chapter 21

I ARRIVED AT SCHOOL with a heavy weight in my stomach on Monday morning. I'd spent all of Sunday locked up in my room crying, unable to get my mind off the betrayed look on Blake's face. I'd effectively ruined my chances of getting him to trust me, and even though I knew I should just let it go, I couldn't. I couldn't be okay with how things had gone between us. I wished he could know I'd never wanted to hurt him with my foolish act. So I kept looking for him around school, feeling the burning need to apologize, or just explain myself.

I didn't see him before U.S. history. I'd thought I could try to talk to him then, but he entered the classroom right before the teacher arrived. He didn't look in my direction even once as he headed for his seat, and my heart contorted so painfully.

The teacher announced a pop quiz, and the classroom erupted in groans and sighs. My heart, however, sped up for a totally different reason. My hands started shaking when the students passed the papers back and I took them from the student in front of me. Slowly, I turned to give them to Blake.

His eyes were on his desk as he reached out, much to my disappointment. But then our hands brushed, and his eyes flitted to mine. I inhaled sharply. There was pain in them, but it was mixed with something else—something that stirred me from the inside out. However, it was so fleeting I could've easily imagined it. His gaze hardened, and he snatched the quizzes away from me, dousing any warmth I'd felt.

The teacher announced the start, but I couldn't concentrate. I was getting jittery. It was torture sitting so close to him, being aware of his every move. Foolishly enough, I hoped our bodies would touch accidentally, my breath catching in my throat each time he leaned closer to me. But they didn't, and that left me with an empty feeling that only grew stronger by the end of class. I could practically feel his hostility emanating toward me.

My courage to apologize almost fizzled out when the bell rang. I picked up my stuff with trembling hands as I thought about what I could say to start a conversation, but he rushed out of his seat and the classroom before I could even call out to him.

I sighed as I stood up and followed Marcus out. He was telling me something as we walked in the direction of Blake's locker, but I wasn't paying attention to him as I watched Blake open it.

"Sorry, what did you say?"

"I think I totally failed that quiz."

I pressed my books against my chest. "That's too bad. I hope I didn't. I answered all the questions, but I don't know if I got them right."

"Ms. Gentry does this all the time. Will she ever get tired of it?"

"I don't think so."

His phone chimed, and he grinned when he looked at the screen. "It's Kev."

I smiled. "Oh? What does he say?"

"He's waiting for me at my locker."

"You two are so cute."

Kev and Marcus were a couple now. They'd gone out on Sunday and started dating, and I couldn't have been happier for them. It was hard to miss how Marcus's eyes started glowing; all his worries disappeared as if nothing mattered in the world for him but Kevin. A dull pain pervaded my chest. It looked so easy—having someone who could bring you the sun when there was only rain. Someone who wouldn't make your heart beat with pain and longing more intense than anything.

His grin got bigger as he texted Kev back. "You think so?"

My eyes moved over to Blake, who stood with his back turned to me as he rummaged through his locker. "Absolutely."

"It's all thanks to you," Marcus said.

"What do you mean?"

"You told me to talk to Kevin. I didn't have the guts to do it, but you helped me, so thank you for that."

Aww, he's sweet. "No need to thank me. I just pushed you in the right direction a little, that's all."

"Still, you're like our Cupid or something." I chuckled. "I'll be going now. Can't keep my man waiting."

My man. So, so cute.

I winked at him. "Sure. We can't let that happen." He laughed, waving goodbye.

My smile diminished as he disappeared down the hallway, my gaze shifting to Blake. Only a few feet separated us now as I neared the corner, but it could've been miles and it would've been the same. My pulse thrummed hard in my throat. This was my chance.

But before I could approach him, some guy rounded the corner, and I bumped into him. The books he carried crashed to the ground, scattering all around.

"Watch it," he snarled as he pushed me away, which attracted everyone's attention.

I barely managed to catch myself before I fell, supporting myself against the locker.

He hovered above me. "Why don't you look where you're going? Look what you've done!" He pointed at the books.

I didn't get to answer him because Blake rushed over and shoved him against the lockers, leaving me speechless.

"What do you think you're doing?" Blake hissed, grabbing the collar of his shirt. My pulse increased rapidly.

He's jumping in to help me.

"Let me go, man." He fought to set himself free, but Blake was much stronger than him.

Blake's fingers tightened around his collar. "I asked, what do you think you're doing?"

The guy cursed into his chin. "You saw it. That stupid bitch didn't watch where—"

"The fuck did you just say?" Blake slammed him harder against the locker, and the guy's head collided hard with the metal.

He cried out. "Hey, I—"

Blake got in his face. "You don't get to call her that. You don't get to even touch her. Got it?" My heart leapt in my chest at hearing his words. The guy didn't reply immediately, and Blake pressed his arm against his throat. "Got it?!"

The guy tried to remove Blake's arm with no success, his face going red. "Yeah, man! I got it! I'm sorry!"

"You better be. If I ever see you near her again, I'll break your jaw."

"All right! All right. I won't even look her way."

"Good." He shoved him away hard, sending him crashing against the ground. His fists were clenched as he watched him pick up his books and leave in a rush, and something in my chest grew tight. He glared at the crowd that still watched. "What are you all looking at? Fuck off!"

The students were quick to disperse, muttering among themselves about what had just happened, while all I could do was just stare at Blake with parted lips and an increased heartbeat.

A trembling smile took shape across my face. He'd just helped me, despite everything. I didn't know what to make of this, but it was hard not to feel hope.

He didn't stop looking in the direction the guy had gone in as I stepped closer to him, having yet to look at me.

I cleared my throat. "Thank you, Blake. I really appreciate what you just did for me."

His hands flexed again. My smile diminished. He didn't move a muscle as he stared straight ahead, and this went on. What was going through his head?

"Blake?"

Without a word, he spun around and moved past me as he returned to his locker, not looking at me even once.

My throat constricted. I went after him. "Blake, wait. I know how things are between us, but I want you to know I'm very sorry. I know how wrong I was, and I wish I'd never done it. I wish—"

"Stop. Talking." He slammed his locker shut and reached for his backpack that was on the ground. "This doesn't change anything," he muttered through gritted teeth as he finally looked at me, carrying anger in his eyes that told me he already regretted helping me. "I meant what I said. Stay away from me."

He turned around and walked away, effectively destroying any hope I'd had.

• • • •

"OKAY, YOU'VE BEEN ACTING weird today. What's going on?" Melissa asked.

Sar and I had gone to Mel's place after school. We were in her room, which was an enormous space that could easily accommodate a plane. Well, almost. It had a balcony that looked over their botanical garden and floor-to-ceiling windows that provided enough light to compensate for all the dark tones in the room. Dark furniture, navy blue walls, a black punching bag, a black bookshelf that took up the entirety of one wall, dark sheets—all of that topped off with black carpet with a skull pattern.

It quite matched my mood at the moment.

"You didn't stay long Saturday morning, so we didn't get to talk," Sar said as she moved to sit across from me on Mel's bed. "Did something happen with Blake on Friday night?"

I gave them the rundown of what had occurred after we left the track, minus the steamy parts, feeling a constant ache in my chest. I'd been able to see the part of Blake I'd never been aware of, and now it was just a memory serving to bring me to tears.

Mel's eyes bulged out. "You ended up kissing?"

I dropped my gaze. "Yes."

She didn't need to say anything because her face was a clear enough message that she didn't approve of it.

"How did it feel?" Sar asked.

A blush spread across my cheeks. "He really knows what he's doing."

Melissa snorted, playing with a pillow on the sofa. "Of course he knows. That guy is a walking prostitute."

Sarah frowned. "That's not helpful, Mel."

"Pardon my mistake. He's not a walking prostitute—he's a walking pro-jerk-stitute." I picked at my nails, unable to look at her as she spoke. "You should've kicked him in the balls and threatened to castrate him if he ever approached you again, not kissed him."

Sarah scowled at her. "Leave it be and try to understand her. She can't help how she feels. And apparently, he can't help how he feels either, and that counts for something, right? He wouldn't have taken her to his favorite place if he hated her."

Mel grimaced. "Yes, but that doesn't change the fact that he abused her for eons. Like I get that he might have feelings for her, which is super twisted, but that doesn't give him a pass to act like he hasn't been a major douche from the start."

"And I know that very well," I told her. "But I'm not you."

She poked her pillow idly. "I know. Sorry. I just don't want him to hurt you."

"What happened after the kiss?" Sar asked.

"Nothing. He brought me here and that was it." I preferred to not mention our argument.

Mel cocked her head to the side. "So are you two on good terms now or what?"

I took a deep breath as a fresh wave of pain washed over me. The betrayed look on his face and the hate in his eyes kept torturing my mind, heightening my regret. I felt like crying, but I had to rein it in.

"Not really."

"Why not?"

I couldn't tell them what was wrong because I would have to reveal Blake's past and his intention to get revenge on his kidnappers. "We just aren't."

"Do you want to be with him?" Sarah asked.

"No."

Mel started clapping. "Someone give this girl an Oscar! That acting—so real!" She wiped the non-existent tears from her face, fake sobbing.

Glancing sideways, I grabbed a pillow and threw it at her. "Shut up."

"I understand how you feel because I also wasn't sure if I could be with Hayden," Sarah said. "I was afraid he would hurt me even more, so I tried to suppress my feelings until I couldn't do it anymore. I decided to risk it and give us a chance. There's always a chance Blake will hurt you, yes, but there's also a chance he will make you the happiest ever."

I just nodded because this discussion was pointless anyway. I took another deep breath to dull the pain in my chest and wrung my hands together. "Anyway, there's something I wanted to tell you."

"You sound like you're going to say you have a husband and two kids," Mel said. Her eyes widened dramatically. "Do you?"

I stuck my tongue out at her. "You're wrong. I have *three* husbands and *ten* children."

"Wow. You're keeping a farm there," she replied, and we fell into a fit of giggles.

"So? What did you want to tell us?" Sar asked.

I stared at my clammy hands, thinking about the right way to reveal this vulnerable part of me. I was finally ready, but my face was already beet red.

"Please don't judge me."

Concern etched into Sarah's features. "We aren't going to judge you, Jess. You know you can tell us anything."

"Yeah, girl," Melissa added. "You have our support 24/7. We're your personal superheroes."

I took a deep breath. "You know I'm going to a therapist for my body image issues. Well, there's something I didn't tell you before. I..." I bit into my cheek. "I may have made myself throw up from time to time." I raised my eyes to look at them, absolutely wary of their reaction.

Sarah's eyes were wide. "Oh no, Jess. How... Why? When did it start?"

I licked my lips. "In eighth grade. My old crush picked on me because of my weight, and at that point, after many unsuccessful diets, throwing up was my only answer." I picked at the pulled thread on my jeans. "Mom sent me to a therapist immediately, and I managed to improve my poor self-image a little, but I always struggled with it. I made myself vomit when it got really hard, just like around three weeks ago. That was the last time I did it."

"Jess," Sarah whispered, touching her hand to my shoulder. I covered her hand with mine and smiled gratefully.

Mel slid off the sofa and jumped up next to me on the bed. "Come here." She pulled me into a tight hug. "Why are you doing that to yourself? I'm not saying you need to lose weight, but if you really want to be slimmer, why don't you exercise? Making yourself throw up is very bad for your health."

I leaned away to look at her. "I know. I really do. I guess the pressure was just too much for me, and this was an easy way to deal with it. But exercising...I tried it, but I never made any progress, and it was hard. Maybe one day I'll try again and be able to stick to it. Then again, I want to love myself the way I am—slimmer waist or not."

"You're right, because pounds come and go, but what matters is what's inside you," Sar told me.

"Sar, the wise one, is right," Melissa said. "Don't rush it. Work on yourself gradually, and you'll see that you'll be happier in time."

I giggled. "You both sound like counselors."

Mel winked at me. "I'll start charging you soon."

"How are you feeling now?" Sar asked. "Have you...have you had the urge to throw up again?"

I shook my head. "No. I've been talking about it with my therapist since then, and she's helped me a lot. She helps me focus on the positives and encourages me to follow my dreams. And whenever I have that urge again, she told me the key is in accepting the mistake, learning from it, and moving on instead of regretting my choice."

"She sounds like my therapist," Sar remarked. "She always says to accept mistakes and learn from them."

Melissa grinned. "Your therapists should be besties."

"Maybe they are," I joked. "Anyway, thanks, girls. This helps me a lot."

"Don't thank us, dummy." Mel bumped my shoulder. "I just don't understand why you didn't tell us this before. We would've helped you."

I played with the ends of my hair. "I was afraid you would judge me. Besides, my road to recovery is long because this is so much more than just body issues."

"I know, silly, but still...you're super, super, super beautiful, on the inside and on the outside. Just take care of your health. As my dearest grandma once told me, health is wealth."

I returned her smile. "Thanks, Mel. I've been feeling like a failure recently, but I know I'm so much more than this. I want to fight it."

Mel flexed her bicep. "That's the spirit!"

Sarah's smile was soft. "You're absolutely not a failure. You're kind, smart, and an amazing singer. You have an incredible talent."

I worried my lip between my teeth. "You really think that?"

Her smile grew bigger. "I know that. Besides, how many people have already told you so on your channel? And they're absolutely right—your voice is angelic, and you can convey so much through your songs. I can't wait for the day when I hear your record went platinum."

My chest grew warm at that thought. A platinum record. That was something I wanted more than anything—for me to be able to reach as many people as possible and touch their hearts with my songs.

I could do that. I had to believe in myself.

"I guess my solo next Saturday is the first big step. I'll finally do a public performance, and I'll also use that opportunity to reveal myself on my channel. Kev is going to film it with his GoPro, and I'll post the video on my channel."

Mel snapped her fingers. "Now that's an excellent idea! You're going to kill it."

I smiled, unease already filling my stomach. I really hoped she was right.

Chapter 22

SEVERAL DAYS HAD PASSED, and each was an embodiment of yearning and dejection. Blake didn't even look in my direction, let alone talk to me, treating me like I'd never existed, and I tried to convince myself it was for the best. I kept telling myself none of it would matter once I went to college and started building my future, but deep down, I knew it wasn't all right.

It was hard seeing him pass me in the hallways, talking with others, or even smiling with someone else. It was hard sitting so close to him in U.S. history. Every night, I cried myself to sleep, tortured little by little by the memory of that sunflower field and fantasies of Blake and me in heated embraces, and it was hard to move on.

And then there was the promise that loomed over his life. I saw him arguing with Hayden and Masen at school a few times, managing to hear snippets of their conversations. I couldn't make out much, but one thing was clear—Hayden and Masen were against Blake's desire for revenge. This only doubled the fear I felt for Blake, making it even harder for me to stand aside as he walked straight into something that wouldn't end well at all.

I poured all my energy into my upcoming solo and used those long hours of playing and singing as my outlet. I grew more nervous as Saturday approached, hoping I wouldn't chicken out at the last minute and realize it was too big a step for me to take.

The song was important in more ways than one since it was my confession and means of apology to Blake. He wouldn't allow me to show him how sorry I was, but he'd helped me on Monday, and that had to count for something. I just hoped my lyrics would reach him and prove to him how I truly felt.

The days rolled by quickly, and the school festival arrived with a bang—the opening ceremony in the gym brought the huge but long-overdue surprise that Principal Anders was history. We'd expected him to show up and give a speech, but instead of him, the representative of the new school board took the stage and announced their decision to appoint one of the teachers, Kalifa Aguda, as the new principal. She was a good teacher who actually cared about her students, so this news was a sign of a great change.

Mrs. Aguda spoke about the changes that were becoming effective in the next few weeks, starting with the security cameras they were going to install on Monday and the anti-bullying training all the staff had to undergo. This was followed by loud applause, and then the festival officially started.

The school had organized various activities for the weekend, now crowded with students and parents who moved from one activity to the next. The psychologists manned the booths in the lobby, and both victims and bullies were encouraged to share their stories. Posters that spoke about the short- and long-term consequences of bullying were plastered all over the hallways, and some students wore badges and shirts with slogans like "Say no to bullying, Say yes to unity" and "Bullying—Nay. Peace—Yay."

Melissa, Shreya Wilkins, and the rest of the student council had contacted a few students who were willing to talk publicly about their experiences with bullying, and they were part of the workshop scheduled for later in the day. Showings of bullying documentaries took place on the second floor, and to attract more people, our biology teacher promised free popcorn and soda for the viewers.

The stands for students to sell their crafts or used belongings were placed near the lobby, and all earnings went to anti-bullying organizations. Mel, Sar, and I were stationed at one of the stands. We sold clay figurines and Sarah's printed drawings that sat on the mini easel stands. Half of them had already been purchased.

Hayden stopped by to see Sar, and Blake was with him. His hands were stuffed in his pockets as he looked at everything and everyone except me, and I could hardly act normal. I tried to catch his gaze, but it was pointless.

His face didn't reveal his thoughts, but I noticed how worn out he looked. He had dark circles under his eyes, and there was something deeply sad in the depths of them that hammered even more guilt into me.

I didn't see him again until the charity basketball game between East Windsor and our school, in which Blake, Hayden, and Masen played. The game, which was scheduled right before the choir and solo segments, was about to start, and girls couldn't stop swooning over the players, flocking around them like flies to honey.

The excitement hung heavy in the air as Sar, Mel, Kev, Marcus, Steven, and I sat in the first row, and it was hard not to stare at Blake, who looked so hot in his black basketball uniform. I wasn't the only one to stare. Many girls stared, and they stared a lot. A few of them even approached him as he warmed up.

Each time I saw him talking to them, jealousy ate away at me along with possessiveness. He wasn't mine, but that didn't stop me from balling my hands into fists and wishing I didn't have to see him talk to other girls. Not even once did he glance in my direction, and it was hard to delude myself into thinking it didn't affect me.

To divert my thoughts, I looked at Kevin, who sat between me and Marcus. They were holding hands, and I melted for the hundredth time at another display of their affection. Dating hadn't come easy for Kev, especially during the first few days when whispers and curious eyes followed him and Marcus as they walked hand in hand around the school, but Marcus—that adorable guy—dealt with it like a champ, supporting Kevin through everything. He didn't let anyone get to him, and it was touching to see him so protective of Kev.

Kev had changed a bit, becoming slightly more confident. He still chose to talk less, but having Marcus by his side did wonders for his self-esteem. He was starting to accept his sexuality and allow himself to be with whoever he wanted, and I was happy for him.

Warming up to Marcus also helped him relax more around Hayden, and I had a hunch that he wasn't crushing on Hayden or me in the same way as before. I was glad, not only for him but also for Marcus.

I grinned at them. "So, tomorrow will be your week-iversary, right?"

Kevin blushed. He was such a sweetie. "Yes." He pushed his glasses up his nose. "Do p-p-people even celebrate week-iversaries?"

I chuckled. "You two can celebrate them."

"I want to take him for ice cream," Marcus half-joked as he looked at Kev with eyes full of adoration.

"You should," I told him. "Kev is crazy about ice cream no matter what time of year."

"There's this small parlor near the river, Icy Shack," Sar said. "Hayden took me there last week. Their ice cream was to die for."

"I went there." Mel piped in from Sarah's other side. "Their ice cream is the best, isn't that right, Steven?" She glanced at him, who sat right next to her with his head buried in his phone.

He barely looked at her, totally distracted by whatever was on his screen. "What? Yeah, yeah, sure."

Mel rolled her eyes. "Steven's brain.exe stopped working." Steven didn't even hear her, his gaze glued to the device.

"Then we can go there," Marcus told Kev. "What do you think?"

Kev smiled. "Let's do that."

I giggled and placed my hand on Kev's shoulder as I leaned toward him. "Just make sure Kev doesn't eat too much ice cream. He doesn't actually know when to stop."

Kevin flushed, while Marcus chuckled. Out of habit, I glanced at Blake, who stood nearby facing us. He glanced away almost immediately, and my smile vanished. I could have sworn he'd been looking at my hand that was still on Kevin's shoulder.

I retracted it, my heart bouncing. Mel said something, but I didn't hear her as my thoughts spun frantically in my mind. It was that easy for Blake to make me flustered.

Sarah's face lit up when Hayden headed our way, and her starry eyes slid down and up his body. Just like Blake, Hayden attracted girls' attention, but he never looked anyone's way but Sarah's, his gaze smoldering.

He crouched in front of her and placed his hands on her knees, and I couldn't stop a smile from forming on my face. But envy flickered in me a second later, reminding me I wanted the same thing with Blake. My treacherous eyes went to him again. I was extremely nervous about the song I was going to perform, even more so because Blake was going to be in the audience.

"You look like you're about to get me naked right here," I heard Hayden whisper in her ear. I blushed, looking all around the gym as I pretended I hadn't heard that.

"I'll get you naked later," she replied seductively in his ear and kissed his cheek.

My fingers curled into a fist of their own volition. Their exchange brought back a whisper of a memory of Blake's lips on me, and it was almost too much. I closed my eyes and took a deep breath. It was hard to believe that had actually happened and wasn't just a product of my imagination.

The game started ten minutes later, and my eyes sought Blake more often than not. I was high on seeing him play, fascinated by his focus and skills. He and Hayden scored the most points, and when our team won, it wasn't even close. Far from it. The whole gym broke out into cheers and unintelligible shouts, and I jumped to my feet to clap like everyone else with a gigantic grin plastered to my face.

The guys rushed to each other and did a group hug. I shouted words of encouragement along with others, and when Blake looked in my direction, it was like a kick that knocked all the air out of me. Our gazes locked for the first time after almost a week. Our eyes communicated what our bodies wouldn't, and it brought me a burning longing that increased with each second we spent looking at each other.

For a few moments, it was like our argument hadn't ever happened. It was like there was just us and this connection that resonated between us, and the world wasn't so dark anymore.

But then Masen clapped Blake on his back and exchanged a few words with him, forcing Blake's gaze away from me, and the spell was broken. Sarah met Hayden halfway before they went in for a celebratory kiss that was movie-worthy, invoking another painful fantasy of Blake and me together.

My phone vibrated in my pocket. I took it out and unlocked it to find a message from Mom.

We're here.

I looked around the audience in the bleachers, squinting to find my parents in the sea of faces. I spotted them sandwiched between other parents in the second-to-last row. My mom waved at me, and I waved back, getting more nervous. I just wanted them to be proud of me when I started my solo.

"My parents are here," I told Kev.

He pushed his glasses up his nose. "You'll rock, Jess. Th-They and everyone will love it."

I tugged at my shirt and flattened the invisible creases. In around thirty minutes, the solos would start, and I would have to perform in front of everyone. I had to do this. I had to.

"I should've learned my mom's breathing techniques. I think I'm going to hyperventilate."

"Don't s-s-stress about it. You'll do just fine."

"We should've done a duet. It would be easier for me to go out there if I had someone by my side."

"You can do it, Jessica," Marcus cheered. "You know what Ms. Donovan always tells you—your voice is so good you'll do well no matter how you sing."

I sighed. "She was sugarcoating it to get me to relax."

"But she wasn't lying," Kev said. "Your voice is p-perfect."

"Thanks," I said on an exhaled breath then went over to greet my parents.

They were excited to see me perform because this would be my first public performance since sixth grade. Mom had told me quite a few times this morning how proud she was of me and assured me I would do great. Dad had given me a thumbs-up and said he was one hundred percent sure everyone would love my solo.

I took my Martin from Mom, who had brought it for me, and returned to my friends. The guitar had never seemed heavier in my hands than now, and I fiercely hoped my voice wouldn't betray me and my stomachache wouldn't get worse, because I felt like I was going to have diarrhea being this wigged out.

Blake, Masen, and Hayden went with their team for a quick shower and a change of clothes before they came back to the gym, and they arrived just in time for the choir to step out on the court.

The flutters in my belly tripled when they took seats on Steven's other side, and for a few moments, I couldn't move from my seat. I was mortified of drawing any attention to myself, most of all Blake's.

Kevin and Marcus stood up and looked at me with raised eyebrows, and I couldn't delay it any longer. I rose to my feet with my heart working in a wild rhythm.

"You'll nail it, girl." Mel winked at me. "Don't think about anything. Just immerse yourself in your music or whatever poetic thing you artists do." She made some dramatic moves with her arms, as if she was acting in a play.

Out of the corner of my eye, I noticed Blake looking at me, and I stiffened. "Thanks, Mel." My voice wasn't mine, and I had to give myself a quick inner pep talk so I could get my body to move.

Sarah's eyes glowed warmly as she smiled. "You can do it."

I managed to smile back at her in response and finally moved my sluggish legs. My body buzzed with awareness. It seemed like the whole audience stared at me as I joined the choir on the dais and left my guitar on the side for later. I had to stand in the front row because of my small height, which only hiked up my anxiety.

I twisted my hands together and looked over my shoulder at Kevin and Marcus, who stood directly behind me. "I'm so nervous," I whispered to them.

Kev patted my shoulder and gave me a few words of encouragement that managed to dispel some of the tension in me. After Ms. Donovan's short speech, we started our piece, and I was able to relax enough not to mess up as the voices surrounded me in perfect harmony.

Before I knew it, it was over and the solos were next. Shelly was performing first, so Ms. Donovan sat down at the piano that had been brought to the stage to accompany her. We remained standing at our assigned places as a sign of support, and my nerves got more frayed with each minute closer to my performance. I should've gone to the restroom before this. I needed to pee so badly.

I listened to two solos that followed with a pounding heart and an aching stomach because the next and last solo was mine. I was terrified that I was going to sing off-key or play a bad note, and all kinds of nerve-racking scenarios dominated my mind.

Submerged in fear, I didn't even hear Ms. Donovan call me to perform next. Kev had to nudge me to get my attention, whispering that it was my turn, and for a moment, I couldn't move. Every single step was hard as I picked up my guitar and went to sit behind the mic. I clutched the neck of my guitar like it was my only defense against the apocalypse that was going to wreak havoc on me and obliterate the ounce of courage I'd managed to gather.

Kevin stepped in front of me with his GoPro and smiled encouragingly, but all I could think about was that he was going to record my failure. I looked away from the lens, beginning to think it was a bad idea to use this performance to show myself on my channel.

I cleared my throat. "Ah, hello," I said, checking the volume of the microphone. My voice sounded like someone was strangling me. I'd prepared a few sentences to say as my introduction, but my nervousness erased them completely from my mind and I couldn't come up with anything to say.

Everyone was silent, too silent, and the loud drumming of my heart filled my ears. So many unknown faces in the audience melded into a mass of various colors that prevented me from finding my parents, and I had to blink a few times to clear my vision. My breathing quickened. I expected to hear insults tossed out at any moment...

You're fat. You can't sing. Go home. You belong in a zoo, hippo. A wailing cat sounds better than you.

I gripped the microphone stand to adjust it to the right height, almost nauseated. I couldn't do this. I was going to open my mouth and nothing would come out. I was going to mess up my notes. I was going to fail, no doubt.

This was a mistake. How the hell did I think I could do this in front of the whole school?

I clutched my guitar. I felt like I could bolt out of here at any moment, but then Blake's words rushed back to me, reminding me of how important it was to stay.

"Running away doesn't make bad things disappear. Tough it out. Fight back. And even if you get hurt in the process, at least you aren't a pathetic coward in the end."

Mel and Hayden had both told me how important it was to face my fears. I knew it myself, yet I always took the easy way out.

I could feel my muscles unwinding, and more air reached my lungs. I searched the audience again and found my parents. Even from my spot I could see my mom's bright smile, which helped me calm down. They were there and they believed in me.

If I ran away now, without even trying to play, I was going to regret it. I had to push through this. It was an extremely personal song, but if I couldn't perform it now, I couldn't hope to perform any of my songs in the future.

I took another deep breath and looked at Sarah and Melissa, who were smiling at me with their thumbs raised. *Okay, I can do this.*

"I'm Jessica." My voice trembled, but I pushed on. "The song I'm about to sing tells a story that started with bullying but turned into something else. It carries a special message, and I hope you'll like it. It's called 'Trapped.'"

Here goes nothing.

I closed my eyes and moved my fingers over the strings, playing the first few notes. My hands shook so much I was sure I was going to miss some, but the melody that came out was good. It was even more than good. It embraced me and led me away from a place full of insecurities to a place of joy, allowing me to forget my fear.

It started with hate
It ended with love
You and me, we're cornered
In the world of dust
In this endless circle
Our story is like shattered glass

I can't stop loving you
I can't start forgiving you

And I'm trapped
I'm cornered
In this world where there's nothing but our pain
And I'm torn
I'm left to wonder
If this has all been just one big game

Fate has played us well

Between heaven and hell

I'm trapped

I opened my eyes and let them find Blake as I slowed down the tempo before the second verse. I felt a jolt in my stomach when our gazes locked, pulled to him by the same invisible thread that always kept us connected.

Sunflowers bloom
But some loves never do
This is my apology
And last confession to you
Scars run too deep to heal
And all that's left is fear

I can't stop loving you
I want to start forgiving you

And I'm trapped
I'm cornered
In this world where there's nothing but our pain
And I'm torn
I'm left to wonder
If this has all been just one big game

Fate has played us well
Between heaven and hell

Blake's eyes never left mine, and the raw expression on his face sliced me open. It was anguish, awe, and yearning combined together, allowing to me sing my heart out—allowing me to connect to him like never before—and my chest clenched with love for him.

I'm accepting my love as I watch you go
At the corner of past regrets, pain, and sorrow
Just a shade under a starry sky, you and me

And then a kiss
Or two
Or three

And I'm trapped
I'm cornered
In this world where there's nothing but our pain
And I'm torn
I'm left to wonder
If this has all been just one big game

Fate has played us well
Between heaven and hell

I am trapped

I plucked the strings and stopped. My chest was tight with emotions that invited tears to my eyes. I couldn't look away from Blake, truly trapped by his gaze, which conveyed his true feelings. He'd never looked at me like this before—a gaze so tender and immensely soft it almost undid me.

Now he knew. Now he knew I loved him. I'd stripped myself of all the layers of lies, doubts, and restrictions and allowed him to see it. I'd allowed myself to see it, accepting the truth. I loved him.

Applause erupted all around, and I looked at the audience with a start, only now remembering where I was. There were no mocking faces or sneers, only wide smiles and expressions of admiration as they gave me a standing ovation, and relief found its way through me.

I'd been able to pour my soul out.

I'd managed to do my solo in front of everyone and bring the house down.

A wave of self-pride stronger than ever before took over me. I had never felt better in my skin than now.

I grinned at Kevin. Only now did I realize I was shaking so hard. The audience still clapped, which eliminated any remaining doubts or insecurities I might've had.

"You were amazing, Jess," Kev said as he turned off his GoPro. "That was awesome."

"Thank you," I mouthed before standing up to take a bow.

I looked at my parents and felt like I could tear up at any moment because they'd never looked prouder of me than they did right now. Both of them were on their feet as they applauded me fiercely. Mom wiped away a few tears, and I placed my hand against my heart.

I'd always hoped for my parents to look at me this way because of my music, and now that it'd happened, I felt like I could conquer the whole world with my voice and my guitar. I could make my dreams come true. I *would* make my dreams come true.

"Jessica, that was wonderful!" Ms. Donovan told me. "I know talent when I see it, and let me tell you—you're going to be a major star one day."

Her praise meant so much I didn't have the right words to express it. So, I just said, "Thank you, Ms. Donovan."

Mrs. Aguda announced the end of the program, and everyone started dispersing. I stepped off the stage with the other choir members, wearing a permanent smile as they congratulated me on my performance. My steps felt lighter when I reached my friends and let them engulf me in their hugs and shower me with compliments.

"You did a good job," Hayden told me. There was no smile on his face, but I saw approval in his eyes.

"Thanks," I replied sheepishly, and then I finally allowed myself to look in Blake's direction. However, his seat was empty.

My eyes searched for him around the gym before I could stop myself. I couldn't find him anywhere, and my lips went downward. Well, I couldn't have expected him to congratulate me or compliment me, now could I?

My parents approached me and pulled me into their embrace.

"You were amazing, honey," my mom said into my hair, her arms holding me tight. "Your voice is one of a kind." She drew away and rubbed her upper arms. "I still have shivers!"

"We're so proud of you," Dad said with a soft smile as he ruffled my hair.

"Dad! Don't do that!" I pulled away from him and ran my hand over my hair to flatten it. "I spent lots of time fixing it." He let out a chuckle.

"Your solo was the best," Mom told me quietly, checking to make sure Shelly and the other choir members weren't nearby. "The others did well too, but there was something special about your performance. And the song!" She placed her hand across her chest. "So beautiful! So emotional."

I averted my gaze. "Thanks, Mom."

My parents' encouragement meant a lot. It drowned out the previous flare of disappointment that Blake was gone.

For now, his absence didn't matter. I'd managed to break through my fear and win against myself, and nothing was going to ruin that.

• • • •

I WAS HELPING MR. MAYNARD set up some of the props for the next day's conference in the gym, so I stayed at school way after the festival activities were finished. I worked alongside him quietly, counting the minutes until we were done and I could head to Mel's place for another sleepover.

"That will be all, Miss Metts," Mr. Maynard said after a while. "Thank you for your help."

I brushed my dusty palms against my jeans. My legs were killing me from standing the whole day, but not even exhaustion could dull my sense of accomplishment. It had been a great day.

"You're welcome. Have a nice rest of the day!"

"You too."

I headed to the parking lot. I left my jacket unbuttoned because the weather was warm. I was close to my car when I checked my phone for any messages from Mel or Sar, but a sudden chill rushed down my spine, and I stopped.

I looked around. I noticed a few students here and there, but no one was looking in my direction. There was nothing suspicious, yet my body was buzzing with a strange awareness that someone was watching me.

I hurried to my car, glancing over my shoulder every few seconds, but I didn't see anyone. I chuckled at myself internally. I was being paranoid for no reason. No one was watching me. I was just imagining things.

I stopped next to my car and fumbled around in my backpack in search of my keys. Just then, I glanced at my driver-side window and spotted a fuzzy reflection of a vaguely familiar male figure with a cap twenty yards behind me. He was staring at me. With a gasp, I spun around to face him and shrieked when someone's chest materialized right in front of my face.

Pressing myself against my car, I snapped my eyes up and met Blake's gaze.

"B-Blake?"

His face carried a broken expression that made my stomach sink, and my mind filled with countless questions that added to my apprehension. Had the figure been him? No, it couldn't have been because that person had stood in the distance and Blake wasn't wearing a cap.

I peeped around Blake to find the mysterious figure, but there was no one. I shook my head. I hadn't imagined it. I couldn't have...

"What...what are you doing?" He didn't answer; his eyes studied every inch of my face closely, and my cheeks warmed. Only now did I notice his eyes were red. "Blake?"

"You had to make it even harder for me," he said in a hoarse voice. "You had to..."

My chest clenched at how torn he looked. He placed his hands against the roof of my car on either side of my body and hung his head low.

"I don't want to trust you. I don't want to want you... I..." He closed his eyes, his heavy breaths falling upon my cheeks. "I'm sorry."

My breathing quickened. "You're sorry? For what?"

He half-smiled, but it was empty. "For many things. For everything. For always being an asshole. For not having a clue how to feel. After last Saturday, I told myself you were going to stay in the past, but that's a lie, and then that song... Fuck. That song." A tear slid down his cheek, and I just stared dumbly at it, shocked that he was crying. He wiped it away swiftly and leaned back.

"What about the song?" I wanted to hear his answer badly. I wanted to know exactly how he'd felt when I sung it.

Another tear escaped his eye as he returned my gaze. "You and me...trapped. Having feelings neither of us want. Going in circles because we can't stay away from each other."

He cupped my cheek. I knew I should move away, but I couldn't. I didn't want to, and it scared me, but I also embraced it.

"I never trusted you to be the person I hoped you to be," he said. "I blew up on Saturday, searching for any possible reason to hate you more, and you gave me the perfect one."

I licked my lips. "I'm really sorry, Blake. It was so wrong of me to do it for so many reasons. I'm so sorry. Please believe me."

"I know." He palmed my other cheek. "I know. I was so mad, but somehow it doesn't matter. It can't even compare to what I've done to you."

"But it matters. Of course it matters. I never wanted to hurt you. It was stupid and completely wrong. I wish I'd never gone into your room."

He just looked at me, searching desperately for something in my eyes. It seemed he found what he was looking for because a trace of a smile appeared on his face.

"The song is beautiful, Jessica." He inched closer to me, and his gaze moved between my lips and my eyes. "You're beautiful. You're so beautiful, and I didn't even see it. I didn't want to see it. I kept telling myself you were bad, but I was wrong. I was so wrong.

"This week has been shitty for me. I couldn't sleep, and as much as I tried to convince myself that what I said to you on Saturday night was right, it didn't feel right. I wanted to see you." His eyes seared into me. "I wanted to talk to you. And when that guy pushed you, it took everything in me not to grab you and hold you in my arms."

He leaned his forehead against mine, his hands framing my face firmly. His desperation was tangible, and I didn't know what to do. I didn't know what my next step would be. It was like walking on slippery ground in total darkness where even one wrong step could hurt me badly.

I placed my hands over his and removed them from my face. I had to put some distance between us no matter how much I yearned for his proximity. I moved away from him and stopped with my back turned to him.

"I wanted the same, Blake, but then again...I'm scared. One moment, everything is good, and the next, everything is bad. I want to find a middle ground with you, but somehow, it always slips away." I balled my hands into fists, staring off into the distance. "I wish things could be different between us. Ups and downs, ups and downs...when can we get past that?"

He stayed quiet. Each second spent in silence brought me more ache, but then he said, "When we learn to trust each other. I want to trust you. I believe I can trust you. Can you trust me?"

I closed my eyes, fighting against my tears. *Trust.* One seemingly simple thing, but it was so hard to achieve it when you had a bad history with someone. All I knew was his cold side and insults, and I was just beginning to see his other side. But we had to take the first step toward trust in order to achieve it, and I wondered if this was our first step, a bridge to something better.

"I want to trust you," I replied quietly.

I sensed him moving behind me, and then he placed his hand on my shoulder. I snapped my eyes open.

"How about hearing me out first, then?" he asked, sounding hopeful.

I sucked in air. "About what?"

"About everything. From the beginning. My fucked-up past...I want you to know everything."

I struggled to even out my breaths. My body was hyperaware of his nearness, and it was hard to fight the need in me. He wanted to open up to me. He was *ready* to open up.

"You were right," he continued. "All I gave you were half-truths. You gave me your song, your honesty, and now I want to be honest with you."

I took a deep breath as I turned around slowly. "Okay. I'll hear you out."

His lips curled up in a small smile, and it was so painfully beautiful. *He* was beautiful.

"Then come to my house right now."

I angled my head to the side. "Your *house*?"

"Yes."

"But your parents—"

"They're on my dad's business trip for the weekend. He has some conference in Hartford, my mom is with him, and our maids have the day off. No one will interrupt us."

My pulse quickened. Blake and me. In his house. *Alone.* My body warmed just thinking about it.

His eyes turned pleading. "I won't hurt you. I just want you to know the truth."

My mouth turned dry. I stood on the edge, weighing positives and negatives.

"Trust me," he added, almost begging me.

Butterflies ravaged my belly as I took another deep breath.

"Okay. I'll come."

Chapter 23

I PARKED MY CAR BEHIND his Dodge Challenger in his driveway and sent a quick text to Mel to tell her I was at Blake's house. Expecting my phone to blow up with her texts, I put it on silent and followed him into his house.

Blake took me to that beautiful garden, and now in daylight, I could see it in all its glory. I stopped next to the pond and studied the flowers of various colors that adorned the space. The way they mashed together left me in wonder.

He stopped close to me, and my muscles locked up in awareness. "What's your favorite flower?" he asked.

"Take a guess."

His eyes smoldered. "Jasmine."

Warmth rushed to my cheeks at the reminder of that moment in the school basement. "You remember."

"How could I forget?"

My heart jumped in my chest. I bent and plucked a small flower from the grass, looking at it but not seeing it.

"Emma hated flowers." I went still. "She was allergic to them."

I looked at him as I stood up. He carried a sorrowful but soft expression. I was burning to ask him about her, but I hesitated.

I decided to bite the bullet since he'd mentioned her first. "How did you two meet?"

He picked up a small, flat rock from the ground and skipped it across the pond. It jumped four times before it ended up on the other side of the garden. For a second, I thought he was going to refuse to answer, but I was wrong.

"She was the granddaughter of one of our previous maids. We were the same age. She lost her parents when she was four, and she came here to live with the only remaining member of her family." He smiled. "It took me just one glance to decide she was going to be my best friend. We were best friends ever after."

A small pang hit my chest. I knew I shouldn't get jealous of Emma—it was awful—but I couldn't help but compare myself to her. She'd gotten Blake's friendship from day one. I'd gotten only his hatred.

"It sounds like she was a nice girl."

His smile trembled. "She was. She was the most amazing girl."

I pursed my lips, holding back a sigh. He talked about her with so much love.

"And when did you start dating?" I asked tentatively.

"In seventh grade. I had a crush on her for a long time, and that's when I finally found the guts to ask her out. We were fourteen when we got kidnapped."

I pressed my hand over my lips. They were only *fourteen*. I tried to push away the image of Emma on the floor with that monster pressing her against it as he... *No.*

"But why? Why did they kidnap you?"

His eyes were on the pond, becoming glassy. "Money." His voice was monotone, as if he'd said this word countless times before he became detached. "They knew my family was rolling in it, so they made a plan to capture me and demand ransom."

I stifled a cry that burned to escape from my mouth. "Why did they take Emma?"

"She just happened to be with me. They never would've taken her if she hadn't gone out with me that day." He clenched his hand and released it right away, his eyes haunted. I could see it. He was blaming himself.

"That's horrible," I whispered, tears filling my eyes.

He crouched and ran his hand over the surface of the water, creating small ripples. "It was horrible. Day after day, hour after hour...minute after minute that felt like a fucking eternity, and I thought I was losing my sanity. I'd already lost hope we would ever get out of that place alive. We were left in that dark basement for days, and at times, they kept us without food or water. They beat me whenever I refused to listen to them, and sometimes it was so brutal I almost begged them to kill me so I wouldn't have to feel that pain anymore. But I couldn't die. I had to stay alive for her." He stopped moving his hand, keeping it an inch above the water. "They filmed everything and sent my parents the videos as an 'incentive' to make them shell out their money."

My throat closed at his words. His tone was emotionless, but I could feel the stormy emotions twirling beneath that impenetrable shield of his, and I wanted to take all his pain away. I wished for a healing touch that would make all his demons and bad memories disappear.

"But why did it take so long for your parents to pay the ransom?"

"At first, my dad didn't want to yield to them. He thought they were just some rookies who would give up once they saw he wasn't intimidated." He smiled bitterly. "He was wrong."

I didn't know what to say. It was hard to believe his father was ready to gamble his son's and Emma's lives just so he wouldn't be cornered into giving in to their demands.

"You saw that video. That was the eleventh day. After..." He closed his eyes. He made a motion like he was trying to grab the water, only to clench his hand so hard the veins on the back of his hand bulged out. "After her death, they kept me there for three more days, until my parents finally handed over the money. I don't even remember the last day, because they beat me to the brink of death and I lost consciousness. I woke up at the hospital."

I was shaking with silent tears that ran unchecked down my cheeks. My chest ached with dull pain that only pulsated stronger.

"Those days were a new kind of nightmare. I went crazy, raging and screaming at them to kill me because I didn't want to live. I didn't deserve to live. She was gone. She died because of me, and I was so mad, so full of anger. They had to strap me to the bed until they were sure I wasn't going to kill myself."

I pressed my hand over my chest. It hurt so much.

"Life wasn't the same after that," he concluded, standing up.

A flock of birds rushed across the sky, wonderfully free and uncon-strained by the cage that life could be. The hues of orange, purple, pink, and red colored the horizon as the day gave way to night—a beautiful sight that contrasted with the ugliness of Blake's past.

"I'm sorry, Blake. I'm so sorry for everything you had to go through. I'm sorry for Emma."

He finally turned to look at me; his face was ghostly pale. His eyes scanned over mine, tracing my tears. "You're crying. Why?"

I took a tentative step toward him. I wanted to pull him into a hug and tell him everything was going to be all right.

"Because I feel for you. I feel for Emma. I wish neither of you had gone through any of that. When I saw that video…" I wiped off the tears, but they kept coming. "It was monstrous. It was heartbreaking. I'm so sorry."

He watched me silently with a blank face. He turned away and looked at the sky.

"My parents kept everything under wraps, you know? No police, no media, *nothing*. No one knew about it. They did everything they could to keep my father's reputation and career intact, letting my kidnappers get away with it."

"But what about…?"

"What?"

"What about Emma? The police must've been notified about her death."

"They weren't notified, because the kidnappers had disposed of her body somewhere."

I cried out. She hadn't even had a proper burial.

"Her grandmother wanted to bring those people to justice, but she had a stroke a few days after they released me. She died."

I gave up on restraining myself and closed the distance between us. I brushed the remaining tears off my face as I placed my hand on his shoulder, remembering too late it was a wrong move.

He flinched and spun around to face me. "*Fuck.* Don't touch me like that," he hissed through his teeth. "Don't ever touch my shoulder from behind."

I cursed myself internally. "I'm so sorry," I whispered. "I won't do it again."

His brows drew tight. "I don't like being touched like that. I can't stand it."

"Why?"

He inhaled a long breath and released it with a curse. "Because that's how they got to me when they kidnapped us. Emma and I were walking together when someone approached us from behind and grabbed my shoulder before they knocked me unconscious. And now it's my phobia. Just like the phobia of basements."

I intertwined my fingers together. "I'm sorry, Blake. I wish there were something I could do to help—with your phobias, with everything. It sounds ridiculous because I know I can't do anything, but still...I'm here if you need me."

There was something in his eyes; it was like ice thawing in the sun, layer after layer. It held me still and left me short of breath.

"You're here if I need you...even after everything I've done to you." Slowly, he took my hand in his, never looking away from me. "I was such a fool. I did the worst things to you, and here you are, offering help to someone who doesn't even deserve it." He shook his head, smiling to himself, but the smile was self-reproaching. "All these years I've felt alone. I had family and friends, but they could never fill that void inside of me. I was always empty, but now, with you..."

I held my breath. "With me...?" I spurred him on, too curious to know.

"We were enemies. We have every reason not to be around each other. You have every reason to hate me. But right now, with you, I feel this is how it's supposed to be." He caressed my palm with his thumb. "And I like the feeling."

I observed our connected hands. I had so many things I wanted to say, but the words were stuck in my throat. He was completely opening up to me, allowing me to see much more than I'd ever hoped for.

I cleared my throat. "I also can't lie to you and say I've gotten over our past, because I haven't gotten over all the things you've done. Some of my scars are still fresh, but all I knew until now was running away from you and blaming you. I don't want to feel bitter any longer and let it poison me. So I want to start over. You can be sure I won't betray you. I won't tell anyone what you've just told me."

A ghost of a smile appeared briefly on his face as he held my gaze. "I know. I knew it the moment you sang those words as you looked at me like I was your everything. In front of the whole school...so brave."

I stopped breathing, growing hot under his eyes. I was taken back to that moment on the stage when we looked at each other, bound by something that was stronger than us or our past. We were both puppets of the irony that led our lives, for how could something so pure as my feelings for him come out of ugliness? How could my enemy turn into someone I wanted to protect?

"Why are you giving your heart to me? I don't deserve you." His words were laden with anguish.

I pulled my hand out of his, blushing. "It's not like I chose this. I didn't choose how I feel, but then again, I believe in second chances. I believe if you want to change, you deserve a second chance."

The briefest glimpse of hope illuminated his face, but then his eyes darkened and he turned away. "It's too late for a second chance."

My breathing halted. "What do you mean by that?"

"I already told you about my promise. I intend to keep it."

My heart squeezed hard. "You want to get revenge on your kidnappers."

"Yes. They got away with it, but not anymore. I've been searching for them for years, and now that I finally found them, I'll get justice for Emma."

Fear invaded my every pore as my eyes followed the ridges of the tense muscles in his back. The scary voice deep within me told me this wouldn't end well.

"That's why you had those photos—you're keeping tabs on them." He nodded. "And that video? You were watching it that day. Why?"

He didn't reply immediately. He took a deep breath in and gave me a searing gaze. "Because I started thinking about a certain girl a little too much, allowing myself to imagine things that aren't in the cards for me." My stomach gave a little jump. "I needed a reminder so I wouldn't forget what's the most important."

Never forget.

"That's why you wrote that note? Never forget?"

He nodded. I closed my eyes for a brief second. I wanted to revel in his words, but I didn't let that distract me from the more pressing matter.

"So you're going to get justice for Emma at the cost of your life? But what do you plan to do?"

The short silence that followed my words was like a premonition of the dark.

"I'll go to their homes and kill them."

I plastered my hands over my mouth, crying out. "No, you can't be serious."

He turned to face me. "I'm very serious."

"But you aren't a murderer. You aren't like that."

He took a step closer to me; his eyes were hard and unforgiving. "And how would you know who I am? How would you know what's inside of me?" He hit his chest with his fist. "For years, I've lived with this poison. For years, I've had this rage that needs to be released. I can't live with this injustice anymore."

"And what do you plan to do? Just barge in all alone?"

He didn't respond, but he didn't need to. His face told me everything I needed to know, and an invisible hand gripped my heart and twisted it painfully.

"That's why you don't want to go to some faraway college," I said. "You want to stay here so you can exact your revenge on them."

"I've never even cared about college. I knew once I found those sons of bitches, there were only two alternatives: kill them and end up in the slammer or die trying."

Fresh tears poured down my face. He was ready to give up his life and future for the sake of dealing with his past. He was ready to kill—

I rushed toward him and grabbed his forearm. "You can't do that. You can't!" I raised my voice, becoming hysterical. "I understand how much you love her, and I understand the injustice, but the authorities need to handle them. You can't ruin your life—"

"Don't you get it?!" He grabbed my upper arms and pulled me against him, his eyes growing teary. "I can't keep living if I don't do it! That was the only reason I pulled through and found the strength to keep living, and each time I wanted to give up, I had that video to remind me not to. My revenge is the *only* reason I didn't kill myself a long time ago."

I choked on air. The agony, the fear, the suicidal thoughts... I hadn't known he held so much pain inside of him. I hadn't known it ran so deep.

My fingers clutched his shirt. "No, *no*. Don't say that. Don't. You're so much more than this. So much more."

Tears overflowed his eyes and slid down his cheeks. "Really? Says the person I bullied the shit out of for six months. Six fucking months." He released me and stepped away, brushing off his tears. "I'm no better than those people."

I grimaced. "Do you even hear yourself? Are you actually putting yourself on the same level as those murderers and rapists?"

He winced, his pale face contorting with agony. He took a deep breath and then another, clenching his hands into fists.

"I have to be on their level if I want to deal with them."

I caught his arms. "You're not a killer, Blake. You're not. Please don't do it. I... If you do that, I..." I sobbed, suffocating with pain. "If you do that..." I couldn't even finish the sentence.

He raised his hand and threaded his fingers through my hair. "I know, and it hurts so much." He brought his other hand to my cheek. "It hurts knowing I'm doing this to you." He rested his forehead against mine. "How things have changed. Everything was easier before I met you. Even when you arrived, it was easier because I hated you. You were nothing to me. But then I started having these feelings for you, and now? Now I feel like shit because I want you to be happy, but I can never make you happy. And you shouldn't worry about me, because I don't deserve to live after everything I've put you through."

I grasped his shirt. "No, don't say that. I can't believe you're actually thinking that. Of course you deserve to live, so don't say something so stupid." I shook with tears, clutching the material in my hands like it was my lifeline.

"Don't cry," he whispered. "You've cried more than enough because of me."

"And how do you want me to react, Blake?" I pulled away to look at him. "You tell me all of this and expect me to...what? Support your plan for revenge? You're going up against murderers only to become one! You know this could get you killed, yet...yet..."

I stopped, letting my words dissolve into nothing. I couldn't convince him to give up on his revenge. No matter what I said, it wouldn't change a thing. I could see the resolve in his eyes, could hear it in his words. There was no other way for him. He didn't even want to try another way.

Maybe he was physically away from that basement, but mentally...mentally, he was still there, trapped in that dark room that now owned his life.

"There is really nothing I can do or say to make you reconsider?" I asked in a trembling voice.

He ran his hands down his face and exhaled loudly. "Don't do this to me. I can't even think about any other alternative, not after all these years. That's why you should forget about me. I brought you here to make you see we can't be together. You should fall for someone else. Not me."

My lips twisted into a smile of pain. I was crumbling inside. I'd never had him, but I still felt like I was losing him, and it was slowly tearing me apart.

"Yet whenever I'm around any other guy, you're jealous. Are *you* able to forget about me?"

His eyes darkened with so much longing it felt like a caress on my skin. Like the touch of his fingers that now trailed my arms to rest on my shoulders.

"I tried so hard these days, but it was impossible. All I wanted was to kiss the hell out of you." He leaned in and pressed his lips to my forehead. The touch was so light, but it had a powerful impact on me nevertheless.

I let out a small, hoarse chuckle. "And there I was, hoping you would look at me at least once."

"I wanted to do that and a lot more, so badly. You were sitting in front of me in U.S. history, and I couldn't think about anything but you. A few times, I was so close to pulling you into some classroom so I could do what I've fantasized about for so long, but I had to stay away from you. It was better for both of us."

Heat surged through me, awakening all my nerves and alleviating the pain. "And what have you fantasized about?" I was playing with fire here, but I couldn't resist. It was stronger than my reason.

He wound his arms around my waist and pulled me closer. The air between us slowly became charged. I sank into him, basking in the feel of our bodies against each other.

"I've fantasized about having all of you." He leaned down and pushed my hair to the side. His lips skimmed over my skin delicately. He groaned. "Don't do this to me."

"Do what?"

"Tempt me like this. I told myself I wouldn't be selfish. You don't deserve more pain after everything I've done to you."

He started to pull away, but something in me reached the bursting point, and I grabbed his shoulders to keep him close to me. "And what if I want to? What if I want the illusion? Just for a little while."

His eyes grew dark and dropped to my lips. "You don't know what you're saying. It's only going to make things worse for us."

Yes, it was going to make everything worse, but now I understood what he'd meant when he said we were on borrowed time. The clock was ticking, rushing us toward our final separation, and my heart won over reason. What was one moment of passion? One moment of indulging in what I'd wanted so badly? I wanted any piece of him, no matter how fleeting and small it was—no matter how selfish or imprudent I was—just for a little while before our time ran out.

All caution cast aside, I pressed my palms against his chest. His heart pounded hard beneath my hands, tempting me to lean in and kiss the spot right over it. "But you wanted the illusion too, that night at the sunflower field. So what's different this time?"

He frowned. His expression was torn as he pondered my words, his desperate eyes reaching all of me, and then...

"Fuck." He grabbed my face, giving in. "It's not fair. I shouldn't have fallen for you. I shouldn't have even met you. Why is life playing this cruel joke on us?"

I could hardly breathe. My chest was tight with need for him.

"Maybe that's life telling you not to go through with your revenge," I whispered, holding on to the thread of hope that he would reconsider. "To keep on living because you have so much to live for."

He grimaced, his gaze moving over each inch of my face. "You have no idea, Jessica. You have no idea how hard it is."

My hand clasped his shirt. "But it can get easier in time. It has to."

I propelled myself up on my toes and kissed his cheek, letting my lips linger on his skin. I started to pull away, but he grabbed my head with both hands and claimed my lips, creating shards of pleasure deep within me. I responded immediately, kissing him back like it was my first and last time doing so. Our bodies entangled as our hands fought to touch more and more, and we lost ourselves in the desperation of the moment.

"You're turning my world upside down," he said between kisses.

"Likewise."

He moaned and left open-mouthed kisses along my jaw as his hands slid down to rest on my back. "I want you so much I can't hold myself back anymore." He nibbled my neck. "So, if you don't want me...just say it. Say it now—"

I claimed his lips in response and kissed him urgently. His words and kisses aroused me to the point where I couldn't go on without having him. He lowered his hands even further and cupped my butt, pressing me against him, and the heat eliminated the cold that'd resided in me the last few minutes. It helped me forget the cruel reality for at least a little while. None of it mattered in this moment.

"Say it, Jessie," he growled impatiently.

"I want you, Blake," I said, quietly but with determination, letting him know I wasn't going anywhere.

That was all he needed to grab my hand and yank me after him, darting out of the garden. The journey to his room was filled with kisses and fervent touches that stripped me of more reason and blurred the rest of the world. By the time we reached it, I was completely delirious for him.

The dazzling rays of sunset bathed the room through the full-length windows, with the shades of purple, orange, and yellow cascading over the floor and the furniture. I got flutters in my belly at the thought that I was in his room again, closer to him than I'd ever gotten before.

Blake took our jackets off, pinned me against the wall, and kissed me hard, our tongues dancing together to the tune of our passion. His hands made a journey across my arms, waist, and hips, never coming to a stop, and I felt like I was going to combust at any moment. His lips slid slowly across my cheek and jaw as they planted kisses on their way to my neck, which strummed my nerve endings.

"I want to feel every inch of you," he said in a husky voice that rumbled against my skin. He sank down to his knees and wrapped his arms around me.

My eyes rounded. "Blake?"

He raised his head to look at me. His eyes were pleading and full of need. "I want to kiss you everywhere."

He kissed me over my shirt, right above the waistband of my jeans, and I let out a moan, heat pooling in between my thighs. I grabbed his head to pull him closer, but then I remembered my body issues. He was going to see all my imperfections, which would certainly put him off.

"Wait." I tried to push away from him, but his hands firmly wound around me to keep me in place. "Don't kiss me there."

His eyes softened as he looked at me. "Kiss you where? Here?" He placed another kiss on my stomach. I gripped his hair. "Or here?" He kissed my right love handle. "Or maybe here?" He leaned to the other side and kissed my left love handle, and to my surprise, I was starting to relax.

His lips curled into a loving smile. "You're beautiful." He placed his hand on my stomach and moved it down only to stop inches above my core. My insides clenched. "Every part of you, no matter how big or small, and I want to prove it to you."

He raised my shirt slowly, never taking his heated eyes off of mine, and peppered my belly with tiny kisses that had me close to begging for more. Just like that night at the sunflower field, all doubts ceased to exist under his gaze and touches, and I stopped resisting the pleasure. There was no disgust on his face as he looked at my stomach fat, just lust. It made me feel beyond desirable, and I gave up on the thought of sucking in my belly so I would appear slimmer.

"I can't erase my insults or fix the damage, but I can try to make it up to you. I can try to show you how beautiful and sexy you are to me."

He unzipped my jeans and pulled them down bit by bit, his breaths coming out more quickly. I could see the coiled tension in his muscles that told me he was restraining himself and going slowly only because of me, and my heart swelled with a sudden rush of love. I was mesmerized as I watched him pull off my jeans and discard them on the floor; I'd never seen this Blake before.

He smiled when his gaze landed on my pink floral panties. "Pink and flowers...I should've known."

I blushed. "Is there something wrong with that?"

His smile illuminated his whole face. "No, I love it. It's even better than I imagined."

I bit my lip to stifle a moan, but then he surprised me when he placed my leg over his shoulder and started kissing my inner thigh, moving his lips even over my cellulite. He looked at me like every bit of me was perfect, and I believed him. I believed all my imperfections were perfect to him, and it was empowering. Maybe I didn't have a thin waist or slim thighs, but I could make this sexy guy look at me this way.

I closed my eyes shut and tilted my head back as my hands reached to grab his hair. He took his time cherishing my skin, sliding his lips up and down my thigh slowly, each time coming so close to my core only to pull away. I was seconds away from begging him to kiss me where I needed it the most.

Just when I thought I couldn't take it anymore, he pressed his lips over my panties, kissing me right *there*, and my world spun.

"*Blake.*" I sucked air in as I returned his fervid gaze.

"I've wanted this for a very long time," he whispered, his eyes incredibly dark. He pushed my panties aside and pressed his lips directly onto my heated flesh, and my whole body jerked with the sizzling bolt of pleasure.

I started to shake uncontrollably, trying to comprehend how something could feel so amazing. He made me feel something so intense and addictive that overwhelmed all my senses, and I wished these seconds could stretch into forever. I wished there was no tomorrow that separated us, only today and this sheathing warmth that seemed boundless.

I climaxed with a scream that tore out of my throat and held him tightly until the last aftershock ripped through my body and ebbed into a haze of ecstasy. His eyes never left mine as he picked me up, carried me across the room, and deposited me on the edge of his bed.

"You're so damn beautiful," he told me, his deep voice sliding over my skin like silk.

I felt so good, so powerful. "Thank you."

"No, thank you."

"For what?"

"For giving yourself to me."

I didn't know what to say to those unexpected words. All I knew was that this longing for him pulsed stronger and gave life to the foolish hope that maybe things could be different. It was dangerous thinking this way, but right now, experiencing this side of reality—this side of Blake—I felt a flicker of hope that he would give up on destroying his life for the sake of his revenge.

He stepped back, and my heart missed a beat or two when he peeled the shirt off over his head and revealed the perfectly contoured muscles of his arms, chest, and stomach. I took him in greedily and tried to memorize as much of him as I could. He had an intricate circular tattoo on the left side of his chest, and I couldn't resist running my finger over it. He inhaled sharply, his eyelids lowering as he observed me touching him.

"What does your tattoo represent?"

"It's the Aztec symbol of courage and strength." I ran my fingers over its edges, and his breathing quickened. "It's a reminder for me to keep going," he added.

I was about to pull my hand away when my fingers brushed over a small rough patch of the skin the tattoo covered. I peered at the quarter-inch round spot, which looked like a bullet scar. My heart contracted painfully. Had he also been shot in that basement?

I frowned at it. "What's this?"

"A remnant of my past. It doesn't matter now." He didn't elaborate, and I didn't push.

He stepped away and took off his jeans, only his black Calvin Klein boxers remaining. My cheeks warmed when my eyes fell on his big erection. He smirked.

"That's what you do to me," he said. "That's how attractive you are." I squirmed on the bed, all flushed and aroused.

He helped me slip out of my shirt and underwear and drew away to look at my naked body. A soft smile played across his lips. I got the old urge to cover myself, but I suppressed it, refusing to let that stupid voice of insecurity ruin this moment for me. This was me, with all my flaws, and I wasn't going to apologize for it or be ashamed.

His gaze was so intense as it slid down and up my body ever so slowly that I felt ridiculous having ever thought he might not like any part of me.

He liked everything, and when his eyes finally stopped on mine, his craving was almost tangible, like nothing else in this world mattered for him but me.

He hooked his hands under my arms and set me in the center of his bed. He sprinkled kisses all over my skin, covering my neck, chest, stomach, and legs before he fondled my breasts and buried his head between them, giving me overwhelming sensations.

Our lips met again as he covered me with his body, but this time his kiss was different. His lips moved over mine like he was pouring all his feelings out, mending my scars one after another—telling me I meant everything to him, and it felt truer than anything.

He pulled away only to take the condom out of his nightstand and put it on. Bubbles of nervousness and excitement rose up my belly. *I'm going to sleep with Blake.*

"I can't believe this is actually happening," I whispered.

The smoldering look in his eyes took my breath away. "Me either." He pulled a strand of my hair away from my face. "Was what you said at that party true? You aren't a virgin?"

"Yes."

He pinched his eyebrows together as if he was in pain. "You don't know how much I wanted to be your first. I know it's selfish, but I couldn't help it."

I ran my finger over his lips. "Does that make me any less desirable?"

He shook his head. "Fuck no. Nothing can make you any less desirable." He positioned himself between my legs and supported his weight on his forearms. "I've never wanted anyone as much as I want you."

I didn't get to respond because his lips covered mine, and he slowly slipped inside of me, drinking in the breathy moan that slipped through my lips. A pure pleasure burst through me and claimed me, becoming more powerful when he started moving. I moved my hips against his, chasing the wave of pleasure.

This was so much more than sex. It was like our souls were communicating with each other, knowing that our time together had an expiration date, and we enunciated it with the contact of our bodies. It was like a happy melody on a gloomy day, like the sun warming cold skin. It was a safe haven that sheltered us from all the pain of the past, and I refused to think about tomorrow.

All we had was now and this connection between us that lasted through all the heartbreaks. I wrapped my arms and legs around him to bring him as close to me as possible.

He slowed down and cupped my cheek with eyes full of adoration. I felt like I was dreaming.

"I think I'm falling for you even more," he whispered suddenly.

My eyes widened along with my smile. I thought I would burst from happiness. "Now I'm *sure* I'm dreaming."

"You're not." He flipped us over so I was on top of him and planted his hands on my hips. "I'm all yours, so take as much of me as you want."

My pulse throbbed faster. I placed my hands on his chest and started to move slowly and then fast. We never looked away from each other, our bodies moving in perfect harmony, and I tried to etch this moment in my mind and store it forever.

He placed his hands on the sides of my face and pulled me in for a kiss. Both of us moved even faster, and when he came, I followed, drowning in the most intense sensation I'd ever felt.

His arms encircled me as I sagged against him, and he held me in a loving embrace. I closed my eyes, listening to his heart racing at a tempo that matched mine. I felt peaceful.

"It's never been this way for me," he said after a while. "It was never like this."

"Like what?"

"Different. Special. Fuck, special doesn't cut it." He kissed the top of my head. "The best moment of my life."

I grinned and snuggled closer to him. "I feel the same."

He held me more tightly in response. I wished we could stay like this indefinitely.

The next day, we would go back to the harsh side of reality.

But today...today, I got the taste of the sweet reality I'd always dreamed of.

Today, he was all mine. And I was his.

Chapter 24

I WOKE UP WITH A START in the dark and squinted at the ceiling. I wasn't sure what had awoken me. I wasn't even sure how I'd fallen asleep. I sat up as my eyes adjusted to the dark in the room that wasn't mine and frowned at the shirt I wore. It was a guy's shirt...

Right.

Blake and I had been cuddling in his bed after our second time, and it seemed I'd fallen asleep in his arms.

I fell asleep.

The clock on Blake's nightstand showed 9:25pm. Crap. I was supposed to be at Mel's place hours ago. She must've sent me a dozen texts. I should get up and—

Blake's whimper cut through my rushing thoughts. I turned around to face him. Now that I could see better, I could make out the features of his face. He was frowning, his lips parted in a quick succession of silent gasps.

"Blake?"

He threw his head to the side and gripped the sheet beneath him with his hands. "No," he said, barely audibly, but with the way his neck constricted, it looked like he wanted to scream it out. His naked chest was rising and falling rapidly. "Don't. No." He threw his head to the other side.

He was having a nightmare. I turned on his nightstand lamp and reached out to touch him, but then I gasped when I saw tears falling down his temples. He was breaking into a sweat.

I touched his upper arm gently. "Blake," I said softly. "Blake, wake up."

He twisted his head to the other side, breathing even more quickly. "No. No!" He jolted.

I nudged his arm twice. "Blake, it's just a dream. Wake up."

"No! Leave her alone!"

The words cut sharply into my chest. "You're just dreaming. Wake—"

"NO!" His scream pierced through my soul, infusing me with so much pain. He flinched and snapped his eyes open.

"Blake—"

"Stay away from me!"

He moved away and pressed his back against the headboard, pulling his knees against his chest and shielding himself with his arms. I just stared at him in shock.

Then, slowly, as if finally realizing it was just me, his wide eyes lost their edge and recognition replaced terror on his teary face.

"It's just me." I placed my hand on his knee gently.

He stared at me, looking more vulnerable than ever. It was heartbreaking. His breaths came out so quickly I was sure he was going to hyperventilate at any moment.

"You're okay." I reassured him and took his hand in mine. "Everything's okay. Breathe slowly." His eyes were glued to mine as he gasped for air. "Breathe slowly, Blake. Just breathe slowly. You're okay."

He took slow breaths, clutching the sheets with a white-knuckle grip.

"That's it. Just keep breathing slowly."

He wasn't breathing as quickly as before, and I started relaxing. I smiled at him.

"You're doing well—"

He burst into tears and buried his head in his hands.

"*Blake.*" I scrambled to sit next to him. I wrapped my arms around him and pulled his head to my chest, cradling him in my arms. "It's okay. I'm here. It's not real. It was just a nightmare."

He whimpered. He shook against me as his tears drenched the shirt I wore, rubbing the back of his hand quickly.

"It's never just a nightmare. It's real. It's fucking real, and it's on repeat."

I stroked his hair as I rocked him slowly. "I'm here, with you. I'll do anything I can to help you."

He stopped rubbing his hand and clutched my shoulder, holding me like I was his only anchor in this world. His sobs quieted, but he was still breathing unevenly. "You can't help me. No one can."

"Do you want to talk about it?" I asked quietly, hoping my voice didn't show how afraid I felt for him.

He stayed quiet, and I didn't push him to speak. I closed my eyes and drew him closer to me. I hoped my presence would help him cope with his nightmare more easily.

He took a shuddering breath. "I didn't tell you everything earlier. There are so many things you don't know. No one knows."

He pulled out of my embrace and brushed the tears off his extremely pale face.

"That kidnapping fucked me up in more ways than one." He met my gaze with red eyes shaded by pain that knew no boundaries. "It gave me post-traumatic stress disorder. PTSD. That's why you saw me at my therapist's office that day."

My mouth rounded in a silent O. I couldn't even begin to imagine what he was going through on a daily basis. I wished it were in my power to help him.

"So, this nightmare is a part of your PTSD?"

He curled up his lips in a bitter smile. "Yes, and it's just the tip of the iceberg."

He gripped the sheets, staring at some spot on the wall. I didn't want to press him for answers, so I waited for him to continue talking.

"It's ironic. Most of the time, I'm afraid to go to sleep because of the nightmares, not that I can fall asleep on most days. But then there are times when my day can get so bad that even nightmares feel like nothing compared to the other things."

My heart sped up. "What are those other things?" I raised my hands in the air. "You don't have to talk about your PTSD if you don't want to."

"I don't want to talk about it, but I've kept everything inside me for so long that it's too much. I need to get it out somehow...some way..."

I wound my fingers around his cold hand and gave him a soft squeeze. "Okay."

He stared at our hands. "It's strange. It's hard for me to trust people, but I'm about to open up to you even more."

I ran my thumb over the back of his hand. "Look at me." He returned my gaze. "You can trust me."

He looked at me intently for a long time, like he was searching for confirmation that I wouldn't betray him.

"Just promise me one thing. No, two things."

"Sure."

"Don't tell anyone about this, and don't judge me."

I frowned. "Of course I won't judge you or tell this to anyone. Why would I judge you?"

"Because I don't feel normal. I can't feel normal ever since the kidnapping. My life became so fucked up that I'm sure you'd run away if you knew all about it."

"I'd never run, Blake. I want to hear you out. I'm here for you. And I won't discuss this with anyone. Pinky swear." I wore a small smile as I raised my pinky finger for him, wanting to cheer him up a bit, but he remained motionless.

He stared at my finger but wasn't actually seeing it.

I dropped my hand. "Um, the bottom line is, I promise I won't say a word to anyone."

He hung his head low and took deep breaths as he grasped and released the sheets time and time again. If this had been any other moment, I would have been distracted by his shirtless torso, but now, all I could think about was how to help him.

"Imagine living your life on alert all the time. You're always hypervigilant because anything or anyone can hurt you. Imagine walking through the unknown where any object, person, sound, smell, word, color—you name it—could be your next trigger. You keep watching out for triggers, but they can be *anywhere*, even your own thoughts or feelings. And when you encounter a trigger, you're brought back to your trauma. Repeatedly. Many times a week. Hell, many times a *day*.

"That's a flashback, and it's the worst because it's like you're seeing a movie of your trauma playing out in front of your eyes, but it's also so much more. You're reliving it. You're there. You struggle to breathe. Over and over again. You're stuck in those moments. You feel the same fear, anger, panic, physical pain, sounds, smell...and you can't prevent it from happening."

"You're...you're saying you actually go through all of that as if it's happening to you again?"

"Yes."

"And you feel...you feel physical pain? For real?"

He swallowed hard. A visible rigidness to his shoulders was always present. "It depends on the kind of flashback, but usually yes. I can feel pain."

I pressed my lips together to stifle a horrified gasp. The claws of his trauma had gotten into him too deep. I never could've imagined he was going through all of this—stuck in a loop, always held captive.

"But what about your real surroundings? How about when you're talking to people? How do you deal with it then?"

He raised his eyes from our connected hands to look at me. "It's downright confusing because I can be completely unaware of my present surroundings, or the flashback can mix with them, so I can see, feel, and hear everything at the same time." He ran his hand down his face and sighed heavily. "You've been around me having a flashback twice already."

I raised my eyebrows. "I have?"

"Yes. Once in the janitor's office when he told us about our detention, and once on the basketball court before we played one on one."

I inhaled sharply, reminded of those times when he'd spaced out. "So that's why you looked like you weren't there." He nodded. "And the hand rubbing?" I pointed at his hand.

"It's my grounding technique."

"What's that?"

"It helps me focus on the present and pull out of the past more easily. I can't quite avoid flashbacks, but I've learned over time to pull out of them more quickly. I can't always pull out, but at least I can manage to deal with them on my good days."

"Good days?"

"Yes."

He rubbed his forehead, looking extremely tired all of a sudden. I wondered if talking about it caused him more stress. I waited for him to continue.

"There are good days, bad days, and just...days. At times, flashbacks can fuck me up so much that I can barely function for the better part of the day."

"And there's no way for you to stop them from happening?"

He smiled ruefully. "No. I can try to avoid triggers, but I can't control everything. So I just use coping strategies I've learned in therapy, but it's hard because I have to do it over and over again, and it never actually stops. It's like trying to reach the top of the mountain, but you always slip down, and just when you think you're closer to the top, you realize you're nowhere close to it. You're in the middle, at best.

"There are extra things that drag you down. Panic attacks, mood swings, uncontrollable anger...so much anger. Little things can anger me so easily, and it feels like my chest is going to explode if I don't get it out somehow. That's where basketball, fights, and racing come in. They help me deal with stress and anxiety."

"And you listen to loud psytrance to drown out your thoughts," I said, referring to what he'd said in his car.

He met my gaze. "Yes."

"But I don't understand. How do you do it? How do you go to school and function?"

The lines of sorrow settled deep in his face. "I don't know. Sometimes, I really don't know. I just do all I can to push through fear and stress. I just...keep on living."

Push through fear...

"I know fear the best. Hell, fear destroyed my life! But I never stopped fighting it. Every second of my life, I'm fighting it. You? You just run away from it, but running away doesn't make bad things disappear." His words from the gym returned to me with a punctuating echo. *"Fight back."*

Now, I could fully understand what was behind those words. I could fully understand why he'd seen me as a pathetic coward. There he was, always fighting through the horrors of his life, and then there was me, running away from them and sweeping them under the rug. It was no wonder he hadn't respected me.

I hadn't respected myself. Or him. But now that I knew what was hiding beneath his exterior, I couldn't see him as the old, ruthless Blake anymore.

I tucked my hair behind my ears. I wanted to know everything, but I didn't want to pry too much. I was amazed that he trusted me enough to share all of this with me. No matter what paths we were going to take going forward, we were allies in this moment.

I wrestled with my thoughts for a bit, until I decided to ask the burning question: "What are your triggers?"

He closed his eyes, grimacing. "I can't actually talk about it, because even that's triggering for me."

"I see." I twisted a strand of my hair around my finger and released it. "Well, bananas are falling from the sky, making monkeys high, and children are hanging from the trees, spending time with bees."

He snapped his eyes open and chuckled. "Are you on something? What was that about?"

"I'm just coming up with whatever I can to keep your mind off triggers."

His eyes shifted between mine for a few seconds, peering deep into me, before he burst into more chuckles. He shook his head. "I should've known you would be like this." He reached out and cupped my cheek. "You really do have a big fucking heart, don't you?"

I blushed, shrugging. "You know, when I was a kid, I used to whine all the time about having to brush my teeth. My mom always had to remind me to brush them, and I hated it because I didn't see the point. I had to brush them over and over again, and it was the most annoying thing because it's for life. Unless you want to have bad teeth." I let out a giggle. "I guess for you, dealing with PTSD is like having to brush your teeth a hundred times a day, but no matter how much you brush them, they keep deteriorating."

His lips lifted in something resembling a smile. "That's a good one, but here's the thing—you can always get fake teeth. I can't get a life free of my mental illness."

It was so disheartening hearing him speak like this. I wanted to say something to lift his mood, but more than that, he needed my understanding. It was true. He had to live with his PTSD, but life didn't end there.

"You're a fighter, Blake. You're able to get out of bed every day and go to school, and that says a lot."

He curled his lips inward. "Yeah, I get up, go to school, and treat people like shit. I'm living the life."

"Then why do you do it? Why do you bully?"

He balled his hands into fists. "Because I'm filled with so much anger. Sometimes it feels that no matter what I do, it will never disappear, and I feel powerless. I know it's sick and wrong, but in those moments, it's my coping mechanism. It feels like it's the only way for me to gain control over my life and my emotions, and for a while, I can get rid of the constant pressure and stress."

I thought about his words, trying to put myself in his shoes. I couldn't sympathize, because I never wanted to hurt anyone and bullying was wrong no matter the reasons behind it, but I wanted to understand him. I wanted to understand his reasons.

"It's like smoking," I said.

He raised his eyebrows. "Smoking?"

"Smoking helps you get rid of anxiety, right? My dad smoked a couple of years ago, and he said he couldn't quit for the life of him. It helped him get rid of stress. But he knew all the while that smoking was bad. He knew he was making a poor choice by choosing cigarettes, not only for himself but also for his family, who were worried for his health, but he still chose to smoke.

"But the relief is always temporary. You always need another cigarette. You always need that next inhalation of smoke that damages your body more and more. It's the same with drugs, alcohol, bullying, and so on. So in the end, it's about dealing with negatives in a negative way. We all do it at some point in our lives, in one way or another. I did it when I made myself throw up. But it's never the solution." I smiled at him. "So instead of bullying, how about you cope with negatives in a positive way? You're already doing it. Basketball, listening to music…there are so many healthy options."

He didn't say anything to that, watching me, captivated.

I blushed. "What?"

He ran his teeth over his lower lip. "Nothing. It's just that I like listening to you. You have a calming voice, you know that?"

My cheeks turned even redder. I couldn't for the life of me understand how he found my high-pitched, childlike voice calming, but it made me happy nevertheless. "Thanks."

"No, thank you. Again. You helped me again, and I don't think you know what that means to me."

"No need to thank me for that. It's the human thing to do."

"But it's not just a human thing to do. There's something about you, something purely good."

He laced his fingers through my hair, and it was getting harder to breathe under his warm gaze. He cupped my chin with his other hand and ran his thumb over my lips, stealing my breath away. My eyes went to his tattoo.

"Um..." I started.

"Yes?"

"There's something I'd really like to know."

He grinned and pulled his hands away. "As if I haven't poured my heart out to you already." He chuckled when another blush permeated my cheeks. "Just teasing you. Come on. Say it."

"I understand that you don't want to talk about triggers, and I hope this won't be triggering, but you mentioned... Am I...?"

"What?"

"I'm sorry, but am I really your trigger?"

He exhaled a long breath and pinched his brows together. "You are, but not in that sense."

"What do you mean?"

He moved and stood up. His body was on full display for me as he walked over to the windows, clad only in his boxers. It was definitely not the time for it, but I couldn't stop my eyes from running down his impressive back, sexy round butt, and long, defined legs.

"In the beginning, my PTSD was so bad I couldn't sleep for weeks and had up to twenty flashbacks a day."

I gaped at him. "Twenty?"

"Yes. I had flashbacks and panic attacks, and when I managed to fall asleep, all I had were the nightmares of that time in the basement. I couldn't go anywhere without breaking down, and this lasted for a really long time. Combine that with the constant anxiety and depression, and you had a complete fucking mess.

"Until my therapy started showing results. I could finally sleep again and had no nightmares. The panic attacks were gone. I only had one flashback a week, sometimes two. I still felt explosive anger, but at least I could deal with my triggers. But then you came, and the hell started again...from the first day I saw you."

"But I don't understand. Why?"

He placed his hand against the glass, looking through the window at the starry sky. The silence stretched until he let out a long sigh.

"This will sound strange, but when you entered the cafeteria on the first day of our senior year, my first thought was that you were so fucking cute. I thought you were cute and so shy, and you needed someone to take care of you. And in that split second, I felt I could be the one to take care of you."

My hand gripped the sheet as I took a quivering breath.

"That was a red flag for me. I thought and felt something that was forbidden—something I felt for the first time since Emma's death—and I didn't like it. I couldn't feel that way. I couldn't let some strange girl get to me after—what? Just one glance? It was pathetic. So I told myself you were most definitely a manipulative bitch and just acting all shy and cute. You weren't someone who should be protected, and you certainly weren't someone I could ever trust. I didn't trust people. I couldn't trust you. That's where that welcome party comes in."

I stared at my hands in my lap, frowning as the images of the first day of school rolled through my mind. "You've never given me the chance to prove myself to you," I whispered into my chin. "You just pegged me as bad and continued to bully me."

He turned around to face me, a veil of regret shading his face. "That day, yes, but that's not all. The welcome party was like my knee-jerk reaction to you. But then, that night, I had the first nightmare. And the next day, the flashbacks started again, followed by panic attacks and more nightmares. The more I saw you, the harder it was, and I blamed you. I blamed you for bringing my symptoms back, and I had to get you away from me, so I did all I could to make you leave, as you now know."

I pressed my hand to my chest, trying to alleviate the rising ache that throbbed there. It hurt a lot hearing this, but at least he was finally giving me the truth. He wasn't sugarcoating it. He was just stating the facts from the past, but that past still had power over me, just like his past still had power over him.

"But you stopped after New Year's Eve. For a while, you acted like I didn't exist. And then you started again before we got detention."

He smiled regretfully. "That's because I was so jealous and angry when I saw you with Robinson. So I started lashing out. I didn't want to admit I wanted you, and I even convinced myself it was all to punish you for affecting me the way you had from day one, but each time I saw you with him or Burks, I felt so possessive. But you weren't mine. Not by a long shot."

I tucked my hair behind my ear. "Do you still blame me? For bringing your symptoms back?"

He looked back through the window and fisted his hand against the glass. "No. I still don't know why your arrival made my PTSD worse, but that's not your fault. It was never your fault. It's all about my sick mind."

I stood up and walked over to him. "Don't say it like that, Blake."

"How do you want me to say it? It's true. I could try to rationalize it, but there's really no excuse for what I've done. There will never be. And I realized too late that hurting you only made things worse. It made me feel like shit. It fueled my guilt...so much guilt that it seemed endless."

He pressed his forehead and hands flat against the glass, his body tensing all over again.

"Sometimes, I'm so tired of myself. I'm sick and tired of constantly navigating through life with my stupid traumas and PTSD. I'm sick and tired of this explosive rage." He hit his fist against the glass hard enough to make it shake. "I'm tired of being this shitty person."

I stopped next to him and looked out the window. The trees surrounding the estate ebbed into nothing in the distance, merging with the starry sky that stretched indefinitely. The full moon created a bright pathway that continued into the dark nothingness, and the contrast between light and dark was mesmerizing. They complemented each other, just like hope complemented despair.

"There is hope, Blake. I can only imagine how hard life with PTSD can be, but as long as we don't give up on hope, things can get better. We can better ourselves. You can be someone better than a bully."

He turned to look at me with dull eyes, his lips pressed into a thin line. "It's too late for me to better myself, but I can do something right for a change." The final tone of his words carried a clear meaning, and the lead in my stomach returned to drag me down.

"Revenge." I barely whispered the word, but its impact was echoing in my mind and heart.

"Revenge," he confirmed, and I closed my eyes, fighting against the tears.

"But I don't understand. How can you face them with your PTSD?" As soon as I asked this question, I realized this must've been what Masen had asked him about after they lost the race to Bobby Q. Blake had PTSD, but he was ready to face his tormentors directly in order to get justice.

"By staying focused on what needs to be done. I'll go through hell if I have to."

His harsh words helped me fully grasp what our reality meant. Everything we'd shared had happened on borrowed time—each kiss, hug, caress, and soft-spoken word. Our bodies dancing the first and final dance until the song was over and the never-ending silence took over our lives.

Blake cared for me, but it wasn't enough. It wasn't enough to conquer his need for revenge. It wasn't enough for him to want to keep living, and that was the sharpest shard that penetrated my heart and created a puncture that took away all the hope and joy.

Anything was better than this. Even if we always remained enemies, it would be better because I would at least have the consolation that he was somewhere out there, *alive*. But this...this...

"Please." My voice was no more than a whisper, carrying the sorrow that pulsed through my whole being. I kept my eyes firmly closed, afraid to look at him because if I did...I would break down, and I didn't want to break down. Blake was right. Making love to him had only made things worse, but breaking down...breaking down here in front of him would taint the time we'd spent in each other's arms, and I couldn't allow that to happen.

"Please reconsider. You don't have to kill them to get your revenge. The cops can arrest them, and I'm sure they would receive a maximum sentence. They would rot in prison."

"I don't want them to rot in prison. I want them dead."

"But don't you see how much it poisons you? I understand that you want them to pay, and they *should* pay, but why do you have to put yourself through something horrible for the sake of revenge? Think about Emma. She wouldn't want you to destroy or sacrifice your life to—"

He pushed away from the window. "Stop. Don't go there." He sat on the edge of his bed. "Don't."

I closed my lips and looked at the moon. A tear slid down my cheek, but I brushed it away quickly and took a few deep breaths.

"I have to avenge her. She died because of me."

I darted to him. "Don't blame yourself, Blake. It wasn't your fault. You didn't kill her. *They* did."

He clasped his head with his hands and placed it between his knees. "They wouldn't have killed her if I'd listened to them."

"That's debatable, and you know it." I sat down on my knees in front of him and laced my cold, trembling fingers through his hair. "They wouldn't have killed her if they hadn't already considered it. They were thugs. Lowlifes. Her death is on their hands, not yours."

He raised his head to look at me, and my heart twisted at the tears on his face. He swept them away, but it did nothing to prevent the new ones from collecting in his eyes. "You think I haven't told myself that? You think I haven't tried to get rid of this fucking guilt? But no matter how I phrase it in my mind, the result is always the same. She wasn't supposed to die. She wasn't supposed to get fucking kidnapped, raped, and killed!"

With a soft cry, I wrapped my arms around him and pulled him into my embrace, pressing his head against my shoulder. It took me a lot not to cry myself, but I had to be strong for him.

"There's no other way for me, Jessie." His whisper was final, punching the permanent pain into me. I couldn't do or say anything to make him reconsider.

I held him until his shivers and tears stopped, remaining silent. I checked my phone for messages and found a few from Mel and Sar.

"Mel and Sar are waiting for me at Mel's place. We're having a sleepover." I finished the sentence with a dose of uncertainty, leaving it open for him to tell me I could stay.

I wanted to stay. I was afraid to leave him alone with his thoughts and nightmares, but he'd closed himself off and put on that invisible shield he always carried around with him.

"It's okay. Go. I'll be fine."

"But I don't want you to be alone."

"I want to be alone." He hardly looked at me as he put his shirt and sweatpants on, his tone leaving no place for argument.

"But—"

"Jessica, it's fine. Just go."

I didn't want him to deal with his demons on his own, but the spell that had held us together today was losing its strength, and the distance between us increased again.

"I see. Okay then. I'll leave."

I texted Mel back saying I was on my way to her place. I kept a blank face, but it was like he could see through me. He stopped in front of me with remorse that darkened his features.

He raised his hand to touch my cheek, and I held my breath, more than aware that I was wearing only his shirt and my panties, but he pulled his hand away before our skin could touch. "It's better this way. For both of us."

I just nodded, trying my hardest to keep it together.

Thankfully, I managed to stay composed on my way out of his room, his house, and most likely, his life.

I stopped next to my car and directed my gaze at the sky, looking for the moon, but unlike earlier, it was clouded and hardly visible, showing that even the mightiest of lights could be conquered by a veil of darkness.

There had to be a way to make Blake's clouds disappear. His light, as weak as it was, couldn't just diminish.

Even though it felt like it might be too late.

Chapter 25

I ENTERED MY HOUSE with heavy steps. I felt like a zombie because I'd hardly slept a wink the previous night. It hadn't helped that Mel had grilled me when I finally arrived at her house with puffy, bloodshot eyes and asked to use her shower, which had raised even more questions I couldn't escape from. We'd ended up talking until it was really late and they could barely keep their eyes open.

I hadn't mentioned anything about my conversation with Blake or his nightmare, only sticking to the sex. Mel's jaw had dropped to the floor when she heard Blake and I had done it. It was funny just thinking about her expression, but I couldn't find it in me to smile now on my way to the kitchen, psyching myself up for the moment of truth.

Seeing the way Blake pushed through his life with PTSD had geared me up for the conversation I was bound to have with my parents. I didn't want to delay it any more. Performing in front of the whole school had been just one step toward making my dreams come true. Telling my parents who I truly was was the next.

The smell of waffles greeted me when I entered the kitchen, and my stomach growled. I'd come home as soon as I woke up, so I hadn't had any breakfast yet.

My mom stood by the kitchen island. She smiled. "Hey, honey. How was it at Melissa's place?"

"It was okay. Mel snores a lot." I took a plate and reached for one of the waffles before taking a seat at the kitchen island.

Mom giggled. "She should sleep on her side or with her head raised to keep her airways open."

I swallowed my waffle in three big bites and took another one. "This is Mel we're talking about—she rolls around in bed like she's practicing samba in her sleep. I think I have a few bruises from her elbows and knees."

"Ouch. So you got to sleep next to her?"

"Yep." I bit into the waffle. "Sar got the better end of the deal. She slept on the sofa. I should sleep there next time."

"You do that. Anyway, there is something I've wanted to ask you since your solo," she said with a small smile, watching me knowingly. "Your song was pretty emotional and...well, personal. So, I assume it's about you, right?"

My cheeks warmed. "Right."

"You never told me you fell in love with someone."

I didn't want to talk about my feelings, and even if I had, I wouldn't have known where to start. "It's a long story."

"I bet, after hearing the lyrics. Is everything okay between you and that boy now?"

I opened my mouth to give her some vague answer, but Dad entered the kitchen and smiled at me, talking to someone on his phone.

"I'll check it tomorrow." He sighed at whatever the person on the other end of the line said. "Robert, it's Sunday. You know better than to call me on Sunday. We'll go over those reports tomorrow. Talk to you later." He ended the call and stopped next to me.

Mom's smile was amused. "They keep calling you on weekends?"

Dad rubbed his forehead. "And it's not even eight yet. Hey, sweetheart." He smiled and ruffled my hair. "How's our most amazing singer? You were extraordinary yesterday."

I bit at the cuticle of my thumb, hoping Mom wouldn't press me to hear about Blake now that Dad was here. "You think?"

"He even recorded it with his phone," Mom said. "He wants to show it at the office."

I frowned. "Daaad! Don't do that! That's embarrassing!"

"There is nothing embarrassing about it. I want to show everyone how talented my daughter is." He and Mom looked at each other and silently communicated something. I was none the wiser about what it was about.

"Hang on a sec," he said before walking out of the kitchen. I just wished he would come back so we could talk about my college decision.

But when he returned and I saw the object in his hands, I grew speechless and my pulse began to race.

He'd bought me a new guitar, and it wasn't just any guitar. I recognized it because I'd googled it so many times, fantasizing about owning it. It was a Gibson Montana SJ-200 Standard, one of the best acoustic guitars in the world. This piece of amazingness cost more than four grand.

This piece would cost their disappointment when they heard about the path I'd chosen.

"I can't believe you bought me a Gibson. Did you rob a bank to buy it?"

Laughing, he handed me the guitar that had a big, red bow attached to its neck. "A bank or two, yes. Do you like it?"

My hands were shaking as I inspected the beautiful vintage design, running my fingers over its polished surface. This guitar was heavier than my Martin, but it felt perfect in my hands.

"Do I like it? I LOVE it!" I jumped from the chair and hugged him, holding the guitar in one hand. "Thank you, thank you, thank you."

I saw Mom smiling broadly over my shoulder, which gave me hope that the conversation about college would go well. They cared about my happiness. They wanted me to do what would make me happy. So maybe they wouldn't get mad...at least not very.

I stepped away from Dad and placed the guitar on the counter, so carefully, as if each move could shatter it into pieces.

"Thank you, both of you," I said, inhaling deeply. "But there is something I wanted to talk to you about."

Dad leaned against the counter next to Mom. "Yes?"

"I'm not going to your law college, or any law college, for that matter." Their smiles dropped.

"What are you saying?" my mom asked. "You won't go to a law college?"

I plastered my suddenly cold hands together. No matter what, I would push through this.

"Yes. I don't want to be a lawyer." I looked at my dad. "I never did. I want to pursue a career in singing."

His face turned stern. "*Singing?*" He said that word as if it was going to bite him.

I swallowed the bile that rose up my throat. "Yes. I want to be a singer. That's my dream."

"Jess, honey, be real," Mom said. "We've talked about this already, quite a few times. It's okay to have dreams, and your voice is incredible, but the real world isn't sunshine and rainbows. Singing will never keep you afloat."

"That's not a sound choice, Jessica," Dad added. "You can't expect to make a living with it."

"Yes, I know very well how low my chances at success are. I know there are thousands—no, millions of singers out there who can't and will never be able to make it in the music industry, but I don't want to give up on my dream just because the odds are against me. If everyone gave up because of the odds, we wouldn't have famous singers—"

My mom let out an incredulous chuckle. "You don't understand how hard those people had to work to reach that point. And it's not just about hard work. It's about dedication, money, and a lot of sheer luck."

I tucked my hair behind my ear. "I know, Mom. I know."

"No, Jessica, you don't know," Dad replied adamantly. "You have an amazing talent, and you should, by all means, continue singing and making music, but keep it as a hobby. You already have a YouTube channel. You can keep creating music for your channel, but get your priorities straight. You already have a job secured at my firm after you go to school, which will make you good money."

"I can also make good money as a singer. In fact, I can earn much, much more if I make it to the top."

"*If* you make it to the top. You said that well. That's a big 'if,'" Dad said. "You're still very young, and I'm sure when you're older, you'll be grateful to your mother and me. Singing is not a good career choice. It's an unsteady income, and you can never know when the things could go down."

"Things can go down whichever career I choose, Dad." I raised my tone, getting frustrated. "If we're going to be that pessimistic then you also don't know if your firm will go bankrupt in ten years or not. We don't know if global warming will kill us all in fifty years or not. No one can be sure about anything these days.

"But I know I don't want to spend the rest of my life doing something I hate. I hate the law and everything associated with it. I don't want to do something I hate for *your* sake." I pointed my finger at them.

"It's not for our sake," Mom said. "It's for your sake—"

"It's not for my sake if it makes me unhappy. Do you want me to be un-happy? Do you?" They stayed silent, wearing flinty expressions. "Yes, maybe I'll be miserably poor. Maybe I'll never have any success. But I'll be at peace with myself because I'll be doing everything I can to make my dreams come true. I won't be sitting in some office and wishing I was out there singing. I won't be withering away with regret as the years go by and my dreams just disappear."

My mom sighed. "Look, Jess, I understand that this period in your life is extremely stressful, and you might even feel cornered. College decisions put a lot of pressure on students because it's a huge step toward adulthood, and it can make you confused. But we're here to support you and—"

"I accepted the admission to a music college in New York," I said, dead-pan.

The expression of shock settled on their faces. I dug my nails into my palms. I'd done it. I'd finally told them the truth. I was terrified, but the words had liberated me, removing the tension from my body layer by layer, and I could breathe a bit easier.

I could look in the mirror and be proud of myself for fighting for who I was at last. This was me, and I wasn't going to allow them to shape me into something I wasn't.

"I'm not confused. I know what I want, from the bottom of my heart. I declined your college's offer, Dad," I said, watching his face go pale. "I know this is disappointing for you, but I've made my decision. And I really, *really* hope you'll be able to support it one day."

"You..." Mom made a choking sound. "You declined the offer? But..." She kneaded the space between her eyebrows with two fingers.

"Jessica, why didn't you talk to us first?" Dad asked, and I winced at the reproach in his tone. His face was the picture of disappointment, just like I'd thought it would be, but the impact it had on me was stronger than I'd imagined it'd be. I was ready to go to a music college against their approval, but I'd hoped they would at least try to understand me and wish me the best.

"Because I knew you would react like this," I replied. "You wouldn't let me major in music. Please understand. I was ready to give up on my dreams and follow your wishes, but it would make me miserable. I just want to be me. I want to live my life the way I want it, with all its ups and downs."

I thought about Emma, whose life had ended before it even started. I thought about Blake, who was ready to sacrifice his life, never even giving himself the chance to live and realize his dreams. Did he even have dreams? Or had those been lost in the same darkness that had swallowed Emma?

"Life is too short and unpredictable for me to waste my opportunities." I slid off my chair and took Mom's hand. "I know you want to protect me and only want the best for me, but please, try to understand me. Maybe I'm young and inexperienced, but I think life is more than just stressing over money. Sure, I'm going to stress about it, maybe even more once I start fighting for my place in the music industry, but at least I will work my hardest to succeed."

We sank into silence, and the atmosphere in the kitchen got heavier with tension. I let go of Mom's hand and supported myself against the kitchen island.

Dad gave me the stink eye. "It doesn't matter if we agree with you or not, does it? Because you've already accepted the offer. You did everything without even consulting us."

I rubbed my chest against the pressure his accusing tone created, battling to keep my eyes on them. "It's true that maybe I should've talked to you first, but have you ever talked to me about what I really want? No, you just assumed I would follow in your footsteps. You never even asked me what I wanted to do in life." A tear slid down my cheek, and I wiped it off. I wasn't going to cry. "Please support my decision. Please."

Mom shook her head. "I don't know what you want us to say. You should've talked to us about the music college first. This is huge, and I don't know what to tell you. I want you to be happy. That is the most important for me, but I don't want you to ruin your life. I need to think about this."

"Yes, we need to think this through," Dad agreed. "You can't just drop this bomb and expect us to accept it. I'm disappointed, Jessica. I expected better of you."

There it was. That word. Disappointment.

"I..." I wrung my hands together. "I understand."

I returned to my waffles even though I didn't have an appetite anymore. Dad left the kitchen, leaving Mom and me in an uncomfortable silence that neither of us broke. We had yet to discuss the finances, but I knew very well if they refused to support me, I was completely on my own. However, there was a silver lining—at least I'd stayed true to myself.

Maybe I would ruin my life and make them more disappointed in me, but it was my life, not theirs, and I was done staying in the shadows of my cowardice. My gut told me this was the right decision, and I wasn't going to let my old doubts trample it down. They would have to understand and accept my feelings eventually, and even if they didn't, it was all right.

Because I was finally starting to feel a bit better in my own skin.

· · · ·

I ARRIVED AT SCHOOL feeling jitters, my heart beating faster at the thought that I could see Blake at any moment. I didn't know where we stood. So many things were happening at once, speeding up this roller coaster he and I were riding on. We weren't enemies, but I wasn't sure if I could even call us friends.

I wanted us to be friends, at least. I was ready to move on and stop harboring negative feelings for him.

And I was finally ready to forgive him.

The night before had provided me with many answers and shed light on who Blake really was. Even though nothing would ever make any of the things he had put me through okay, he wasn't that horribly cruel person anymore, and it hurt to know he was ready to throw his life away and become something awful—a murderer—in order to find justice for Emma. It hurt that he could lose his life any day.

A dangerous thought had begun to echo louder than others, putting me in limbo. I was starting to think about saving him, about doing anything to stop him from going through with his plan, which seemed impossible, because what could I do? I was powerless, just a blip on the horizon of hate and anguish he'd held himself in for years.

I busied myself with festival activities around the school as the day progressed, but he was always on my mind, and I kept looking for him in the crowds that filled the hallways.

The second day of the festival brought even more people to our school. The booths run by psychologists were a hit, and the sales of the students' crafts went more than well, but the most anticipated event was a conference similar to TED Talks that was scheduled for noon in the gym, where students were going to share their bullying experiences and invite people to spread understanding and work on unity. Mel was one of the speakers.

Sar, Kev, Marcus, and I were headed to the gym when I bumped into a short redhead carrying a stack of books in her hands. The books fell on the floor upon the impact, scattering around my feet.

"I'm sorry," the blue-eyed girl said with a small smile before bending to pick up her books.

"It's nothing," I said. "I'll help you."

I crouched and reached for the rest, reading their titles: *Pained*, *Trapped*, *Scarred*, and *Damaged*. I picked them up one by one and placed them on top of the one she held in her hands, which was titled *Bullied*.

"Thank you," she said.

"You're welcome."

"If you want to buy these or any other books, you can do it over there." She pointed at the bookstand nearby.

"Sure."

"See you around," she said then walked away.

We passed through a crowd of students, and I noticed a few of them casting curious glances at Kev and Marcus, who held hands. I smiled to myself because they didn't let anyone or anything interfere with their relationship. People could talk and point fingers at them as much as they wanted, but love prevailed, and only that mattered.

I was glad Kevin was starting to accept himself for who he was. It was inspiring and beautiful seeing him get his happy ending because that cute cinnamon roll deserved it more than anyone.

I wondered where mine was.

The bleachers were already half-filled when we entered the gym. We took seats in the third row, and I waved at Mel, who stood on the stage next to Shreya Wilkins and the rest of the student council. She waved back with a grin.

Blake, Hayden, and Masen entered the gym moments later, and relief flooded through me because Blake had showed up. I'd been worried he wouldn't seeing how shaken he'd been after his nightmare. I didn't even realize I was holding my breath until they came over and my eyes locked with his. Instantly, the room narrowed to the two of us. His face was serious, but there was heat in his gaze, warming my body, and I was taken back to his room at sunset. I remembered vividly each caress, each kiss, each moment spent in his arms... I couldn't look away from him, longing to touch him.

Hayden and Masen went over to sit next to Sarah, while Blake took the empty seat next to me, and my heart began pounding. I stared straight ahead, unable to look at him. I was hyperaware of his every move.

"Hi," he said.

My cheeks flushed. "Hi," I croaked out.

It was ridiculous. He'd seen all of me—*kissed* all of me—yet there I was, blushing furiously at one simple greeting.

No, it wasn't simple. Nothing about Blake was simple, and the thought that he was so close to me, his knee touching mine and his hand resting so close to my thigh...it was impossible not to want that hand on me.

I tried to focus on anything else but him, listening to Marcus and Kev on my other side talk about whether Kylo Ren was hotter than Anakin Skywalker, but it was pointless. My mind was all about Blake. *Blake, Blake, Blake.*

"You look strange. Are you okay?" he asked, his breath fanning my face because he was leaning toward me. It was difficult not to look back at him when he was this close. *Of course I look strange when all I want is to kiss you and get those clothes off you—*

"I think that's the question I should ask you." I tugged at the hem of my shirt. "I was worried about you."

"Why?"

I stared at the loose thread on the seam of my jeans. "You know why."

"It's something I've dealt with for four years now," he said quietly, so only I could hear him. "I went through much worse than what you saw, so don't worry about me."

"I have to worry about you."

I could feel him smile. "Because that's what you do. You worry about people and want to help them."

"It's impossible not to worry about the people you care about," I let out, my face warming.

I saw him watch me out of the corner of my eye in a prolonged silence that caused my pulse to go wild.

"How about you?" he asked.

"Me?"

"Who's going to help you?"

I stifled the strangled sound that wanted to come out of my throat and finally looked at him. His lips were curled into a tiny smile, and I found myself staring at them. I wanted to kiss him. A lot.

"What's with that sudden question?"

"I was thinking about it last night. I thought about how I've never helped you with anything."

"You helped me when that guy pushed me in the hallway."

"That's nothing."

"That's everything." I looked away from his suddenly fervid gaze and tucked my hair behind my ears. "Besides, you don't have to help me. I can help myself. It's high time I stop relying on others to help me."

"Yes, but still..."

"Still what?"

His eyes darted between my lips and eyes. "I want to be there for you. I wish I could be there for you."

I closed my eyes. "But you can't." I didn't add the word that was hanging between us like a guillotine blade: revenge.

He opened his mouth to say something, but one of the teachers tapped the microphone and called for our attention. The whole gym went quiet, and I tried to focus on her and not on Blake's eyes that didn't leave my face.

She made an introductory speech, and then Mel took her place behind the mike and started her speech, talking about how important bystanders were.

"They can make a difference," Mel said in a strong, unwavering voice. "It's extremely important to help people in need instead of just ignoring it.

Bullying can scar someone for life. Just imagine what it's like to be bullied every single day. Just imagine how it feels when bystanders just watch the abuse and do nothing to stop it.

"Do you know that suicide and bullying are closely connected? Do you know that suicide is now the second leading cause of death among teens and young adults? Most often, our help can make all the difference. It can change lives and give hope to people who need it the most. So, let's help. Let's show those in need that life is more than days filled with hopelessness and cruelty."

The applause spread through the room, and I smiled with pride at Mel. She was so inspiring.

Blake shifted closer to me, and I grew still. "I couldn't stop thinking about you last night," he whispered directly into my ear, causing tingles to explode all over my skin. I dug my nails into my palms and willed myself to breathe evenly. "I couldn't stop thinking about your smile. Your kisses. *Fuck*, those kisses..."

I bit my lip. His hand was even closer to my thigh now, his pinky almost touching me.

"I thought about how I want to be that person who will take care of you."

I turned my head to look at him, but it was a mistake because his face was only inches away from mine, and all I had to do was just tilt my head toward him and we would be kissing. It was too tempting, which was why I had to snap my head back and fix my eyes on Mel.

"It's not fair, Blake, because you won't ever be that person. You have your priorities settled." I didn't want to sound bitter, so I said this in a neutral voice, wanting him to know I wasn't accusing him of anything.

"I know." His whisper carried so much pain.

"Then what are we doing now? What are we? Friends? Acquaintances? Nothing?"

His fingers slipped over my thigh in a feathery touch and stopped. "Just two people who are trying to figure out how to go on with their feelings."

I looked at him. "That's not good enough, Blake. I...I don't know how to act around you. I don't know what to expect from you."

"Don't expect anything. I can't give you anything."

"Then why is your hand on my thigh?"

He pulled it back as if he'd been burned and looked away. I willed myself to breathe evenly. This was bad. It was becoming torturous to sit next to him and know there would never be anything between us. I'd thought I would be able to handle it, handle his nearness and act like everything was okay, but right now, I couldn't. I couldn't get rid of the constant fear that reminded me of how limited our time together was.

I needed to get out. I needed some fresh air.

Mel ended her speech, inviting witnesses of bullying to stick up for victims instead of keeping quiet, and one junior came out to share her story, but I couldn't stay here a moment longer.

Feeling the sudden urge to get some space, I whispered to Kevin that I was going to the restroom and stood up. I had to pass Blake first, and I held my breath when I stepped in front of him, more than aware that my butt was right in his face because the space between the rows was so narrow. I let the breath out only when I was off the bleachers and scurried out.

I burst through the gym doors and rushed down the empty hallways in search of...what? Clarity? Answers? Anything that would dull this ache and longing that were becoming unbearable. Music. Music was the answer.

The sunrays blinded me when I stepped outside, and I shielded my eyes with my hand as I went to the parking lot. I needed music badly, and my headphones were in my car.

"Jessie!" I spun on my heel and halted, my eyes widening when I saw Blake running toward me. "Wait!"

I stared at his ridiculously sexy body as he rushed over. Each muscle was accentuated, flexing and unflexing, and it was too much. My body didn't care about logic or reality. It didn't care that I would never be his priority or above his need for revenge and the lost love of his life. It just wanted to take and give.

He stopped a bit too close to me as he grabbed my face to pull me in for a kiss, and I lost myself in the contact of our lips. It felt too good. His hands went down to the small of my back and pulled me flush against him as his tongue stroked mine with great need. I clutched the lapels of his jacket, not caring if anyone could see us or not.

Was it too foolish to have this overpowering hope in my chest that survived each bump in our road? Was there any chance, no matter how tiny, that Blake would give up on ruining or risking his life?

I pulled my lips away, wishing this was more than just a stolen moment. "Wait—"

He pressed his face into the crook of my neck and continued kissing me, battling against my reason.

"Wait," I repeated, willing my hands to push him away, but I was so needy for his kisses, already leaning closer to him for more... I pushed him away and took a step back. "Do you have any clue how scared I am for you?" I asked. "Do you know how scared I am that any day now, I won't even see you anymore? I'll come to school and hear you're *dead*, or jailed for life. And the more I think about your revenge, the more horrible scenarios I come up with, and I feel so lost because you're so hellbent on that revenge and..." My words dwindled away when he cupped my cheeks with his hands.

"I know." He leaned his forehead against mine. "I know, and I'm so sorry. I don't want to lead you on. I don't want to hurt your feelings. I want to be with you, but..."

"But you won't change your mind. Nothing will ever make you change your mind because you don't even want to consider a life free of your revenge."

He grimaced and dropped his hands. "Don't, Jessie. Please don't say it. I—"

"The world is so much more than you think, Blake. It's not all negative. It can be happy and full of joy, and I wish you would let yourself experience it. But you won't even try."

I turned around and continued walking toward my car with a suffocating feeling clawing at my chest.

"Jessie!" he called after me, but I didn't stop, my eyes set on the pavement in front of me. I wanted to lose myself in music and forget about everything.

I fished my keys out of my pocket. "I want to be your friend, Blake. Maybe even something more, but that doesn't matter," I said when I heard him stop behind me, opening the car door with my shaky hand. I bent to reach inside. "It can't matter when you could lose your life—" I froze, my eyes going wide when they met the end of a gun.

"Finally," Isaac, Blake's friend from the track, drawled with a crooked smile. He was sitting in my back seat with his gun pointed directly at me. "Now we can get this party started."

Chapter 26

BEFORE I COULD EVEN process what was happening, Blake rushed between me and the gun incredibly fast and shoved me behind him, shielding me.

"Blake, are you crazy?" I shrieked. Terror bolted right through me because he was risking his life to protect me. "You can't—"

"What the fuck do you think you're doing?" Blake asked Isaac, and the realization hit me hard. It was *him*—the guy I'd seen behind me here yesterday. That was Isaac. That was why he'd looked familiar.

Isaac's smile grew bigger. "Blake, my man! I have to say, this has just become ten times better. We planned to take your girl as a bait, but now that you're here...this is perfect! It's like, like..." He snapped his fingers. "Like poetic justice, yes!"

His casual way of speaking only added to my jumbled up thoughts. I scanned the parking lot for any witnesses, but there was not a living soul.

"Isaac, what the fuck are you on?" I wanted to peer further around Blake to see Isaac better, but Blake's arm held me back. "Stay back," he hissed at me.

Isaac chuckled. "What? You thought we were friends? Think again, man."

Blake's muscles locked up. "You were feeding me the info on Bobby Q and his guys."

He grinned. "And I fed them the info on you."

"What?"

"I told them about your plan to get back at them. They had a good laugh, really. Almost as good as mine when you told me why you were looking for them. Seriously, it's totally ridiculous, but you get brownie points for the thought."

"You hung around me from the start. You acted as if we were friends. So why?" Blake said through clenched teeth.

Isaac's smile dropped, giving way to a scary expression. "Let me jog your memory," he said in a completely changed voice, one that was deep and rough, sounding like a totally different person.

298

Blake let out a choked gasp. "No." He staggered. "*No.* It can't be you."

"Oh, it's me, all right." He cocked his head to the side. "And let me tell you, her pussy was sooo tight..." His eyes found mine. "Right before I put the bullet in her head."

Everything in me went cold. A silent cry formed on my lips as the meaning of Isaac's words settled in my mind. Isaac was the one who... He was...

Blake's whole body went rigid, his breathing accelerating rapidly, which activated alarms in my head. I feared he was having or was about to have a flashback.

I rubbed his hand that was still on my waist the way I'd seen him do and whispered, "It's all right. I'm here."

The words were supposed to reassure him, but how I would be able to reassure him when I was terrified myself I didn't know. My gaze made another sweep of the parking lot. There was no one at all. The damn cameras were supposed to get installed around the school the next day, and I wanted to scream in frustration.

"Okay, enough chitchat. Here's how this is going to play out. Both of you are going to get in this car. The chick will be driving. And if you even think of refusing or running, there will be consequences."

This seemed to pull Blake out of his daze; his terribly cold hand gripped mine as he pushed me further behind him. "She isn't going anywhere with you," he said in a hoarse voice, and I clutched his jacket. "You can do whatever the fuck you want with me, but I won't let anything happen to her."

Isaac chuckled. "How noble, tough guy, but you don't have a choice. I won't hesitate to shoot you if I have to." He looked at me. "Would you want that?"

"*No!*" I cried out in sheer fear. "No, Blake. Don't be stupid! Listen to him."

"Jessica, run into the school and—"

"No, I—" I started, but he pushed me backward and away from him.

"Run in and alert them—"

"Not so fast," said a strangely familiar voice behind me, and I felt something solid pressing into my back. I grew stiff, every muscle in my body turning tense. It was a gun.

My heart rate went through the roof. "B-Blake...," I said breathlessly.

"If either of you takes a step, she's dead," the newcomer said, pressing the gun harder into me and paralyzing me from head to toe.

"*Lawrence?*" Blake looked over his shoulder, his face ashen and eyes full of fear.

"Recognizing my voice after all this time, Jones? Touching. Now, do what Isaac said. Get in the car, or I'll pull the trigger." He turned the safety of his gun off, the soft click resounding in my mind loudly like a hammer against metal.

Blake's eyes met mine over his shoulder. His expression of regret sent shards of icy pain into my heart. My mind raced to come up with any solution to this but had no success.

"Please, Blake, do what he said," I pleaded in a trembling voice, worried he might do something that would put him in danger. Anguish rolled over his face, and he held my hand in an almost unbearably tight grip as if he didn't want to let go of me.

"No," he whispered regretfully. "This was not how it was supposed to be." He glared at Lawrence. "If you hurt her, I'll kill you."

"I'm the one holding the gun here, so don't make me laugh. *Move.*"

I willed myself to release his hand. The lack of his touch and strength against my skin made me feel like I'd lost the last pillar of support, but I didn't let it show on my face. I needed to stay strong for both of us, so I put on a brave mask as I gazed back at him. He grimaced and moved reluctantly, dragging his feet across the pavement as he went around my car to the passenger side.

"And don't try anything funny," Lawrence told him.

"Or what? You'll grab the camera to record us before you kill us?" Blake asked him with a sneer before he sat inside my car. So Lawrence had been the one holding the camera in the video. It was no wonder his voice was somewhat familiar to me.

"Your humor is drier than your grandma's pussy," Lawrence replied, and I grimaced with disgust. He nudged me with his gun, signaling me to move.

I took a wobbly step closer to the car, but then Lawrence pulled my phone out of my back pocket with his gloved hand.

"You don't need this anymore," he said and flung it into the distance, where it landed with a loud crash.

I yelped, watching this with round eyes. As long as I'd had my phone with me, there had been hope I could use it, no matter how far-fetched that might have been, but now...

"Get in the car," Lawrence ordered, pressing the gun into my back to make me move. I took another wobbly step and then another, my cold fear getting stronger because each step, each breath I took, each *second* felt like it would be my last.

I got behind the wheel and pulled the key out of my pocket, trembling. I was only able to insert it in the ignition after the third try. Isaac reached with his gloved hand for Blake's phone and threw it out the window before he told me the address, which was on the outskirts of Enfield.

I looked around once more as I started the car. Not a single person. But even if there was someone, what could I do? Both Blake and I would be dead before I could even alert them.

Dead. I shuddered with a fresh wave of fear and looked at Blake, who stared straight ahead. His face was almost unrecognizable with the strong emotions passing across it. What were they going to do to us?

"Drive." Isaac's sharp order had me wincing in my seat. I barely remembered that I had to buckle up, but I stopped myself before I reached for the seat belt. Maybe, just maybe, the cops would pull me over for not wearing it, and that could be our chance to get out of this. But no, Isaac and Lawrence would see through me once the seat belt warning went off, so that wasn't an option.

My panic increased as I shifted into first gear. I could ram the car into something and hope they would get hurt enough for us to escape, but then I would also risk Blake or me getting hurt. Maybe I could just drive too fast and hope to get stopped for speeding.

But as I proceeded to the exit on my right, planning to drive through the busiest streets, Isaac instructed me to go to the left and then follow the road that led away from the busy streets and areas where I could expect to see cops.

I did as I was told, terrified about what was waiting for us after this ride. I took one quick look at Isaac. He'd raped and killed Emma. It was difficult to understand how one person could be so evil.

"Why are you doing this shit?" Blake asked. "You short on dough again?"

They chuckled. I glanced in the rear-view mirror to see them give Blake a derisive look.

"Not really, tough boy," Lawrence said. "Did you really think we would just sit and do nothing while you plotted your childish revenge? I thought we taught you to be more obedient and stop snooping around in other people's business, but I guess you haven't learned your lesson."

Blake let out a choked breath. "So, while I plotted to take you and Bobby Q down, you plotted to—what? Kidnap me and torture me to death?"

"Nope. Just killing you was good enough," Isaac said sardonically. "But then Bobby Q and I saw you getting real cozy with this cutie here, and it was like a sign from above because what's better than coming full circle, right?"

"This has nothing to do with Jessica. Let her go."

"And miss the fun we can have with her?"

I gripped the wheel, nauseated by the implication in those words. I feared how Blake was going to handle this for the second time.

"I'll kill you," he growled through his teeth, to which both Isaac and Lawrence laughed.

"Oooh, I'm shaking," Isaac mocked.

"You will be when I'm done with you," Blake muttered under his breath and covered my hand on the gearshift. I glanced at him. "I'll protect you," he mouthed silently, and I could see it—guilt, regret, fear, determination.

I offered him a small smile, wanting him to know I trusted him. I felt safe with him.

"Who would've thought, eh?" Isaac said in his cheerful fake voice, his aim remaining fixed on Blake. "That I would find you when I joined T's gang last year? The world is so small. And you didn't even recognize me!" He let out a poisonous chuckle. "But that's the point of ski masks. No one can recognize you with it, get it?" He smacked his hand against his thigh, breaking out into laughter that grated on my ears.

"So, what? You knew who I was from the start and decided to pretend to be my friend? You even changed your voice so I wouldn't recognize it."

Isaac grinned darkly. "Yes."

"Why?"

He shrugged. "For fun. It was hilarious to see you hang around the person who fucked and killed your girlfriend."

Blake fisted his hands on his thighs. He did it so tightly his veins bulged out. I swallowed the bile in my throat.

"But I never expected you to come to me and ask about Bobby Q," Isaac continued. "That was huge."

"I only asked you about Bobby Q because I heard you two moved in the same circles."

Isaac smacked his lips. "Gotta love the irony. And now, here we are."

I curled my lips in disgust. He'd done unspeakable things to an innocent girl but was roaming free around the world, and for a moment, I understood Blake's burning desire to put an end to his miserable life. I wondered if a life sentence would be enough for the likes of him.

"Was that you yesterday?" I asked Isaac.

"Yesterday?" Blake asked me.

"There was a guy in the parking lot when I left the school. He looked familiar, but he was standing in the distance and wearing a cap, so I couldn't be sure. Then you showed up, and he was gone."

Isaac nodded with a grin. "Yep, that was me."

Blake cursed. "What were you doing there?"

"Just keeping tabs on her."

"Son of a bitch," Blake growled.

"You're not going to get away with this," I told him, despite knowing how improbable that was. They had gotten away with Blake and Emma's kidnapping.

Lawrence barked a mocking laugh. "We'll see about that."

The ride felt long and short all at the same time, killing all my hope that we could get out of this before we reached the address. My heart dropped into my stomach when an ominous-looking gray Victorian house came into sight at the end of the road. There was nothing here but meadows and more meadows, which increased the dreadful feeling that this wouldn't end well.

Isaac ordered me to park in the small driveway and hand him my car key; his aim at my head never faltered.

I gave him the key and got out of the car, shivering when a gust of cold wind swept over me and blew my hair into my face.

"Both of you, move," Lawrence ordered when Blake refused to step away from the car. He was more composed now, all traces of fear gone from his face and replaced with a quiet fury.

"I'll make you regret this," Blake warned.

Isaac rolled his eyes. "Spare me the dramatics and fucking move already."

Their guns on our backs were a constant reminder not to do anything rash as we headed toward the house. I looked at the sky. The sun was high above the horizon, making it a beautiful day, and my chest hurt. It felt like I was going into a prison I would never come out from, and I was afraid this was my last time to see the light of the day.

"What are you going to do with us?" I asked Lawrence as I stepped inside the dark house that contained a musty smell and old furniture.

"You'll see soon enough."

We ended up in a living room that looked almost like my grandparents' with its floral wallpaper, large framed photos of pastures, upright piano, rocking chair, and ancient worn-out sofa. There wasn't anything we could use to defend ourselves, except for a lamp on the small stand next to the sofa.

And there, standing next to a curtained window, was Bobby Q, dressed in black and looking as scary as could be. Now, in daylight, I was clearly able to see the pale scar line that started at his chin and ended on his cheekbone.

"Look who we've brought," Isaac told him with a huge smile, motioning at Blake with his head.

"Motherfucker." Blake spat the word out and took a threatening step toward Bobby Q, but Isaac pressed his gun to the side of his head. I cried out, clamping my hands over my mouth.

"Where do you think you're going?" Isaac asked him.

Blake curled his hands into fists, his icy gray eyes full of hatred as he glared at Bobby Q.

Bobby Q smirked. "Jackpot. Hello, Jones. It's nice of you to pop up and make everything easier for us."

"Cut to the chase. What do you want? Spit it out," Blake said.

Isaac chuckled. "Whoa, boy, slow down. You sound a bit too on edge."

"You kidnapped us," I said. "How do you expect us to react?"

Lawrence whistled behind me. "Roar. This one can bite."

Bobby Q's gaze was cold as he assessed me, sending chills down my spine. "I'm going to have so much fun with you later."

Blake dashed toward him. "Son of a—"

Isaac fired his gun, and I screamed. The bullet landed super close to where Blake had stopped, making a hole in the carpet.

"Next time I won't miss, so consider this your only warning, Blake," Isaac said in a low tone, which sounded muffled to me under the increasing pressure in my head. I stared at the hole in the carpet with my heart thrashing against my rib cage. More and more dread crept through me until I couldn't think properly, until there was only panic.

"Search him for weapons," Bobby Q ordered.

"Take off your jacket," Isaac told Blake and waited for him to do it, leaving nothing to chance. He threw the jacket on the sofa and passed his hands over Blake's body. He smirked when he pulled a pocketknife out of Blake's back pocket.

"Carrying this to school?" Isaac said, raising the knife in the air for emphasis. "Tsk-tsk. You won't need that anymore." He tossed it on the sofa next to Blake's jacket.

Blake glowered at him. "Go fuck yourself."

"No more weapons?" Bobby Q asked Isaac.

"Nope."

"Now the girl."

"Don't touch her," Blake shouted, looking ready to jump at Isaac and rip his throat out, but Isaac didn't pay attention to him, taking my jacket off and patting me down for weapons without missing a beat.

My skin crawled in disgust at his touch, which was followed by queasiness when his hands brushed over my intimate parts. I felt horribly violated. I dug my nails into my palms so hard I thought I might draw blood.

"You never know with girls these days," Isaac said before stepping away. I fought to even out my breathing.

"I swear I'm going to fucking kill you the first chance I get," Blake said, glaring at Isaac with hatred that knew no boundaries, and I believed him. The conviction in his words was unmistakable.

"Not if we kill you first," Bobby Q stated in a bored tone.

Blake glared at him. "If you wanted to kill me, you could've already done it. You didn't have to waste time on all this shit."

"You know how we do things around here, Jones," Bobby Q joked with a half-smile on his face. "It's not an accomplishment if we don't kidnap a person..." His gaze found mine. "Or two."

"But unlike last time, you're not hiding behind your goons and expecting them to do all the dirty work for you," Blake said. "You're showing your face, which can only mean we aren't getting out of here alive."

"Who knows?" Bobby Q grinned. "Maybe, maybe not."

I shuddered. I was scared to even think about that possibility, but it was becoming more plausible with each minute. I knew the exact address of this place. I doubted Isaac would've given it to me if they planned to let us live.

But no, I couldn't think that way. I had to stay positive.

"I just want to know one thing," Bobby Q said as he spun the massive ring he wore on his right hand. "How did you know what I looked like? I was there only twice, and I wore a mask each time."

"I saw you come through the window before you took us to that basement. You should've put your mask on earlier."

Bobby Q sneered. "Are you shitting me? No one has that good a memory."

"They do when you have an ugly-ass scar that's visible from a mile away."

Bobby Q was quick, throwing a cross at Blake's face before anyone could even see him move. Blake staggered, his cheek splitting open where Bobby Q's ring had hit it. I pressed my hand against my mouth to stifle a cry. The metal of the gun at my back destroyed any possibility that I could do something to help Blake, and I hated being this useless.

"Take them to the basement," Bobby Q said. Blake flinched. *No, not the basement.* "Leave them there to reevaluate their life choices for a while."

"No," I whispered. Blake grew pale at once, and a sudden burst of anger carved a path through me. He was reliving his trauma all over again because of the same horrible people that had caused it.

"Walk," Isaac said, yanking him by his upper arm toward the hallway. Blake's steps were slow, laden. He had no choice but to face what he feared the most, and it wasn't fair. I wished I could at least touch him or hold him to dispel his demons.

"What are you waiting for? A blessing? *Move*." Lawrence nudged me with his gun.

My legs felt heavier than ever as I followed Isaac and Blake out of the living room. We descended the narrow stairs that led to the basement, the surrounding silence in the house falling heavy on my ears. There was no one who could help us. There was no one who could even hear us. We were on our own.

Blake stumbled when we got inside the small, stale room, which was completely empty save for the ropes stacked in the corner. It was lit by a light bulb that was so weak it seemed like it could burn out at any moment, and I wondered if that was the whole point. Maybe they wanted us to be in complete darkness.

Blake's words about his experience in the basement four years earlier came back to me with a vengeance, and I couldn't stop thinking about the worst. No food, no water. Dark. Punishment. Emma...Emma had gone through hell before she...

A whimper wanted to tear out of my mouth, but I had to keep it together. I mustn't lose it.

"This time you won't be able to untie yourself that easily," Isaac said as he grabbed one of the ropes. "Maybe that's better. That way you won't be responsible for someone's death." He winked at him, sharing a vicious laugh with Lawrence. *Bastard*.

Blake went even paler. I was sure the words had a devastating effect on his mind.

"Did you know?" Isaac asked me, tying Blake up as Lawrence held us both at gunpoint. "We kidnapped Blake and his lil' girlfriend four years ago. And guess who died then?" He secured Blake's wrists behind his back before he moved to wrap his ankles together. "His girlfriend! But not before we got to play with her. Men have needs, you know? And what can a man do when he has such a perfect pair of young tits and pussy in front of him?"

My heart felt like it would burst from its rampant pulse. I was nauseated.

"But in the end she died because of the tough boy here. He didn't listen. He wanted to play the hero, and that poor girl tried to protect him. So sweet." His fake dulcet voice added more weight to the lead in my stomach. "In the end, she paid the price because of him." Isaac stared coolly at Blake. "She died because of you."

He pushed Blake to sit on the floor against the wall. It concerned me how unwell Blake looked as he stared off into the distance.

"No," I said firmly. "She died because of you." I pointed an accusing finger at Isaac before Lawrence twisted my arm behind my back to tie my hands. "You're the one who killed her. It's your fault and your fault alone." I yelped because Lawrence tightened the rope around my wrists too hard.

Isaac raised his eyebrows at me. "So you heard the sob story from Blake, eh? I guess it's a good story to tell if you want to get into a girl's panties."

Blake didn't react, and I doubted he'd even heard Isaac because he was lost in his own world.

I spit in Isaac's face in a sudden spurt of courage and anger. "You're sick."

Lawrence stopped moving, as if waiting to see how this would unravel. Isaac wiped my spit off his face with a grimace and took a slow step toward me.

"Bitch." He slapped me across the cheek, hard, and I stumbled against Lawrence. My skin burned like thousands of needles had prodded my skin.

Cursing Isaac, Blake scrambled to get to his feet, but Isaac stepped above him and hit his temple with the handle of his gun, which sent him back down.

"Sit the fuck down," Isaac bit out.

"No, Blake." My legs moved toward him of their own volition, but Lawrence grabbed my hair and yanked me back, creating a burning pain in my scalp.

"I'm not done," he hissed into my ear. "So don't fucking move. You either, tough boy. Make a move, and I'll pull her hair out."

With a whimper, I looked back at Blake as Lawrence tied my ankles together, my eyes prickling with tears. We didn't look away from each other until Lawrence finished and pushed me to sit down next to him. I lost my balance and slid against the wall, landing on the ground with a thud.

Lawrence and Isaac laughed at my expense, getting sick pleasure out of all this. I tested the ropes around my wrists. They were too tight. There was no way I could ever get them loose.

"See ya in a while," Lawrence told us with a wink, and they left the basement.

Chapter 27

A THICK SILENCE DROPPED on us. Blake's ragged breathing and the loud thumping of my heart were the only things that filled it. My skin stung from the tight ropes, and my cheek pulsated dully in waves. I listened for any sounds from up above, but there were none.

The shock was slowly wearing off, and I started realizing the full gravity of the situation. We could be trapped for days. They could torture us however they wanted and we would most likely end up dead. How much time would pass before they were back?

My stomach churned as my breathing grew uneven, and I willed myself to calm down.

"Are you okay?" he asked me. "Does your cheek hurt?"

I looked at him and winced at the blood that trickled from the side of his head down his face. His cheek was already bruised, the cut on it bloody. "A little, but I'm okay. You?"

He wore a grimace as he studied my cheek, and I assumed a bruise was forming there. "Trying to be." He cursed. "Those sons of bitches." He leaned his head against the wall and closed his eyes, taking a deep breath. "I'm sorry."

"You don't have to be sorry for anything."

"Yes, I do. It's my fault."

"No, Blake, it's not your fault. Don't do this to yourself. It's not your fault they're deranged."

"But you would never have gotten into this situation if it weren't for me."

"Hey." I shimmied closer to him, until our bodies were almost touching. I bumped his shoulder with mine, managing a small smile. "You know guilt doesn't look attractive on you," I teased him, hoping to distract him enough to slow his erratic breathing. The tormented look on his face had been constant ever since we stepped in here. "Or fear. Where is that big, scary Blake?"

He didn't answer; his eyes were firmly closed as he took deep breaths.

"Just give me some time," he said after a while. "Talk about something."

"About what?"

"Anything will do."

"Okay, so..." I looked over the depressing gray bricks surrounding us in search of anything to talk about. "I love to sing in front of a mirror and pretend I'm in my own music video."

I formed a smile, even though I didn't feel like smiling. If this had been any other day, I would have been embarrassed, but now, I needed a distraction myself, a piece of normalcy in this completely abnormal situation.

"I take my deodorant and pretend it's a mic, and I sing my heart out. I've lost my voice too many times because I've pretended I'm Adele, hitting all those ridiculously high notes. Once, my youngest cousin, who was nine at the time, caught me doing it, and he couldn't stop laughing about it. He said I sounded like a chicken on helium. He even told my other cousins, and they goofed on me for weeks."

I wasn't aware of when my tears had started. I missed my cousins. I missed my family.

"I've been singing ever since I was little. My mom said I used to sing other children to sleep in kindergarten. You could say they were my first audience." I let out an empty chuckle and blinked quickly to clear the tears from my vision. "And speaking of firsts, my first kiss was so stupid—if you can even count it as a kiss. I was four, and a boy in my preschool class decided it would be nice to put his lips on mine in front of everyone. He said he saw his parents do it and wanted to see what it was all about." I giggled, shaking my head.

"What did you do?"

"I didn't do anything then, but I wrote on his face with a Sharpie while he was sleeping the next day. By the time he woke up, his whole face was covered in purple hearts and flowers."

He smiled for the first time, still resting his head against the wall with his eyes closed. "Good girl." He wasn't breathing as hard as before. "I never told you how I felt when I heard you sing at Hayden's place," he continued. "You had that look on your face I'd never seen before. You were so into it, and it was like I was seeing a completely different person. You had me dumbstruck right then and there. You're an amazing singer."

A flicker of warmth spread through the solid cold in my chest. "Thank you. I've always been so insecure about my voice, so...yeah. Thanks."

He looked at me. "You have nothing to be insecure about. You're smart, talented...beautiful. You're so beautiful, Jessie."

His words and the soft look in his eyes soothed me, making me feel like we were just two people hanging out with each other. There were no ropes that bit into our skin and limited our freedom, no walls confining us to un- certainty and fear. All this fear...we weren't getting out of there alive, were we? All these memories...they were just blips on our horizon that would soon be filled with darkness.

He moved closer to me so that our lips were only inches away from each other. "Kiss me," he whispered.

I leaned in and pressed my lips against his, feeling like crying and losing myself in him all at once. I was afraid. I was afraid this could be our last kiss, something deep within me telling me something terrible was going to hap- pen, even though my mind still refused to accept that possibility. I tugged at my ropes reflexively. I wished I could hug him and hold him close, but I couldn't, and it was too painful.

He pulled away, his eyes the softest shade of gray. My chest tightened at the blood on his face, and I wanted to do anything to make it go away—to help him heal. To stay with him and let us both heal. Together.

"Thank you for distracting me," he said. "Now..."

He blinked, and the softness in his gaze was gone, replaced by calcula- tion. He twisted and turned his body so that he was on his knees, looking like old Blake—in control and strong.

"Kneel with your back turned to me," he instructed me.

I angled my head to the side. "Why?"

"So you can try to reach for my belt." I looked at his black leather belt with a frown. "The buckle is actually the handle of a knife. You need to grab the buckle and pull it to the right to take the knife out. I'm going to cut our ties off."

My eyebrows rose high. *Wow.* "I never would've thought you'd have something like this up your sleeve. How did you come up with that?"

His eyes were dark and cold. "I learned my lesson the hard way. This is the best way to hide a knife."

"I see. Wait a sec." I wriggled so I could get to my knees and kneeled in front of him, positioning my hands right over his groin. "Admit it—you did this just so you could have me close to your crotch." I grasped the buckle.

"That was exactly my plan all along." I yanked the handle and pulled the knife out. "Good. Hold it that way. I'll just turn around and take it from you."

He moved around, and I looked over my shoulder as he looked over his. He reached for the knife, and I made sure he didn't touch the blade as I handed it to him.

"I'm going to cut your ropes first. Stay still."

He started working, the serrated blade coming dangerously close to my skin, but I trusted him not to hurt me. We didn't speak until he managed to cut through the rope, which loosened it enough for me to free my hands.

"*Yes.*" I exhaled, barely containing my voice that wanted to shout out my joy.

"Now cut mine."

My heart pounded faster as I took the knife from him. If they returned now... I pushed the blade against the rope, making sure it didn't come in contact with his skin. I managed to cut it, and he freed himself.

He smiled at me. "Thanks."

Next were the ropes around our ankles, which he cut in a few quick moves, and we were free.

I stood up. "What are we going to do now?"

"You won't do anything except run away. I'm going to deal with them."

"What? No. You absolutely can't do that. There are three of them!"

"In case you haven't noticed, the back door is right behind the staircase. They were cocky enough not to lock that door"—he pointed at the basement door—"so that's one less problem to deal with. I'm going to make sure the coast is clear for you to—"

I grabbed his forearms, getting colder and colder. "Do you even hear me, Blake? We should run away together! We'll find someone with a phone and call the cops."

"Jessie." He took my hands in his. "I can't miss this opportunity. I can't just run away when I can finally get my revenge."

"No, Blake. Please. Think about this. Please. I'm begging you not to do it. Let's escape together and call the cops on them. They will get a long time in prison for what they did to Emma."

He just watched me for a long time, and each new second was agonizing because my hope clashed with hurt, which consumed more of me. If he wouldn't reconsider...

"Or...or you can just shoot them in the leg or something," I added, getting desperate. "You can injure them badly. Yes. You can injure them and they will, like, bleed a lot and it will be satisfying, right?" I was babbling now, trying anything I could to make him change his mind. "You can make them suffer by torturing them long and slow, and it will still be cruel, right? There are a lot of ways to torture them—"

He squeezed my hands. "Jessie—"

"Please," I whispered. A tear slid down my cheek. "Please don't leave me."

He cupped my cheek and brushed my tear away with his thumb, looking at me with sadness that was unparalleled. "I don't want to leave you. I want to make you happy."

"Then make me happy. Give us a chance. There are other ways to get your revenge. Please, Blake."

"Jessie, I..." He dropped his hand from my face and closed his eyes. He took a deep breath. "I don't know what to do. I have no fucking clue."

"Live," I said. "Find a way to break away from your past and live. And I'll be here. I'll wait for you to come out and help you the rest of the way." I placed my hand over his heart, a few more tears escaping my eyes. "I'll help you see that you have so much more to live for. You can be happy again. I'll do my best to make you happy."

He studied my face in the long seconds that ticked by, his heart thumping madly against my hand. I could hardly breathe. I fiercely hoped I was getting through to him.

He wiped one tear from my face, then another. And another...

"Okay," he said, after what seemed like forever.

My heart stopped. "Okay?"

"Okay. Let's get out of here."

Relief unlike anything before surged through me, and I pulled him into my embrace, wrapping my arms around his waist tightly.

"Thank you!" I said into his chest. "Thank you, thank you, thank you."

He kissed the top of my head. "Save your thanks for later. Let's go before they return."

He took my hand and headed for the door. The pounding of my heart sounded too loud to my ears as he reached for the door handle, and a hundred bad scenarios passed through my mind as I waited for him to turn it. I exhaled a long breath when he opened the door and there was no one on the other side.

We climbed up the stairs to the first floor then he stopped at the top step. "Wait for me here while I check if the back door is locked," he whispered, releasing my hand.

A grim thought that it was my last time to hold Blake's hand flashed through my mind, and I stood glued to the ground. *This is bad.*

He peeked around the wooden banister to look down the hallway we'd come from and treaded silently to the back door, which now seemed too far away. My body was itching to move, to check if they were anywhere close—to rush Blake out of that door—but I didn't do anything, counting seconds that seemed like hours.

He tried the door, but it was locked. *Bad. This is so bad.* Beside that door, the hallway was a dead end, which meant the only way out was how we'd gotten here in the first place. We would have to pass the living room, which was connected to the hall, so there was no way for us to leave unnoticed.

"What now?" I mouthed as I took a step closer to him.

"Wait," he mouthed back, raising his hand in a stop motion. "I'll look around for another way. Don't move."

"No, Blake—" I started, but he didn't listen, walking in the direction of the living room.

I fisted my hands. I knew he shouldn't go there. They were going to see him and—

A crash coming from the living room made my blood run cold.

"Blake," I whimpered.

Another crash ripped through the air, and I darted around the banister to the sounds of fighting and grunts. I'd barely made it two steps when Isaac came out of the living room and rushed toward me with his gun. With a scream, I bolted around the banister and down the stairs to the basement, panic setting my lungs on fire when he fired the gun at me.

I screamed again, staggering into the basement. What could I do? I couldn't escape! In just a few seconds, he would reach me and kill me... My eyes darted frantically around the empty room—

The ropes!

But...

No, I had to do it.

I grabbed the rope and stopped next to the open door at the last possible moment. Isaac rushed inside, unable to see me hiding to the side, and I acted on instinct.

I threw the rope around his neck and pulled as hard as I could, adrenaline flooding through my system.

"*Bitch*," he choked out as he elbowed me in the stomach.

I was left without air as a sickening pain burst forth in my abdomen, and I almost let go of the rope. Pushing through it, I yanked the rope even harder, wrestling with him as he tried to take me down. His choking sounds mixed with my loud grunts when he tried to elbow me again, but I barely dodged it, and the rope cut deep into my skin when I pulled it even harder.

He choked and spurted, backing us up. "I... Kill..." He rammed me into a wall, trapping me between him and the firm surface as shouting and crashing rang out from the living room.

His elbow found my stomach again, which knocked all the air out of me. I cried out, nauseated by an unbearable pain. I couldn't take it anymore. I was about to release the rope, but then he collapsed head first, hitting the floor unconscious, and I almost ended up sprawled on top of him.

I regained my balance. My hands still yanked at the rope, my mind refusing to accept the possibility that he was unconscious, thinking he must be playing tricks on me...

But seconds passed, and he didn't move. I released the rope and slumped down to my knees as the horror of what I'd done surged through me. Was he dead? No, he couldn't be dead.

I pressed my fingers to his neck and felt a faint but present pulse. I cried out in relief. He was alive—

A shattering scream cut through the air, and my stomach dropped.

Blake. I had to get to Blake immediately.

I supported myself against the floor to stand up, but immense pain ripped through my abdomen, bringing tears to my eyes. I wheezed, telling myself to ignore the pain and exertion, and forced myself up to my feet until I spotted a bulge in the back pocket of Isaac's jeans that looked like a phone.

I could use it to call the police! *Yes.*

There were more sounds of crashing, and I forced myself to move faster. *Blake, hang on.*

"Please don't wake up soon. Please, please, please," I whispered to Isaac and pushed my hand inside his pocket. *Yes!* It *was* a phone.

I dialed 911 with trembling fingers and forced myself up to my wobbly feet as I listened for any new sounds from the living room, dreading seeing Bobby Q or Lawrence at any moment. *I hope Blake is okay. I hope he isn't banged up or...or dead. I hope—*

"911, what's your emergency?"

"Please, help! My friend and I have been kidnapped, and there are three of them. They have guns. I...I think my friend is hurt. Please, send the police immediately." I talked a mile a minute, my heart rate through the roof as I stared at Isaac's unmoving body. He could move at any moment...

"Do you know where you are?"

I gave her the address, and then she asked for more details. I had to repeat myself a few times because most of my words came out jumbled.

"Please hurry," I whined.

"The police are on the way," she told me. "Stay put and wait for them—"

The gun went off in the living room, and a scream lodged in my throat. *Blake.*

The phone slipped out of my hand and fell down.

"Miss? Hello? Miss?" I could hear the dispatcher calling me as I reached for Isaac's gun on the floor. I rushed out of the basement, ignoring the pain in my stomach. The weapon felt strange in my hand, heavy with the added weight of the silencer, and I didn't know what I was going to do with it.

I halted and peered around the wall into the living room. Blake and Bobby Q were fighting in the middle of the space, the chairs, coffee table, lamp, and gun thrashed around them. Several bruises already tainted their faces. Their punches were quick and brutal, and my stomach curled up into a tight knot when Bobby Q threw a one-two punch at Blake, making him stagger against the wall.

"You're done for, Jones," Bobby Q taunted.

I raised the gun at Bobby Q as I stepped into the room, but something in the corner caught my eye. Lawrence was slumped against the wall on the floor, unconscious, with Blake's belt knife stuck in his stomach. A huge amount of blood soaked his gray shirt and pooled around him, and for a moment, I couldn't move, fearing he was dead. I tore my gaze away from him.

"D-Don't move," I told Bobby Q.

He snapped his head to look at me, which was enough of a distraction for Blake to close in on him and punch him in the jaw. Bobby Q toppled over the couch and dropped to the floor, but he quickly scrambled to get up, and I aimed at him again.

"Don't move," I repeated. I hoped he couldn't see just how much my hands were shaking. "If you move, I'll shoot you." He grew still.

Blake supported himself against the back of the couch, panting. "Are you okay?"

My face distorted when I saw blood dripping from his mouth down his chin. "Yes."

"Where's Isaac?" Bobby Q asked me.

"Passed out in the basement." I looked at Blake. "I called the police, and they're on their way." Bobby Q reached for the gun on the floor. "Don't move!"

He smirked and retracted his arm, wiping some blood off the corner of his mouth. "You won't shoot me. You don't even know how to hold a gun." He pointed at the gun I held, and I straightened my grasp around it, holding it with both hands.

"Maybe she won't," Blake said. Something dark converged around him as he picked up the gun from the floor. "But I will." He aimed it at Bobby Q.

I let out a small gasp because of the sudden look on his face. I could feel the darkness that was unlike anything I'd ever felt from him—not even in those days when he bullied me the most—and it was like I was seeing a completely different person. My fear of what he could do returned, only it was so much stronger. This wasn't the same Blake. This guy...this guy was capable of killing a person.

This was his chance to avenge Emma, and now, with a gun in his hand, he had the perfect opportunity to deal with his kidnappers. I looked at Lawrence. I couldn't see his chest moving. What if Blake hadn't pushed that knife into his stomach in self-defense? What if he had been trying to kill him?

"Blake, what are you going to do?" I asked in a panicky tone when he took a few menacing steps toward Bobby Q. His face was filled with undiluted hatred, his teeth bared as he hovered above him. My stomach coiled with increasing tension. "Blake, the police will come and handle him. So please..."

He didn't even listen to me, taking another step toward Bobby Q, the end of the gun only inches away from his face.

Bobby Q's cocky expression was finally gone. "Don't do anything rash, okay?" he told him. He could see it in Blake's eyes too. He could see that Blake was capable of finishing him off in an instant. "You don't actually want to kill me. So put down that gun and—"

Blake pressed the gun against Bobby Q's forehead and snarled at him. "I want to kill you," he said in a voice I didn't recognize. "I want to blow up your brain just like Isaac did to Emma. I want to kill all of you."

I took a shaky step toward him. "Blake, please, put the gun down."

Blake nudged Bobby Q's forehead with the gun. "No. He needs to die. All of them need to die."

My heartbeat was deafening in my ears. "No, don't do this. You've decided not to do it. They will be jailed for life. They will be punished."

Blake growled. "*No.* That's not enough."

"Listen to the girl, Jones. Be smart."

"*Smart?* That's rich coming from you. How many deaths do you have on your conscience?"

I took another step toward him, Isaac's gun hanging loosely in my hand. "Don't, Blake. You're not like him. You're so much more than that. Please think about yourself, your future. Think about me. Don't do it. Please, don't do it."

He just glared at Bobby Q as he stood rigidly; his hand clenched the handle of the gun more tightly as his finger twitched over the trigger. His muscles were quivering, and I expected him to shoot any second...

Too quickly for me to comprehend, the gun was taken out of my hand and pressed against my temple.

"Drop the gun, or she's dead," Isaac said hoarsely as he grabbed my shoulder to keep me in place.

Blake's eyes widened at Isaac's gun. He met my gaze then looked at the gun again, and his face twisted with anguish and fear that matched mine. I grew queasy with fear that made my limbs cold. It was limitless.

"Okay," Blake choked out. "Okay. Just don't hurt her." He dropped the gun to the floor and stepped away from Bobby Q, and for a second, our eyes locked on each other.

Isaac aimed his gun at Blake and pulled the trigger.

I screamed. The world narrowed to the bullet that hit Blake's head, just like it had hit Emma, and the horrid and ghastly sight punched the air out of me.

Blake dropped to the ground and remained there motionless, dark blood streaming from the top of his head down his face. Just like Emma. *Dead.*

"NO," I screamed, sinking to my knees. He'd been shot in the head. He wasn't moving. He wasn't moving at all. "No, no, no, no!"

The police sirens reverberated in the distance, but I couldn't feel anything but this crushing feeling in my chest that spread through all of me and hammered more and more pain into me. He was dead. Blake was dead. *He's dead. Dead. Dead. DEAD.*

"Shit. The fucking cops," Bobby Q said, sounding like his voice came from the end of a dark tunnel. His face was blurry as I looked at him, just like the rest of my surroundings as the edges of my vision went white. "I'll go get the car ready, and you get rid of the girl."

He ran out of the room, and I looked at Isaac, unusually apathetic as shock detached me from reality.

Isaac hovered above me. "Sorry, sweety pie, but play nice in heaven, okay?" He winked and raised his gun at me, and I closed my eyes, too empty.

Blake is dead.

And I'm going to die too.

The gunshot rang out, followed by a scream. I jerked, but there was no pain. I opened my eyes in confusion. Isaac fell to the floor and let go of the gun, blood flowing out of his stomach. I snapped my head at Blake and choked on air. The gun was raised in his hand, pointed in the direction where Isaac had stood a moment before.

"Blake!"

He was *alive*.

I knocked the gun away from Isaac, who was curled into a ball and holding his stomach as he whined in pain, and then I crawled to Blake, taking in the huge, gruesome wound on the top of his head. The sickening amount of blood trickled from it all over his face, making it unrecognizable. I thought I must have died and was seeing a fantasy. Blake was *alive*. Fresh tears streamed down my face.

"Blake, you're alive," I croaked, grabbing his shoulders.

He dropped his arm and looked at me with a faint smile. "You're okay," he whispered, his eyes fluttering shut. "Thank fuck."

I dug my fingers into his shoulders, feeling like I was going to hyperventilate. "No, Blake. Open your eyes. Don't close them."

The front door burst open, and three officers appeared at the threshold with their guns drawn. "Police!" one of them said, but he stopped himself when he spotted us. "Miss? Are you okay?"

I took Blake's hand in mine. "Please, call an ambulance," I said quickly. "That guy"—I pointed at Isaac—"shot him in the head!"

The officer said something into his radio and stepped inside with the others, looking around the room. "The ambulance is already here." His colleague went over to check Lawrence, while the other guy leaned over Isaac.

"Jessie..." Blake let out, his hand getting colder in mine. "I...I..."

"Save your strength and don't talk," I told him, smiling and brushing my tears away. "You're going to be all right. Just hang on. The ambulance will get you to the hospital, and you're going to be okay. I promise. I'm here with you."

He struggled to open his eyes, and when he did, the warmth in them undid me, breaking my heart over and over again.

"You did great, Jessie...you're so brave."

I wiped more tears away, but they kept coming and coming. "Just like you. You saved me."

His lips fought to hold his smile. He tried to squeeze my hand, but his grip was so weak. "I love you," he said.

He loves me.

And that was where I lost it. I broke into more tears, sobbing, and I clutched him like he was going to disappear right this second. The paramedics rushed into the room with a stretcher and surrounded us, but I didn't want to let go of him. I'd never even told him those exact words.

"I love you too, Blake," I said with a heartfelt conviction, feeling it was too late. His eyes closed of their own volition, and his hand became limp in mine. My panic tripled. *No, no, no, no...* He had to be okay.

"Miss, you need to move so we can do our job," someone said, pulling me away from Blake as the paramedics gathered around him.

"I love you so much," I murmured, reaching out for him, but I grasped only thin air. "I love you, Blake."

Don't die.

He didn't move. He didn't even *breathe*.

"We're losing him."

No.

"He has no pulse."

No, no, no.

"Start CPR."

NO.

Someone made me sit on the couch and told me something, but I couldn't hear anything. I couldn't see anything but Blake, and it was like an eternal cold seeped into each part of me and I wasn't living anymore. They kept compressing his chest, the motion repeating into forever as they placed pads on his chest that were connected to some small device next to him.

"Still no pulse."

"Apply the AED."

Everything became muffled, and as I watched them trying to revive him in the countless seconds that rushed by, I lost all hope. He wasn't waking up.

He was dead.

It was like someone had drawn a curtain over me, and the world lost all sense.

Chapter 28

I STARED AT THE THERAPIST across the desk as she wrote something on her clipboard. Each minute brought me little shards of ache. I'd been in her office for the past twenty minutes, but it felt like days, especially after that hour I spent with the emergency doctor as he examined me. I had a huge, ugly bruise where Isaac had elbowed me, but the doctor had determined there was no further damage, so I didn't have to stay in the hospital.

He sent me to a therapist for discharge counseling, but not before I gave a detailed statement to the cops on what had happened in that house just a few hours earlier, and it was like a fresh round of torture.

Just recollecting everything was enough to suffocate me with pain, which felt like it would never end. I'd seen him die with my own eyes. Just like Emma.

"I need to see him," I said to the therapist, anxious to get out.

She moved her gaze from her clipboard to me and offered a polite smile. "I understand, but please be patient. You need to go through a full check-up—"

"I'm fine." I was close to bolting out and going to Blake's room.

"There may be psychological effects—"

"There are none," I insisted. To hell with pleasantries.

I couldn't have cared less about niceties or whether she would see me as desperate or not. I couldn't care after seeing the person I loved die and come back to life in front of my eyes. Not after having almost died myself.

Somehow, after all of that, all my previous insecurities and doubts seemed so trivial now. So unimportant. It didn't matter when I was staring death in the face. It didn't matter when my every second now was a gift—a gift from Blake because he'd saved me. He'd saved my life, completely disregarding his, and it felt like I would never be able to repay him for that. Not in a million years.

There were no more restraints that kept me away from him. There was no more shame or insecurity. Nothing mattered anymore but being by his side and giving him all the love in this world, telling him I forgave him for everything and needed him with me.

The therapist smiled pleasantly. "You may feel okay, but we need to make sure you actually *are* okay. It's highly possible for you to sustain trauma after what you've gone through."

I wanted to laugh at her. Or just laugh. Laugh, laugh, laugh. I'd felt like laughing ever since the paramedics applied the AED and his heart started beating again after going into cardiac arrest. He had actually been dead. For whole two minutes, he'd been dead, but the damage that had been done to my heart was permanent. I knew very well the pain of losing him now, and it was stamped into me for good. I never wanted to lose him again. I wanted to laugh until the pain and trauma were just a faint memory.

"Yeah, sure. But can we do that later? You can analyze me all you want after I see him. I haven't even seen him yet."

I hadn't seen him since they rushed us to the hospital. I'd sat next to him in the ambulance, holding his hand as the paramedics talked about how lucky he was because the bullet had miraculously only grazed his head instead of hitting him, and all I could think about was the hilarious irony that had allowed him to keep living. If that bullet had been only a tiny bit lower, it would've hit his brain, and he would've been dead for good.

The bubbles of laughter rose up my throat, but I suppressed them because I knew if I started laughing now, I would burst into tears and never stop.

The bullet had only taken a piece of his skin, creating a wound on the top of his head that needed five stitches but wasn't serious according to the doctors. He'd gone into cardiac arrest because of a chaotic heartbeat caused by shock, but because he had been resuscitated quickly, it appeared there was no brain damage. They had mentioned they would keep him under observation for a few days, after which he was free to go home. Free to continue living as if nothing had happened.

But it had happened, and it had marked us forever. It had ensnared us, only this time, we had each other to push through. And it was going to be okay. It had to be.

She sighed and pushed her glasses up her nose. "All right." I jumped up out of the chair and grimaced when a dull pain pierced through my stomach. "*But,*" she went on, "I hope we'll continue our conversation later."

I nodded at her, already on my way out. "Sure."

I'd barely stepped out of her office when I got pulled into a hug, and Mom's brittle voice filled my ear. "You're all right. Thank goodness."

"Mom!" I leaned into her, unable to withhold my tears anymore. I cried in her arms, seeking her warmth and support like it was the only thing that shielded me from the hell of this world. I could've died and they could've lost me...

I clutched the fabric of her jacket. "I love you, Mom. I love you so much."

"I love you too, sweetie. I love you the most in this world." She kissed the top of my head, sobbing together with me.

I met Dad's gaze over her shoulder. His usually stoic face was a picture of pain and fear now.

"We came as soon as we got the call," he said as he pulled Mom and me into his embrace.

"Are you okay? Are you hurt?" Mom asked, stepping away to inspect me for any injuries.

"Yes, I'm okay. I got hit in the stomach, but the doctor said it's not serious."

"Oh, sweetie." She kissed my forehead. "Those horrible, horrible people."

Dad's brows pinched together in worry. "They told us you were kidnapped along with Mayor Jones' son. I just got off the phone with Nathaniel, who confirmed it."

"It's true. They showed up in the school parking lot and took us."

Mom grew pale. "The school parking lot!"

"Why did they target you?" Dad asked, assuming his lawyer stance.

I let out a long exhalation and sniffed a few times, brushing away my tears. As much as I wanted to give them all the details, it had to wait. I needed to see Blake.

"It's a long story. I'll tell you later because I need to see him now."

"Him?" Mom asked.

"Blake. He saved my life. I'll see you later." I turned on my heel, but then I stopped myself and looked at her over my shoulder. "He's the boy you asked me about. He's the boy I fell in love with."

"What?" both my parents said simultaneously, but I didn't elaborate, rushing to Blake's room.

I'd just turned the corner when I saw Sarah, Melissa, Kevin, and Marcus coming in my direction. Their worried faces broke into relief when they saw me.

Mel pointed at me. "She's not a ghost! She's very much alive. We've been looking everywhere for you!"

The sight of them brought on fresh tears, reminding me of everything I could've lost.

"You're here," I said.

Sar hugged me. "It's okay. We're here."

Mel, Kev, and Marcus joined us, making it a group hug, and we all started laughing. My friends. My beacons in the dark.

"Thank you for coming."

"Of course we're here, silly!" Mel said when we separated. "Who would've thought you would join Sarah's 'kidnapped' club?" She shook her head. "Those sons of cockroaches. They deserve to be cooked in the deepest pot of boiling water then thrown to rats."

Sar squeezed my shoulder. "It's all over now."

"Are you okay?" Kev asked me. "Did th-they hurt you?"

I couldn't really tell them my physical wounds didn't compare to what I felt inside. So I just said, "Yes, I'm okay, but how did you know I was here?"

"A student saw them force you into your car," Sarah said. "He rushed into the gym and shouted that we needed to call the cops because you and Blake had been taken away, and Principal Aguda called 911. We immediately came here when we heard you were found."

So the whole school knew about it. It was no wonder there were reporters outside who were trying to enter the hospital to get the scoop.

"I still can't believe it," Marcus said. "I thought that student was pranking us."

"You can imagine Mrs. Aguda's expression when she heard what he said," Mel said. "We were at an anti-bullying festival while her students got kidnapped right under her nose! I can already see her organizing an anti-kidnapping festival to make sure this doesn't happen again."

"What happened there?" Sar asked with concern on her face that doubled the pain simmering inside me.

"Is it true that Blake died and was brought back to life?" Marcus asked, his eyes wide.

My chest hurt. I didn't want to remember that moment. I didn't ever want to talk about that moment.

"It's true, but let's talk about that later." I continued toward Blake's room. "I'm on my way to see him."

"We've seen him," Sarah said, walking in step with me.

"You have? How is he?"

"Hayden, Masen, and Steven are with him now. He's awake, and he's okay. He asked for you."

My tears blurred my vision. "He did?" I quickened my steps. I wanted to pull him into my embrace and never let go of him. I felt like it had been weeks since I'd last seen him, and my legs couldn't carry me fast enough.

"Yep. He even cried tears of joy for you and ordered a hundred bouquets of red roses to be delivered to your doorstep," Mel said, pressing her hand against her chest dramatically.

I rolled my eyes at her. "Really now?"

She looked at me solemnly. "Cross my heart and *never* hope to die."

Kev adjusted his glasses. "He was t-talking to the officers when we saw him."

"The guys who did this to you are in for a very long time in prison," Marcus said.

I truly hoped so. Unlike Bobby Q, who was in custody now, Lawrence and Isaac had been rushed to the hospital, but they were under surveillance and would be transferred to jail.

I was relieved Lawrence hadn't died. Blake's knife had ruptured his liver, but the paramedics had managed to treat him before he bled out. As for Isaac, the bullet had hit his spleen, but it wasn't fatal, even though he'd lost a lot of blood. They were both going to recover, but I wanted them to receive the highest punishment.

My heartbeat quickened when we reached Blake's floor.

"I love you," he'd said.

His words ricocheted through my mind like fireworks, alleviating the pain. He'd managed to break out of hatred and love me back. We'd managed to find a way to each other. And now that the nightmare was over, we were finally free to get a new beginning.

I didn't bother knocking, losing my breath when I wrenched the door open and found him lying in the hospital bed with bandages covering his head. He was smiling as Steven talked, and the sight almost made the ball of tension in me burst. For a painful moment, I saw him get shot, fall to the floor, and remain motionless in a heap of blood. My body swayed on my unstable feet as my vision blurred once again.

He's alive. Alive.

His gaze met mine, and a sharp pang hit my chest. I was barely aware of everyone around us. I was barely aware of anything as I rushed to him, grabbed his shoulders, and pressed my lips to his like he was going to dissolve at any moment.

He responded immediately, his arms wrapping around me and pulling me in so that I was sitting against him as his lips molded to mine. I held him tighter, ignoring the pain in my abdomen, the intoxicating taste of him rolling over my tongue. *I love you, I love you, I love you.*

"Let's give them some privacy," I thought I heard Sarah say, but I couldn't be sure because I was so lost in him.

The sounds of retreating footsteps filled the room, but we never broke our kiss. I couldn't stop the tears from pouring out, both happy and sad. All I needed was for us to find some sense after everything we'd been through.

He surprised me when he cupped my cheeks and kissed my tear away, and then another, and then one more. My heart was so full of him.

"You died. You actually died right in front of me, and I thought I lost you forever," I cried out, clinging to his shoulders.

"You didn't lose me. You'll never lose me."

His fervent words hammered happiness into me, and more tears poured out, soaking my whole face.

"How do you feel? Does your head hurt?"

"Yeah, but it's nothing serious."

I let out a strangled chuckle. "Nothing serious. The bullet grazed your *head*. I can't believe how lucky you were. So lucky." I chuckled again and again, feeling like I was on the verge of hysteria.

"Hey." He peered into my eyes with a crushing softness in his gaze. "Hey, I'm okay. It's strange since that bullet didn't do any damage other than leaving a nasty scar, but I think I'll be able to live with that."

He winked and smiled at me, but I didn't return it, tracing each inch of his face with my eyes. He was covered in bruises and small cuts, and it hurt just looking at them.

"Are *you* okay?" he asked me.

"I'm fine."

He shook his head. "You're not okay. Come here." He pulled me against his shoulder, snaking his arms around me, and I sank into him, seeking his comfort and warmth like it was the only thing that could keep me sane at the moment. I shook as I shed silent tears.

"I'm here," he whispered into my hair as he stroked it. "It's over now, and it's going to be okay."

I clutched his shoulder. "I'm the one who should say that. Look at me. I'm all whiny and crying when you went through a lot worse—"

"Hey." He made me look at him and smiled softly. "Don't worry about me. You can cry all you want." He ran his thumb over my cheek. "I'll be here to take care of you."

His words opened the dam, and I couldn't stop myself from bursting into more tears. I cried and cried as he slowly rocked me in his arms, all that fear, pain, anxiety, and stress flowing out of me. It was over. That horror was over.

My tears had long stopped and dried, but he didn't let go of me. Peace unlike ever before took over me. I wasn't going to break. He wasn't going to die.

"I was so worried about you," he said. "I was scared shitless when Isaac went to find you, but I couldn't do anything to stop him, because Lawrence had pinned me against the floor."

I leaned back to look at him. "What happened there? With Lawrence?"

"He tried to take my knife, but then Bobby Q pulled out his gun, and I knew I had to act fast if I didn't want to end up dead. I had to use my knife.

It was the only way for me to free myself and fight back before Bobby Q killed me. You saw the rest. What happened with Isaac?"

I took a deep breath and told him how I'd used the rope to defend myself. "I was afraid I'd killed him, Blake. I was afraid I'd gone too far."

He observed me with awe, a small smile flickering across his lips. "But you didn't. You just defended yourself. You did nothing wrong." He took my hand and pressed an open-mouthed kiss to my palm that I could feel all the way through my body. "I'm so proud of you, Jessie. You were so strong back there."

My chest inflated at the look in his eyes. It felt like I was dreaming, only this time there were no nightmares. Just sweet dreams, which fueled me with hope that tomorrow would be a new day, a better day.

I leaned in and touched my lips to his. This time our kiss was slow and sweet, our lips brushing against each other softly, and I savored the moment.

I was warm all over when I pulled away. "You saved my life. I don't think I can ever thank you enough for what you've done for me."

He planted a small kiss on my forehead. "There's no need to. I would do it again."

He would do it again. I just looked at him, the depths of his searing gray eyes pulling me in. How things had changed between us. From enemies to this. From a person I feared and hated the most to the person I loved and needed the most. I wanted him to know how he made me feel. I wanted him to know I was okay with our past. I wanted to tell him everything.

"I love you," I started. "All this time I was fighting against it, against the pull, but I couldn't beat it. I thought I was going to finish school, leave Enfield, and forget about you, but I don't want to forget about you. I don't want to be away from you.

"I've let go of our past. I was holding grudges all this time and reminding myself how bad you were, but you've changed, and what you did for me in that house...no, from the moment you stepped in front of Isaac's gun to protect me in the school parking lot—I'll never forget it. And now I just want to be next to you and love you. I just want to make you happy. And I..." I placed my hand on his cheek and ran my thumb softly over one of the cuts that marred his cheek. "I forgive you. For everything."

His eyes darted between mine as he studied me quietly with no smile on his face, and the prolonged silence played with my nerves.

"Say something," I let out on a breathless chuckle.

"It took you a while," he said with a smirk and a mischievous glint in his eyes.

I raised my eyebrows as the faint blush coated my cheeks, but then his gaze softened.

"That's okay. It took me a while too." He leaned in and pulled my lower lip between his, tugging at it once before he kissed it. "It took me a while and that fucking gun aimed at your head to realize you're the most important thing to me. Nothing matters but you." He laced his fingers through my hair. "All this time I was so stuck on my past I didn't even see I was missing out." He leaned his forehead against mine. "I was missing out on the best thing that has happened to me, and I almost lost it. I almost lost you." He nuzzled my nose. "But not anymore. I'm not leaving you. Ever."

A sweet ache nestled in my chest as warmth and happiness claimed each inch of me. A happy melody formed in my mind, playing out in a quick tempo that matched my fast heartbeat. I couldn't look away from his eyes that spoke so much to me, feeling the warmth that helped dispel the ever-crushing feeling of his death. He was here; he was alive. Not dead. Not anymore.

Too overwhelmed by my feelings for him, I pressed my lips against his and gripped him by his hospital gown. I felt like no kiss would ever be enough. I was going to kiss him again and again, day after day, and shower him with the love my heart begged me to give him.

"Thank you for forgiving me," he said in between kisses. "Thank you for being the person you are."

He held me by the back of my head and deepened our kiss, and it was all I'd ever needed and much more.

"You got under my skin, Jessie, and I love every second of it." He moved my hair away from my neck and left a kiss under my ear. I let out a satisfied sigh, my eyes fluttering closed. "I can't get you out of my head." He placed another soft kiss on my neck. "I can't stop thinking about you or when I'm going to see you again." He drew away. "You're all I can think about these days, and it sickened me that I couldn't even do anything. It was like my hands were tied again because I had to make things right and avenge Emma."

"How about now? You wanted them dead. Do you...do you feel like you've failed her?"

He looked out the window into the evening darkness. His brows furrowed as he mused on something. Slowly, the corner of his lips quirked up.

"No. You were right. She wouldn't want me to destroy or sacrifice my life. She would want me happy. And I'm happy because I have you." He looked at me. "I'd rather see them dead, true, but they will get what they deserve because I'm going to make sure they're serving life."

"How are you going to do that?"

"My dad has connections. It would be no problem to convince a judge to sentence them to life without parole, and at the worst prison in the state. A lot of nasty stuff can happen there that will make them 'reevaluate their life choices,'" he said, quoting Bobby Q's words. He smirked, and I was offered a glimpse of that cruelty I'd seen when he held Bobby Q at gunpoint. "I guess the video I kept all this time won't just be a torturous reminder of those days. It will come in handy as evidence."

"I'm just glad they won't be able to hurt anyone anymore." I palmed his cheek and smiled. "It's over."

He smiled back at me. "It's over for them...but it's just the beginning for us."

My heart contracted. My lips curled into an even bigger smile, but then the door burst open, and a barrage of questions filled the room. I jumped away from Blake's bed like I'd been caught red-handed as his parents pushed their way through a crowd of reporters with cameras and microphones that had flocked to the corridor outside Blake's room.

"Mayor Jones, what can you say about the kidnapping?"

"Mayor Jones, is it true that your son was kidnapped four years ago?"

"Sir, we heard your son was shot in the head. Is that true?"

"Is he alive?"

"No, you're looking at a vampire," Blake said in a low tone with a sneer.

The security officer kept his parents separated from the reporters, shielding them as they came inside. The reporters pushed forward to get some photos, but the security officer didn't allow it.

"No cameras allowed," he said, preventing one of the reporters from getting in. "You're not allowed to enter. Step back." He closed the door, which left Blake, his parents, and me in awkward silence as they stared at me. I blushed.

"Hello," I said quietly to break the ice, giving them a small wave.

"Jessica Metts?" Nathaniel said.

"You came back from Hartford to see me," Blake said, his face blank. "Surprise, surprise."

Daniela and Nathaniel approached his bed and stopped on his other side, splitting a look between Blake and me.

"We were supposed to return tomorrow, but once we got the call, we came as quickly as possible," Daniela said.

She was a picture of composure as always. There were no worry lines on her face as she looked at her son; there was nothing. If it was my mother in her place, she would be a bawling mess by now. However, I could see a hint of anguish in the depth of those gray eyes, reminding me so much of Blake.

"How are you holding up?" Nathaniel asked him.

Blake assumed a bored expression. "As you can see, I'm in one piece, so don't be so heartbroken about me." His sarcasm brought a frown to their faces.

"We're worried about you, son," Nathaniel said. "You could've died." He shook his head and closed his eyes for a few moments in an unusual and brief display of vulnerability. "And to think the same people kidnapped you again. It's ridiculous!"

"But this time you can't hide it from the public," Blake retorted with a sardonic smile on his face. "I'm sorry about your reputation, Dad, but you can't keep it intact this time. I wonder what the media will say once they hear you wanted to keep everything on the down low."

"Will you stop with that attitude, Blake?" his mother asked. "We're not your enemies. We've done what we thought would be best for our family—what would be best for you. You developed..." She looked at me, stopping herself before she said what she'd intended to say. "You developed some *issues* after that, and it would've been worse if the whole town had gossiped about you. It would've been a constant reminder for you."

Blake curled his lip at her. "How touching. You did it all for me." He rolled his eyes. "And you can say what it is. She knows I have PTSD."

Daniela let out an almost undetectable gasp. Her eyes widened imperceptibly as she took me in. "You told her?" She was looking at me differently now, like she was seeing me for the first time, and I could almost see the wheels turning in her head. "Why are you here exactly?"

I felt myself blushing profusely under their inquisitive stares. "I—"

"Why is she here?" Blake asked, staring at them. He took my hand. "She's here because she's my girlfriend."

Girlfriend. I gaped at him.

Nathaniel's brows rose. "Your girlfriend?"

Blake smiled softly at me. I felt hot and so shy in front of his parents, but that didn't defuse my happiness.

"Yes, girlfriend." He didn't look away from me, smiling. "And I love her."

It was official. My heart would burst any moment now.

He looked at them, narrowing his eyes. "Any problem with that?"

Daniela and Nathaniel shared an uncomfortable glance.

"No." Nathaniel was the first to speak. He cleared his throat. "No, not at all."

"Good," Blake answered and squeezed my hand, his eyes glimmering joyfully as he looked at me. "Because I wouldn't have it any other way."

Chapter 29

ON MONDAY, IT SEEMED like the whole town knew the mayor's son had been kidnapped for the second time. The media went nuts, trying to dig into Blake's past as much as they could, and the headlines talking about both kidnappings seemed never-ending. People were shocked to hear that Blake had gotten kidnapped when he was only fourteen years old, along with his girlfriend who'd been raped and brutally killed, which sparked public outrage.

The news outlets were starving for drama, so when they heard a girl had been involved in the second kidnapping too, it was like offering blood to sharks, drawing their unwanted attention to me. The reporters had been calling the whole day trying to get an interview with me, but Mom refused every one of them. By Tuesday, she couldn't handle the phone constantly ringing in our house, so she unplugged the device and cursed journalists—or as she called them, vultures—six ways to Sunday.

The mayor was quick to hold a press conference in an attempt to reduce the damage this could cause to his reputation. He claimed they'd needed to keep the first kidnapping a secret because they feared for their son's safety, which only gave rise to more questions. However, he skillfully dodged them by talking about Bobby Q, Isaac, and Lawrence and the long time they awaited in prison. He ended with a promise that he would do everything in his power to make sure they received the punishment they deserved, which earned him a round of loud applause.

The way Nathaniel dealt with the public outcry was revolting, and I felt sorry that Blake's dad couldn't be someone who cared for his family more than his public image. Blake didn't make a big deal out of it since he was already used to it, but it only made me want to show him even more that he was loved and cared for. He wasn't alone in this world. Not anymore.

Since we were on spring break, I used the free time to be with Blake and work on my music. My mind replayed the scenes from that house on repeat, and my music helped me shut it out at least for a while. It helped me forget the dark side of this world that I never wanted to experience again. However, I couldn't stop the tears as I played my guitar, letting all those negative feelings flow out of me before they ate me alive.

I cried and cried, welcoming each new breath I inhaled more than ever. I could see many things in a new light and appreciate what I had, which fueled my strength to pursue my dreams no matter how hard it would be. One step at a time.

At night, memories unveiled themselves in front of my eyes like a movie reel. Emma. Blake. Me. Lost and broken dreams. Second chances. But I had Blake's nightly call to help me deal with bad feelings. After almost an hour, his deep voice would lull me into dreamless sleep, and it would almost be as if nothing had happened.

On Thursday night, I edited and uploaded the video of my solo on YouTube, right after I changed the name of my channel from Valerie to Jessie, using Blake's nickname for me as my new stage name. I was finally revealing myself to the public, and as I watched the video load and play on my screen, I felt a strange mixture of anticipation and relief. I was taking another big step forward after my festival solo, and it was just the beginning.

The next step would be live performances, and I already had some plans for the summer. My stomach twisted just imagining it, but all the anxiety would be worth it. It would be worth it to perform for many people and see their faces as they got immersed in my music.

I smiled. One day. One day, I would make it happen.

My new phone rang, and my smile grew bigger when I saw Blake's ID.

"Hey," I said as I sank into my bed and settled myself against the pillows.

"I just saw your video. You look like an angel when you sing."

I squealed and blushed. I wanted to hug my phone to my chest. "You really think so?"

"Yeah. All those views you have? Half of them are from me."

I giggled. The previous night, I'd told him about my channel and my dream to become a singer, and he had spent hours browsing through my videos and liking them. He teased me, saying I was about to pee myself with how excited I was each time he clicked on a new video, but it was hard not to be in seventh heaven when he was quickly becoming my number one fan.

He even asked me to send him one of my songs so he could use it as a ring-tone for my calls.

"I'm just glad I have any views at all. I was so nervous when I posted it."

"Don't be. I'm sure everyone will love it. I'll have to fend off your admirers real soon."

I started chuckling and couldn't stop. "Already jealous?"

"Can't help it when I have such an attractive and talented girlfriend."

There it was again. I couldn't get any happier, and my longing for him pulsated stronger. We'd seen each other only this morning, but it felt like it'd been days, and I missed him. I'd never known being his girlfriend would feel so, so good. I still had to pinch myself to prove to myself I wasn't dreaming.

"You're so full of compliments today."

"Is that a problem?"

I grinned. "No, I just feel like you're going to spoil me soon."

"I wouldn't mind that."

"I miss you."

"I miss you too. I can't stop thinking about you. But you already know that." There was a raspy quality to his voice that underlined his words, and I got a strong urge to make out with him until we were both breathless and totally lost in each other.

"It doesn't hurt to hear it again." There was a knock at the door. "Hold on a sec," I said to Blake and sat up. "Yes?"

My mom peered inside. "Can you come down? Dad and I want to talk to you." She looked serious, with a hardly visible smile tugging at her lips.

"Sure. I'll be there in a minute." She nodded and closed the door. "Blake, I have to go. My parents want to talk to me about something."

"Okay. We'll talk later."

My chest warmed. I was already looking forward to it. "I can't wait."

I stood up as soon as I disconnected and left my phone on my bed. I wondered what they wanted to talk about.

When I'd been discharged from the hospital, they had sat me down in the living room for a long talk about the kidnapping. Mom and I had broken into tears when she pulled me into a hug and held me as I shared the most horrifying details.

I'd never seen them more scared, and I wished they didn't have to go through this. I didn't want to think about how they would've felt if anything had happened to me. Maybe they were too strict and unrelenting when it came to some aspects of my upbringing, but they loved me the most in this world, and I knew no matter what, I was never alone. I would always have them.

They were seated on the couch when I stepped into the living room. "What's up?"

They glanced at each other. "Last night, Dad and I talked about your college decision."

I froze mid-step. "Okay." I lowered myself into the armchair next to the couch and clasped my hands together in my lap. They didn't look off the wall, but that didn't alleviate my sudden anxiety. If they wanted to tell me they wouldn't support me and help me with expenses...

Mom's lips curled into a tiny smile. The worry lines seemed to have etched themselves into her forehead since Sunday, and it was like she had aged years in a matter of few days. "We support you."

I was sure I must've heard her wrong. "What?"

Dad smiled at me. The dark circles under his eyes matched Mom's. Both of them looked like they hadn't slept a wink the night before. "We support your decision to go to a music college," he said.

I gaped at them. "You do?"

Mom nodded. "Yes." Her smile disappeared, giving way to pain. "We want only the best for you, but not at the expense of your happiness. What happened on Sunday..." She shuddered. "It opened our eyes. You were right. Life is too short and unpredictable for you to waste your opportunities. We've pressured you too much, without ever really asking you what you want."

"We want you happy, Jess," Dad said. "And if becoming a lawyer will make you unhappy, we won't pressure you to do it. All that matters is that you're safe, healthy, and happy."

My heart danced madly in my chest as I looked between them. "Do you really mean that?"

Mom leaned toward me and placed her hand over mine on my lap. "Yes. And it's high time we start believing everything is going to be all right no matter which path you choose, isn't that right, Owen?" She looked at Dad with a smile.

"That's right. You have an extraordinary talent, so prove us wrong. Prove you can make a future for yourself. Fight through good and bad."

"And don't worry about the money, because we'll help you with it as much as we can," Mom added, making my heart beat even faster. "Follow your dreams, honey. Make us proud."

"Thank you, thank you, thank you!" I squealed in excitement and wound my arms around her tightly. "You're the best!" I squealed even louder as I hugged Dad. "I'll make you proud. You'll see."

I couldn't stop grinning, jumping up and down like a little kid. They were letting me follow my dreams. I almost expected someone to tell me this was an early April Fools' joke, but they were serious and it was real.

"I love you," I told them.

Mom left a kiss on the top of my head. "We love you too."

"But if you change your mind one day and decide to become a lawyer, you can come to work at my firm any time," Dad added.

"Sure. Thanks," I said, but I knew deep down that I would never stray from my path.

"And bring Blake to our house sometimes," Mom said with a grin as she winked at me. "We would like to know your boyfriend better."

I groaned. "Mom, no! It's completely embarrassing."

"That boy saved your life, Jess," Dad said. "The least Julie and I can do is thank him in person."

I sighed. "Fine. I'll have him over one of these days. Just don't interrogate him too much, okay?"

Mom feigned a shocked gasp. "We would never!" She chuckled.

Yeah, right. I acted annoyed, but in truth, I was happy. I had their support and approval.

Things were turning out well after all.

• • • •

BLAKE AND I RETURNED to school right after spring break, on Monday, and it was like all eyes were only on us. Wherever I went, people were whispering and watching me, and even more so when I was with Blake. They wanted to know the details of our kidnapping, and some of them even asked Blake if he'd seen any lights or his body from above in some weird out-of-body experience when he died, looking at him like he was some mythical creature.

Like that wasn't enough, the whole school knew Blake and I were dating, and it was a hot piece of gossip. Girls didn't stop staring at me, and I felt more self-conscious as the day went on.

"Did you want to disappear when everyone found out you and Hayden were together?" I asked Sar on our way to the cafeteria, glancing between her and him. "Because people are staring at me. A lot."

"Yep," she answered. "It was embarrassing, but they stopped staring that much eventually."

"That much, huh?" I let out a nervous chuckle.

"Don't pay attention to them," Hayden told me in his even tone of voice. "They're just jealous."

I sighed. "I'm not so sure about that."

"What do you mean?" Sar asked.

"I know I shouldn't feel this way, but I..." I blushed. "I kinda feel inadequate as Blake's girlfriend. The way some girls look at me...it's like he deserves someone much, much prettier."

"You're right," Hayden said, and I snapped my eyes to him, mortified, but then he continued, "You shouldn't feel that way." My chest deflated in relief. "Because Blake doesn't care about that. He likes you the way you are, and who gives a fuck what others think?"

My blush intensified. I knew that. I was taking baby steps when it came to self-acceptance and body positivity. I knew I was going to have setbacks from time to time, but I wasn't going to let it drag me down anymore. I was pushing forward, and I knew one day, whether I had more or less pounds, I was going to love my body just the way it was.

"I know. I just have to learn to ignore all their stares and mean comments."

"I've seen the way he looks at you," Sarah said, her eyes glimmering. "Believe me, he's crazy about you."

"You got that right," Blake said from behind us as he wrapped his arms around me, pulling me into him. I sank back, my pulse starting to pound.

Blake liked to cuddle. He used every opportunity he could to touch my hair, kiss my forehead, or hug me, and he loved when I initiated our kisses. That was why I pressed a quick kiss to his lips over my shoulder, more than aware of the dozen pairs of eyes homed in on us from all sides.

"Hello to you too," I said to him. I noticed the darker tint to his eyes as he looked at my lips. He wore a black cap, which hid the bandage that covered his wound, and it only made his delectable gray eyes stand out more in the shadow of the bill. The previous paleness of his face was replaced with a healthy color, and the bruises on his cheeks were faded and scarce. It was incredible how quickly he'd gone back to normal, after only a week.

He looked at the blonde next to us, who stared open-mouthed. "What are you looking at?" he snapped. "You've never seen two people kiss each other?" She blushed and scurried away.

Hayden looked at Blake with amusement. "I'll quote you," he drawled. "'You might want to fuck each other later, when there's no audience.'"

Blake tightened his grip around me. "Fuck you, princess."

Hayden narrowed his dark eyes at him. "Wanna say that again with a broken jaw?"

"No more injuries, okay, guys?" Sarah said before kissing Hayden's cheek. "First you with the car accident and getting jumped out, and now Blake. Both of you have already gone through more than enough."

Hayden said something, but I didn't hear him, because the words "jumped out" got stuck in my mind. Only now did I remember that Blake was still in the gang, and to get out—*if* he wanted out—he would have to get jumped out too. That was the only way T, their gang leader, would allow him to leave.

My stomach plummeted. I sneaked a glance at Blake and dug my nails into my suddenly cold palms. I couldn't lose him. Not a chance.

More eyes landed on us when we entered the lunchroom, but I was hardly aware of them. Kev and Marcus waited for us at our table, and I waved at them, feigning enthusiasm.

"Are you okay?" Sarah asked me quietly.

I pulled her closer, letting Blake and Hayden join the line first, and whispered in her ear, "Is there really no other way out of the gang except getting jumped out?"

Her brow furrowed as understanding dawned on her. She looked at Blake. "Did he say he wants out?"

"He didn't, but if he does, he has to go through that, right?"

She sighed. We stopped behind Blake and Hayden, who were talking to each other, but not close enough to hear our whispers.

"He can leave Enfield. We're graduating in two months, so that could be his chance to escape from here until they forget about him."

I bit my lip and took a look at the food choices with no interest. I'd already lost my appetite. "But that's a big if. What if they never forget about him? Would he need to hide forever? What if they wait for him to come back and hurt him for leaving? What if—"

"What are you rambling about?" Hayden asked, looking at me over his shoulder, and I blushed.

"Nothing," I said. I didn't want to talk about it now. I met Blake's gaze, unsure if they had heard anything.

There was always a chance Blake didn't want to leave the gang. He'd said he'd never cared about college, and if his life in the gang provided him with coping mechanisms for his PTSD, he would most likely stay there. I didn't know how to feel about that.

We took our food and continued to our table. Kev and Marcus were in the middle of their conversation about Marvel superheroes when we arrived.

"Superheroes are boring," Hayden declared as he put his tray on the table and sat across from them.

I sat down between Blake and Sarah. This was Blake's first time to sit at our table, which did something unusual to my heart. It was such progress compared to just a few weeks earlier.

"They're not boring." Marcus popped a piece of his steak in his mouth. "Captain America rocks. And he's super sexy." He winked at Kev.

Kev blushed and righted his glasses. "Yeah. Chris Evans is, is, is eye candy."

Blake rolled his eyes. "Scarlett Johansson is eye candy."

I gaped at him. Did all guys have the hots for her? She was all my cousins talked about. Her and Megan Fox. "Really?"

He shrugged, chuckling at my expression. "What? She even reminds me of you, although you're much, much hotter than her." He accentuated that by running the tip of his finger over my mouth before he kissed me, slowly and heatedly.

A groan sounded near us, and I looked up to see Masen rolling his eyes before he, surprisingly, flopped down next to Marcus and lowered his tray to the table as if he'd always sat here.

"Pussy-whipped," he said to Blake, but there was none of the usual casualness or cockiness in his demeanor. He was pissed off. "So, what now? We're going to sit here with your chicks?" He looked at Blake and Hayden with more-than-evident displeasure on his face. "Pussies."

Hayden glowered at him, fisting his hand on the table. "Nobody forces you to sit here, so fuck off if you don't like it."

"What's going on with you?" Blake asked him. "You didn't get to jack off last night or what?"

I blushed as I glanced at Sar, Kev, and Marcus. They looked sheepish too as they observed the interaction.

Masen dug his fork into his food. "It's that nutcase. She deserved what she got."

"She?" I asked, hoping he wasn't actually referring to Mel.

He looked at me the same way he had when I'd helped Eli with the apples. "Your crazy friend, Melissa."

"She's not crazy," Sar said.

I frowned. "What happened?"

"What *will* happen is that I'm going to kill this degenerate asshole slowly and painfully, and I'm going to enjoy every second of it," Mel said, appearing behind Masen with her hands on her hips. She looked at us. "What is he doing at our table? He better teleport his ass away, or I'm going to eat somewhere else."

Masen sprang to his feet and got into her face. "Make me. Not that you can do much now that you're suspended."

Say what?

"Okay, what's going on?" Sarah asked, already on her feet.

"You're *suspended*?" I asked Mel in a high-pitched voice.

"Of course she's suspended," Masen sneered. "That's what she gets for punching Steven and acting all aggressive."

Whoa, whoa, whoa. "What?" I asked dumbly. She'd punched her brother *again*?

Mel looked at me; her features were briefly shadowed with hurt before she schooled them into blandness. "Steven said some things, and I just snapped."

Masen chuckled. "She just 'snapped.'" He made the air quotes, gloating. "Yeah, right. It's too bad the principal showed up right then."

She glared at him with her bared teeth. She looked on the verge of hitting him, but then she glanced around the cafeteria. The new lunch monitors seemed ready to intervene at any moment, so if she did anything, she would only make things worse for herself.

"No, it's too bad *you* had to show up with her and make things worse," she said to Masen. "You lied through your teeth. You actually told her I punch students all the time and have aggression issues, you pile of cow crap."

My eyes got even wider. I glanced at Sarah, who looked as confused as I was.

Masen shrugged his shoulders. "Where's the lie in that? You do have aggression issues, and you hit your brother all the time."

Veins bulging out on her temples, she pushed against his shoulder and raised her fist like she was going to punch him any moment now. "I dare you to say that again. I dare you." Masen looked over her shoulder and smirked.

"Hey." One of the lunch monitors stopped behind Mel. "What's going on here?"

Masen cocked his eyebrow smugly. "And I dare you to hit me. Maybe that will finally get you expelled."

"If you don't stop right this moment, you're going to the principal's office," the lunch monitor said, scowling at Mel and Masen.

"Mel, listen to him," Sarah told her. "You're already suspended, so don't make things worse."

Mel didn't look at anyone but Masen, glaring at him like she wanted to pummel him into nothing. The aversion was thick between them, and when she lowered her hand and unclenched it, it looked like it took everything in her to do just that and not sock him.

"I'll wipe that smug smirk off your face if it's the last thing I do," she said under her breath then spun on her heel to leave.

"Mel!" I called after her, already moving to reach her.

"Don't follow me," she tossed over her shoulder. "I'm going home." She rushed out of the cafeteria, leaving the whole table in heavy silence.

Sarah frowned at Masen. "That was a low blow."

Masen sat down, looking at her coolly. "A low blow? She's like a rabid dog, and no one does anything to stop her. She deserves this."

"No, she doesn't," I told him. "She's going through a difficult time with her parents in the middle of their divorce, so cut her some slack."

"So, what—we all have to let her treat us like punching bags just because she has issues? You can forget about that."

"You're the same," I told him, and his face dropped. A sliver of danger flashed in his eyes. "You also have issues—"

"You better think twice before you say anything, Metts," he told me, and I remembered his warning. I wasn't supposed to say anything about Eli.

"And you better stop talking to her like that," Blake growled.

I took his hand. "It's okay."

"No, it's not okay," Blake said. "You have some big-ass issues with Brooks? That's fine, but don't get Jessica wrapped up in that clusterfuck."

Masen looked between Blake and me with a clenched jaw in silent anger, and I expected him to start arguing, but then he threw a big smile on his face and winked at us. "Whatever, man. We're cool."

For a few moments, I could only gape at him, reminded of Mel. She was the same. She could hide her real feelings in a second, acting like her charming, usual self despite how hurt she actually was on the inside, and it was scary how good both of them were at that. During the rest of the lunch, Masen's smile didn't vanish, his crude jokes, laughter, and charm filling the conversation, and it was like nothing had happened.

I massaged my temples, thoroughly confused by Mel and Masen. Things were definitely going to be challenging between them, maybe even more than they were now, and I didn't have the faintest idea how it would all work out.

Chapter 30

"YOU'VE COME A LONG way, Jessica," Susan told me, placing her clip-board on the upholstered arm of her chair. "I'm impressed by your will to improve despite the setbacks along the way."

I looked at my chipped pink nail polish. "I still feel like I have a long way to go. I feel like I could fail if I don't try hard enough."

"It's okay to be afraid. Just don't stop. I'm amazed that you're this de-termined after what you went through a week ago. That can take a toll on a person."

It's okay to be afraid. Just don't stop. It was strange how the way Blake pushed through his life with PTSD could be inspiring for someone as easily disheartened as me. I had him to look up to whenever I thought about quit-ting because even in his darkest moments, he had the strength to stand up and keep walking. So I was going to keep walking and make something out of myself.

"Yes, it took a toll on me, but it also helped me realize, in a way, that I have so much to be happy about. I have my family, my friends, my boyfriend." I smiled, and a faint blush painted my cheeks. "I have my mu-sic and hobbies. I'm healthy and alive. I have so many reasons to be happy. I took everything for granted, but now I see how lucky I am to have all of this."

"You're absolutely right. You have so many reasons to be happy. How about your body? Do you feel happy?"

I inhaled deeply as I glanced at her golden pencil that now lay still on top of her clipboard. "It would be a lie if I said I don't want to change any-thing about myself."

I looked at my stomach. I was wearing a tight-fitting shirt that didn't hide my fat rolls, and I imagined a waist without them. Unlike before, that image didn't bring me painful longing whenever I thought about it. I want-ed a thinner waist, but I wasn't beating myself up about it or blaming my body for not being the way I wanted it to be. I was good enough like this.

"I'm learning not to compare myself to others and to set realistic expec-tations for myself. The build of my body clearly doesn't allow me to have a thigh gap or smaller hips, and I'm just learning to accept it and move on. We can't have everything in life, and that's okay." I glanced at my lush breasts that were even more prominent now that I was wearing a push-up bra, and I thought about Sarah. "My friend once told me she wished for bigger breasts like mine, which is ironic since I wish for a slim body like hers. We always want something we can't have, right? And it seems like it's really hard to be satisfied with what we already have.

"It's like shopping. You buy one thing, and it's not enough. You always want something new, something more expensive, something prettier. I always wanted a better and prettier body, but now I just want to slow down and appreciate myself for who I am. I want to stop considering my physical flaws something to be ashamed of.

"Actually, I don't want to consider them flaws at all. Why are they flaws? Why is my cellulite or body fat a flaw? Unless my weight deteriorates my health, why should I be against my thicker thighs or thick waist? Why should society be against my thicker thighs or thick waist? And I don't want to punish myself with throwing up or guilt-tripping. I don't want to punish myself for the way I am. One day, maybe, I'll reach my desired weight. Maybe I'll never get to that, but no matter what, I want to be free of regret and self-dissatisfaction. And I'm working on it. One step at a time."

She watched me with approval written all over her face, her soft smile growing bigger.

"You've really come a long way," she repeated. "I'm amazed at the difference between before and now, and I'm certain one day you'll get there. Just focus on yourself and don't let outside voices conquer you. You're your own biggest strength and support."

That ended our session, and I exited her office feeling more positive than before. The week had been chaotic, but life went on, and time would heal the wounds.

Blake, who'd had his session at the same time as me, was already waiting for me in the waiting room. His lips turned up into a radiant smile when he saw me, which made his gorgeous face even more beautiful, if that was possible. I noticed with a flutter in my chest that he smiled and laughed more often now.

These days hadn't been easy for him either, because that Sunday had exposed him to an insane amount of stress, which had led to new nightmares and flashbacks. But according to him, it hadn't been as bad as it could've been. He was on antidepressants that did their job well, which, combined with the time we spent together, amounted to him being in a much calmer state than usual.

"Finished?" He stood up and left a kiss on my forehead.

"Yep. Let's go."

We walked hand in hand outside and got in my car, the sunset creating a cozy picture in the distance.

"So, the sunflower field?" I asked.

"The sunflower field." He leaned in and captured my lips. The kiss was languid, until he deepened it and stole my breath. Always hungry for his kisses, I cupped his face and pressed myself closer to him. We separated moments later, both gasping for air.

"You know I'm addicted to your kisses, right?" I told him as I started my car.

"You know I'm addicted to you, right?" His sensual voice did something strange to my core.

I giggled as I pulled out of the parking lot. "Now I do. How was your session?"

"As usual, boring as fuck but necessary. She was glad to hear about you. She thinks I'll be able to deal with my PTSD symptoms more easily now that you're by my side. Support and all that." I truly hoped so. I wanted to be of help to him. "And how was your session?"

"It was okay. I like talking to Susan."

"Yeah? Why?"

"Because she always makes me feel calmer and closer to accepting myself the way I am." I smiled and accelerated, passing the car in front of us. "She's satisfied with my progress."

He placed his hand over mine on the gear stick. "I love the way you are," he said gently, and I glanced at him. There was longing and a slight hint of regret in his expression. "I wish I could erase my insults and fix the damage, but as I told you, that's not possible. So, I'll show you each day how special and beautiful you are. I really don't care how much you weigh. I just want you happy."

I smiled at him, wishing I could pull him into a crushing hug. "I know. I mean, it still feels a bit unusual since you called me fat until recently, but you can compensate by telling me how pretty I am and how much you love me a hundred times a day." I winked.

He laughed. "That's nothing. Let's make it three hundred times."

"Three hundred and fifty times."

"Deal." I giggled, and he planted a quick kiss on my cheek. "You were never ugly or fat to me. If you could only see yourself the way I see you, I'm sure you'd never doubt yourself again."

"I bet all you see are my big boobs and butt," I joked.

He chuckled. "I can't deny that. They're sexy as hell." He stroked my hair, running his fingers through the strands slowly.

"Hey, you're distracting me."

"I love distracting you," he said in his sexy, low voice, which sent a shot of pleasure through my belly. He didn't stop teasing me the rest of our ride, and I was almost tempted to pull over and have him kiss me again and again long before we reached our destination.

There was still enough light when I parked at the same spot as the last time, a few feet away from the sunflower field sign, and I could see everything I hadn't been able to that night.

The whole area was decorated by vivid wildflowers, and the trees in the distance had just started to leaf. It was a peaceful view. I jumped out of the car and skipped over to the edge of the field, mesmerized by the budding nature and the darkening colors of the sky. The earthy fragrance was overpowering, widening the smile on my face.

"Jessie?"

"Yes?" I turned around, and he snapped a photo of me with his new iPhone.

His eyes warmed as he looked at the image. He smiled. "Perfect."

Giggling, I ran to him and wound my arms around his neck. He'd been taking photos of me every day. "*You* are perfect. But won't you get bored of taking my picture? You already have so many of them."

He grinned. "Are you complaining?"

I bit my lip as my smile stretched. "Not at all." I kissed him and gave myself over to the warmth that blossomed in me each time our lips connected. His lips were soft, so soft, creating music with mine in my mind, an uplifting song that talked about two lovers finally united in light.

When I pulled away, we were both dazed and panting. He hugged me and put my head on his chest, letting me soak in his closeness.

"I'm so happy, Blake," I whispered as I looked at the vacant field that would soon be full of beautiful sunflowers. It would change. Just like Blake and me.

"Me too. I'm happier than I ever thought I would be. Hell, I never thought I'd be happy to begin with."

I raised my head to look at him. "But here we are. We went through hell, but we've survived, and now we have each other."

He cupped my cheek and laced his other hand in my hair. "It's strange. I never thought I would have this, and now that I do..."

"Yes?"

"I want to protect it at all costs." He took my hand and pulled me to my car. "There's something I want to tell you."

We sat on the hood next to each other. A bird chirped in the distance, adding to the peaceful melody of nature with no cars passing to ruin it.

"I wasn't afraid of death. After Emma died, I didn't have any other reason to live except my revenge, and I thought if I died, it would be okay. I would be free of trauma and pain. But in that house, with you next to me, I was afraid to die for the first time. I was afraid to leave you, and my last thought before I passed out was how I wished I could see you again."

A bittersweet feeling crushed my chest. I interlaced my fingers with his. I would never forget that moment, the shine in his eyes as he told me he loved me before the current of death dragged him away.

"I got a second chance at life, and I don't want to waste a second of it. I don't want to lose you. I want to see you. Your smile. Your beautiful eyes. Want to hear your sweet laughter. Your songs. I want all that and so much more, which is why I've decided to accept admission to Columbia. I want to go to New York with you."

My pulse doubled. I grabbed him by his forearms, ready to squeal and jump in excitement. "Really?"

He smiled. "Really."

"Really, really?"

He chuckled. "Mhmm."

"Yes!" I pumped my fist in the air and planted a loud kiss on his lips. "Yes, yes, yes!" He laughed as I peppered his face with kisses. "We're both going to New York!"

"Yep. I mean, I don't know if law is my thing since I've never cared about anything, but I have to start with something. Maybe it will turn out that I like it."

I licked my lips as I conjured up an image of Blake dressed in a suit in a courtroom. "Mmm, you would be a sexy litigator."

He cocked his eyebrow. "Who told you I was going to be a litigator? Maybe I'm going to be a prosecutor and put motherfucking bastards behind bars."

"Even better. You're going to punish all those murderers and look sexy while you do it." My smile dropped at the sudden reminder of his ties to the gang. "But wait...what about the gang?"

He grew serious. "That's another thing I wanted to tell you. I talked to T last night."

I raised my eyebrows. "You did?"

"Yes. I talked to him about leaving the gang."

My heart kicked against my ribs. "Will they jump you out?"

His lips curled at one corner. "Not really."

At first, I thought I'd heard him wrong. "No? But how? Why?"

He gazed softly at me. "Remember the scar underneath my tattoo?"

The round spot that looked like a bullet scar. "Yes."

"I got it when someone tried to kill T a while ago. I was standing next to him when it happened, so I reacted out of instinct and shielded him, taking the bullet for him."

I gaped at him. "You took a bullet for him?"

He half-smiled. "Crazy, right? I still don't know why I did it. Maybe that was me trying to end my miserable life, or maybe I was actually trying to protect him. Either way, he owed me, and he said if I ever wanted out, he would let me go. A life for a life. But I didn't want out because life there helped me keep my mind off my problems and deal with anxiety. But more importantly, it allowed me to dig deeper for Bobby Q and his guys." He gazed at the dark sky that was now decorated with a few stars. "When Hayden wanted out, I went to T and told him to let Hayden leave instead of me. But he didn't want to hear it, said it didn't work that way. I couldn't help Hayden."

My heart ached. He was ready to do anything for the people he cared about. Emma. Hayden. Me.

"But in the end, it turned out to be a good thing," I told him, and he looked at me. "Because Hayden survived, and you can get out without consequences."

"Right. So, now I'm officially out of the gang. I'm free."

Yes, yes, yes! I began bouncing up and down on the hood, laughing like a maniac. He didn't have to risk his life. He was *free*.

"YES!" I smacked my hands together. "We have to celebrate this!"

"Definitely." He smiled and placed his hand on my waist, his gaze full of adoration. "You're amazing, you know that?"

"Not more than you."

"No, you're the most amazing. The sweetest, most caring, most addictive..." His lips brushed my cheek softly. "You gave me your heart and helped me when I needed help the most, no questions asked. I'll never forget that moment in the school basement when you helped me with my panic attack." He cradled my head with his hands. "Maybe that's what made me fall in love with you." His voice dropped to a whisper.

I sucked in a breath, my eyes dropping to his lips before he kissed me, tasting me slowly. My whole being was filled with love for him that increased every day. Each day, he gave me a new reason to be happy, and I could finally fully understand Sarah's words from her birthday party.

Love is resilient. It can be born on ground filled with hatred and negativity and still survive. It can change a person, and seeing Blake finally allowing himself to heal and be happy, I understood that love isn't just about the entrapment. It isn't just about the unwanted feelings that keep you in a place you want to escape from. It can also be about healing and second chances. It can be about a door into a new world that allows us to grow and come out stronger than ever.

In the midst of all-consuming negativity, our hearts had managed to find their way to each other. We'd managed to find a shelter from all the pain and nurture our love, and now we were free to love each other with no bounds to keep us shackled.

His eyes were almost as dark as the sky above when he drew away to look at me. His hands roamed up and down my arms languidly. "So, if I'm really that amazing, what do I get for it?"

I put my finger on my lips, pretending to think. "Hm. A dozen kisses?"

His eyes twinkled with amusement. "And?"

I tipped my chin down. "And? Let's see...sex?"

He chuckled and ran his finger over my lower lip. "Tons of it, yes. And?"

I chuckled in disbelief. "You want more?"

He grinned. "Absolutely."

"I'll let you beat me at Monopoly again."

"I won that fair and square, but sure, I'd love to win again. So? What else?"

My smile was enormous. "Okay, I get it. You want me to sing for you."

His smoldering gaze made me so warm. "Bingo."

My heart began to pound in my chest. My performance anxiety came to the surface, but I'd promised I would sing for him today, and I wanted to see awe in his eyes as I played my new song for him.

I slid off the hood and opened the rear door to retrieve my new guitar from the back seat. "Promise you won't laugh." I sat back down next to him, holding the guitar in my hands.

He cocked his head to the side. "Like I laughed the first two times I heard you sing?"

My cheeks went red. "I know you didn't laugh, but I'm nervous, and while I know you wouldn't, it doesn't hurt to remind you to—"

He interrupted my rambling by pressing his lips to mine, giving me a long, warm kiss, and my toes curled.

"Don't ever be nervous in front of me." His words were a warm whisper upon my skin. Our gazes locked. "I love you, Jessie."

And just like that, my anxiety was gone. I rested my fingers on the strings, and my lips curled into a smile. "I love you too."

I played the first few notes tentatively, then more confidently, and the poignant tune poured out into the night air. I fixed my gaze on his, moved by the stars in his eyes that matched the ones dotting the sky, soaking in this moment.

No matter what tomorrow might bring, it was all right. We were going to overcome all the lows one by one. And I was ready for it.

You and I are like flowers
That bloom at night
Courageous, teasing
Opposing the dark
Shining our own light

And it's mesmerizing, enticing
The way you watch me move

Like the sunrays on your skin
Like the love that you give

The flames flicker in the dark
Creating a path of light
That bursts through hearts filled with love
And ends our happiness drought
And it's heaven, the way you kiss my skin
Making my heart go wild

And I feel free
I'm becoming stronger

The flames flicker in the dark
Creating a path of light
That bursts through hearts filled with love
And ends our happiness drought
And it's heaven, the way you kiss my skin
Making my heart go wild

And I'm freed...

Stronger than ever

Afterword

IMPORTANT PTSD DISCLAIMER:

Blake isn't a representation of all people with PTSD, and this author's intention wasn't to portray this disorder or people with PTSD in a negative way. Each person with PTSD experiences their condition in their own way, and PTSD symptoms and their frequency/intensity may vary from person to person.

• • • •

AS SHOWN IN MY CAMEO in chapter twenty-five, the titles of the *Bullied* series hold yet another special meaning. Blake's condition is post-traumatic stress disorder, or PTSD. The first letters of *Pained*, *Trapped*, *Scarred*, and *Damaged* spell PTSD.

• • • •

THANK YOU FOR JOINING Jessica and Blake's emotional ride and for reaching the end. I hope *Trapped* helped you get through difficult times and put a smile on your face. *Trapped* is for all of you who feel insecure or unhappy with yourself. It's for all of you who feel there is no way out of the shackles that prevent you from going on, for all of you who want to make your dreams come true but just don't know how or don't feel strong enough.

Just remember that happiness and strength lie within you. You shine your own light, and your uniqueness is the true beauty, so be yourself and keep going. One day, everything will come to its place.

In the end, here is a quote from me:

"Follow your heart and believe in yourself because you don't lose when you fail. You lose when you give up."

• • • •

JESSICA AND BLAKE'S story has ended, but there is one more story in the *Bullied* series. Stay tuned for Melissa and Masen's story in book five, *Scarred*.

Be sure to subscribe to my newsletter to get notified about this and all my future releases and receive sneak peeks, giveaway info, and more!

Sign up here: https://www.verahollins.com/newsletter/

Acknowledgments

THIS TIME I WANT TO begin by thanking my readers—my great pillar of support. I feel very grateful for each and every one of you and for your highly encouraging messages, comments, and reviews. Thank you for the time you put into reading my books and for your enthusiasm about my characters and their world. Your encouragement always pushes me forward. <3

To all bloggers: thank you for taking a chance on my books and for helping them reach more readers. There are a lot of books out there and so little time, which makes me appreciate everything you're doing all the more.

To my beta readers Auni Borhan, Rita Joana Gonçalves, Rachel Domingos, Breannca Bussert, Jean Manoti, and Mehvish Azmi: thank you for your very helpful responses and suggestions!

To my ARC team: you're so amazing and supportive! I can't thank you enough for helping my books get discovered.

To Jo, Kylie, and everyone else from Give Me Books promotions, thank you for all your amazing work.

To Caitlin from Editing by C. Marie and Stacey from Champagne Book Design, thank you for your excellent work.

To Catreena: thank you very much for all your posts. I really appreciate your time and effort.

To my FB reading group Evil Bunnies: you're always so wonderful, and I feel so lucky to have you as my readers. Thank you for your continuous support and enthusiasm!

And to my love and number one fan, Rasha, thank you for always cheering me on and believing in me. Love you lots.

About the Author

Vera Hollins is the author of the *Bullied* series, which has amassed 40 million reads online since 2016. She loves writing emotional, dark, and angsty love stories that deal with heartbreak, mental and social issues, and finding light in darkness.

She's been writing since she was nine, and before she knew it, it became her passion and life. She particularly likes coffee, bunnies, angsty romance, and anti-heroes. When she's not writing, you can find her reading, plotting her next book with as many twists as possible, and watching YouTube.

Read more at https://www.verahollins.com/.

Made in the USA
Monee, IL
09 April 2021

65227636R00201